They'd thought the case was over, but now they weren't sure...

Frank put his napkin down on the table. "Did—Does Uncle Mike have a wife and children?"

"I thought you said you're friends?"

"Well, we are. New friends. We met last month. We do the same kind of work with people."

"Yes. He's a talking doctor," Benjamin said. "He had a wife. But what's it called when the wife leaves?"

"A divorce?" Sam said.

"Yes. And she stayed in Florida. With their children. But they're older than us."

Sam continued to feed Margie the soup. It gave her some time to let her mind wander.

Thank you, Benjamin for confirming that Mike Sheffield had to travel with Henry Slater. No wonder his wife wanted a divorce. Mike would rather play with Henry than with her. What wife would tolerate that? Or maybe she wasn't into the culture. Um, was it a divorce, or was she another victim? How many more bodies do we need to uncover?

Sam felt the jab of Dara, her spirit guide, in her abdomen. She'd learned to trust that response since her conversation with Dr. Trenton in the Aries case. Her feelings were consistently on target—especially in the case she thought they'd completed, just two days ago. This time she was sure. There'd be more leftover bodies still to uncover.

Forty-eight hours ago, a serial murder case that spanned nine years ended. Or did it?

Four children intrude upon the scene of the suicide of Henry Slater, claiming he's their dad. Dr. Frank Khaos and Detective Sam Wright become their temporary guardians. The goal—to find the children's biological mothers. Or has Henry Slater added them to his dossier of kills? Through the investigation, the NYPD detectives and FBI Special Agent Brett Case uncover a kidnapping ring and do find the mothers, but are they fit—and willing to take their children back? As Sam and Frank fall in love with them over nine weeks, and the reality sets in, Libra, the Scale of Justice, kicks their butts. What's right for the children is against the law.

Another case falls into Agent Case's lap. A murder spree and drug involvement with Jarrett Miller, Vicki Trenton's first husband. To make matters worse, Miller has ties to the biological parents of Dr. Khaos whom he has to travel to Florida to confront as a stipulation to the execution of Slater's will.

How will Frank deal with the two people who've been his Achilles' heel his entire life, and will he and Sam get the family they desire so much?

KUDOS for *Libra*

In *Libra, The Sign Behind the Crime, Book 4*, Detective, Samantha Wright, and Forensic Psychiatrist, Frank Khaos, discover that Henry Slater, the serial killer they apprehended in the last case, has four children. But who and where are their mothers? Are they really Henry's children, or was he running a children kidnapping ring? As Sam, Frank, and the team search for answers, they soon discover that this case is a lot more than they bargained for, especially when innocent children are involved. Like the other three books in the series this one is intense and chilling—one that will keep you on the edge of your seat all the way through. ~ *Taylor Jones, The Review Team of Taylor Jones & Regan Murphy*

Libra, The Sign Behind the Crime, Book 4 by Ronnie Allen is the continuation of the serial murder case from *Scorpio*, the third book in the series. The serial killer, Henry Slater, is dead, but the consequences of his crimes live on. Detectives discover that Slater has four children, whose bedrooms are hidden behind a wall. The kids show up forty-eight hours after Slater dies, claiming to have been at the nanny's. So now the main question is, where did Slater get the children? Are they really his, and if so, where are their mothers? Were the children kidnapped from their parents, or do the detectives have even more bodies to find. It was thought that Slater killed seventeen women, but now it appears that number could be higher—much higher. *Libra* answers many questions and solves a few remaining mysterious left from the first three books, as well as presenting some intriguing new ones. With marvelous character and fast-paced action, it will grab your interest from the very first page. All in all, an excellent addition to the series. ~ *Regan Murphy, The Review Team of Taylor Jones & Regan Murphy*

ACKNOWLEDGMENTS

Book 4 in The Sign Behind the Crime Series is here. It was such an exciting time writing this book because it's the culmination of a thread that spanned the series. And yes, it's a happily ever after ending, the happiest you'll ever find in a novel.

As always, I want to thank my cherished critique partners and beta readers who have been with me from the beginning. Sherry Wilson, Sue Pellegrino, and Judi Oglio spotted some areas in Scorpio, Book 3, that I was able to incorporate in and create the plot for this book, Libra. And this year, Carol Cohen joined us. These four women gave up hours of their time with dedication and passion to help me create a book that I am proud to release.

I have new consultants in this book. Elly Molina, world-renowned spiritual consultant and the author of the Amazon best seller, *Children Who Know How To Know*, also published with Black Opal Books, was my guide for my psi-child, Benjamin. Her insight helped me to enrich his character and credibly portray his abilities. Any deviation is on me; this is a work of fiction.

My son and car expert, Dave Allen, provided me with information about navigation systems that helped me develop a subplot.

Lisa Dinaso Bastedo, AKA Hunter, allowed me to use her tag name and skills as a hairstylist and colorist. Seriously, readers, if you're in NYC or in California you must sit in her chair! In Central Florida, you have to see Freedom, John Freedom Henry, who appears as himself in this book, and who also gave me tips on color. I thank him and Lisa for allowing me to use their names and personas.

As always, I'm grateful to Black Opal Books and their editors, Lauri and Faith, who stuck by me through four books, and Jack in the art department who created my vision for the covers.

And my husband, Bob, who understands what being an author means: More work for him.

I sincerely hope you enjoy this book, and keep a box of tissues handy.

Best,
Ronnie

LIBRA

The Sign Behind the Crime
Book 4

Ronnie Allen

A Black Opal Books Publication

DEDICATION

To every parent and grandparent, biological and adoptive.
May you love, cherish,
and support your children in every aspect of their lives.

CHAPTER 1

It was over—less than forty-eight hours ago. The serial murder case that spanned nine years and took seventeen lives now put to bed. None of their own were lost, though it came close. Too close, with one of his favorite rookies, Samantha Wright. He'd relax. At least there was no bloodshed in here to clean up. Henry Slater had been the toughest of his cases to date, in his twenty-year career with the NYPD.

Detective Lex Withers blew out a breath of relief as he observed crime scene techs still putting down markers throughout the Upper West Side Manhattan apartment—over two hundred markers. Two teams of investigators were there now, all wearing Tyvek protective gear with nothing left up to chance. No telling what that Slater character would do to exterminate all of them. Withers trusted the system. Yeah, he was feeling pretty good now. Feeling good he was a cop.

When his cell rang, he went out into the hall to answer it. Markers lay on the carpet, and a long table holding photography equipment hugged the wall. He nodded, acknowledging what an arduous process this would be as he leaned against the spotless bone and gold wallpaper, talking on his phone.

At the other end of the hall, an elevator door slid open. With his back turned, Withers didn't notice. The eldest child, Benjamin Slater struggled to push his sister's stroller over the tracks, and then he started to roll it down the hall as the next oldest, Mel, held the toddler, Henry's, hand. They didn't get far.

Squeaky wheels on the stroller caught Withers's attention, and he turned around. Stopping his conversation mid-word, he disconnected the call without saying "goodbye," then put up his hand for the children to stop. "Whoa. Hold on." Smiling, he approached them. "And who might you be?" His gaze scanned the older children before settling on the infant in the stroller.

The children just stared at him, then at the markers, then at the cluttered table but remained silent. Withers gave them their space. He knew damn well who they were. Frank Khaos was spot-on. There *were* little Henry Slaters out there. Their forensic psychiatrist did indeed have more nieces and nephews. The detective removed his badge from his pocket and showed it to them. "I'm a detective with the New York City Police Department. My name is Lex Withers."

The older boy's eyes widened in astonishment. "A real police badge? I never saw one up close." His gaze darted around the hall. "And why are there cops outside our house?"

Mel trembled. "And where's our dad?"

"And who is your dad?" Withers asked. The question was merely for confirmation. The older boy was a miniature Henry Slater with hair, and come to think of it, a miniature Frank Khaos, too. Damn!

"Henry Slater," Mel said.

Withers bit the inside of his cheek to prevent expletives from flowing out of his mouth. Some choice words certainly filled his brain. This wasn't what he wanted to confront right now, though he already knew it. "All right. Listen to me, okay?" The children nodded. He continued. "We're going to help you, so there's no need to be afraid of us, understand?" The children nodded again. Withers smiled. "Good. I need you to help me out, too, and answer my questions, okay? Who else lives here with you?"

Benjamin didn't seem to understand why the detective asked that. "Us and Dad. Who else would live here?" He started to move the stroller around the detective. "Excuse me, we have studying to do."

Moving in front of the boy, Withers blocked him. "Studying? On a Sunday?" The detective nodded in approval. "So you live in the apartment? All of the time?"

"Yes. Please tell us what happened, sir," Benjamin said.

Withers smiled at the politeness. "Okay, I will. Come on. But you have to stay inside the path we blocked off."

Benjamin and Mel looked surprised. "Why?" Benjamin asked as he wrapped his arms around Henry, holding him close. "You're scaring my little brother."

"Us, too," Mel said, shaking.

"We'll explain everything. But you have to come with me."

In the walk down the hall to the apartment, Withers's mind reeled. Henry Slater was dead, and he continued to be a nemesis in the afterlife. Withers himself was beginning to sound like Sam Wright. Her, and her psychic intuition crap. Too bad, she was always correct. *What else is this case going to bring?* Withers called his partner to come outside into the hall.

"What's going on?" She stopped mid-sentence, seeing the children. "Lex…"

"And this lady is my partner, Detective Bella Richards. Now, tell me your names."

Benjamin swallowed hard. "I'm Benjamin. This is Mel. That's Henry, and Margie is her," he said, pointing to the infant.

Bella softened. "Um, sweetheart, we didn't see any children's bedrooms, and we're looking through the entire apartment."

Benjamin stood silent. Then he whispered, "Our bedrooms are behind a wall."

That statement shot Withers an unnecessary jolt of adrenalin. He forced a smile to cover-up his sinking heart.

"Show us." While waiting outside, he peeked into the doorway and yelled, "Curtain."

A six-foot tall white curtain rolled, closing off the right side of the apartment from the doorway to the bathroom where Henry Slater offed himself. Withers hoped the kids' rooms weren't on that side.

Benjamin led the way into the center hall in the apartment. Withers could tell his tough bravado was a front. His hands trembled on the stroller handle, as did Mel's, as the two children huddled together, taking small steps. *Brave kids.* Crime Scene roped off a path by which people could enter and leave. The children stopped dead and looked up at the detectives.

Withers read the fear in their eyes. Damn, the curtain didn't conceal half of what he wanted to prevent them from seeing.

The apartment had been transformed into a science lab. Long tables stood on top of white paper covering the tile floor. Photography equipment and sterile packaging supplies were on opposite ends of the table. Markers lay on the floor. More tape lay across the doorframe of Henry's master bedroom, to the left. Technicians barely gave the kids a glance. The two older children became teary-eyed.

Benjamin whimpered. "Something bad happened to our dad."

"Yes," Withers said. Not having the heart to tell them the truth, he lied. He'd need Frank Khaos on this one. "Your dad's in the hospital. He got very sick. Now, we need you to help us, okay?"

Mel sniffled. "Can we go see him?"

"No. Not yet. Now where are your rooms?"

A crime scene tech overheard them "What rooms, Detective? We covered the entire apartment."

"Our rooms are hidden," Mel said.

Oh man! Slater told Frank at their family meeting on Friday that his parents hid him in the closet. Is that what he's doing to his kids? Crap, Slater, what kind of son of a bitch were you? If we walk in to closets, I know Bella will freak. Hell, I'll freak.

"Down there," Mel said, pointing to the left.

The narrow hallway to the babies' rooms was free from any furniture or wall-decoration. Crime scene tape ran across the open door to the baby girl's room. If these kids were as smart as their father was, they wouldn't let that go. Withers wanted to walk past it.

Benjamin jolted at the sight of the tape. "What happened in there?"

He had to answer. The kids deserved some honesty. He certainly couldn't say that Detective Sam Wright came close to losing her life in that room. "We don't know yet. It's procedure to look at everything."

Benjamin stared at him, compressed his lips, but said nothing. Withers knew a lot was going through the kid's mind. Had to be.

This was unexpected. He shot a concerned look toward his partner to break the ice.

Bella understood. "Is that Margie's room? It's so beautiful."

Benjamin gave a harrumph. "That? That tiny box?"

Bella stiffened. "Tiny box?" She put her hands on her hips. "That tiny box is bigger than my bedroom. Shoo, kid. Show some appreciation. Everyone who went in there loved it. The pink and brown wallpaper, the matching bedding. Everything. I know a detective who'd love that for her little baby's room, especially the pink carpet. Her name is Samantha."

Benjamin smirked "Good for her. Keep that one away from us."

The adults looked at each other in bewilderment. "Benjamin, what's with the attitude all of a sudden?"

Whoa, like father, like son. This one we'll have to watch.

Benjamin shook his head. "You're not telling us the truth, Detective Withers. So I don't have to act nice."

"What do you mean?"

The boy sulked and waved a dismissive hand. "Forget it," he said, shrugging.

Withers needed to make it right. "How old are you, Benjamin?"

"I'm eight and a half. But we're accelerated. I'm in fifth grade."

"Fifth grade?" Bella said impressed. "Are you accelerated, too, Mel?"

Mel let out a breath of exasperation. "Yes. I'm six, if you must know, and I'm in third grade. And Henry is three. He's in nursery school. He hasn't been tested yet, but I'm sure he's as gifted as us."

Okay, little brother copies the older one. "Where were you yesterday, and Friday after school?" Withers asked in an interrogative tone.

"Why do you want to know?" Benjamin asked, mimicking the detective. "We didn't do anything wrong. We swear," he said, beginning to tear up. "We never do anything wrong. We're not allowed."

Withers mellowed. "I know you didn't. It's okay, son. Who was taking care of you the past two days?"

"Our nanny," Mel said.

"And where does she live?"

"On the twenty-fifth floor. Right below us. Can we get into our rooms, please?" Benjamin rotated his shoulders. "These book bags are heavy."

"Sure," Withers said. "What's your nanny's name?"

"Locklear Henderson. Our rooms are through there." He opened up the door to baby boy's room.

Withers stepped away. He wasn't going to overthink this now. This was the time to keep his emotions out of the game and go by the book. All he knew right now was that these kids would need long-term care on every level going forward.

He made a call for a unit to pick up the nanny and bring her to the Manhattan-North precinct. He then signaled to two crime scene techs to join them.

"Henry, did you sleep in here when you were a baby? This room is awesome!" Bella said.

The three-year-old frowned and pursed his lips. He shook his head.

Benjamin sighed heavily. "You don't have to pretend to be nice to us, Detective."

"I'm being nice because I'm a nice person."

Benjamin gave her a quick glance. "Our dad tells us not to trust anyone." He walked into the room and moved the rocking chair against the wall to the side. "Dad must have had a lady friend up here."

Withers hiked a brow. *This kid sure has great inference skills*, he thought. "What makes you say that?"

The eight-year-old looked up at him. "Whenever he does, he moves this to here, to block the wall."

"And he told Locklear to keep us until today, so I guess she slept over," Mel added.

"And let me guess. I bet her name was Samantha." After glaring at Bella, Benjamin bent down toward the baseboard. "Just don't go all nuts. I can guarantee you have never seen anything like this."

"Stop the drama, kid." Benjamin jumped back from the adult. "Slide the wall open," the tech said with a softer tone.

Benjamin pressed a button on the baseboard, holding his finger on it. The door slid open. Everyone stood mesmerized. Withers couldn't take it in all at once. *Thank God, it's not a closet.*

"You just gave us a couple of weeks of extra work, kid."

"Come on in. We'll show you around." Benjamin snickered at the adults who stood dumbfounded.

Withers and Bella followed the children into a massive space—a one-bedroom apartment with the walls removed. Hand painted murals of sports figures and games lined the walls on both sides of the room in the color schemes of bright oranges, yellows, reds, and some browns for a grounding effect. The low-textured carpet, divided into four parts, picked up the colors from the wall. Two twin beds were on the left, with a wood dresser matching the bed frame, interspersed between desks with filled to capacity bookshelves, containing children's books and games. A twin bed and a crib were on the right.

"Are you just going to stand there?" Benjamin picked Margie up and out of the stroller and crinkled his nose. "Ugh. She just pooped."

Withers smiled. "Give her to me. I'll change her." He reached out to the baby.

Benjamin stood hesitant, wrapping his arms around the infant. "Do you know how?"

"Yes. I know how. I must have changed over a thousand diapers in my day." Benjamin groaned. "I have children," Withers said, taking Margie in his arms. "How old are you, baby?"

Benjamin laughed. "You have children?"

"What?" Withers said as he took the child to the changing table.

"Then you should know that at her age, she can't answer you. She's ten months."

"Oh, man," said the tech. "Come on, show us around. A diaper change doesn't warrant an audience." He urged the children forward.

"This is my bed," Mel said, bouncing on the soccer themed bedspread. "And my dresser with my clothes is here."

"And those beds on the other side are for me and Henry," Benjamin said as he placed his book bag on the desk chair. "I have to pee." He went into his adjoining bathroom.

The tech followed him, and Withers noticed Benjamin's scornful glare. "Hey, I just want to see what it looks like," the tech said. After he glanced in, he did a quick turnaround. "Hey, Detective, ya gotta see this."

"In a minute." After the diaper change, the baby squirmed in Withers's arms. He forced her onto Bella who clumsily took her. "Bella, keep an eye on her." He chuckled. Walking into the bathroom, he halted. "Holy sh...cow.

Benjamin, this is bigger than my bathroom in my house."

"I'm sure it is," the boy answered snidely.

Again, Withers slid past the attitude, but he surely planned to address it. "Did you help your dad pick out the design?" He ran his hand over the three dimensional wall art. "It actually looks like you're on a pirate's ship in rough seas. The colors and everything."

"No, Dad did this by himself. He covered the walls with cement and carved the picture. Then he painted it. But it is a replica of a real ship. And the pirate drawings are real pirates."

Withers had to switch his tense deliberately to make sure he didn't alarm the boy. "Your dad *is* a very talented man. Even your towels have matching pictures."

"Dad had them specially made. You should see Mel's bathroom."

"You each have your own bathroom?" The tech asked.

"I share this one with Henry. And Mel shares with Margie…well, when she gets older."

"Where is it?"

"Right across."

Withers couldn't stop from looking around. Every bit of space contained something educational. A computer station stood at the far end of the room against a wall. A wall unit next to it held computer games. *Wow. Slater sure made up for what he lacked as a child with his own. He told Frank that he never had books or games.* Withers walked into Mel's bathroom. The shock of the navy and white with splashes of red caused his eyes to blink involuntarily. Mel stood by the doorway.

"Got a problem?"

"No. I do not have a problem. So you're in the navy?"

"I don't have plans to, no."

"Dad did this by himself, too?"

"Whoo," Mel said, twirling an index finger in the air. "You're smart, Detective."

"And you kids have smartass attitudes. How does your

dad deal with that? I spoke with him and he seemed strict. And didn't your brother tell me just a few minutes ago that you're not allowed to do anything bad?"

"We don't with Daddy. But Daddy says if people lie to us about anything, then we can answer back. Because we can't trust them. And Benjamin said you lied to us, and I believe my brother."

All well and good. Better off to lie to them today. I have no qualms about that. And I know exactly who to call to knock them down a peg or two.

"Bella, help the kids pack for a few days. I have some calls to make."

Withers left the bedroom area, walked through the baby boy's room, down the hall into the living room. He stood still in a somber moment, leaning against the only wall that wasn't taped off. He ran his hands over his mouth. Damn, his son was eight and a half. He could just imagine what would be going through his mind if he suddenly disappeared from his and his brothers' lives. It would be the unthinkable. Then again, his sons would have their mom.

Come to think of it, where are their mothers? Did Slater kill them, too? Closing his eyes, his heart wrenched, thinking about what his department had to do.

He decided to wait on the calls and he returned to the bedroom.

Still holding Margie, Bella sat down on Mel's bed. "Need some help to pack?"

"Where are we going?"

"We'll figure it out."

Benjamin brought over an overnight bag. "Here, Mel."

Mel took the case, pouting. "We can stay with Locklear."

"Not at the moment."

"Why not?"

"We'll decide after we speak with her."

"I'm okay. Go pack Henry and Margie."

Bella compressed her lips and rose from the bed. She

slipped Margie into her stroller and strapped her in.

Benjamin had jeans and long sleeve polo shirts on his bed. Withers sat down next to him. "Need help?"

"No." He looked away. "What's going to happen to us?"

"I don't know that yet. We're going to where we work, and we'll talk to a lot of people. All I can promise you is that nothing bad is going to happen. You'll all be safe and kept together."

"Now you're telling me the truth, sir."

Withers let out a nasal breath. "Yes, listen to me. Mel told me why you spoke less than respectfully before. Sometimes we adults have to protect children from hearing certain things. It's not as if we're lying. We're just deciding what's necessary for you to know at that time. Understand?"

"No. Dad says we shouldn't be protected from hearing anything."

Withers compressed his lips. *That's what Henry Slater Sr. told Sam when he had her in the bedroom. "You can't pamper kids," were his exact words after he tormented Frankie on the phone.* "Cops have a different opinion on that one."

"Why can't we stay here?"

"Well, the police have a lot of work to do."

"Why?"

Withers paused long and hard. *How do you tell a child that his dad was a serial killer?* "A lot happened and the police need to investigate so we can do what's best for you and your siblings."

"We can help them."

"Nope. You're minors and now that Detective Richards and I found you, you're our responsibility. Does that make sense?"

Benjamin bit his lip and exhaled deeply before he nodded. "What do I need to take?"

"Let's see." Withers counted the jeans and polos. "There's enough here. Now pack underwear and socks. And pajamas." He got up and went over to Mel.

Navy and brown jeans along with long sleeve sweat-shirts lay on the bed. A few of the shirts had decals of famous football players in the center. Withers smiled. "When you grow up, Mel, do you want to play football like these guys?"

Mel swallowed hard. "No. I heard what you told Benjamin. I just have to pack my pajamas and I'll be ready."

"Okay. Ready?" Withers asked Bella.

"Yes, all set." She put the baby's bag on the handle of the stroller and handed her partner Henry's bag.

"Ready, guys? Grab your coats and gloves."

"Okay," Benjamin and Mel said together.

"Hold on," Benjamin said. "Grab some containers of food from the fridge for Margie. Dad makes her baby food. And her bottles are in there, too."

"Good boy. Taking care of your baby sister. I like that," Withers said.

"Yeah, well. You wouldn't know. And there's cooked food for over a week in the fridge and freezer." Benjamin walked toward the tape barrier but a crime scene tech stopped him.

"Who made all the food?" asked the tech.

"Our dad."

"No can do." The tech looked up warily at Withers. He compressed his lips. "Based on what happened, Detective, we're not letting prepared consumable products out of our custody."

Withers caught on fast. *Would Slater poison the food he prepared? To take the kids with him?* The thought nauseated him. "Where did your dad get the milk for Margie's bottles?"

"Some place where they give mommy's milk to dads. I don't know where," Mel said.

The tech smiled. "How is it packed?"

"I don't know what you call it. It's in the freezer. And he mixed it with goat's milk."

"Hold on." The tech left and returned a few minutes later with vacuum-packed bags of breast milk. "These were brought in as is from a milk-bank. We checked them. Not tampered with so you can take these. And, Detective, when these thaw, the milk needs to be consumed within twenty-four to forty-eight hours. I'll pack these in ice. We found a cooler in the closet."

"Okay. Thanks." Withers yelled to the senior crime scene tech, "We're leaving. I'll write up this report." He turned toward Bella. "Wait here. Give me a minute."

He walked into the hallway outside of the apartment, took a deep breath, and pressed a key on his phone. He knew Frank and Sam had gone to the cemetery today so Sam could pay her final respects to her friend, Carrie Baines.

"Frank Khaos."

"It's Withers. A major development just popped up in the Scorpio case. We need you and Sam at Manhattan-North, ASAP."

"Okay. We're just leaving the cemetery. On our way."

CHAPTER 2

Withers hadn't given Frank specifics, so on the drive up, both he and Sam went through possible scenarios. They knew Slater didn't survive, so what could have Crime Scene uncovered? More money? Sam had gotten her resolution. What she'd had vowed to her friend Carolyn Baines came to fruition. The man who'd murdered her was dead himself. It was less than forty-eight hours after the suicide. Frank didn't know what to expect. Withers kept his tone of voice mellow. Was it something minor, or did he do that on purpose because he was with people? He knew Withers was still at the apartment and would be for at least another week. Frank didn't know him outside of the job, but one thing he did know. Detective Lex Withers was dedicated to everything he took on. He was a damn good detective, and Frank respected him. When he got the call, Frank didn't question the man further.

Forensic Psychiatrist Dr. Frank Khaos and Detective Samantha Wright opened the door to the war room in the Manhattan-North precinct. The bland walls made the people within them stand out. Sitting around the conference table more than the expected people accosted them. Frank nodded, as his gaze hit Withers and Richards, along with Nick Valatutti, Sam's partner, and Lieutenant, Ted Martin.

Then Frank laid his gaze on the four children sitting opposite the detectives. He couldn't take his eyes off them. He looked at Sam. He knew it—her love for children. With her serene expression, she was already in love. *Wow, Sam, hold on. Way too soon for that.* Sam couldn't stop smiling at the beautiful little faces. Frank shot Withers a glare and merely got a nod in response. Sam was right again. She'd had wondered if Henry Slater had children. And even Frank thought he'd have nieces and nephews out there. More importantly, they resembled him—and his son, Frankie.

"Get comfortable," the lieutenant said. "This is going to be a long afternoon."

Frank and Sam took off their coats and hung them on the wooden rack in the corner, and took a seat by the conference table. Not expecting to go in to work today, they were both dressed uber casual in dark denim jeans and solid colored T-shirts. Sam had on a multi-shaded, blue-floral, fleece, zip-up-the-front sweatshirt over her pink T. All the while, the children didn't take their gaze off Frank.

"Dr. Khaos, meet your nephews, and niece," said Lieutenant Martin. He introduced the children, pointing to them. "This is Benjamin, Mel, Henry, and the little one, Margie. Children, this is your Uncle Frank. And this is Detective Samantha Wright."

Benjamin sniggered at Sam then turned his attention to Frank. "You look like our dad, but he wouldn't wear that."

Frank looked down at his black T-shirt. "Why? It's clean."

"He isn't the T-shirt type. And he doesn't have tattoos on his arms."

Frank chuckled. "What you see is what you get. Deal with it."

Benjamin, wide-eyed, stared at his uncle as he pressed back into the chair, obviously intimidated by Frank's tone. Then he looked toward Sam and spoke with a low voice. "And are you the Samantha who was in our house?"

"Yes, I am, sweetheart."

Margie squirmed in the stroller. Sam got up and took off the harness holding the baby, lifting her up and embracing her, letting out a soft moan.

Margie babbled and grabbed onto Sam's hair, as she sat

back down on the chair. Sounds of delight emitted from the baby's mouth.

Sam swooned holding the precious child who wore a pink and yellow one-piece outfit. She rested her cheek on the side of the baby's head. "Oh, my God, so sweet."

Frank looked at her, groaning, as Withers handed Sam a bottle. Frank could just imagine what was running through her mind. Probably it was the same thing going through his. What were they going to do now? He would do what it took to protect these children. They were family. His family. His blood.

"This is too cold for her." Sam put the bottle on the table and flexed her hand. "Who wants to go heat this up?"

Nick laughed. "At her age, she can drink cold milk."

"No," Mel said. "Daddy still heats it up for her."

"I'll go." Nick patted Sam on the shoulder before he left the room. Sam smiled.

Mel looked down at the floor. The child blinked repeatedly, sniffled, and swallowed. Frank could tell that Sam's heart wrenched. She moved forward in her seat and tilted her head toward Mel. "What's the matter, sweetheart? I know. You've all had a shock."

Mel sat up but hesitated. The child froze. Benjamin whispered something. Mel sniffled and nodded then got up, went over to Sam, and stood between her legs. "You're so beautiful."

Sam smiled from ear to ear. "Oh, thank you, sweetheart." She pulled a tissue from her bag and handed it to the six-year-old.

Mel blew her nose. "I want to be beautiful, like you."

Frank did a double take. Sam gasped and handed him the infant. He seemed to guess what was next, as did Sam. His gaze took in all the shocked faces on the adults in the room.

Nick returned and he smiled seeing the baby with Frank. Then he had to have seen his colleagues' faces. His smile vanished.

Frank took the bottle and immediately Margie wrapped

her hand around it and put the nipple into her mouth. She nestled in the crook of his arm, bending her knees with her right leg over her left. Frank laughed at how comfortable she made herself.

Sam removed the baseball cap that covered Mel's head. Her hair was bobby-pinned to her scalp. "Oh my goodness, Mel, who put your hair up like this?"

"Me."

"Why, sweetheart?" Sam started removing the pins, and Mel's unruly and uneven hair fell below her shoulders.

The detectives looked like they were about to die. Apparently, they hadn't suspected Mel was a girl. At six, it could be hard to tell.

"Dad wants me to be a boy," Mel said, breathing heavily, holding back tears. "But I want to be a girl, like you. I am a girl."

Withers pounded the desk, startling the children. Richards collapsed into her chair. There were no words. Frank closed his eyes to prevent himself from exploding in anger. He couldn't let loose with Margie in his arms.

Ignoring them, Sam removed all the bobby pins, putting them on the table, and barely held back tears, herself. "What's your real name?"

"Melissa."

"From now on, you're going to be a girl." Sam fluffed out her hair and then pulled Melissa into her arms and held her tight.

Melissa fought her and pulled back. "We don't hug." Sam looked sad. "Daddy says 'we don't need that.'"

"I know that about your dad, but most people love hugs. I love hugs. Want to give it a try?" Sam opened her arms.

Melissa looked toward Benjamin, obviously for approval. The boy stared at Sam for a moment then nodded to his sister.

Melissa meekly went into Sam's arms. Apparently comfortable, the little girl wrapped her arms around Sam's torso and rested her head on Sam's chest.

Wow. It looks like big brother has the final word. Frank put his hands up and out. He couldn't let his true feelings show. "How did this ever happen?"

Melissa turned her head toward him. "From the time I was little."

Frank blew out a deep breath to prevent obscenities from pouring out. "Why did he do that?"

"Daddy says girls aren't as smart as boys." Melissa hugged Sam as she let some tears sprinkle down her cheeks. "And—I'm—trying—so hard—to show—him—I—am." She used her fist to wipe away the tears.

Sam caressed her. "What about in school?"

She looked up and swallowed the tears. "In school, I'm a girl and we wear uniforms, but as soon as we get back to the nanny we change into regular clothes."

Sam smoothed out Melissa's hair. "Didn't your nanny ever talk to your dad about it?"

"No, she was afraid of losing her job. And she's a really good nanny."

Withers really didn't understand it. "So there was no one you could tell?"

"Not until now. I never met a lady I could talk to who wouldn't tell on me to Daddy. Benjamin told me I could trust Samantha, and she likes Margie. So maybe she'd like me, too."

Sam hugged her tightly. "I do like you, Melissa, and you'll always be able to trust me. We'll make this right. I promise."

"Hold on. All you have is boy's clothes at your house?" Withers asked.

"Yes."

Frank's blood boiled. "Did you ever tell your dad that you were unhappy?"

"No. It was his way all the time."

Benjamin leaned forward in his chair. "We're not allowed to give our opinions. That's why Melissa couldn't tell anybody."

Frank groaned. "What did you wear when you went out with your dad?"

"We never did."

"You were in your house, all the time?"

The little girl nodded and sniffled, holding back more tears. "Most of the time."

"So you wore boy's clothes all day?"

Melissa nodded. "At night, too."

"Well, we are going to change that." Sam revolted. "In ten minutes. I'll be right back, Melissa. Stay with everyone." Sam kissed her cheek. Melissa startled at the affection then backed up. Sam glanced toward Frank, worried, then turned toward the girl. "What's your favorite color, sweetheart?"

"Pink, like what you're wearing," Melissa said like a child with no hope of getting what she wanted.

Frank blew out a deep breath. *Yeah, Slater wasn't an affectionate guy. These kids aren't used to any warmth from adults. We'll change that, fast.*

Sam ran her fingers through Melissa's hair, got up, grabbed her coat, and left the room without saying another word. Melissa watched her leave then sat down next to Frank.

"So now what?" Benjamin asked. He held back tears, himself.

Frank didn't miss a beat. "Until we find out what's going on, you're coming to live with Sam and me."

"Hold on, Khaos," Lieutenant Martin said. "CPS is on their way."

"I don't give a damn about protective services, I'm their biological uncle."

"We don't know how long it will be."

"And I don't give a damn how long it will be. It's permanent, as far as I'm concerned."

"It's not that simple."

The door flung open and the elderly social worker entered with a newbie children's attorney. Not waiting for an introduction, she took her seat at the conference table and grabbed folders out of her tote bag.

She frowned. Frank assumed from now being delegated not one child, but four. The young female attorney held a softer expression.

Benjamin ignored the new adults. "Where do you live?"

"In Brooklyn."

"Ewww," Benjamin and Melissa yelled in unison.

Frank put his hands out. "What's wrong with Brooklyn?"

"Brooklyn's a dump."

"It is not! Who told you that?"

Melissa sat up tall as if proud. "Daddy. He won't go there."

"Your dad was born in Brooklyn."

"Yes, we know," Benjamin said, shaking his head. "And he told us he'll never go back there."

The social worker looked impatient. "I'm Mrs. Kruger. Are you making arrangements for the children, Dr. Khaos?"

"Yes. I want them to come live with me. I have a large house and my son would love to have his cousins."

"But where is their mother?"

"Uh, you mean, mothers, ma'am. We each have different ones, but we don't know where they are," said Benjamin.

Melissa added, "We don't know their names, either."

Frank closed his eyes for a moment. Did Slater kill more women? "When was the last time you saw them?"

"I guess when we were babies. Younger than Margie," Melissa said.

"I guess you're Melissa," Mrs. Kruger said. "Can you please tell me more about that?"

"About what?" The child didn't seem to understand.

"I've been doing this a very long time, Detectives, Lieutenant, and I'm sensing you have a big problem on your hands."

Oh, man. Frank wrote *where did Slater get these kids and how?* on a piece of paper and passed the sheet to the lieutenant, who, in turn, nodded, after reading the chicken scratch, and passed the paper on.

Sam returned, carrying two bags from a children's store. Everyone stopped talking and stared at her. "What? I'm a fast shopper and this is just one outfit, pajamas, and a coat. Come on, Melissa, you're going to change."

The little girl smiled, probably for the first time in a long time. Sam took her by the hand and squeezed it tight. She glowed. Swinging their arms, Sam left the room with her.

"I can just imagine what Samantha bought her, with her taste," Benjamin said with a hint of jealousy.

Frank laughed. "Excuse me? Taste? What's that about?"

"That woman liked the baby's room," he responded, shaking his head.

Mrs. Kruger cleared her throat. "Can we please get back to the children's residency? I don't have all day."

Benjamin met her eye to eye. "We don't want to go to Brooklyn. We'll stay in the city. And you have to keep us together."

He certainly knows how to stand up for himself and his siblings. That's a good thing. He must also feel less restricted not in front of his father.

"Well, don't you have demands?" Mrs. Kruger retorted. "There's no guarantee of any of that. Even if you went to a group home instead of to foster care, you wouldn't be in Manhattan or kept together."

"If they came with me and Sam, they'd be kept together."

As Frank spoke, Sam entered with Melissa dressed in a three piece pink and brown fleece sweat suit, with a matching long sleeved shirt under the jacket. She smiled, when everyone stopped and stared at the little girl and compliments came from everyone. Even the staunch social worker smiled.

"Wow, Mel—"

"It's Melissa from now on, Benjamin."

"You look great, Melissa."

Frank chided the boy. "What did you say about taste?"

"Okay, so I take it back." Benjamin sat back in his chair, looking smug.

Melissa sat next to Sam at the table and hugged her. Sam, beaming, wrapped her arms around the girl.

"So what about it? You want to come live with us?"

Sam sat up startled. "That would be wonderful!"

"In Brooklyn?" Benjamin paused. "Do you know how to cook?"

"I'm learning."

"Learning? How old are you?"

Sam did a double take. "What's that got to do with it?"

"We only eat gourmet meals."

Frank bellowed out laughter. "You're kidding me, right?"

Benjamin leaned back and folded his arms across his chest. "No, I never kid."

Neither did his dad. "Excuse me?" *Whether, it's the right time or not, this kid needs to know some middle ground.* "Come over here, now." Frank signaled with his index finger.

Benjamin reluctantly got up and sauntered over to Frank with a smirk on his face.

"Oh, boy." Withers chuckled. "Sure you can handle this, Frank?"

"Oh, yeah, I'm good."

Benjamin reached Frank. Standing in front of his uncle's knees, the boy's smirk transformed into a pout. Frank stared at him without saying a word.

Benjamin exhaled deeply. A minute of silenced passed.

"Now, respectfully, tell me about your gourmet meals."

The boy sniffled. "I'm sorry, sir. I just don't know what's going to happen to us."

Frank cringed at the word *sir*. That didn't suit his personality at all. "It's okay, bud." He placed his palm on the boy's shoulder. "Listen, I'm an informal kind of guy. And sir makes me feel so old. Let's drop the 'sir.' Okay? Uncle Frank will work just fine."

"Okay, Uncle Frank. Dad only cooks gourmet."

"And what is that, exactly? Like four or five course meals?"

"More like three. And only healthy."

"Okay, good. Me, too. What kind of courses?" Frank didn't know what to expect.

"We always start with a salad, always. Chopped, so Henry can eat it, too."

"Okay. Then what?"

"Then a chicken, meat, or fish, and vegetables. But we eat on fancy plates—"

"China," Melissa interrupted him.

"And he makes the food pretty," Benjamin added. "He just doesn't slop it on the plate, like they do in restaurants."

"There's no slopping on the plate in restaurants," Sam said. "Which one did that?"

"I don't know. We never went to one. But Dad told us."

"You never went out to eat in a restaurant?" Sam asked.

"You never went out to eat Chinese food or Italian?" Frank asked. Benjamin shook his head. Frank frowned. "We'll have to change that. Speaking of food, I'm starved. Did you guys each lunch?"

"No."

Henry got antsy in the chair and he started to whine.

Sam reached for the three-year-old. "Come here, sweetheart."

The boy revolted. "No!" He punched Sam in her chest, flailing his arms. "Go away! We don't like you!"

Sam backed off, startled.

After swiftly handing the sleeping infant to Withers, Frank grabbed Henry as Sam sat back down with jaws dropped. "Hey, stop it, Henry." The kid screamed in an all-out tantrum. "Whoa, whoa, whoa." Frank wrapped his arms around him, and carried him to the couch against the wall. "Henry, stop."

The little guy continued to scream. He kicked Frank's legs.

Frank couldn't sit. "Shush, shush, shush, it's all right, Henry." With patience, Frank rocked him like a baby. Henry stopped fighting after a few minutes, still breathing heavily and sobbing.

Melissa and Benjamin sat, stunned.

"He never ever does that!" Benjamin bellowed.

Mrs. Kruger shook her head. "With behavior like this, that child will be hard to place."

Frank continued to hold him tight to his chest. Frank rested his palm on the back of Henry's head. "No one is being placed. They're coming with us."

Henry cried on Frank's shoulder. "I want Daddy. Tell her to go away," he cried out, pointing to Sam.

"Oh, man. I know you do. I know you do, bud. Why don't you like Samantha?"

"Daddy said we don't need any mommies. Just him."

Withers blew out a deep breath. "I think we gave the FBI another case. I'll put in a call to the New York office." He began to get up with sleeping Margie in his arms. "Order me whatever." He strapped the baby into the stroller before he left.

Frank patted the boy's back. "Well, I disagree with your dad. My son, Frankie, loves Sam and she's going to be his mom."

Henry rubbed his eyes with his fisted hands, still pouting.

Benjamin frowned. "What do you mean, 'going to be his mom'?"

After Henry calmed down, Frank brought him back to the table and sat with him on his lap. "Sam and I are getting married and we're going…well, now that you're coming to live in my house, Sam's moving in today, too." He shot Sam a wide grin.

"I guess I am." Sam reached over and hugged Frank's arm. "Are you hungry, Henry?"

"Yeah." He frowned at Sam, sticking out his lower lip, as he sat on Frank's lap. "But we don't like you. You're not coming."

"We like Samantha, Henry. She's nice," Melissa said.

"Is he in nursery school yet?"

Melissa nodded.

Sam sealed her lips into a sliver and then put on the drama. "Oh, my goodness, Henry. You hurt my feelings, so bad." She crossed her hands over her heart. "You made my heart hurt."

The three-year-old's expression changed. He stared at her.

Sam laid on a pout. "I'm going to cry."

Henry slipped off Frank's lap. He gingerly approached Sam. "I hurt your feelings?" He stood in front of her. His high-pitched three-year-old voice sounded sincere. It took a lot for the other adults in the room to hold back laughter.

"Yes, you did. Come here, sweetheart," Sam said in a pleading tone.

He climbed up onto her lap.

"You're learning all about feelings in nursery school, aren't you?" The boy nodded. "What did your teacher tell you?'

Henry sniffled. "To be nice and not hurt anyone's feelings cause it could make them sad."

"She's right. You made me sad. And what are you supposed to do, when that happens?"

"Say you're sorry."

"So what are you going to say to me?"

"I'm sorry I hurt your feelings, Samantha."

Sam hugged the boy. "It's okay, I accept your apology."

He shook his head. "But we still don't need a mommy."

"That's not true, Henry," Frank said. "Your cousin Frankie loves Sam and he wants her to be his mom."

"I know!" Melissa jumped up out of the chair. "Why don't you go ask Dad who our moms are? But we won't need them anyway, when he gets out of the hospital, right?"

she said as she threw her hands out to the side.

Frank and Sam both gasped at the same time. Frank immediately realized the inevitable.

All right, Withers, you laid it on the shrink. I am the one who makes family death notifications, and I did have personal experience with it, telling Frankie his mom had been taken from us. It's not something I want to repeat. But, okay. It needs to be done, but not today.

Frank changed the subject fast. "Call in from the deli. Do you kids have any allergies to foods?"

"No," Benjamin said. "No allergies, but we don't eat bread with that gluten or any foods, like, that come in packages with bad stuff."

"Like no, ham, Bologna, cheeses."

"Yeah, stuff like that. No bacon, sausage, boxed cereals. And you need baby food for Margie. I know what's it's called. Organic. Dad only buys organic food. I don't know why but the man in the white suit at our house wouldn't let us take any of her food. Dad made it special."

Frank nodded. "Well, for today, she'll need some jarred. It's all right. We'll make her food at our house."

"I'll go take care of the ordering." Nick got up. "Mrs. Kruger would you and Miss Schaeffer like to join us for lunch?"

The lieutenant handed Nick the precinct's credit card.

"No, thank you. We have paperwork to do." Mrs. Kruger's cell rang and she excused herself to take the call, answering it as she left the room.

"Does he know what to get?" Benjamin asked.

"I think so, why?" Frank's delivery was firm with an additional glare.

"Never mind."

Mrs. Kruger re-entered the room too fast, and Frank could read her expression. She looked like a person would after their power was usurped. "I don't know what strings you people pulled, but I just got off the phone with Judge Holmes from Family Court. Usually, this process takes a lot longer before granting guardianship. He'd gotten a call from the FBI of all things. I'm not questioning it because the bottom line would be that the children are well cared for. Just give me a few minutes to amend these papers. Where can Miss Schaeffer and I go to work on this? And is there a notary in this building? On second thought, we can work in the corner over there."

Frank turned around at hearing the door close. "Reach him?"

"Oh, yeah," Withers said as he tilted his head toward the social worker. "I filled him in on everything. Agent Case is on his way."

"Who's Agent Case?" Melissa asked.

Withers smiled. "He helped up with some things with your dad. It's nothing for you children to worry about. We have everything under control."

The attorney, Miss Schaeffer, approached the table. "Dr. Khaos, we'll just need you to sign these guardianship papers." She placed the papers on the table in front of him. "I need you to initial and then sign the highlighted lines."

Frank flipped through the papers. "Okay. Standard. I've seen these before."

The notary came in and witnessed the signing. Frank carried through with intent, the notary did his job, and he and slid the papers back to her.

"All right, Dr. Khaos." Mrs. Kruger and the attorney rose. "Everything is in order. I wish you and the children luck." She and the attorney raced out of the room.

"What kind of a doctor are you, anyway?" Benjamin asked, still with the attitude.

"I'm a psychiatrist. Forensic."

Benjamin's face lit up. "You work with the brain?"

Frank smiled, his lips curling in approval. "Yes."

Benjamin bolted up and pulled his iPad out of his backpack that hung on the back of the chair. "I love the brain!" He opened to an app and ran over to Frank. "See? This is an app that shows every part!"

Frank wrapped his arm around the boy. "I'm impressed, Benjamin."

"See, this is the frontal lobe." Benjamin pointed. "This is the hippocampus."

"That's terrific. And the names aren't even written there. How did this interest come about?"

"I love science. It's my favorite subject. And I want to grow up to be a doctor because..." Sadness overcame the boy's excitement.

"What's the matter?"

"Tell him, Benjamin. He could help Dad."

"Help Dad with what?"

"Dad gets bad headaches. And no matter what he does they don't get better. Well, sometimes, they do. He's got to be real careful with what he eats."

"And how he sleeps, too," Melissa added. "He needs three pillows."

"Sometimes, he'll go away for a day, and we'll sleep over at the nanny. He comes back all better."

That's when he went out for murder. Oh, man!

"Did he ever go to a doctor?"

"No. He doesn't even believe in doctors. I didn't tell him I want to be one, either."

"Did he ever take you to the doctor, even for your vaccinations for school?"

"For that yes, but we really don't get sick."

Nick opened the door, carrying bags of food. He placed them on the table as the children watched Lex and Bella distribute the lunches.

Melissa and Benjamin's gazes darted to the white wrappers back and forth to each other, then both of them sat back into their chairs, grimacing as they stared at their names on the packages. They seemed to have been communicating with just their facial expressions, almost telepathically.

It was obvious to Frank what they were thinking. "Didn't your dad ever bring in prepared foods?"

Melissa shook her head. "No! Never. We only ate what he cooked."

Oh, man. These kids are too sheltered. Frank smiled, keeping it inward.

Margie had awakened and sat up. Sam pulled the stroller over to her. She opened a couple of jars of the baby food: puréed chicken, and peas and carrots. The baby giggled excitedly seeing the jars. Sam held the jars on her lap. Gingerly, she fed Margie with tiny bits of food on the spoon.

Good thing Nick was a parent, Frank thought. He made great choices. He doubted if Sam would have known what to get. "Sam, you can give her some more on the spoon."

"I'll get the hang of it." She brought the spoon to Margie's mouth and spoke in a childish tone. "Right, baby-doll. I can do it."

The children looked confused, especially when Frank put their tuna sandwich in front of them. Melissa and Benjamin backed away from the table and leaned into their chairs again. They vehemently shook their heads.

Do they actually think that behavior is going to allow them to escape? "What's the matter?" Frank asked as he unwrapped the paper around the sandwiches. The white paper doubled as a plate.

"Where's the china?" Henry asked.

Everyone in the room laughed and dug into their sandwiches.

"Henry, this is a police precinct," Lieutenant Martin answered. "No fancy plates here, son. Use the paper as a plate."

"Yeah. We're roughing it." Frank laid a napkin across Henry's lap and started to slice his piece of sandwich. "Eat. Listen you, two. Your brother will copy you, and you have to show him it's okay. Got it?"

Benjamin succumbed. "Yes, sir—uh—Uncle Frank."

"No. I want it that big." Henry looked at his brother and sister. "I wanna hold it myself."

Melissa swooned after taking a bite. "This is soooo

good. I never tasted anything like this before. Oh, gosh."

Frank handed Henry his food. "Hold it good. Otherwise, it'll fall out."

Some of the tuna plopped onto the napkin in his lap. Henry was determined. With his fingers, he stuffed the tuna back into the bread.

"You're an independent little guy, aren't you?"

Henry looked up at Frank making a mean face, scrunching his nose. "Yes."

Frank shook his head.

After she swallowed, Melissa asked, "What's next, Uncle Frank?"

"We'll go to my house. We have a lot to do," Frank said, looking at Melissa and Benjamin. "And I'll need your help and Frankie's. The crib is in the garage."

Benjamin looked toward Frank with a mouthful of food. "How old is Frankie?"

"He just turned eight."

"What grade is he in?"

"Second."

"Second? And he's eight?" Melissa smirked.

Frank did a double take. "What?"

"I'm six, and I'm in third grade."

Frank stared at Sam, surprised.

"And I'm in fifth grade," Benjamin said with superiority.

Withers must have thought it was time to fill him in. "Oh, yeah, Frank. I was informed by these children," he said, forcing a smile, "that they're accelerated."

Frank sat speechless—not his usual behavior. He couldn't even think of a response in the moment.

It was a good thing Special Agent Brett Case opened the door. Accompanied by his fifteen-year-old son who carried a highchair and a booster seat for a chair, the agent carried a shopping bag and car seat. He wore his blue FBI jacket with the initials in yellow on its back. "Hey, guys." After putting down the packages, he took the highchair from his son and brought it over to Sam. "Here, put her in this. You'll kill your back leaning over. This is my son, Kyle."

Everyone said greetings. Frank introduced the children to Special Agent Case and the kids looked at him with their mouths agape. He and Frank laughed. Sam lifted Margie out of the stroller, moved it out of the way, and put her into the highchair. The baby giggled in delight.

"Hi, Kyle," Frank said, extending his hand to shake. The fifteen year old reciprocated.

Agent Case looked down at Henry, with his legs criss-crossed on the seat and the napkin over them. The tuna fell onto his lap with every bite. Case laughed. "Come here, guy." He removed the napkin and put it on the table.

Henry yelled, "No. I eat like this."

"Uh, oh," Kyle said.

Frank glanced up at the teen. Yeah, he'd figured Case would be a stricter parent than he was.

Henry yelled at the agent, again. "No!"

Agent Case compressed his lips but didn't say a word. He scooped up Henry in one arm, as Henry flailed his arms and legs.

"Let go a me, you mean FBI man!"

Case ignored the tantrum and with the other hand placed the booster seat on the chair. With Henry yelling, Case put him into the seat, and pushed the chair toward the table. "There ya go."

The little boy pouted, but he lifted the sandwich and with tiny fingers stuffed the fallen tuna back into the bread.

"Now isn't that better? You're the same height as every-one else. And now you can have the salad, like everyone else." He brought the salad tin toward him and removed the cover. He handed Henry a plastic fork. Case pulled out pre-pared baby food from the bag. "Here. You'll have this for a few days until things settle down. My wife made it."

"Thank you so much, Brett. That was so thoughtful of her," Sam said. "And it must have been awhile since she's made some."

"You're welcome. And not really. We have four at

home. Our youngest is his age," he said, pointing to Henry. "And we're expecting in June."

"I didn't know that!" Sam said, looking up at Frank.

"Yeah, you missed that conversation. We were in the van following you."

Case coughed, Frank guessed to prevent the children from questioning his last comment and the agent pulled a chair from the corner to the table. "Give me an update." He sat next to Benjamin.

"You're a real FBI agent?"

Case nodded.

"Wow."

Case smiled. "So tell me, Benjamin, how long were you living in this apartment?"

"Uh…" The boy paused as if calculating the time in his mind.

"I'll help you out. How many school years were you in the apartment?"

"Oh! This year, and the year before." Benjamin paused. "And the year before. This is our third school year."

"Okay, excellent. What's the name of your school?"

"Scholars Academy."

"And where is it?"

"In Manhattan near our house."

"How do you get there?"

"By school bus."

Frank listened intently to the exchange. Case certainly knew how to elicit responses from a child. Probably because he had his own. Frank doubted if Case interviewed many children in his homicide investigations, though.

"How long are you on the bus?"

"Um, I know," Melissa chimed in. "Fifteen minutes. We had to time it as a homework assignment."

"Very good. Thank you, Melissa. Do you remember where you lived before?"

The little girl smiled. "Yes. In Florida."

"What part of Florida?"

"Miami. We like it better there. We don't like the snow."

Case chuckled. "Yeah. It is something to get used to. Detective Withers, check out that Miami address we have." Withers nodded. Case faced him. "Have your people made contact with the nanny?"

"Locklear?" asked Melissa.

"Yes," Withers said. "I got a message from the team that she wasn't home."

With her fork, Melissa picked up some of the tuna that fell onto the paper. "She's on vacation."

Bella groaned. "Where did she go?"

"She went to visit her sister in Ireland."

Bella leaned toward the girl. "When did she go?"

Benjamin elbowed his sister. "I'll talk. When she put us into the elevator, she had her suitcase."

Withers blew out an exasperated breath. "Why didn't you tell us this at your house when we asked about her?"

Benjamin shrugged. "Dad always tells us to only give short answers and not more…well, something like that."

Case shot Withers what appeared to be an unappreciative glare. "You kids know so much. I'm impressed. Do you know how long she'll be gone? And we need a full answer."

Melissa nodded. "Three weeks. She and Dad worked it around his schedule. So we know he'd be home three weeks." She sounded relieved. "That'll give him time to get better in the hospital."

"Right." Case shot Frank a saddened look. He turned away from the children. Frank guessed he needed time to compose himself. Turning back, Case asked, "Who did you live in Miami with? Was Henry born there?"

"No. He was just three. He came to live with us in our first year here," Melissa said. "Oh, and Margie just came to us, too."

"Margie just came to you? When was that? She's ten months, right?"

"Yes, but I don't know exactly when," Melissa said.

"Okay, tell me this. Did Margie come around Thanksgiving in November?"

"I know! I know," Benjamin said, jumping up and down in his chair. "She came at Christmas."

"Yes!" Melissa shouted. "That's right. Daddy said she's our Christmas present. We got other presents but he was teasing."

Oh, man, where did he get these kids? They resemble Frankie and me. Our coloring, facial features. Benjamin could pass for Frankie's brother, except for the longer hair. Melissa's face is rounder, probably after her mom. The little ones? They both have Slater's oval eyes—come to think of it, mine, too.

Frank watched Sam wiping the baby's mouth and lifting her out of the high chair. He extended his arms out to the infant.

Margie leaned in toward Sam, not wanting to go to Frank. "Mama," she whispered.

Sam lit up. "Oh, my God!"

Benjamin's eyes widened. "Mama? She never says that!"

"Does she say, 'dada'?" Case asked.

"Yes, all the time."

Case and Frank stared at each other, probably with the same thing going through their minds. Frank slumped back in his chair. Case must have gotten the message. *That's right, Case. This one's on you. You can be the mean FBI man.*

Case got up with a tense posture and went over to Sam who'd already bonded with the infant.

"Let Dr. Khaos hold the baby, Detective Wright."

Sam had to have caught on to the formality. She hesitated. Frank reached for the infant.

Margie hugged into Sam. Frank put his hands on the baby and pulled her toward him. "Mama," she cried.

Sam stiffened. Frank was confident she wouldn't break down in front of her colleagues.

"Come over here, Detective." Case walked to the door, opened it, and led Sam into the hallway before closing the door. She stood in front of FBI Special Agent Brett Case. He continued. "Listen to me and listen good, Detective. Margie apparently remembers her mother. And that's not you. I'm warning you. Do not become attached."

Sam sniffled. "I know."

"Good. Our goal, your team's goal, is to find the children's biological mothers. Understand?"

Sam exhaled deeply and nodded. "Yes."

"And I expect you and Dr. Khaos, while the children are with you, to continue to try to get as much information as you can. We'd like their reunion with their mothers to happen as quickly as possible. Got that?"

"Definitely, Special Agent Case." Sam turned to go back into the room.

When Margie saw Sam, she called out to her. "Mama."

CHAPTER 3

Frank and Sam drove their cars to Frank's Mill Basin, Brooklyn, home in the section with the largest properties. He pulled into the driveway in his Explorer first, and Sam followed in her Murano, parking behind him. Perfect timing. She'd left the precinct with Nick twenty minutes earlier to get a lift to her house. No matter what, they'd need two cars. It was a good thing that Agent Case brought a car seat to the precinct. Frank had Frankie's seat that he outgrew in the trunk. It came in handy for Henry, and Benjamin was tall enough for the seat belt. Sam took Margie and Melissa with her. Margie's stroller converted, so Melissa sat in the gifted booster seat.

He'd had called his in-laws before he left the precinct—when he had the energy. Frankie was so excited to meet more cousins. And he couldn't wait to see Cameron and Andrew again. Frank smiled. Yes, he'd be getting together again soon with his brother Carl. This reminded him. He'd have to call Carl ASAP. He needed to know what happened today.

Frank's mind reeled. In the course of an hour today, his life changed. How would he deal with this—going from one child to five, and Sam moving in after only being engaged two days? He was usually slow in making life-altering decisions. The universe certainly pelted him with the unexpected. He closed his eyes for a moment in a silent prayer to his mom up in heaven. He needed her protection more than ever, now. Theresa had never let him down, even when she was alive and he was in Iraq, he felt her energy surrounding him. She'd dealt with plenty of his craziness over the years from the time she and Peter adopted him when he was ten. She was making it her duty to make sure he paid it forward, all right—by now adopting four children. How could he not? They were his brother's blood, his blood. *Hold on, Frank. You're jumping the gun here. It may never come to adoption if, and when, they find the children's mothers.*

His adoptive parents forgave him for all of the grief he had put them through. Now it was his turn to forgive. *But could he? Could he forgive his biological brother for murdering seventeen women across the United States?* That would be a tough nut to crack.

Until he met Sam, Frank didn't give a thought to the astrological signs. His was Libra.

Oh, man! Thinking about it, he was a true Libra—forgiving. He never liked confrontation. He was the negotiator by career choice. Now, it spread to his personal life. He didn't know why these thoughts hit him now, but they did.

Yeah. He was a Libra all right—on every level.

The front door of the house opened, and Frankie ran down the ten steps to meet them before Frank opened the car door. "Dad!"

The sound of his son's voice jolted him out of his self-analysis.

Sam was the first to get out of the car, and she went around the passenger side rear to help Melissa. Frankie ran into her arms. "You're moving in, Sam? Really?"

"Yes, I am!" She kissed him on the top of his head.

Melissa stepped out of the car, and Sam introduced them.

After the eye-to-eye then body lookovers, Melissa broke the ice. "Frankie, you look just like my brother!"

"Really? I look just like my dad."

Frank got out of his car with Henry and Benjamin and noticed the mischievous look Frankie carried on his face—

the hidden smile as he twisted his mouth. "Frankie, be nice."

Frankie went face to face with Benjamin. "We do look alike," he said as he used his hand to measure their height. "And you're as big as me, too!"

"I'm even bigger! When were you eight?"

"In January."

"I'm eight and a half."

So far so good. "This will be great, Frankie. You'll have friends right in the house with you." *I hope.*

Sam held Margie as Frank pulled out the stroller base from the trunk and reassembled it. Trying to put Margie back in the stroller was impossible. The baby wiggled so much in Sam's arms, she gave up. Frank sucked his cheeks in. Right away, he realized—as if he didn't at the precinct— that Margie had Sam wrapped around her little finger, and at ten months, that finger was definitely little. Sam was already a pushover with these kids. Something, he'd have to change.

Benjamin looked around in awe. "Why is there so much snow on the ground?" He looked as if he was afraid to take a step.

Yep. Definitely sheltered, Frank confirmed.

Frankie didn't seem to understand his cousin's question. "Because it's winter." He took the lead and charged onto the snow-covered lawn that ran around the expanse of the brick house. "Bet you can't catch me."

After bursting out laughing at Frankie, Henry was the first to take the plunge, running into the snow, falling in up to his waist. Melissa yelled after him, sounding as if she was the little mom of the four. She traipsed into the snow, wobbling and falling, herself. Benjamin took a few small steps into the white mound. He picked up some snow in his gloved hand, appearing not to know what to do with it. He compressed it in his hands and then stared at his gloves. Shaking his hand did nothing to dislodge the snow. Margie squirmed in Sam's arms, wanting to go down onto the snow. In her snowsuit that had booties to cover her shoes, and gloves attached to the sleeves, she was the most protected. Sam made sure the gloves were secure, fumbling with one hand. Frank laughed at her. She responded with a crooked smile then put the baby down. Margie took one crawl, got snow on her mouth, and sat up. She looked up at Sam with a quivering lower lip. Sam bent down to pick her up, but the baby pushed Sam's arm away. Then the little one clapped her hands and the snow puffed onto her face. Then she put her arms up, and Sam picked her up immediately, brushing the snow off her.

Henry struggled to take steps and his laughter turned to crying quickly. Frank scooped him up into his arms and brushed the snow off him. He realized the older kids weren't wearing boots. "Come on, guys. Inside. It's getting dark and the temperature is dropping."

"I want to play, Dad." Frankie jumped with big strides over to Benjamin and picked up snow in his glove. He made it into a snowball and handed it to the newcomer. Benjamin took it and smiled. Frankie made another snowball and tossed it gently onto Benjamin's chest. This time, the newcomer scowled. "Hey, this is what we do with it. Have a snowball fight," Frankie explained.

Benjamin shook his head while backing away and bumped into Frank.

"Not now, Frankie. We have a lot to do. Come on. We need your help putting together the crib and setting up the guest rooms. Let's go. Grandma and Grandpa have dinner ready." Frank opened the garage door. "Grab your bags from the car."

Benjamin handed Melissa her bag then he took his and Henry's. Turning back quickly, he realized he needed Margie's and grabbed it from the open trunk.

Frank nodded, impressed. "It's terrific the way you take care of your brother and sisters, Benjamin."

"Yeah, well, we're all we have right now. I don't know how long we'll be here."

"We'll stay together for as long as we can. Hopefully, that'll be a long time."

Benjamin looked up at him suspiciously but didn't respond. He looked down as he followed Frank into the garage.

Leaving the stroller in the garage, they entered the mudroom where Frank's in-laws met them. Both career military, they always held serene postures. Nothing ever riled them. Nothing overwhelmed them—except for the murder of their daughter.

Now they smiled at the five, cold, snow-covered children and gave Frank a long stare. *Okay, they may not be overwhelmed, but they think I'll be*, he thought. Now wasn't the time to tell the children these were his late wife's parents and that he was very close to them. He introduced Kathryn and Walter as Mom and Dad, Frankie's grandparents. They held warmed socks and slippers in their hands for all of the children.

Kathryn bent down toward Henry. "Let's get these wet clothes off you." She began to pull the zipper on his coat down, but he grabbed her hand.

"I can do it, myself," he said, shuddering.

"Well, you're too cold, so I'll help."

She spoke firmly, and the youngster apparently got it. His coat, shoes and wet socks came off without a problem.

The coats and gloves were hung on racks, shoes under the bench.

Melissa hugged herself, rubbing her arms. "It's so cold." They scrambled into the house. "Ah, warm. Much better."

Frankie didn't get it. "Didn't you guys ever play in the snow before?"

"No," answered Benjamin, for the first time appearing to Frank to be shy.

"How can that be?" Sam asked.

"Dad wouldn't let us play in the snow."

"Why not?"

"Snow is dirty in the street and it melts fast."

"Come on, guys, get your wet clothes off. Benjamin, you're in Frankie's room. We'll set up the crib in the room next to Sam's and mine, and Melissa, you're sharing with Henry, for now. So let's go upstairs and get into dry clothes."

Melissa stopped dead. "I only have boy's clothes in my bag."

Sam smiled. "I got you covered. I bought you two outfits."

The little girl stared at her. "You lied? At the police station you said one outfit."

Frank shot Sam a look that could kill. She had to make it right. "It's one set that came with a few choices, so I bought all of the pieces. Come on, Melissa, I'll show you, upstairs." Frank glared at her. Sam blew out a deep breath. "What, Frank? I like to be prepared. And I'm glad I did. Hey, don't you remember I taught for ten years before joining the department? I know kids need more than one change of clothes."

Before he went up the staircase, Benjamin turned toward Kathryn and Walter. "What do we call you, anyway?"

The seniors glanced at each other. "Grandma and Grandpa will do just fine," the older woman said with a warm smile.

Melissa pouted. "We never had a grandma and grandpa, ever."

"How come?"

"Dad told us his parents lived very far away, and he doesn't see them anymore."

Grandma's voice softened. "That's so sad, sweetheart."

"It was only bad at school when we were in a play or when people came to see us in the classroom. Other kids' grandparents came."

When Melissa became teary, Frank intervened. "Upstairs, now. Let's get you all into dry clothes. Give the baby to Mom, Sam." He stared at his wife-to-be.

Mom held out her arms for Margie. As Frank expected,

it was a no go, at first. The baby held onto Sam's hair, whining, "Mama."

"Come to Grandma, Margie. Mama will be right back." Kathryn took the baby, held her tight, and turned her away. "Go."

Sam stood hesitant, while Frank rolled his eyes. He actually had to push her toward the stairs. "Come on, Sam. You have to get your tough on."

They heard Melissa arguing with Henry over who was going to take which bed prompting them not to waste any more time on nonsense. Frank bolted up the rest of the thirteen stairs to find Henry crying in the corner. He was soaked down to his briefs. Frank knew he'd done it to himself.

"Come on, let's get you washed and changed. I'll show you where the bathroom is." Frank got his clothes off, giving him a chance to examine the little guy. Not one mark scarred his light skin. *Thank God, these kids don't appear to be physically abused.* "Come on, Melissa, you get changed, too."

"Not in front of you, Uncle Frank."

"Ah, okay, you're at that age. Come on, Henry, let's give the girls their privacy." He winked at Sam and left the room.

♥♥♥

"Finally, girl time!" Sam exclaimed, lowering her tone to that of a child, proceeding to take out the second outfit from the shopping bags that lay on the twin bed. Melissa giggled but Sam saw her holding back. "What, sweetheart?"

"We're used to being with adults but you're acting like a little kid!"

Sam stared at her with jaws dropping. "Guess I'm trying too hard to make you feel at home, huh?" She felt her sweatshirt and T-shirt then the pants. "Just your pants need to be changed—oops, and your socks." Sam handed Melissa the clothes, and she sat on the bed to change.

As Melissa pulled on the pants, she looked around the room. "Not that. Dad expects us to act grown up all the time, especially with strangers. And you're talking baby-talk. It's okay with Margie, but not with us. This room is so pretty." After she dressed, Melissa went over to the wallpaper, and ran her fingers over the Paisley pattern. "Wow, I love these colors. The pinks are my favorite." She ran her finger down the striped wall then raised her finger to her mouth. "I bet this wallpaper is hand painted." The curtains seemed to have drawn her in. As if mesmerized, Melissa handled the matching textured silk, ceiling-to sill-curtains. She lifted the top layer and moved it to the window frame. "I'd like it better if the sides were pulled back." She held the fabric, stretching her arm out, and moved back to get a better view. Tilting her head to look at it in different perspectives, she nodded. "Definitely better."

"Melissa, you're six years old. How do you know all of this?"

"Did you forget that my dad is a designer and artist?"

"He's teaching you?"

"Yes. He has a design studio."

"Where?"

"Oh, in the apartment. And he has tons of art stuff. We stay in there with him while he's working, and he asks us what we think."

"That's wonderful."

"I think I want to be a decorator when I grow up." She continued to look around and walked to the dresser opposite the twin beds. "See, like this? I think it would be prettier painted white, than left in the plain colored wood."

Enough with the decorating. She'd like to remodel it herself, except for the fact that Frank's late-wife, Jen, did it all and he'd made it a point to tell her he'd change nothing, ever.

"You said you have to act grown up with strangers. Are you with strangers, a lot?"

Melissa turned toward Sam and then a painting on the wall caught her eye. She went up to it and answered Sam, but the painting held her focus. "No, never. I mean with Locklear and if any of her friends come over. But she's not supposed to. This could be like the ship in Benjamin's bathroom, but I think my dad could do a better one."

"How do you know?"

Melissa turned abruptly apparently not understanding the question. "Have you seen any of his art?"

"Uh, yes." Sam paused to refocus. "But I meant how do you know Locklear isn't supposed to have friends over?"

Melissa stared up at the painting. "We heard Dad yelling at her. Not exactly yelling, he never yelled, but he sounded angry. I'd sure like to feel this."

"You'll have to ask Uncle Frank. What happened?"

Melissa plopped down on the bed next to Sam. "Well, you met Dad, right?"

"Yes. I did. He was so nice to me."

"He didn't yell, did he?"

"No. Not at all."

Melissa scrunched up her nose. "Why were you in our house, anyway?"

"Well," Sam paused. "First tell me about how you knew he was angry. I don't want to forget that part."

"Okay. He came to pick us up and Locklear's friend—"

"A man or lady?"

"A lady. Her name is Chantal. And she was playing with Margie on the floor. And it looked like she and Locklear were having a serious conversation."

"How could you tell it was serious?"

"They were whispering then looking at me and Benjamin and then whispering more. I couldn't make out the words. And Margie was laughing. Dad came in, and he motioned with his finger like this—" She demonstrated with her index finger bent toward her. "—and said, 'over here, now.' He whispered something, and Locklear looked like she was going to cry. Then he got us together without saying another word and we left."

"I guess your dad wanted Locklear to give her full attention to you. I could understand that. So Benjamin saw this, too?"

"Yes, and we just hoped that Dad wouldn't fire her, but he didn't." Melissa let out a breath of relief.

Frank passed by the door with Henry already in pajamas. "Dinner's ready. One bathed and four to go. Meet you downstairs. Come on, guy," he said, holding Henry's hand.

"Melissa, hungry?" Sam asked.

"A little. We just had lunch."

Sam checked her watch. "That was four hours ago. What time do you usually go to bed?"

"Benjamin and me by nine. Henry by eight, and Margie, earlier."

"Well, tonight will be a late night for all of us. Let's go downstairs."

Benjamin and Frankie already seated around the dining room table dug into their salads. Frank had put Henry into a booster seat, served him, and Margie was in a highchair, with seats for Sam and Melissa next to her. Frank's parents sat at the end of the oval table. A white tablecloth with lace trim covered the table, with cream-colored plates and matching silverware in front of each place. A chopped mixed salad sat in the center as the first course.

When Sam came in with Melissa, the little girl's gaze scanned the entire room. She nodded as she looked at the cream embossed wallpaper but grimaced at the table settings.

Sam and Melissa took their places and immediately Margie squirmed to climb out of the highchair. Everyone was distracted from acknowledging Melissa's disproval.

"No, Sam, don't take her out." Frank gave Margie a stern look. "No." He got up to get the baby food, that Special Agent Case's wife made, from the warmer and brought it over in a divided baby serving plate.

As Grandma served the salads to Sam and Melissa, Frank attempted to feed the baby. As he brought the spoon to her mouth, she shook her head with closed lips. Frank attempted the old airplane trick with the food-filled spoon coming in for a landing. Too bad, Margie's hangar closed.

Sam snickered. *Go ahead, Frank, show me you can beat me.* "Let me see if I can feed her." She turned the highchair around, and as soon as she lifted the spoon, Margie opened her mouth. "Yum, yum, right?" Sam was in heaven. Though not her own biological children, she felt fulfilled. *Too soon? Maybe.* But, yes, she was totally willing to adopt as she and Frank had discussed just last week, and today confirmed it. Even though Frank did say he wasn't afraid of having another child, and he mentioned it in front of her own father, she'd wait and see. *And who knew how long the kids would be staying? Right. Way too soon for her to become their mommy.*

All she knew right now was that her life was becoming complete—a wonderful husband-to-be, an amazing stepson, four beautiful and healthy nieces and nephews, and wonderful in-laws who adored her. Everyone ate so peacefully, and she was shocked the kids were so quiet. *After what I've been through the past few weeks, I deserve peace.*

Grandma served bowls of homemade chicken soup full of carrots, celery, and boiled bite-sized pieces of chicken in front of all but the baby. The sweet and savory aroma woke Sam up from her focus on Margie. She watched the children and smiled as she dug into her own bowl of soup. She blew on a tablespoon. Margie grunted and pointed to the soup. "You want some, Margie?"

The baby grunted again.

Frank got up and pulled a bowl from the cabinet, filling it with the soup. After mashing the veggies, cutting the chicken into tinier pieces, he brought it over to Sam, who was already feeding Margie from her bowl. The scornful look she got as he sat back down gave her the idea that now was the perfect time to change the subject. "Melissa, tell Uncle Frank your decorating ideas."

Frank nearly choked on his soup. He coughed and soup dribbled down his chin. He grabbed his napkin just in time. "Excuse me?" he said. Melissa sat with serious intent. He sighed. "Redecorating ideas?"

Sam saw his body tense up. *Will he stay in his staunch 'I'm not changing a thing' stance or will he humor the six-year-old?*

He took another spoonful of soup, and while he chewed and then swallowed, he stirred the soup. He barely glanced up at Melissa. "And what might those ideas be?"

"Here she goes." Benjamin rolled his eyes. "I wouldn't get her started if I were you, Uncle Frank."

Now Frank laughed. "Why not?"

"Every house we go to, she tells people what she thinks they should do."

Sam perked up. She was still on the job to get as much as she could from them. "I thought you said you didn't go anywhere with your dad."

"Not like outside," Benjamin said. "We went to his friend's apartment a lot."

"Yeah, Uncle Mike," Melissa added "And when Dad was decorating his apartment, I picked out a lot of the stuff."

Sam had an idea she was talking about Mike Sheffield but she had to ask. "And where does Uncle Mike live?"

"On the floor below us."

Frank groaned. "Mike Sheffield?"

"You know Uncle Mike?" Melissa said.

Frank distracted himself by helping Henry wipe his mouth. "Yeah, we were—" Sam immediately patted his arm. "—are friends," he said.

"You better call him," Melissa said.

"Why?"

"He'd want to know Dad is in the hospital."

Sam saw Grandma grasp onto her husband's hand underneath the table. Frank had brought them up to speed on the entire Scorpio case—that the children's dad was deceased and so was their "Uncle" Mike, by their dad's hand, or rope to be exact. And that Mike Sheffield was Henry Slater's accomplice in the seventeen serial murders. Well, they had to confirm the last sixteen. The FBI was in the process of tracking Sheffield's traveling to the casinos that Slater had hit.

After worried looks from Frank's in-laws, Sam changed the subject. "Let's get back to Melissa's decorating ideas."

Frank sucked in his cheeks. With pursed lips, he focused on Melissa. "Sure, tell me your ideas."

Benjamin bit his lip but then said what was on his mind. "Melissa, look at him. He really doesn't want to hear it."

Frank had to know what he was doing. He immediately relaxed his facial expression. "How do you know?"

"I'm good at…I don't know how to say it. I can look at someone and tell stuff."

Frank smiled. "What kind of stuff?"

Sam grinned. She knew Frank understood exactly what Benjamin meant. Just like with Frankie, Frank wanted to increase his expressive abilities and made him explain things. Frank was also on the job. Another pressure.

"Like the way a person looks."

Smiling, Frank explained it. "You mean you're good at reading someone's body language."

"Yes. I think that's what they call it. That's how I knew when not to talk to Dad."

"How did your dad look?"

"It's hard to explain. Dad just sat there and looked straight ahead."

"Yes," Melissa said. "He was in a daydream. I did it in school and my teacher woke me up."

"Good. Daydreaming in school isn't a good idea. Well, I will listen to Melissa, but tell me first about your Uncle Mike. You told Special Agent Case this is your third school year in New York. Did you meet him when you moved here?"

"No," Benjamin said. He put a spoonful of chicken soup in his mouth and swallowed. "He moved here with us."

Sam perked up. "Really? From Florida?"

"Yes."

Frank put his napkin down on the table. "Did—Does Uncle Mike have a wife and children?"

"I thought you said you're friends?"

"Well, we are. New friends. We met last month. We do the same kind of work with people."

"Yes. He's a talking doctor," Benjamin said. "He had a wife. But what's it called when the wife leaves?"

"A divorce?" Sam said.

"Yes. And she stayed in Florida. With their children. But they're older than us."

Sam continued to feed Margie the soup. It gave her some time to let her mind wander.

Thank you, Benjamin for confirming that Mike Sheffield had to travel with Henry Slater. No wonder his wife wanted a divorce. Mike would rather play with Henry than with her. What wife would tolerate that? Or maybe she wasn't into the culture. Um, was it a divorce, or was she another victim? How many more bodies do we need to uncover?

Sam felt the jab of Dara, her spirit guide, in her abdomen. She'd learned to trust that response since her conversation with Dr. Trenton in the Aries case. Her feelings were consistently on target—especially in the case she thought they'd completed, just two days ago. This time she was sure. There'd be more leftover bodies still to uncover.

"I'm full," Frank said, wiping his mouth and pushing his chair away from the table. He checked the kid's bowls and saw they were near empty.

"Me, too," the children all said with their voices trampling each other.

"Sam and I will clear the dishes, Frank," Mom said. "Dad will help you bring up the crib."

Melissa jumped up. "We could help, too."

"How about, you let the boys help, and Melissa, you can help Grandma and me, and keep Margie occupied?"

"Okay!" the little girl said excitedly.

$$\text{\emph{c}\emph{se}\emph{s}}$$

The next two hours dragged for Frank and his father-in-law, though it was nonstop strenuous work. Leave it to Jen to pick out the most complicated crib to reassemble—with the added designs on separate pieces of wood. Unpacking the frame was a struggle. It was wrapped tight in plastic and duct tape to prevent it from yellowing in the heat of the garage. Frank decided to forget about the decorative pieces. They'd take at least another hour. And he was already beat. The kids looked like they were falling asleep on their feet. Jen demanded the crib be white in case they had a girl. When all the plastic lay on the floor, he paused at the memory. They were going to have a girl. She was pregnant when gunned down by Dingo Withers. The emotional side of Frank reared its head, filling his eyes with tears. His father-in-law wasn't doing any better. Oh, man! Even though he'd move on with Sam, and he knew it was right, he couldn't get past this moment. He literally froze, immobilized. It wasn't until Frankie yanked on his pocket to get a move on that he snapped out of it. Frank ruffled the top of his son's head as a thank you. Frankie understood what his father meant and looked away.

It took three trips from the garage up to the bedrooms to get all of the parts of the crib and that was with the three boys helping. Henry carried the plastic baggie of nuts and bolts that opened and fell all over the stairs. Another ten minutes wasted as the older boys went on a search to find the pieces. It was more of a game to them then a serious assignment. Frank let them be. The boys were bonding— loud and boisterous but bonding. Frankie always loved it when a friend slept over for one or two nights, max. This would be a long-term arrangement and Frank wanted the boys to be friends. Spending all of their time with their dad, Henry and Benjamin didn't have much socialization time with kids their age outside of school. He saw that Benjamin had even been a little awkward in the snow. Undoubtedly, these children would have problems yet to be uncovered and the next few days or upcoming weeks would be the honeymoon period. Not to mention his son. This would be an adjustment for Frankie—no longer the only child.

The crib itself wasn't hard to assemble once the opposite sides were aligned, but Frank and Jen's dad were eight years younger the last time, and Jen, with belly nearly popping, and her mother helped. Now they had the assistance of three more-than-clumsy kids, with Frankie being the only one who could hold a side upright. It was apparent that Frankie was the more-athletic child, thanks to his own involvement in Mixed Martial Arts and Brazilian Jiu Jitsu and Frank's encouraging Frankie to earn a yellow belt in Tae Kwan Do. Okay, one of his first goals would be to get these kids into martial arts. *But first things, first. Let's survive this first night.*

They assembled the crib and change table in the bedroom next to Frank's master. When it was finished, Frank tugged on the side railing to make sure it was sturdy. He didn't remove his hands. It was as if they stuck. This had been Frankie's nursery and the decor and wallpaper was still the infantile animal print in yellow, white, pink, and blue. Frank had kept the door to this room shut—to block out the memory, though he told people it was for less to clean. When Frankie needed a big-boy-bed, Jen wanted him in another room, farther from their master, so when they were busy trying to add another member of the family—for the nursery—they'd have some peace and mommy-daddy time. Frank inhaled deeply then smiled.

Come to think of it, he needed to tell the kids about his rule. *If the bedroom door is closed, don't come in unless you're bleeding or the house is on fire.* Frank wondered if Henry had such a rule. Did he entertain lady-friends in the apartment when the kids were there? He made sure they were gone when Sam was there.

A warm arm sliding around his waist pulled him out of his reflection. He hadn't even noticed that Benjamin and Frankie disappeared out of the room, and Henry lay collapsed on the carpet. Oh, man! He was in a deep one. Frank reciprocated and hugged Sam, smiled at Melissa, then let go of Sam to get crib sheets out of the chest against the opposite wall. Blue, but they'd have to do for now. After handing them to Sam to put on the mattress, he scooped up Henry to put him into his bed in the room next door.

He stopped when he was in the hall. "Melissa, did the detectives pack nighttime diapers for Henry?"

"I don't know. The lady detective packed him. But he does need them."

"Okay. We're covered. Sam, in the bottom drawer there are toddler diapers. They should fit for now."

The shower started in the bathroom next to Frankie's room. Then laughing. Too much laughing. With Henry in his arms, Frank peeked inside. "Guys, make it fast. It's late." It was beyond late.

Another half hour to shower the kids then tuck them into bed. Henry had been out, Melissa dozing off, but Benjamin and Frankie were pulling a stall technique—reading a book.

"Wow!" Benjamin exclaimed as Frank entered the room. "Uncle Frank is this really you?" Frank smiled and nodded. "Wow! You jumped out of a helicopter!"

"That's right. In Iraq."

Frankie turned a couple of pages. "And that's my mom next to my dad. They're taking care of a soldier who got hurt."

"You took care of people on the dirt? Where's the hospital?"

"None around there. We had to make do."

"Is Frankie's mom a doctor, too?"

"No," Frankie said, with gloom. "She was his nurse."

"She looks almost like Samantha. Where is she?"

Frankie looked up at his cousin with tears in his eyes. Frank sat down on the bed and hugged his son as Frankie hid his face on his dad's chest. It took Frankie a few moments to compose himself and apparently, he decided to brave it. "My mom was killed when I was five." He sniffled. "This past November, Sam found the man who did it, and now he's in prison for the rest of his life."

Benjamin looked somber. "At least you knew your mom. I don't know mine. Uncle Frank, do you think Sam can find her and all of our moms?"

"Come here," Frank said, pulling Benjamin into his arms along with Frankie. Now came the task of comforting two choked-up kids. "That's exactly what we're going to do. But right now, all you have to know is that you're safe and loved. Okay?"

Benjamin buried his head in Frank's chest. Frank bet that this was the first time Benjamin attempted to cry, probably having to hold onto his emotions in front of his dad. Frank didn't stop him. After a few minutes, Frank had to.

"Come on, into bed now. It's been a rough day for you guys."

Frank looked toward the wall above the boy's head, compressing his lips.

And I sure hope we find your moms…alive.

CHAPTER 4

When the sun peeked through the bedroom window, Frank opened his eyes, still lying on his back. He turned his head and caught a glimpse of the clock on the night table next to his bed. Sitting up fast, he pulled the blanket off. "Crap! Nine-thirty?" He almost didn't believe it. Sleeping late was not his thing.

The high-pitched "Hey," that came from next to him made him turn around. His gaze went to Henry—still asleep—who struggled to tug the brown Jacquard blanket back up. Then his gaze hit Melissa sleeping on her side facing Sam, and lastly to Margie, who laid half on Sam, half on the bed—all with their eyes shut tight and that included Sam. *How in the hell did that happen? Without me knowing?* That was a first. Ever since the military, he'd been a light sleeper. He'd be the one up with Frankie at the slightest whimper. Three kids in his bed? Uh uh. Not good. He looked at the foursome sleeping so peacefully. Ah, what the heck? He'd let them sleep.

Frank got up, pulled on sweat pants and then his T-shirt. After taking care of his needs in the bathroom, he went into Frankie's room to check on him and Benjamin. The boys were just beginning to stir.

Frankie sat up quickly. "Dad, I'm late for school."

"No, you're taking off today." His son looked surprised. "I shot your teacher an email last night. You're covered."

Benjamin opened his eyes. "We can't miss school."

"I know. I like that you feel that way. But we have to

take care of things to register you. Tomorrow we'll go. Get washed and ready for breakfast. Hungry?"

The boys couldn't get out of bed fast enough. Frank laughed.

Frank passed Sam in the hall holding Margie as she walked into the baby's room. "How did that happen last night?" His gaze scanned her body. Pajamas? She was actually wearing frumpy granny PJs? In a monotone navy blue? She prepared better, rather more modest, than he did at least.

"How did what happen?"

"Sam. Three kids in our bed. Not good."

"Margie started to cry and I went in to her. Listen, I was exhausted. I wasn't going to fight her."

"And the other two?"

Sam laughed. "I don't know. Magic?"

"Not funny, princess." He kissed the top of her head. "Get the kids ready. I'll make breakfast."

Still in their pajamas, Sam included, the troop sat around the dining room table as Frank served sunny-side-up eggs he made in a special pan that had indented sections to maintain their shape. He placed flawlessly rounded circles of egg—with the yolk positioned in the center—on each plate. The kids stared at them. Frank laughed. "What? Your dad made them plain scrambled?"

"No," Melissa replied with an attitude. "He made them with the exact same pan."

"Ah. And it's exact or same, not both," retorted Frank. "They mean the same thing." Melissa rolled her eyes. He wasn't letting this go. "Hey! Did you wake up with an attitude today?" He flipped over the waffle maker and opened the top. He cut the waffle into four sections and handed them out.

"No," she pouted.

"Then what's the matter?"

"I want to go back to our house, our own room. When can we go?"

Frank paused. The time was getting closer to tell them. "The police are still there. It's not good to be in the apartment with all of their equipment."

"Why not?" Benjamin asked.

Frank's cell rang. "Hold that thought. Khaos."

"Hey, It's John Trenton."

Frank served Sam and himself eggs and waffles, holding the phone between his shoulder and ear. "Hey. What's going on?"

Sam was feeding the baby oatmeal with mashed banana, but Margie grunted and pointed to the egg and waffle on Sam's plate. Without hesitation, Sam took a tiny amount of egg on a spoon and fed her. The baby sucked the egg, delighted, and opened her mouth for more.

Frank couldn't pay attention to her and the call. He turned his back on Sam and plated more eggs.

"Did you survive the first night?"

Frank laughed. "Yeah, the kids are great."

"Glad to hear that. Honeymoon period."

"Don't I know it?" Frank took the loaded plate to the table.

"Lieutenant Martin called me in to work the Scorpio case while you and Sam are off this week. I just wanted to give you a heads up."

"Hold on a minute." Frank got up. "Sam, hold down the fort. I'll be right back." He walked out of the dining room and into the den. He opened the blinds to let in the sun before he sat on the leather couch in front of the window and put his legs up onto the coffee table. "Okay. Cool. What did he tell you so far?"

"It's still too fresh. When he called me this morning, he caught me up on yesterday. I'm going to meet with him now. Brett Case is also coming in. Then if Withers can meet with us, we'll go over to the apartment. I want to see the children's quarters."

"That's something I'd like to see, too."

"Okay, I'll keep you posted. In the meantime, take care.

Five kids are more than a handful. Oh, before I let you go. The captain approved our leave for April to go to Florida." The phone disconnected.

Frank's mind came to a full stop.

Crap! I forgot about that. I have to fulfill Henry Slater's will before it can be executed. How in the hell did I allow myself to be sucked into that? Confronting my bio parents? I still don't see Trenton's point of view on that. Shrink or no shrink, he actually wants me to thank my bio parents for placing me for adoption so I could have a better life? Sorry, Doctor Trenton, this time forgiving will be very hard for me. Plus, I'm sure his kids get the bulk of his estate, which Slater failed to tell us at the time, and now I'm their guardian.

He blew out a deep breath.

That makes it imperative for me to carry through on Slater's dying declaration.

The worst was yet to come. He knew he and Sam had to tell the children their dad was deceased. And he had to do it today. Knowing Benjamin's skills of putting two-and-two together, the kid must be surmising something is up. He'd never lie to a child—no matter his or her age. The memories of how he told Frankie his mom was killed came back to haunt him.

He sat on this couch. He remembered the exact time that he broke the news. It was three-o-five in the afternoon, when he told his son. Jen had been gunned down at ten a.m. On his birthday. And it was noon by the time they reached him at the Manhattan hospital. His lieutenant, Miguel Rojas, came personally with the hospital administrator. He couldn't believe it. He wouldn't believe it. It still seemed surreal. He'd collapsed screaming and demanded to be taken to see her body in the morgue. A sight he'd keep from their son. All the way, he kept hoping they'd made a mistake. Jen did two tours in Iraq with him, and she returned to the states without so much as a scratch. As did he. Only for her to be gunned down by a cop. That damn bastard crook-

ed cop. At the morgue, they prevented him from laying on Jen's bullet ridden body. Three bullets to her torso was what it took to deform his beautiful soulmate and murder their daughter in her womb.

Frankie was just five and in the second month of kindergarten. Frank held his son tightly in his arms and told him, "Something bad happened to Mommy." Frankie might not have understood at that moment but at the funeral when he saw his precious mommy lowered into the ground, the kid just lost it. So did Frank. And Jen's parents. On the positive side, Jen was given the priceless military funeral that she deservedly earned.

The sounds of raucous children running into the den brought him back. Thankfully so, or was it? "Hey, finished eating?"

"Yes, but you didn't," Sam said as she placed Margie on the carpet with some toys.

"I'll grab a shake."

"You okay?" Sam obviously read his despondent look.

"Oh, yeah. How about you kids getting dressed and we go over to visit Sam's parents?" Frank asked the children. "I'm sure they'd love to meet you."

"The only parent we want to meet is our own." Benjamin stared eye-to-eye with him.

"What's on your mind, Benjamin?" Frank knew this was it.

"Would you tell us the truth?"

"Always. Come here." Benjamin sat on his lap. Melissa snuck in between him and Sam, and Henry sat on Sam's lap. Frankie sat on the other side of his dad.

Benjamin's lower lip quivered as he paused. "Is our dad going to be okay?"

Frank exhaled deeply and glanced at Sam. "No."

"Did he die?"

Frank blew out a nasal breath and just nodded.

"What?" Melissa screamed.

Sobbing audibly but without tears, the children buried

their heads into Frank's chest. Henry sobbed from example. The little one didn't seem to know what to make of it.

Intellectually they know they should cry, but they don't know how to get to real emotions. "I know," Frank said, rubbing their backs and kissing their heads.

Sam's tears flowed as she hugged the children.

No matter what their dad did, he was still their dad, the one who protected and loved them—if Henry Slater Sr. knew how to love. There were no words at this moment.

Melissa sat up. "What happened?"

Oh, man. That was too fast of a recovery. "He took a pill of some kind and collapsed."

Benjamin stammered. "How—do—you—know?"

"I was with him."

"Then why did you let it happen?" Melissa raised a fisted hand but stopped before slugging Frank on his chest. "I hate you!"

Frank pulled her in close to him. "I couldn't get to him in time. He closed the bathroom door. I know, baby, it's so hard to understand."

"Sam," Benjamin cried. "Were you there, too?"

"Yes," Sam swallowed, stalling. "But I was in another room."

"Why did he do that?"

Frankie looked as if he was about to spill it all. Frank starred at him and shook his head.

"What, Frankie?" Benjamin demanded. "Do you know about it?" He sniffled out the words. "You know and we don't!"

Frank thought hard for a moment. As a kid, he'd been through a rough life, himself, and the people around him haven't been honest. It screwed him up for years. Until he was told by his adoptive parents, that his foster parents were killed in a car accident. It wasn't that they abandoned him at four, as he'd thought all those years. He nodded to Frankie that it was okay to talk to his cousins.

"I spoke to Uncle Henry, your dad, too."

"How did you speak to him?"

"I failed a test and I called Sam. Your dad answered the phone."

"You failed a test?" Benjamin grimaced.

"That wasn't the important part. He wanted Sam to marry him, and I wouldn't let him."

Melissa threw out her arms. "What? What about us?"

"He didn't tell me about you."

Benjamin stiffened, apparently in shock. "Why not? Uncle Frank, did he tell you about us?"

"No, he didn't."

"But why not? He loves us." Melissa collapsed onto Sam's chest. "No, I don't believe you."

"It's true, Melissa," Sam said, stroking the girl's hair.

Benjamin sat up and Frank could see in his eyes that the eight year old was reflecting upon something. "Why was he keeping us secret, then?"

"We're looking into that. It could explain why he never took you anywhere and you stayed in the apartment all the time, except when you went to school."

Benjamin turned toward his cousin as though he probably thought he'd get a more honest answer from the one his age. "What else, Frankie?"

"Yeah, then I met him at your house with Uncle Carl and our other cousins."

"We have another uncle?"

"Uncle Carl. And he has three kids. Andrew, Cameron, and Abby. And Abby is in jail for something. And the police were there with the ESU."

"What's the ESU?"

"The Emergency Service Unit," Frank explained.

"The same police that were in our apartment yesterday?" Melissa asked.

Frank felt a lump in his throat. He swallowed before he answered. "No, that was a different department."

"Why? What's going on?" Benjamin inhaled deeply, his cheeks reddening as if bracing himself. "Tell us, now!"

Frankie bit his lip and looked up at his dad.

Frank had to muster up the courage. "All right..."

᭡᭡᭡

John Trenton walked through the lobby in the Manhattan-North Precinct. In the six years he'd been a consulting forensic psychiatrist with the NYPD his reputation through the five boroughs preceded him. Although most of the department knew of him, he hadn't met all of them personally. Thankfully, since Nick Valatutti was in on the Scorpio case and he'd be here today, Lieutenant Martin had requested that Trenton come in, along with the Queens team—Lex Withers and Bella Richards—who were at Henry Slater's Upper West Side apartment right now. Except for the brief phone call this morning, Trenton would have to get to know Lieutenant Martin.

Entering the war room, the lieutenant cordially greeted him. "Have a seat, Dr. Trenton. Just when we were hoping that this case was winding down, we were hit by a major avalanche."

"Well, it wasn't a total surprise, Lieutenant," Detective Valatutti said. "Detective Wright surmised there might be children. And so did Dr. Khaos."

"Yes, Detective, I read the full report, and Lieutenant Hicks of Queens filled me in. I'm glad the children appeared when they did, though. From the standpoint of a parent, the thought of them appearing on the scene of their father's suicide would have been emotionally disastrous. Dr. Trenton, are you up to speed on the case?"

"Somewhat, as much as I've gotten in our meetings with Special Agent Case and the detectives," John said, hanging up his coat on the rack in the corner of the room. "But I haven't analyzed any paper work yet." Before he sat at the table, he unbuttoned his sports jacket. "And it's going to be emotionally disastrous anyway. I can't imagine how Dr.

Khaos and Detective Wright are going to break the news to them. Dr. Khaos's son knows because a cousin, who's also in custody for home invasions, blurted it out. To learn their dad is a serial killer is going to haunt them a long time. I know the goal is to reunite them with their mothers, and that will be another trauma. They've been raised together and now to separate them—bad move, in my opinion."

"Okay, point taken. I happen to agree with you."

Excellent. This guy is a caring human being. I could work with him.

"Agent Case is bringing over the will, and you'll dissect it to find the answers to what we need."

"Which is?"

"Where are these children's mothers?" Lieutenant Martin asked. "Are they alive or did they fall victim to Slater? On the one hand, I hope they're alive, and, on the other, it'd be better for them to have met their demise. Going along with what you said, Dr. Trenton, if the mothers are indeed alive, the children have to go back to them. It's the law."

"We can possibly delay the reunions for a while for the investigation," Detective Valatutti added. "It's easier to keep the children here for questioning, rather than hunt them down across the country. Then again, none of their testimony will be valid in court."

"Correct."

A receptionist showed in Special Agent Case.

🙖🙖🙖

Taking some silent time, Frank and Sam sat holding hands on the couch in the den. Frank's legs rested on the coffee table, while Sam rested hers across Frank's thighs. Sitting up, she leaned into him. Their conversation with the children had been the hardest thing either one of them had ever done in their lives. Frank knew kids were resilient. Frankie seemed to be after his mother's death, and Frank grew up, in spite of himself. He was also of the belief that no one ever escaped trauma in their life, and anyone who said their life was perfect or their children were perfect were lying. He encapsulated Sam in his arms, ready to kiss her. Loud voices from upstairs stopped them dead.

"Uncle Frank! Get up here," Melissa yelled, repeatedly, from the top of the stairs.

Frank pursed his lips and for a moment of needed rest, laid his head onto the back cushion before he bolted, ran up the stairs, and into Frankie and Benjamin's room. He found Henry scrunched close to the ceiling on top of Frankie's bookcase.

Frank reached for the boy. At six-four, with his arms extended, he just about had him. "What are you doing?"

"I climbed."

"Well, you're not supposed to. Get over here." Frank pulled him into his arms. Henry was hysterical laughing. "It's not funny. I'm not laughing."

"We're laughing," Benjamin said as he and Frankie lay on their backs on one of the beds.

Frank glared at them. "Don't egg him on. It's not funny."

"Yes. It is," Benjamin said, sitting up.

"You don't do that again." Frank carried him out of the room.

"Yes. I will."

Midway down the stairs Frank upped the ante. "You will? Then you're having a time out."

Henry stiffened. He stared at Frank as if his world had ended. "No!" he screamed. "No time out. I don't wanna go in the cage!"

Frank halted at the bottom of the stairs. "Cage? Kids, get down here, now!" He carried Henry over to the recliner in the living room and sat him down. Henry rested his hands on the plush tan suede armrests. "Lay back." Trying hard to keep a firm expression on his face, which was difficult because this kid was so darn cute with his curly head of dark blond hair and chubby cheeks with dimples, Frank pulled up the footrest so the recliner tilted back. Then he pulled the throw that hung over the arm and put it over Henry, cuddling him. "You rest now until I tell you that you can get up." Henry pouted but he relaxed. Frank sat down on the freestanding couch in the center of the room. "What is the cage?"

"Yeah, it's a cage for time out," Melissa said.

"Like an animal cage?"

"Sort of."

"And where is the cage?"

"In a room next to the kitchen."

"How often do you go into this cage?"

"Whenever Dad said we were bad." Melissa looked over at Henry. "He's sleeping. No! Don't let him sleep."

"Why not? He needed a nap. That's why he was cranky."

Margie crawled over to Henry and stood up holding onto the edge of the footrest of the recliner. Sam's eyed widened as the baby pointed. Sam picked her up, kissed her cheek, and put her under the blanket with her brother. She closed her eyes.

"No, don't let him." Melissa vehemently shook her head. "We're not allowed to nap. Dad says that if we sleep during the day, we won't sleep at night. And he likes a good night's sleep."

"It's okay. Let him. We need to take care of this." Frank put in a call to Withers at the apartment.

"Withers."

"Yeah, it's Frank. Did you find a cage in the apartment?"

"A cage?"

"The kids told me it's for time-out."

"Are you freaking kidding me?"

"You're on speaker. No. I'm not. Benjamin, tell Detective Withers where the cage is."

"In the room next to the kitchen."

"Another hidden room?"

"Hey, Detective, did I hear you correctly?" yelled a crime scene tech.

"Yeah, you did. Benjamin, how do we get to this room?"

"First, go into the kitchen."

"Okay, we're here."

"On the wall next to table and bench."

"Yeah?"

"On the board by the floor, there's a button."

"Got it."

"Push it and door will slide open."

Frank heard the door mechanism and then a few moments of nothing.

Withers yelled, "Holy crap! What else are we going to find?"

Frank became antsy. "Lex, what's going on? Show me!"

"Yeah, hold on, Frank." Withers hung up and called back using Facetime. "Take a look at this." He panned the phone for Frank and Sam to see the room.

"What is that stuff? That's a drawing board?"

Melissa looked at the phone. "That's Daddy's art studio. I told Sam about it."

"Where's the cage?"

Withers continued to pan the room.

"Stop. Right there. There's the cage," said Melissa.

Frank saw Withers turn around abruptly. He pointed. "This? This is a cage?"

Benjamin bopped his head. "Yes. That's where we go when we're bad."

Sam's jaws dropped as Withers moved the phone to cover the structure. "Oh my God! Melissa, that's not a cage. That's a dollhouse. A giant, adult-sized dollhouse. Lex, take us inside."

Lex moved the camera to inside the dollhouse that had pink and blue tiles on the roof. "Frank, you can fit in here."

"I see that. What's that? A bench? Melissa, give us a tour."

"Okay." She pointed on the screen. "That's the bench we sit on to read. And in the corner are the books Daddy wanted us to read. And when time out is over, Daddy sits on the bench with us to test us on the book. Over there, are the stuffed animals we could cuddle. Detective Withers, open the window on the side."

With the tip of his index finger, Withers slid the window up. He looked through it at Frank and shook his head,

Melissa continued. "See? When we were in there, Daddy was in the kitchen cooking, or we were doing homework at the table, so he could always see us."

"Why didn't he just send you to your room?"

Melissa let out a huff of exasperation. "Obviously, Uncle Frank, you didn't see our room."

"No, I did not. How long did you stay in there?"

"I don't know the exact time, but see the fridge?"

Withers brought it into the camera's view. "A real fridge?" He opened the door.

"Yes. Daddy never wanted us to be hungry, so he always brought us a snack."

"Oh, man!" Frank laughed. "So what snack did he bring?"

"Stop making fun, Uncle Frank," Melissa admonished. "This is serious. A bowl of fruit with humus or cottage cheese."

"Tell us about the outside. Did you build this with Dad?"

Benjamin sat up proud. "No. I did. Melissa was too little. See the fancy tile-work?"

Frank and Sam nodded.

"I bet you can't guess what style it is." Melissa taunted them.

"I wouldn't venture to guess," said Sam. "But I'd sure love to play in there."

Putting her hands on her hips, Melissa didn't hesitate to show her disapproval. "Of course *you* would."

"Hey," Frank responded to her attitude.

"Sorry. It's Victorian."

"Whoa!" Frank exclaimed. "And how do you know about that?"

"Daddy taught me." Melissa blew out a deep breath, preparing for the explanation. "Daddy said a dollhouse is perfect for the Victorian style. It's got a slanted roof, and many bright colors. This one is only one floor, though."

Frank's eyes opened wide. "I am very impressed."

"I told Sam. I want to be a decorator when I grow up. Detective Withers, can you bring all of Daddy's art stuff here?" Melissa choked up. "I want to still work with it."

"Sure, Melissa, when we pack up the apartment. Speaking about packing up. We sent out boxes of the kids' clothes and things to you this morning, and his office is already boxed, too. A lot we'll bring to the precinct and some will go to our guys at the lab."

Frank heard tapping on a wall and then a tech yelled into the phone. "Ask the kids if there's a moveable wall here. The paneled one on the other side of the room."

"Yes," Benjamin yelled into the phone.

"What is it, Benjamin?" Withers said with frustration in his voice.

"It's something secret. Dad never showed us what was in there. There's no button to open it. A keypad is on the wall."

"Hold on. We can get it." A minute passed. Frank heard the sliding of wood. Another moment passed. "Everyone, out of this apartment! We're done! Out now, Detectives!"

Frank heard voices, scrambling feet, and skidding sounds of heavy equipment on the floors. "What was behind that wall?"

"An aquarium, Doc," responded the tech. "An aquarium of scorpions."

CHAPTER 5

Sam sat on the couch, stunned, after Withers's quick disconnect in discovering the scorpion aquarium. She and Frank very well knew what that meant. No one would be allowed into the apartment until animal control neutralized the critters. That could take a week or more. Her heart sank thinking that Melissa's wish for her dad's art supplies may not happen. When those guys went in to spray, preserving the crime scene—yet alone a room not in question until a few minutes ago—was not on their agenda. She'd sure as heck do what she could to make sure the property remained intact. Would they let her in to supervise? Not a chance in hell, she thought, especially being on leave for a week. She'd never missed more than a day of work since she began her teaching career fifteen years earlier. Um, this gave her pause for thought. *Would I be able to cope being a stay-at-home mom for these children, or my own, one day? Take it easy, Sam,* she admonished herself. *Way too soon to even think that.* Though their needy faces as they played on the carpet gave her the answer—hell, yeah!

Hopefully, what was needed for the case had already been removed. Damn! That art room could tell them a lot, especially if Slater kept client files in there. Contracts would be even better. Frank patted her thigh. They were so in-sync with each other, even though barely three months into their relationship, but she knew he was probably thinking the same thing—about preserving the art supplies. She was sure—with their love for children—that's where Frank's mind went, too—not the crime scene.

Benjamin stared at her from where he was sitting on the carpet with Frankie and Melissa, playing with some transformers. "Samantha, what are you thinking about?"

He startled her out of the reflection. "What, sweetheart?"

"What were you thinking about?"

"How do you know I was thinking about something?"

He exhaled deeply as if he was insulted that she'd ask. "I can tell things."

Immediately, Sam caught on. What if this kid was already in tune with his abilities? His psychic abilities. She was certainly going to encourage it. Withers had already told her about his inference skills. "Well, you're right on target. I was thinking about the scorpion aquarium."

"And what else?"

Wow! He can read me. "Did you know about it?"

"Not that. But Dad has a big scorpion tattoo on his back. And he's a Scorpio, November second. I'm a Gemini, June tenth. And Melissa is an Aries, March twenty-first. What are you?"

"I'm a Scorpio, too."

"What's Uncle Frank?"

"A Libra. Listen, as much fun as it is to stay in PJs all day, how about getting dressed and going over to meet my parents?"

"Why?" Melissa asked, with a snicker.

"Because, I want to show you off to them. They'll love you. Just like Uncle Frank and I love you."

Melissa got up and, with pursed lips, went over to Sam. She tilted her head and put her hands on her hips. "Love us? How can you love us? You just met us yesterday."

Sam did a double take and looked toward Frank with mouth agape. "Come here, sweetheart." She tried to take Melissa in her arms. The six-year-old pulled back. "I'll tell you one thing. When a mom meets her baby or adopted child the very first time, the very first moment, the bond is there."

Melissa looked more despondent than she did before. "Then how come my mom didn't love me and my dad did?"

"We're going to find that out, sweetheart, and for right now, you're loved with all our hearts. Okay?"

Melissa nodded, without a smile.

Sam blinked back her tears. "After we go to my parents, you and I are having a girl's day out. Okay?"

"What's a girl's day out?" Melissa said suspiciously.

Sam spoke in a girly girl tone. "You—and—I are going shopping for school clothes, and I have a surprise for you."

Melissa huffed. "Okay. But please—stop with that little girl voice. It's getting on my nerves."

Frank bellowed out laughter.

"So, you know what I mean, right?" Melissa asked.

Frank nodded. "Yeah, I know what you mean."

"So do I," Frankie yelled. "But you'll get used to it."

"I can't help it. I was a teacher before I became a cop. So, let's all go get dressed."

"Really? What grade?"

"I started in kindergarten and moved up grades until fifth."

"Maybe you should go back there," Melissa chided.

"No!" Benjamin yelled. Melissa turned toward her brother. "Sam, found out who killed Frankie's mom," he told her, "so maybe she can find our moms. She has to stay a cop."

Melissa's jaw dropped, and then she compassionately looked at Frankie. "I didn't know that." She looked down at the carpeting, pouting. "Guess we're all messed up."

"No you're not, sweetheart. Come here." Sam pulled Melissa into her arms. This time the little girl went and laid her head on Sam's chest. "You've all had a hard time, but don't you worry. Uncle Frank and I will make it right." Sam kissed the top of her head and a solemn moment passed. "And so will everyone on our team."

Henry and the baby were still sleeping peacefully on the time-out recliner. Sam so badly wanted a distraction to lighten the mood. "Ooh, ooh, ooh." She took out her cell phone and opened the camera.

Melissa lifted her head. "What are you doing?"

"I'm taking a picture."

"No, you're not allowed to."

"Why not?"

"Dad wouldn't ever allow it. He said bad things happen to children when their pictures get out."

"We'll be very careful. And we want to have memories. Just for us."

"Melissa, Dad is dead." Benjamin introjected. "It doesn't matter what he said."

Melissa moved out of the way with her head down. Sam took the picture. "Hey, Melissa, want a selfie with you and me?"

She scrunched her freckled nose. "What's that?"

"Come here." Sam held Melissa close and held up the camera. "Smile." After the click, Sam showed it to her. The little girl giggled.

୧୬୧

The glare from the sun on the folders on the table distracted him. John squinted as he, Nick Valatutti, and Brett Case sat around the conference table in the war room in the Manhattan-North precinct. Open forensic folders and Henry Slater's Last Will and Testament covered the table. Half-eaten sandwiches and coffee cups added to the tabletop decor. Obsessive-compulsive, orderly John became more confused by the hour. As organized, as Henry Slater appeared to be, his financial records were a mess, as least as far as what his will projected. *Was that deliberate?* They had gone through it page-by-page, line-by-line, and they still hadn't reached the part that mentioned his biological children.

They'd put a call into the attorney who created the will, only to get a disconnected number. What a shock? While
Agent Case starred at the handset in bewilderment, Detectives Lex Withers and Bella Richards opened the door,
wearing intense frowns on their faces.

Agent Case looked just as annoyed. "You can't be
done?"

"Far from it." They pulled chairs out from the table and
sat. "The all mighty Henry Slater had his own supply of
scorpions. Live ones. A lot of them."

"You're kidding me?" John said. "It's illegal to have
scorpions in a New York City apartment."

"Tell that to the decedent," Withers said sarcastically. "It
was a large aquarium in his art studio—another hidden
room—concealed by a paneled wall. Thankfully, we didn't
see any loose, but the apartment had to be vacated."

"Got that part," John said. "But Slater couldn't buy them
in a pet shop or even have them shipped to his address. He
had to bring them across state lines himself."

Agent Case leaned forward in his seat. "And that matters
because?"

"All right," John said. "Hear me through. I'm going to
do a think aloud."

Agent Case snickered. "Would you please explain to me
what that is?"

"Going with thoughts as they come into my mind. Not
necessarily making sense yet."

"Yeah, you did that at the halfway house, looking for evidence in the Bobby Mitchell murder case last month." Bella sat back in her seat to take it all in. "Okay, go ahead with
your *think aloud.*"

John shook his head. "Okay, we know Slater committed
murders in fifteen states along the East Coast, including two
in Jersey to make seventeen. But we do not know if his
children's mothers came from those states. I'd guess not.
Because he wouldn't want to be seen again. Make sense?"
The team members nodded. "And it's our primary goal now

to locate their mothers," John continued. "The Southern and Mid-Western states allow the sale of scorpions. The store-owners had to know he was an out-of-towner. It's also policy for a responsible business owner to ask the reason for the purchase, especially if they're in bulk. Possibly Slater gave the mother's address to the owner of the store. Number one, to establish his residency, and number two, so they don't question the purchase. Giving his New York address would nix the sale. So I'm guessing Slater visited the mothers of his children. I'd like to have a language specialist, especially for the older children, and yes, the three year old and the infant too, yes, even with her babble, to speak with them, possibly to determine accent or region. That would help us narrow down birth. Okay, back to scorpions. Pet store franchises keep records that we should be able to access with a warrant, Agent Case. They also have security cameras in place. There are lots of break-ins and thefts of animals. So, it was revealed that the little one, what's her name?"

"Margie," answered Agent Case.

"Margie came to live with them around Christmas time. That's just five weeks ago. Can you get a warrant for every major franchise that sells scorpions throughout the US? Maybe we can track the surveillance footage and see Slater with one of the children, Margie, specifically, and her mother."

"Do you realize how much work that's going to be?" Withers said, annoyed.

"Absolutely. And I'm sure Agent Case's office can put all this into a database and find something."

"Yes, we can," Agent Case said. "You're right. I'd guess larger franchises, as well. They'd have younger employees who wouldn't necessarily be on the ball. A mom and pop store's employees might get more suspicious. Probably older. Possibly the owners, themselves. It's not going to be 'poof' immediate, but it can be done. Okay, what else, Doc?"

"Very conveniently the nanny disappeared, so did the

building superintendent. We know for sure Slater didn't kill the nanny. She was with the children Sunday after Slater died on Friday. But the superintendent, I'm not so sure about. Slater knew the end was near. He killed his swinging partner, Mike Sheffield, because of it. What's going on with that search?"

Nick opened the file on the desk in front of him. "Lex, since you're going to be busy, I assembled a team. They've been going door to door in the apartment building. As Henry Slater told everyone in the family meeting, celebrities do live in the building. Most of them were on location. The other residents seem to keep to themselves. Apparently, it's rare for the children to use the elevator in the hallway. Only one neighbor on the twenty-fifth floor ever saw them."

Withers nodded. "He does have a private elevator in the apartment that goes straight into the garage."

John referred to his notes. "First, can we get the nanny back to the states?" he asked the agent.

Case nodded. "Yes. We need her contact info, and I doubt if the kids know her address abroad. I do want to get a warrant for her apartment. Hopefully, we can find her destination in there."

"Okay, good. Lex, what can you tell us from being in the apartment?"

"A lot, John. Everything was meticulous. Even the kids' clothing drawers, clothes all folded. We packed up a lot for three of them. That crap about him wanting Melissa to be a boy scares the shit out of me."

"Leave it to Sam." Nick laughed. "A few days with her, Melissa will be a little princess."

"Oh, yeah?" John asked.

"Oh, yeah. That woman invented the word *Fashionista*." Nick grinned. "She could go head-to-head with you, Doc." John laughed. Nick continued. "I'll tell you, in the Aries case, with Sam newly assigned, she batted it out of the park with what she knew about the fashion world. Helped us solve that case, big time. What else about the apartment, Lex?"

"His fridge and freezer were stocked with prepared meals. Like there wasn't an inch of space available to put in anything else. An investigator only allowed me to take out prepared breast milk. They removed the food and brought everything to the lab for testing for poison. We'll have to wait on those results. Slater knew the nanny was going to be on vacation, so the food wouldn't be for her to feed the kids, and we believe he planned his suicide, so why so much food? Did he count on Frank taking it to feed the kids at his house?"

"I bet he did," John said. "Or that Frank and Sam would live in the apartment. That's what he told Frank at the family meeting, right?" The team looked at John, startled. John shrugged. "Lieutenant Martin let me listen to the tapes before you all came in. But breast milk?"

"Yep."

John jumped on that. "Hold on. So, Margie was nursed by her mom for at least eight months before she came to live with Slater. And he's continuing to get it for her. Okay two things are coming to me. We're either looking for women who agreed to be a surrogate, but no, that doesn't make any sense to me. What women after giving birth and nursing for eight months would hand a baby over? Anyone?"

"Are you kidding me?" Brett answered immediately. "That bonding is too strong. I can see a surrogate handing a baby over as soon as he or she exits the womb, but even to hold him or her—that would destroy it for my wife."

"Mine, too," Withers and Valatutti responded together.

"Now, I get the feeling Slater would have told people he had surrogates for mothers. Lessens questions," John said.

"So what are we looking at?" Bella asked.

"Four murdered women," said John. "Or—"

"A baby snatching ring," everyone blurted out at once.

∽∾∽

Sam and Frank, with the entourage of five children, lined up on the steps of Sam's parents' house in the Madison section of Brooklyn, the house that Sam grew up in, waiting for her dad to open the door. Both her parents greeted them—her mom dressed in a gray sweat suit and her dad, in jeans and a long sleeved polo—with broad smiles.

The troop piled in and Frankie ran to give them both hugs. "Grandma, Grandpa, I have brothers and sisters, now."

"I see that," Grandpa George said. "How about introducing us?"

"That's Benjamin. He's older than me. That's Melissa. That's Henry, and that's, where did she go? Oh, over there," Frankie explained. "Crawling—by—up the stairs. Dad, get her."

Frank did a quick turn around. "Oh, man, Sam!" He caught the baby going up the third step. "Come here, you. Where do you think you're going?" He cuddled Margie in his arms as she heartily laughed and returned her to the love seat perpendicular to the couch where Sam's parents sat.

"I know you both have a lot on your plates now, but have you thought about a date?"

"Mom!" Sam shot Frank a look of astonishment. "It's only been four days."

"A date for what?" Melissa asked.

Grandma Marilyn blurted it out. "For Sam and Frank's wedding." Sam cringed.

George nodded. "Sorry, princess, Mom and I are too old to care about what we say or think."

"Yes!" Frankie yelled. "I've been bugging him for months. You gotta plan a date."

Frank burst out laughing as Sam buried her head on his chest.

"We never went to a wedding!" Melissa exclaimed.

"Well," Grandma said as she out pulled the spring issue of *Brides Magazine* that was wedged into the love seat frame. "Here, you can look through this book with Samantha."

Melissa took the issue that was almost too large for her six-year-old hands. "Wow! That is so beautiful." Mesmerized, she walked over to Sam almost tripping on her own feet. "Wait! I got a great idea!"

Sam took the magazine and Melissa into her arms. The little girl leaned against her. "What Melissa? What's your great idea?"

"I'll plan the wedding. I can draw the stuff and I can decorate."

"Whoa, hold on there, Melissa," Grandpa George said. "What about us? The girl's parents plan the wedding."

Sam felt Frank's torso warming up. That meant his anger flared—or at least him not being keen on the idea. "Excuse me? You two are planning—" Frank pointed between himself and Sam. "—our wedding?"

"Yes. Without a doubt," George said. "We're very old fashioned."

"Then what are Sam and I supposed to do?"

Marilyn let her words flow so naturally as if there was no other alternative. "Come as guests."

Frank held back his laughter and, in a combination with anger, at the thought, probably in respect for her parents, but Sam knew that was never going to fly. "Mom, today's couples when they're our age, we make our own wedding."

"And I'd like to hear what the kids have to say, too."

Melissa scowled. "Yeah, right, Uncle Frank. You wouldn't listen to me when I said I wanted to redecorate your house, you're going to listen about a wedding?"

"What? You want to redecorate my house? When did that conversation happen?"

"Well, it didn't, remember? Last night, you almost choked at dinner."

Frank paled. Sam had to change the topic quick. "You

know what? How about, Melissa, you and I go shopping now as we planned?"

"Shopping?" asked Marilyn. "Where to?"

"I need clothes for school. My brothers have theirs, but I need girl's clothes."

Marilyn shot Sam an inquisitive look. "What kind of clothes did you have before, sweetheart?"

"Uh, do you know about kids?"

"Yes, I do. I'm a pediatrician. What's your pediatrician's name?"

"Mine is Dr. Hill."

"Yours? Do you by chance all have different ones?"

Sam and Frank sat up and paid attention.

"Yes. Benjamin, what's your pediatrician's name again?" Melissa asked.

"Dr. Berry."

"Do you know Henry's or Margie's?"

"No, they go to different ones."

Marilyn and Sam looked at each other. Marilyn sat up on the couch and folded her hands on her lap. Sam knew her mother had some strong thoughts on the matter. "Mom, come into the kitchen with me. I need to talk to you about your wedding plans for us."

Benjamin looked up as the women rose. "Samantha, I thought you said you'd never lie to us."

"I wouldn't."

"You're lying now. You're not going into another room to talk about the wedding." Sam compressed her lips. "You're going to talk about why we have different baby doctors."

"That is suspicious, Benjamin," Grandpa George said. "But why don't you let the women talk about it? It's to help you children, after all."

Benjamin exhaled deeply. "How is it going to help us? Dad died. But, yeah, if it'll help Sam find our moms, go ahead."

Sam and her mom darted into the kitchen. Sam smiled at

the new faux art mural on the largest wall. The same guy from the East Village who did her master bedroom, painted this for her parents—just yesterday. As expected, he ripped them off, too, but he was so worth it, as she at first thought. But after seeing Henry Slater's decorating, she changed her mind, quick. The green and purple tones made the flowers appear to jump off the wall. Sam could swear the young girl on the wall carrying the vase was her, maybe twenty years earlier. Leave it to Mom to want her permanently embedded into their house—especially since her heart now belonged to Frank. Sam didn't even ask her mom if it was her. She let it slide. At least, now was not the time to ask about it.

"Mom, what are you thinking?"

Marilyn leaned against the sink with her arms folded across her chest. "First, what did she mean by girl's clothes?"

"It's very hard to understand. Her dad wanted her to be a boy, so other than in school, he forced her to wear boys clothes."

"That's very disturbing."

"Tell me about it. The school didn't know, but as soon as they got home to the nanny, they had to change."

"What happened when they went out?"

"They never did. He kept them secluded in the apart-ment. They never watched TV or went to a restaurant."

Frank appeared in the doorway and leaned against the doorframe with his arms crossed over his chest. Marilyn acknowledged him with a nod and then Sam turned around. "Come in, Frank."

"Sam, there's only one conclusion I can make. When a parent takes children to different doctors, it's usually to hide the other children's presence or even existence. I'll make you a bet that this man, though he very well might be their biological father, he kidnapped these children or had them kidnapped, from their mothers. And because he keeps them so hidden, I bet their mothers are out there."

Sadness overcame Sam. "I agree, and because the mothers are probably out there, we'll find them. If that's the case, they'll have to go with them. Mom, I know it's way too soon, but I'm having a hard time trying not to fall in love with them."

"I know, Sam. I know. Think about how appreciative those women will be, knowing you're taking care of their babies. So right now, pull yourself together and go have your time with Melissa. Daddy and I will watch the others with Frank." Marilyn looked up at Frank with an equally sad expression.

Good thing I didn't put on makeup. Nothing to smudge during her teary-moment. Returning to the living room, she asked Melissa if she was ready to go.

"Okay. Where are we going?"

"There are some stores on the avenue, and you need sneakers and boots."

"Looks like someone is going to be spoiled today." Marilyn smiled warmly and Sam could tell her mother's heart was breaking for the children, as much as her own.

Frankie had a gleam in his eyes. "I know! Grandma Marilyn, do you want go with them?" Frank's lips curled up in approval. Sam grinned. "This way, we'll be all boys together, except for Margie."

"If it's okay with Samantha."

"I'd love for Grandma to come. Right, Melissa?"

"Yes!"

Sam hesitated. "Sure you two men could handle three boys and a baby?"

"Yes. Go," Frank said. "Not too long. How about we all go for Chinese for dinner?"

"I'd love it!" Sam gave him a hug and kiss while the kids reacted with "ewes."

Frank pulled out his credit card from his wallet and handed it to Sam. "Don't max it out."

Sam smiled like a little kid in a candy store as she twirled the card in her fingers as she left the house.

❧❧❧

As soon as the women were out the door, even before Frank could say a word to Sam's father, his cell rang. Looking at the caller ID, he knew he had to take it. "George, can you handle them? I have to take this."

"Of course."

Frank handed Margie over to him, and for once, the baby went without complaint. "Hey, John." He walked into the kitchen and pulled out a chair facing the mural. The first thing he focused on was the girl with the vase.

Crap! That's Sam!

"We've been in meeting for the past three hours. Have a lot of questions."

Frank couldn't stop looking at the mural. "Yeah, so do we, along with some answers. What have you got?"

"The scorpion tank suppliers could give us a lead. Brett Case is getting surveillance footage. It's a stretch, but we'll use it. We also seem to think the kids were kidnapped from their mothers."

"We're on the same page there. Sam's mother is a pediatrician. She had some pretty strong feelings that's the case."

"All right, good. There's a team out looking for the building superintendent and Brett will try to get a warrant for the nanny's apartment. At the very least, to find her destination so we can bring her back. We still haven't found birth certificates. Can you find out the children's birth dates? Case wants to enter their names into NCMEC."

"Great idea, but for the National Center For Missing and Exploited Children you need their exact date of birth, their birth name, and a photo. Get this, Slater never took pictures or allowed pictures to be taken. Guess he didn't want any identification. Hold on, Benjamin told us his and Melissa's birthdates. Let's see if he knows the other two. Melissa went on a shopping spree with Sam and her mom."

John laughed. "Yes, Nick told me about her."

Frank sneered, glad John couldn't see his reaction. "I'll call Benjamin, but there's something I have to tell you. How old were you when you started to become psychic, maybe not psychic, but have the uncanny ability to put two-and two-together?"

"I know exactly what you're saying. I was a toddler. Lex said Benjamin has great inference skills. You think it's more than that?"

"Much more. Before we go to the birthdates, I have to tell you something. These kids recover way too fast. We just told them their dad died an hour ago, and now they're all happy planning a wedding."

"Very concerning. Were their reactions intellectual or emotional?"

"At this point, intellectual. No real tears. We'll need to go deeper for sure. Hold on a sec." Frank went to the hallway and called Benjamin. The boy came into the kitchen the first time he was called. Frank put the phone on speaker. "Benjamin, I want you to meet someone."

"Okay."

"This is Dr. Trenton. He's a forensic psychiatrist, like me."

"Hi, Benjamin."

"Hi, Dr. Trenton."

"Benjamin, I'm talking with people you've already met, and they've told me wonderful things about you and your siblings."

"So?"

"I just wanted to tell you. Can you answer some questions for me?"

"Yes."

"Do you know all of your birth dates?"

"Yes."

"Okay, good. What's yours?"

"I'm June tenth. Melissa is March twenty-first. Henry is January eleventh. He was just three. And Margie, I don't know. But it's in April."

"That's fine. Thank you. Benjamin, did your dad ever bring home a box with scorpions in it?"

"We just saw the tank this morning."

"But did you ever see a box being brought into the apartment? A box with holes poked into it, possibly?"

"For oxygen to get in?"

"Exactly."

Benjamin scrunched his nose as if thinking. "Yes, a few times. Once, he put it on the kitchen table, and he got mad when we went near it. Then he pulled it away and told us to go into our room to study."

"Do you remember when the last time was?"

"Yes. I remember because it was the same day he brought Margie home. We were so excited about our new sister that we forgot about the box. Do you think he got Margie in the same store—no, that can't be. You can't buy babies in a store. But wait! How about in the same state? Uncle Frank and Sam said you're going to find our moms. Right?"

"That's right. Tell me what you're thinking."

"The box had a big stamp on it that said the words Fragile and Texas. Texas is a state. And animals are fragile. I just remembered that now. I don't know why it just popped into my head."

"Excellent, you're doing great. Was there a label on the box?"

Benjamin closed his eyes as if to visualize it. Sam did that many times. Frank assumed the boy was doing the same thing. "There was paper over the top of the box, like to keep it closed."

"Excellent. Do you remember if the store name was on there?"

"No. I didn't look at it."

"That's perfectly all right. You helped us a lot. What are you thinking about now, Benjamin?"

Benjamin looked at Frank then turned his attention to the phone. "Why?"

"Detective Withers and your Uncle Frank told me you understand things and reasons for things and you can connect them. That's very mature for your age."

"Oh, yeah. I can tell things."

"Well, you know what? So can I, starting from when I was much younger than you."

"Really?"

"Yes. And I want to talk to you about it but when we meet in person, okay?"

Benjamin smiled. "Okay."

"I wanted to tell you, Dr. Trenton, that we're taking them to school tomorrow."

"That's wonderful."

"Yes, it is." Frank hugged Benjamin. "So we need you to go talk to their headmaster and teachers so we can get their records transferred over. Like, first thing in the morning, so it's not a surprise to their school."

"Will do. Benjamin, what's the headmaster's name?"

"Dr. Sulley is the principal. And my teacher is Miss Redding. Melissa's teacher is Miss Monty. She was my teacher last year. And Henry's teacher is Miss Sandy. I don't know her last name. Sandy is her first name. He's in nursery grade."

"Pre-K?"

"No. The grade before Pre-K."

"Thank you, Benjamin. Now we know whom to ask for. What grade does the school go up to?"

"Nursery to eighth grade. Oh, and don't forget to ask if you can bring us our books."

"Thank you, we won't. Anything else you want us to tell them or ask for?"

Benjamin sniffled and put his head down. "No."

"If you think of something, tell your uncle and he'll call me, okay? Okay, Frank. At least, now we know where to start. Speak to you soon." John disconnected.

"You, okay?" Frank asked Benjamin.

"I guess."

Frank and Benjamin returned to the living room where Margie was asleep on the couch, and Frankie and Henry play wrestled on the carpet, noisily. Frank was surprised that Walter let them, knowing how protective he was of Sam. Benjamin sat back on his legs watching them. He looked uneasy.

"What's the matter, Benjamin?" Frank asked.

"Dad wouldn't like that at all."

"No?"

Benjamin shook his head. "We're not allowed to do that."

"No roughhousing?" Frank asked. Benjamin's brows furrowed. Frank exhaled deeply. "No physical playing?"

"No."

"Well, in this house, we play, but safely. You'll get used to it."

An hour passed with Frank and George having conversations with Benjamin and Frankie—all educational discussions. From what Frank could tell about the kids so far, Henry was the one who was free-spirited.

The noise from the girls opening the door stopped conversation. Frank heard the shuffling of bags rubbing each other. "Uh, oh." Frank saw Sam and her mother who both beamed with ear-to ear-smiles. *Where's Melissa?* "Missing someone?"

"Nope." Sam opened the door gallantly as if presenting royalty. "Meet, Princess Melissa." She opened the door all way, and Melissa entered with a fresh haircut with bangs and her dark brown hair cut shoulder length.

She held out her hands displaying her fingernails polished a light pink. "Finally, I feel like a girl."

CHAPTER 6

Frank; Sam, holding Margie in her arms; four more children; and Sam's parents planned to meet Frank's in-laws in the waiting lounge of their favorite Chinese restaurant on Flatbush Avenue. Parking was nearly impossible, including after rush hour. Brick and mortar stores took up the commercial avenue that ran through almost the entire borough. Frank tried to avoid this main thoroughfare as much as he could, except for going to this restaurant, a little past The Junction near Brooklyn College. He and Sam intended to get the Slater kids immersed in Brooklyn life immediately. You couldn't live in Brooklyn without savoring the tastes and aromas of ethnic foods. This restaurant was the best. It catered to gluten-free and MSG-free customers including their rice and noodle dishes.

The children stared at the large red Buddha statue in the corner in between two Bonsai trees. The red and gold wallpaper with a Chinese garden mural embedded in the fabric held their attention and Melissa touched the three dimensional pattern. From her pursed lips, Frank guessed she was thinking of redecorating ideas. He smiled and then rustled Henry's hair, paying attention to the boy clutching onto his leg, pushed onto him in the crowd. The little guy looked as if he was going to cry. Frank lifted him up into his arms. Henry wrapped his arms around Frank's neck and held on for dear life. *Okay, the assertive one doesn't like crowds.*

At least paying attention to Henry took his mind off his nervousness. With Frank's free hand, he clutched Sam's hand. Sweaty. Both of them. Today, the parents would meet. It would go well, Frank hoped. Not that it would matter. He and Sam were too old to need approval, but he hated family conflict. The parents were of the same age, late sixties, his in-laws retired from the military and Sam's parents still worked at their medical practices. From the way it appeared so far, the big difference would be that Sam's parents would be pushovers with the kids and his in-laws were tough. Sam's mother proved it already, not allowing Sam to use his credit card or hers while shopping today for Melissa's new wardrobe or salon appointment.

Sweet and spicy aromas filled the lobby and the children sniffed and inhaled deeply. "Smells good in here," Benjamin said.

"Wait till you get inside," Frankie said. "Dad, how much longer?"

"Just a few minutes till Grandma and Grandpa get here."

Frankie looked toward the door when a cold breeze hit him. He moved in between other patrons to make himself seen. "Grandma, Grandpa, over here."

Frank smiled. Should he introduce them as Major Kathryn and Colonel Walter Brandman and Drs. Marilyn and George Wright, or leave the titles out? In his contemplation, the seniors beat him to it and introduced themselves with handshakes and warm smiles.

"Khaos, party of eleven," came through the loudspeaker, and Frank held the door open for everyone to enter. The hostess led them to the section with larger parties and the loudest conversations. Benjamin and Melissa furrowed their brows.

Grandma Marilyn and Grandpa George took their hands in what Frank knew was a comforting response. Then he saw the still expressions on his in-laws faces. To them, that was a pampering response, not what they'd do. Nor would it be what Frank would do under ordinary circumstances. But this wasn't the ordinary. These children had just lost their father, their only parent as far as they knew, and they were thrust into the unknown. As far as he was concerned, the children were dealing with it quite well. But he wouldn't let his in-laws in on his thoughts right now.

The hostess brought over a high chair for Margie and the waiter brought the booster seat. Neither one of the children wanted to sit in them. Margie fought Sam, wiggling so much Frank could tell his fiancé was in a place she didn't want to be. Frank put Henry into the booster seat with a firm "stay there," and he pulled the baby out of Sam's arms. After absorbing a glare from the colonel, Sam blushed. Frank put Margie into the highchair then immediately handed her a teething toy that worked for the moment.

The server handed the adults menus that held their attention. But not for long. Melissa brought it upon herself to update the military grandparents on what she'd planned. "Guess what, Grandma?"

Kathryn, who sat next to Melissa, turned toward her. "What, Melissa?"

"We're planning Uncle Frank's and Samantha's wedding and I'm in charge."

All of the adults did double takes. "You're doing what?" Grandpa Walter bellowed out in laughter.

"Yes," Marilyn explained. "We adults were taken out of the equation today." She pointed to Frank. "And that seems to include you and Sam, too."

"Oh, no!" Frank said. "Who gave you that power?"

"See?" Frankie said. "I told you my dad wouldn't let us do it."

"You guys discussed this?"

"And they need me to be in charge because I have the best ideas," Melissa said proudly. "But don't worry, we didn't do anything yet. We just got the idea to do it."

"Whew, I thought you had the limo coming to get us already."

"No, Uncle Frank, things like this take time." Melissa bobbed her head as she spoke. "If you want it done right, you can't rush."

Sam moaned in delight. "And where did you learn that, sweetheart?"

"Daddy always said that to the people he decorated for."

"You listened when he was on the phone?"

"Yes. We were with him in his art room a lot, and he always called the people with questions."

The server interrupted, ready to take their orders. Frank looked at Sam's parents. "I usually do the ordering. Shall I?"

Her father was quick to respond. "No, I like to order myself, thank you."

After snickers from his in-laws that Frank noticed, he used his own judgement and conceded. "Okay, go ahead then I'll do the rest."

This is an opportune time to get some more information about Slater and block out Sam's father. "Did your dad remember all their phone numbers?"

Benjamin laughed. "No, too many people."

"Where did he keep their phone numbers?"

"He had this big book. And it had the people's orders and things."

"And where did he keep that book?"

Benjamin scrunched his nose. "Why do you need to know that?"

The waiter addressed Frank. "Dr. Frank, you ready to order?"

Frank rattled off eight dishes from soups, to appetizers, and main courses. Each had modifications to order. The children looked amazed, and Frank watched their reactions—furrowed brows, grimaces, scrunched noses, and stuck out tongues—all except Frankie who gave the fisted hand up for "yes." Frank handed his menus back to the waiter.

Benjamin repeated the question.

"Well, these people hired your dad, and we really should call them to tell them he won't be able to finish the work."

"Oh, don't worry about that!"

"Melissa, don't tell me, you plan to complete those projects," Grandpa George chided.

"No. But everybody loved Dad, they'll understand."

Frank thought for a moment before he answered. "In business, though, Melissa, people may not care as much as you think. Do you know if your dad worked with anyone who would take over, in case he had to travel to one of his work places?"

"No, he didn't," Benjamin said, pouting. "He did it all by himself. That's why he let us stay with him in the art room. If he didn't, he wouldn't see us that much. He was always working."

∽∾∽

With the baby in the crib and Henry tucked into bed, Frank thought the easy part was done. He went to Frankie's door where Sam was eavesdropping, swooning from watching the trio. Frankie, Benjamin, and Melissa lay on their stomachs on Frankie's bed with the *Brides Magazine* between them. They turned each page, looking in wonderment at the wedding gowns.

"Yes. This one is it," Melissa exclaimed.

"No, wait." Benjamin turned the page. He tapped it with his finger. "This one is it."

"I want to see more before we decide," Frankie said. "Like this whole book."

Melissa turned the page and stared at the table setting. "Look at this. Hold on. Hold on." She pointed to a box painted white, made out of Styrofoam, filled with white carnations. "See the box? I can do that easy and even better. Dad has plenty of that white stuff in his office, and Detective Withers said he'd get it for me, and we can order the flowers. I bet Dad has all the people we can call."

"No. I don't like that one," Benjamin said. "I think if it were Dad, he'd pick out something fancier."

"This is not happening," Frank whispered to Sam. He entered the room. "Come on, guys, bedtime. It's a school night." He gently pulled the magazine from Melissa's grasp and got a pout in response. "You'll have plenty of time to look at all of this. I promise. In bed, now. We're all going to bed." He tucked in Benjamin and Frankie, while Sam tucked in Melissa in her room.

With their bedroom door closed tight, Frank lay naked on top of Sam in bed. The kids, slept peacefully, or so Frank thought. "Oh, man, do I need you now, princess." He caressed her face in his hands and brought his lips down to hers, as his hands slipped to the back of her head. Wrapping her arms around his neck, Sam didn't want to let go. She spread her legs and, with bent knees, braced her lower legs on Frank's buns. Peace and quiet. What he craved. What he knew Sam craved. He'd never been around so much non-stop chatter since he was in Iraq. The silence seemed deafening.

Too bad, it was short-lived.

Henry pushed opened the door with such force the little guy almost fell into the room. He made it to the bed, head first and scrambled up onto it before he realized that Sam and his Uncle were both in dispose. Thank God, they were both covered, Frank thought.

"What you two doing?" the little voice inquired as he sat up, wide-awake.

While Sam had a hard time concealing her laugh, Frank wasn't so sympathetic. "Now, go into your room." He threw the blanket over Sam's head.

"No. I sleep here." Henry plopped onto his back, rolled onto his side and pretended to be asleep.

Frank shook his head. He kept telling Sam that she had to be more firm, and like his in-laws said at dinner, so did he. The colonel couldn't believe he was so easy going with these four. Frank was military. Special Forces. Tough to the core. He'd never let Frankie get away with it. Why now? Because he still didn't know for sure if these kids had been abused by their dad or not, that's why. He rolled off Sam and grabbed up his briefs from the floor just before Melissa came in.

He pulled them on while under the covers. "Take your brother and go back into your room."

"Eww. What are you two doing?"

"What? Didn't your dad ever have a lady friend stay overnight?"

"No. Never!"

"Did he ever keep the bedroom door closed?"

"No." She put her finger up into the air. "Oh, only once. No, uh, maybe more."

"And you were expected to stay out, right?"

She nodded.

"Well, same here. So take Henry and go back to bed. It's a school night."

She went over to where Henry lay and took his hand. He pulled back, giggling. "Come on, Henry."

Frank leaned over to him. "Now," he said, the sternest they'd heard him speak.

Henry must have realized his uncle meant it. He got up with Melissa. Before they left the room, Henry turned toward the bed. "Okay, go back and play with rubber dolly."

Frank perked up. "Rubber dolly?"

"Yes," Melissa said. "Daddy has a rubber dolly he sleeps with."

"That rubber dolly," Henry said.

"This is Samantha. Not a rubber dolly."

"No. Samantha went home. That's rubber dolly."

"Okay, Henry. And where does he keep this rubber dolly?"

Sam squirmed under the blanket. Frank felts kicks in places that were not pleasant. He fought to keep the *rubber dolly* still, finally lying over her.

"Under the bed."

Having a hard time controlling laughter, Frank forced a straight face. "Oh, okay, go to bed, now. I'll be careful to put the rubber dolly under the bed in the morning."

The kids left and closed the door with a bang.

He leaned off Sam, and she pushed the blanket down. "Damn it, Frank. You almost suffocated me." She sat up out of breath, pushing her hair off her face. With labored breathing, she slugged his chest.

Frank ignored that. "Sam, that's messed up. Did you see anything like that when you were kept in Slater's bedroom?"

"No, it didn't dawn on me to look under the bed. And he had me tied up, if you remember. Where was Dara when I needed her?"

"Sam, I think fear for your life interfered. Come on, let's get some shut eye."

"No. Hold on. Something's very wrong."

"What are you thinking?"

Sam did her own thinking aloud. "Slater exaggerated things to his children, like telling them they're having a time-out in a cage, while it turns out to be an elaborate doll house. Now it seems he calls a lady-friend a rubber dolly. He misconstrues things to them. What does that mean? Are they brain-washed?"

"It's got to mean something. Right now, I'm too tired to think. This is a big adjustment for me."

"Excuse me? Just you? What about the children and me? You were at least a parent. I've got to leave a house I put my heart and soul into a full year before I moved in—just four months ago—and now, spontaneously I'm leaving it."

"I know, Sam, I get it. But I'm going to fall asleep mid-conversation in a minute."

And he did. Just as he did in the military.

CHAPTER 7

John Trenton, Lex Withers, and Bella Richards got out of Withers SUV in the parking lot of the Scholars Academy on the Upper West Side in Manhattan. The three NYPD employees looked up at the massive red brick Victorian style four-story building. On both sides of the school, brownstones took up the rest of the block, alternating with off-white stone and red brick on the front. Stone columns stood on either edge of the ten steps leading to the entrance from the parking lot. A red neon sign—*EXIT*—was affixed on top of the redwood door.

As they approached the steps, John pointed to the sign and then his gaze caught the path leading to the front of the building. Even during winter, with snow on the lawn, the bushes lining the path were snow-free. The front entrance was a duplicate in style to the rear. They went up the steps. John pulled on the lion-head door handle. Locked. Finding the intercom, he rang the bell.

"May I help you?" said the elderly female voice.

Lex rubbed his hands together as frost pillowed from his breath. "We're NYPD. Need to speak with Mr. Sulley."

"One moment, please." The clacking of high heel shoes on wood flooring permeated the intercom. The woman opened the door. After the detectives showed their credentials, the woman moved aside. "Come in, please. And it's *Doctor* Sulley. I wouldn't make that mistake unless you want your visit to be short lived."

"Wouldn't think of it, ma'am," said Bella. The detective

walked past the woman with sleeked back salt and pepper hair, wearing a tailored silk white button-down-the-front blouse, navy blue knee length skirt and stockings, and four-inch heel navy pumps.

John took notice of her appearance and attire—simple but definitely elegant and designer. He recognized the Italian leather shoes. He'd bought the exact pair for Vicki right after the first time they'd come to live in Manhattan. Twelve hundred bucks. To him, they were worth every penny. To Vicki, not one cent. She'd insisted he return them, which he did after she fell walking in them for practice in the condo. Getting a bruised knee in the bargain, his athletic gun-toting wife couldn't balance herself. She threatened to shoot him the next time they were in Florida. Too bad, it did happen—being shot—three years later in Florida by Barbara Montgomery in the Gemini case. Crap! Why was he thinking about those shoes now? It was over four years ago. In his reflection, John wasn't aware of the silent walk down the hallway to Dr. Sulley's office. The woman opened the door for them.

"Thank you, dear. Come in, please."

John furrowed his brows at the way Dr. Sulley addressed his secretary, or so he assumed.

"She's my wife. Over fifty-three years now."

John smiled and extended his hand to shake. "I'm Dr. John Trenton and Detectives Lex Withers and Bella Richards." He watched Mrs. Sulley as she closed the door behind them.

The office was wood paneled, with filled-to-capacity bookcases lining the walls. The oversized colonial desk with desk accessories matching the light sand colored leather couch and club chairs added a sophisticated feel to the office. The conference table, appointed with the same details, didn't show even a speck of dust.

John felt at home in here. It was similar in decor to his office in Manhattan Psych in which he spared no expense. If he was going to spend most of his day in there, he had to be comfortable. He guessed this school administrator felt the same way.

"How may I help you?" Dr. Sulley pointed to the conference table. "Come, let's make ourselves comfortable."

After sitting around the table, Withers took out his notepad. "Dr. Sulley, how long have you owned this school?"

"Over twenty years."

"What were you doing before?"

"My wife and I were college professors. In education. Teaching theories and best practices for teachers in elementary school classrooms. That's where we started our careers. In the classroom. In 1964. We met teaching in our first school in the Bronx and have been together ever since."

"Nice," John said, smiling.

Withers apparently wanted to get down to business. "We need to talk to you about the Slater children."

"Benjamin, Melissa, and Henry?"

"Yes."

"Where have they been? Is everything okay?" Dr. Sulley depressed the intercom. "Millie, come in here right away, please." She entered and joined them, taking a seat at the table. He continued. "We're talking about the Slater children."

"How well did you know their father?" Withers asked.

Mrs. Sulley sucked in her cheeks. She sat up straight in the chair. "That man was going to be the death of me."

"Why, Mrs. Sulley?" John asked.

"He wouldn't let the children breathe. He regulated everything around them. Their diet. Well, I could understand him wanting the children to eat healthfully, but he was extreme. We only serve healthful foods here. We even have a special caterer, but he insisted they bring their own lunches and snacks. No one could cook as well as he, he would tell me. He was so protective, he wouldn't allow them to go on class trips the first year, and we take the children to wonderful places. We finally convinced him to allow it because the teachers use those trip experiences in the classroom. We also had to promise him, when a child was having a birth-day party, we'd send them to another class. And it wasn't religious, mind you. Now he's all right with it since the children know what they can and cannot eat."

"How did the children react to those restrictions?"

"Like obedient little soldiers." She shook her head. "Not like children should be. They were also younger, easier."

"Why did you keep them in the school, then?" Withers asked. "Money?"

Dr. Sulley hesitated then pursed his lips. "No, Detective. The children are needy, like some of our other students from single parent homes. And we were able to convince Mr. Slater to be slightly more open."

"Needy? As in how?" John asked.

"They needed warmth, nurturing, sometimes they're withdrawn. Emotionally they're very repressed. They wouldn't open up about it, and we didn't push."

"You have a guidance counselor on the premises?"

"Yes, with a full time nurse, as well, but—"

"But what?"

Mrs. Sulley was quick to respond. "Mr. Slater didn't want them to speak to the counselor. Another reason I was unhappy with him."

"I have a feeling I know why."

"Why, Dr. Trenton?"

"Did you know that at home Mr. Slater wanted Melissa to dress like a boy?"

"No! That can't be." Mrs. Sulley shook her head. "Melissa is a precious little girl. She needed a haircut over the past few months, and I couldn't understand that one. They were impeccably dressed."

"Yeah, it can be," Withers responded. "She had her hair pinned up under a baseball cap when we—" He pointed be-tween him and Bella. "—met her. We thought she was a boy. She has only boy's clothing in her room, and boy's furniture, wallpaper, everything. They were here for three years, and you didn't know that?"

"Oh, my God!" Dr. and Mrs. Sulley responded at once.

"How can you let a parent get away with telling you they won't let their child see the counselor?" John asked.

"We don't if there's any sign of abuse, but there was none. And Melissa didn't come to us to tell us. She acted like a little girl who wanted to please her father."

Withers paused to phrase his comment, John assumed, not to alienate these school administrators. "Okay. Hear me out. When we took custody of the children, they knew something was up, and we'll tell you about it in a minute. Melissa broke down and told a female detective."

Mrs. Sulley sighed. "I'd bet that was the first time she displayed any emotion."

John nodded. "I'd have to agree."

Bella looked around the room. "How much does it cost to send a kid here, forty, fifty grand?"

"Are you assuming we're in it for the money, Detective? I'll assure you we're not. It looks more expensive than it is. Fifteen thousand for the school year. Three thousand for the summer camp."

"That's pretty inexpensive for a New York City private school, isn't it?"

"Yes, Dr. Trenton. Uh, what's your specialty?"

"Forensic psychiatry."

Dr. Sulley did a double take. "What on earth happened? The children haven't been here for two days. That's unlike them. Now you've gotten us very worried."

John received a jolt from Max, his spirit guide. Hs feeling was correct. These administrators had genuine concern for these children. "Henry Slater was under FBI and police investigation." John glanced at Lex and Bella. They nodded. They'd allow him to do the questioning.

"For what? He has a successful decorating business, and I believe he works with casinos in that venue."

"Did he talk to you about his work?"

"He told us, yes, because he had to travel, so their nanny would pick them up at times or she'd meet them when the bus dropped them off. She also came to their in-classroom events. What struck me as odd was that he always had to travel whenever there was something going on in the classroom, even parent-teacher meetings. But the children verified it."

"How? How did they verify it?"

"They told me they spoke with their dad through Facetime. They never missed a day talking to him. I have to correct myself. He did manage to meet each teacher at least once during the school year. I have the teachers fill out a response form about each parent, so we know what struggles we'll be up against. Every report about him was glowing. The teachers found him charming and totally interested in his children's success. They never missed an assignment or homework. He signed everything. Now, you tell me what's going on. We have an obligation to protect those children."

"We're glad you feel that way," Withers said. "The children are safe. They're living with their uncle and his fiancée, in Brooklyn."

"Mr. Slater told us he didn't have any siblings."

John continued. "He has two biological brothers placed for adoption, at birth. They didn't meet each other until…this situation."

Mrs. Sulley put her hand over her heart. "Oh, my! They have to be attending school."

"We know that," Withers said. "They're starting today in Brooklyn. We'll need their records transferred. That's one of the reasons we're here."

Mrs. Sulley wagged an index finger at the detective. "Uh, no. We can't transfer records without their father's written consent."

"That will be the hard part." Withers paused. "Henry Slater is deceased." He nodded at John to take over again.

Mrs. Sulley reached for her husband's hand. "Oh, my God! How did that happen? Was he ill?"

John swallowed hard. He hadn't cleared it with the department as to how much he could say or not say. "Okay, I'll tell you as much as I can. Henry Slater had killed seventeen women in casinos along the eastern coast, the last one in Queens. The victim was a friend of one of the detectives on the case, the woman with whom the children are living now. We found Mr. Slater's brother by examining familial DNA. His brother, who came up, works for the department, a forensic psychiatrist, like me." The Sulley's sat with jaws dropped. Before they could respond, John said, "We're trying to find their biological mothers. Did Slater tell you what happened that precipitated him to be a single parent?"

"That's absolutely not believable, Dr. Trenton," Dr. Sulley said. "He was a bit rigid in his persona but in no way was he a killer."

"What you described in how the teachers responded to him is exactly part of the psychopathic personality. Did he tell you why he's a single dad?"

Mrs. Sulley bobbed her head. "Yes. He came to New York from Florida with Benjamin and Melissa three years ago. Benjamin was five, and Melissa was too young to be admitted. He told us their mother died of ovarian cancer the year before."

"So they both have the same mother?"

"Yes."

Lex and Bella looked at each other suspiciously. "That's not what the children told us."

Mrs. Sulley sat stunned with her palm covering her mouth while her husband continued to respond to the questions.

"And what was that?" Dr. Sulley asked.

"That they each have different mothers. And that they don't know who they are. What did he say about Henry?"

"He told us he wanted a large family, since he didn't have one, so he adopted. The same thing for the little one, Margie. The children may not understand what was going on so they said what they did."

"No, Dr. Sulley, " John said firmly. "If Benjamin lost his

mother at four, he'd remember it. There'd be memories. Parents who lose a spouse have pictures, want the children to remember them, talk about them. He doesn't have any pictures at all. This could explain his rigidness, not wanting them to go on the trips. He doesn't want them being seen. We need to see the birth certificates, please."

Mrs. Sulley scrambled out of her seat to get to the file cabinet. Her fingers trembled as she thumbed through the files to get to S. She pulled out three folders, one for each of the admitted children. Placing them in front of John, she leaned over his shoulder and flipped pages until she reached the attached certificates.

John sat stunned and just stared.

Withers pulled the files between him and Bella. "Okay, while Doc is in La-La Land, we'll look at these. Okay, same mother for the older two. Sara Phipps, married name Sara Phipps Slater. Birth date, Benjamin, June tenth; Melissa, March twenty-first; Henry, January eleventh."

John refocused. He pulled the file back toward him. "Those are the dates Benjamin told me. Look at these name spellings. Far from the traditional way. The children don't know about this Sara Phipps, I'm sure. Did you ever get an idea that these birth certificates are counterfeit?"

"No," Dr. Sulley said. "Why would we?"

"No, you wouldn't, I guess." John turned toward Lex and Bella. "I can't start profiling based on these."

"True, then any theories we form on that would be bogus. Okay, first things first," Withers said. "The children need their birth certificates for admittance to a New York City public school—"

"We just can't hand the birth certificates—"

Without saying a word, Withers pulled the warrant from his pocket and slid it across the desk to Dr. Sulley.

Ignoring her husband's comment, Mrs. Sulley interrupted. "Oh, no. No way would they make it in public school. Not with the education they've gotten here."

"I beg to differ," Withers said. "New York City schools

give a very good education. My boys are doing fine."

"Glad to hear that. But they're used to, what, thirty-five children in a class?"

"Just about."

"Here, we have fifteen, max. All lessons are individualized and mostly hands-on experience. There are two teachers in a room at the minimum."

John's mind wandered. He liked these people. He and Vicki had discussed getting their son, Ricky, into school. The nine-year-old had come a long way over the past year being homeschooled. Maybe now would be a good time. "We'd like to speak to Benjamin's and Melissa's teachers and Henry's too, as well as see some of their work in the classroom."

Mrs. Sulley smiled. "Perfect, Dr. Trenton, I'll take the three of you to see Melissa's teacher, Miss Monty. She was Benjamin's teacher last year so she'll tell you about both children. And, before I forget, there was one incident, but I'll let the teacher tell you."

John got the feeling it was something endearing not troublesome. "That's fine."

"What do you need transferred to the new school? I'll tell our secretary to get it all ready."

"Immunizations, did they have those?"

"Yes, I believe they did."

"We'll also need their pediatrician's numbers," John continued. "And report cards. Also the original birth certificates you have. We'll be able to verify authenticity."

"No problem on any of that. Now, Henry is in the nursery class, and he's age appropriate for that. Melissa came in Pre-K and she was so advanced, probably from all the work at home with her father, that mid-year, we moved her to Kindergarten then first grade. They're also tall for their age, so moving up seemed practical. Last year, second, this year third. But in all honesty with the class size in the public school system, I'd personally recommend second grade placement for her."

"That's very valuable information, Mrs. Sulley. Thank you."

"You're welcome, Dr. Trenton. The children are my utmost concern. And likewise for Benjamin. He's in fifth grade here, but I'd recommend fourth in his new school. And there probably won't be a choice. But he needs a very special kind of teacher."

"How so?"

"Benjamin...how do I say this so do you don't think I'm not all there?...Benjamin has certain skills, abilities, that most children can have—" she sucked in her cheeks. "—until... well, adults squelch their imaginative expression."

John caught onto exactly what she meant. "So he has psychic abilities and intuition?"

She exhaled deeply. "Yes, and more than that. He has premonitions, sees visions in his daydreams, and if he's in tune with the adult communicating with him, he can tell what he or she is thinking. Lying to him will make an enemy for a very long time. From your expression, I can tell you understand what I mean."

Detective Withers confirmed it. "He sure does. He's our department psychic."

"Seriously?"

"Yes. I've been psychic and clairvoyant since I was a toddler."

"Then maybe, Benjamin should be living with you."

"I wouldn't want to break the siblings up, but don't worry, I will be speaking with him and the detective he's living with, Samantha Wright, has many of the same abilities. She was also a teacher before she joined the department, and I know she'll encourage him."

Bella added, "That one? She sure would."

"I'm glad to hear that. If you'll come with me, I'll walk you to the classroom and get Miss Monty coverage so you can speak with her in private."

John appreciated this school as a perspective parent as well as an outsider. He bet his parents, Esther and Sam, would like it, too. Even though they called Max, his spirit guide, his imaginary friend when he was a toddler, they never discouraged communication. They probably weren't a fan when Max forewarned him of their impending presence, but on the other hand, John conformed before his parents told him what to do. That had to relieve their parenting stress. John smiled at the memory and followed Mrs. Sulley around the hall from the point of view of an incoming parent.

They came to a white marble spiral staircase with solid mahogany handrails engraved in an early 1920s leaf pattern style. *Henry Slater must have examined these thoroughly. That man was meticulous in details.*

"Stairs or elevator? It's right there."

The trio looked at each other and all came out with "stairs" at the same time.

At the top of the staircase, Mrs. Sulley led them around to where the classrooms started on this floor. John and Lex smiled and nodded in approval to each other. Student work took up all of the bulletins boards hung across the walls between the classrooms. Some teachers went beyond the boards onto the white tiles. Laughter permeated the hall from Miss Monty's classroom, the third classroom from the stairwell. John stopped to examine the bulletin board. The social studies topic that featured children's artwork compared imported foods from Egypt, China, and the Middle East. He was impressed. That was beyond the topics Vicki covered with Ricky—who was third grade age, though well below academically. John looked at the board on the other side of the door. Math—that he could identify with. The board illustrated problem-solving techniques for subtraction with exchange. Mrs. Sulley let him look without interference.

Lex and Bella entered the classroom but stood by the doorway. John joined them a minute later. Mrs. Sulley approached the teacher, and she acknowledged the visitors with a warm smile. This woman was a looker. Dark auburn hair in a ponytail, dark brown eyes, and a very pregnant belly. John smiled, wondering how much longer she had to go. She seemed to be nearing the end of the second trimester, and she resembled Vicki when she carried the twins. She wore a solid white tunic sweater, with navy slacks. John guessed those were the school colors. As his gaze scanned the room, he saw all of the children in the same colors. Mrs. Sulley signaled to the visitors to come into the room.

They went to the back of the room to observe, not wanting to interfere. Fifteen children appeared in center activities throughout the room, communicating methods of solving the task. No yelling. No fighting. Lots of laughter, and seemingly plenty of fun. Every area of the room had something going on— crowded bulletin boards displaying the children's work, carpeted areas for reading centers, multiple computer stations, a reading loft with comfy pillows, a center for table games, and a library with books of every dimension. John compressed his lips. He missed not having any classroom experiences with Ricky. His own parents loved coming into his class.

Lex must have read his demeanor. "Hey, think this school would work for your son?"

"Believe me, I'd love it to, but he's refusing to try."

"Who's the boss in your house?"

"I was hoping it was me, but apparently not. He's come a long way with homeschooling but still fearful, maybe of leaving us. I don't know."

Mrs. Sulley overheard them. "You're homeschooling, Dr. Trenton?"

"Yes. It's a long story. We adopted last February. He's nine now and very behind in school."

"How did that come to be?"

John exhaled deeply preparing for the hurtful memory. "Ricky had been abused."

Mrs. Sulley interlaced her fingers and brought her hands to her chin, placing her touching index fingers over her lips.

This woman truly listens. John let out a nasal breath then felt comfortable in explaining. "Sexually, up until he was five. I rescued him from a hostage situation in Florida. I was down for the Jewish holidays in September, five years ago, and he wanted to come live with us then. But I had just met my wife and the courts wouldn't let me bring him to New York. It took us three full years to reconnect. He'd been thrown out of every school he went to for behavior issues. We figured we'd homeschool until he caught up. But to tell you the truth, I'm missing not having school experiences with him."

"Why don't you and your wife come in to speak with Dr. Sulley and me? Your story isn't a stranger to us." She looked toward the door when she heard Miss. Monty's relief teacher enter. "Ah, perfect. Thank you, Miss Burger."

"Now, I expect a good report. Am I going to get one?" Miss Monty smiled at the class.

"Yes, Miss Monty," came from eight-year-old mouths.

"Come with me, please. We can talk in the lounge."

The lounge was an open space with seating in quadrants. Artwork covered the walls. Special care was taken in painting the picture frames the school colors of navy and white, though not always successful. John liked that apparently no adult interference corrected the children's efforts. The low-shag carpet was a lighter blue complementing the navy seating upon it. Miss Monty led them to a couch grouped with club chairs as John looked around the room as he walked. She sat in a club chair, John in one next to her, and the detectives took the couch. As she felt the baby move, she smiled and put her hands on her stomach.

John smiled. "When are you due?"

"Not until the end of May."

"Your first?"

"Yes, and my last."

John startled.

"Oh, don't mind me."

"Believe me, honey," Bella reassured. "I get it."

Miss Monty laughed. "So, what is going on with Melisa

and Benjamin? They've been absent for two days. I would have called tonight."

Rather than catching her up on the conversation with the administration, John wanted her take on the children and their father. "What can you tell us about their work in the classroom?"

"Meticulous. That would be the one word to describe them. Even with their penmanship, they write slowly, as if they were afraid of getting the angle wrong. I tried to get them to relax but that made them more nervous. Melissa would shudder and throw her paper away to start over rather than erase something. Benjamin, the same thing. Why are they absent?"

"They're safe and living with an uncle. We'll tell you everything, Miss Monty, but right now, what can you tell us about Mr. Slater? Have you met him?"

She chuckled. "Oh yes, I met him," she said, patting her stomach.

The detective shot each other curious looks and Miss Monty's comment halted the conversation—for a moment.

Pointing to her belly, Withers exclaimed, "That's his?"

"Oh, no, no, no. I think he just opened me up to become aware of my maternal urges."

John got the feeling it was a lot more than that. He felt Max's jolt.

"And what?" Bella said sarcastically. "You became pregnant through osmosis?"

"What? No."

Withers squirmed in his seat. "Would you mind elaborating?"

"It's a long story."

"We need to hear it," John said emphatically.

Miss Monty let out a deep breath. "Okay. Last year Benjamin was in my class. He never got less than a hundred on a test. This time, he failed a spelling test, and I knew it was on purpose. He got every word wrong, twenty of them. I told him to have the paper signed and to bring it back tomorrow. He didn't. For five days, he gave me every lame excuse—his dad was busy, his dad wasn't home. The usual I-didn't-do-my-homework excuses. I called Friday night and spoke to Mr. Slater for the first time. He was shocked but he thanked me for calling. And that he'd take care of it. On Monday, Benjamin came in with the paper signed, and I asked him what his dad told him. He said that he was punished severely. That word struck a cord. I asked him what 'severely' meant. He said his dad spanked him and his dad told him, it was a severe spanking. He told me he had to stay in his room and write all twenty words, a lot. With describing it like that, I had to call Dr. Sulley and the guidance counselor."

"I'd agree. But was it severe, in the sense of what most adults consider severe?"

Miss Monty's eyes widened. "No. Not at all. Why are you asking that, Dr. Trenton?"

"All right. Finish the story and I'll tell you."

"Dr. Sulley and the counselor actually checked his bottom. Not one mark, no red spots, nothing to indicate anything severe, actually nothing at all. The guidance counselor asked him to hit his palm with the same strength his dad hit him, and Benjamin gave him what you'd call a love pat. They decided to call Mr. Slater to come in and talk with us. Monday afternoon he came and I was called into the office as I was getting ready to leave. We met for the first time. Benjamin was with us. I looked at Mr. Slater, he looked at me, and Benjamin said, 'So?'" Mr. Slater asked him what he meant. Benjamin started to giggle and he blushed. Then he responded, 'You can't figure it out?' It hit us like a ton of bricks. Benjamin was trying to fix us up. Mr. Slater got so upset, and he started apologizing for his son. He's the sweetest man. I explained to Benjamin that I couldn't go out with his father because it's against school policy. It's true. At this school, teachers are not permitted to fraternize with parents. And I asked Benjamin if he wanted to get me fired. Of course he didn't. So we left it at that. At the end of the year, Benjamin approached me again. He still wanted me to go out with his dad. The last day of school Mr. Slater came to pick up the children, and he brought thank you gifts for the teachers. I heard Benjamin whispering to him, 'Ask her out.' It was so sweet, I blushed. He told me that Benjamin wouldn't stop nagging him until we did, so he asked me out for lunch. It was in front of Benjamin, so I said 'it would be my pleasure.' A week later, I received a call and he asked me out for a casual dinner." She sighed. "I made a good guess because he doesn't describe things accurately."

John moved in toward her. "Sorry to interrupt, but we've seen that. What do you mean?"

"Well, like he did with the severe spanking, for one. What have you seen?"

"He gives the children time-outs and they think they're going into a cage."

Miss Monty gasped.

John held up his index finger. "But it turned out that the cage was an elaborate adult-sized dollhouse with even a refrigerator for snacks. So what about casual wasn't correct?"

"Because I'm in a uniform, so to speak, all day, when I go out, I like to dress up. I did, and it was good thing, too. He picked me up and we went to the most expensive French restaurant in the theater district. He's the most charming, courteous man, and he'd be a great catch for a woman who wants to get married and be a stay-at-home mom. That's his vision. Not mine. I told him I didn't even want children."

She must have seen her audience stiffen. John saw the detectives expressions turn stoic, he felt his face tighten, too.

"What's the matter?"

"This part is crucial, Miss Monty. How did he react to that statement?"

"About not wanting children?"

"Yes."

"Well, I think he wasn't pleased. It was more like angry.

He put his fork down and asked me why. I told him it was my choice and I really didn't owe anyone an explanation. He didn't agree with that and continued to push. Uh, why is this important? It's rather personal."

John nodded. "All right. You've been forthcoming with us. Mr. Slater is deceased." John paused, waiting for her reaction.

Miss Monty held her baby bump and looked faint. She closed her eyes and slumped into the chair. John jumped up to take her pulse.

Detective Richards wasn't so sympathetic. "And you expect us to believe that little bundle of joy isn't his?"

With labored breathing, Miss Monty pulled herself together. "No, it's not that, believe me." She grasped onto John's forearm. Her gaze traveled between the visitors. "Those poor children. Now both their parents are gone."

"Better now?" John asked.

She nodded.

"We need to know everything, Miss Monty. Please don't hide anything from us. This is an FBI investigation."

"What?"

"Henry Slater murdered seventeen women."

"Oh, my God! What? How?" She looked up at the ceiling, her mind appeared to wander.

"Miss Monty?" John touched her hand to bring her back.

She burst out in tears and threw her hands up to cover her face. "Why? Why did he murder women?" With labored breathing, she looked pleadingly at John.

"Is he the father of your baby?"

"Yes. And no. Why did he murder women?"

"He murdered women whom he wanted a relationship with, but they told him they didn't want children," John explained. "So how come you're still alive?"

"What a dismal thought!"

"But it's true," Withers said. "And that's the million dollar question. Tell us the rest of the story, and don't leave anything out. What is this? Yes and No? It's not like you can be a little bit pregnant."

"In vitro."

Bella grimaced. "What about the good old fashioned way?"

"Aside from that, let her tell us what led up to it." Withers apparently didn't like the aside.

John smirked.

"After I told him that I didn't want children, he asked me why and he didn't let up. He asked me if I'd meet a man I was madly in love with who I knew would be a wonderful father and could support us would I change my mind. I said, in that case, maybe. He was satisfied for the moment. He then told me I was the type of woman he was looking for. He wanted an educated woman. I have a doctorate in elementary education. I was shocked that he knew so much about me. It was definitely off putting that he researched me, like analyzing data, comparing different cars. He took me home, and I figured I'd never see him again. That was fine with me. He's—uh, was—too controlling."

"Okay, so how did you go from there to here?" John pointed to her stomach.

"I told all of my friends about him, all his good points, and mostly they were all good. He was raising four adorable, sweet children. And for someone who didn't want a child to begin with, I'd be a stepmom to four. For me, that's a lot to take on. I'm also an associate professor at the university, and I teach at night. I want to go for full professorship, so being a mom wasn't in my plans. Then three of my friends gave birth in the same month. They're around my age, thirty-nine. I went to see all of them, and all of a sudden, I couldn't believe it, when holding those babies, I fell in love. Something inside of me did a three-sixty."

"And?"

"What I tell you, can it be in confidence?" she whispered. "Dr. and Mrs. Sulley can't find out."

"We'll see," Withers answered. "But we need the full story."

"Out of the blue, Henry, uh, Mr. Slater called me and we went out again. I told him what happened and that I changed my mind. We couldn't continue a relationship because Melissa was going to be in my class this year. And if I became pregnant with his child, Benjamin, being so intuitive, would be able to tell and he'd rat us both out. I have to say that Mr. Slater was manipulative and he has an answer and solution for everything. If we had gone to a fertility doctor the first question we'd be asked is "How long have you been trying?" Well, we weren't. He suggested because of our ages, that we have in vitro and tell the doctor I was his surrogate. That's the way he came to have Henry and Margie—"

"Whoa!" Withers interrupted. "Dr. Sulley just told us that Henry and Margie were adopted."

"I don't think that's true. Why would he lie to me?"

"I think your infatuation with this man let him get to you," Withers said.

She frowned. "Anyway, he wanted me to be a surrogate, and when the baby was born he'd take it."

"It?" Bella didn't mince words. "As in something inhuman?"

"Sorry. I'm just so rattled right now. Him or her. And I'm seeing a man now who knows about it, and he's expecting me to carry through on the surrogate thing."

"Well, now you can't," Bella said. "So what are you going to do?"

Miss Monty's teary gaze shot to the ceiling. Sniffling, she said, "I have no idea."

CHAPTER 8

Sitting in the den as Sam got the kids ready for school, Frank disconnected his cell after John caught him up on the meeting with the school administrators and the emotionally disconnected teacher, Miss Monty. All he kept thinking and saying was "Are you kidding me? Are you freaking kidding me?" He was happy, at least, that the school encouraged Benjamin's abilities, which he and Sam appreciated and understood. Right away, he thought of his mom, Theresa, and her psychic strengths. *Could it be that she brought me and Henry Slater together for the sake of the children? Nonsense, Frank, what are you thinking? It was science. The DNA, nothing more, nothing less.*

He caught John up on the info they got from the kids—the cage situation, which Withers told him about, at length. It seemed that Slater misconstrued things to Miss Monty, as well. On a lighter note, Frank mentioned Melissa's plans for his and Sam's wedding, and he almost forgot about the rubber dolly. He and John at least got a good laugh over that one. The first thing John would do is validate the authenticity of the birth certificates with Brett Case and his people. Case would also put pressure on animal control and try to get into Slater's apartment to remove the scorpion tank. Then Withers would be able to go in to retrieve the rubber dolly and send it to forensics. What it could tell them, he had no idea. Frank leaned back on the couch with his eyes closed for a solemn moment, steadying his brain.

At least Sam got the children dressed and she made

breakfast—scrambled eggs, hash browns, and gluten-free rye bread toast. He smiled when he heard compliments coming from the quartet. Margie apparently stayed in her high chair because he didn't hear any stressful babbling which usually meant she wanted out, and fast. It looked like his princess was getting the hang of motherhood. Now he had another niece or nephew in the oven. What if Miss Monty wouldn't want to raise the child? From what John explained, she wouldn't want any responsibility of being a parent. Crap! What would that mean for him and Sam? He very well knew Sam wanted her own. Another thought hit him. Would Sam want to wait until they got married to try? Knowing Sam's parents, they'd be pissed big time if she didn't. Why the hell was he thinking about this, now? Five children were more than enough. And he and Sam had more than enough to deal with.

They got to the school just in time for Frankie to get on line by his class in the cafeteria. Sam wheeled the stroller into the main office on the ground floor of the school while Frank headed toward the reception counter with Benjamin, Melissa, and Henry. The trio was ready for school, backpacks with their notebooks and all. Henry had insisted he go to this school even though Frank and Sam had told him otherwise. Frank wanted to enroll him in the same nursery school Frankie had gone to, which was a few blocks away and would be their next stop.

The secretary, Mrs. Freed, greeted him cordially. Glad he had a good working relationship with the school, Frank hoped it would be easier to admit Benjamin and Melissa without all of the necessary paper work. He handed Mrs. Freed the forms Sam had downloaded and he had filled out for admission of students to the New York City public school system.

She scrutinized each answer. "You have guardianship?"

"Yes." Frank handed her the paperwork the attorney gave him.

"Do you have the death certificate?"

"No, not yet."

She grimaced. "How about the children's birth certificates?"

"The school in Manhattan has them, but at this point we don't know their authenticity."

"That complicates things."

Sam intervened. "It doesn't matter. You can't deny them admittance. The children just came to live with us on Sunday. It'll take time to get all of their paperwork together." She paused. "You can admit them provisionally." Mrs. Freed gave her a quizzical look. "I was a teacher for ten years before I joined the department," Sam continued. "In the northern section of the borough."

Frank didn't give Mrs. Freed a chance to respond. "The school also recommends placing them down a grade. They were both accelerated by two years."

Benjamin and Melissa yelled out at once. "We're not going down a grade!"

"Oh, no," Benjamin added.

The principal approached the counter and stared directly at his two new admits. "Who is yelling in my school?"

Melissa frowned. "Your school? Who are you?"

"I'm Dr. Cohen, the principal, and I expect a certain decorum among our students. And as far as your grade placement, it isn't up to you children, nor is it up to your former school."

"Then who is it up to?" Benjamin asked.

Dr. Cohen smiled at the boy. "I'll have a teacher work with each of you for a while, and they'll assess your placement."

Benjamin stared directly at the principal. "Then all our good work in our school won't count? That's not fair."

Sam stood up for him without missing a beat. "He's absolutely right." She nodded to Benjamin apparently glad he spoke up.

"And you are?"

"This is my fiancée, Samantha Wright. Former teacher, now detective."

"I see. What's the school's contact number?"

Mrs. Freed handed him the forms. "It's right there," she said, pointing to it.

"Have a seat on the bench, I'll call in the grade leaders to work with the children, and Mrs. Freed will call their former school for their records."

"Dr. Sulley is expecting your call," Frank added.

The children looked anxious. Melissa hugged Sam, and Benjamin leaned in to Frank.

Frank put his arm around the boy. "Hey, it's okay. Go sit down on the bench." He spun around, moving his eyes all around the office. "Where's Henry?"

Sam became frantic. She ran out into the hall, and looked in all directions. The security guard sat behind a desk situated on a platform leading to the main entrance.

"Did you see a little boy with a light blue bubble jacket, curly hair, and a Sponge Bob back pack? He's three."

"No, ma'am, I didn't. He certainly didn't leave the building."

A cafeteria worker overheard them. "Oh, no. He was leaning against the door, and I thought he was a straggler. I put him on line for Mrs. Trevor's class."

Sam let out a breath of relief.

"He's in room one-twenty-three."

"Stay with the kids, Sam. I'll get him." Frank ran down the hall, through the cafeteria, and to the opposite hall. He knew the room. Mrs. Trevor was Frankie's Pre-K teacher.

He entered the classroom, looked around, and saw Henry, all at home, at the computer station with a group of four-year-olds. When Frank called his name, Henry ignored him. Frank laughed then looked around for the teacher. A young substitute approached him.

"Hi, may I help you? I'm Miss McClain."

"Is Mrs. Trevor absent?"

"Yes, she is."

"That explains it. My nephew, over there, left us in the office. Someone thought he was from this class. I'll take him now." Frank walked over the computer and tapped Henry's shoulder. The little one looked up and turned back to the game. "Henry, this is not your class."

"Yes. It is."

"No. You're going to your school later."

"This is my school." He pushed on Frank's leg. "Go away."

"This is pre-K. You're in nursery school. Come on, we have to admit your brother and sister."

"No. I'm staying."

Frank explained the situation to the teacher. He didn't want to be the cause of a tantrum, not because he didn't want to upset Henry, but he didn't want to set off twenty-five other four-year-olds. This young teacher didn't look as if she could handle that. She listened attentively to him and then told him he could leave Henry there until they were done in the office. She didn't seem to mind being the babysitting service. At least he and Sam would know the little guy would be taken care of. Frank graciously accepted the offer, told Henry he'd be back for him, which went over like a lead balloon, the three-year-old not even paying attention. Frank darted out of the room and made it back to the office to see Sam sitting on the bench holding Margie on her lap. Teachers had taken Melissa and Benjamin in for testing.

Frank sat on the bench next to Sam and opened his arms for Margie. She went to him and immediately put her head down on his shoulder. "How's it going?"

"They're only in the office about ten minutes. They went willingly with their book bags."

Frank's cell rang. He manipulated Margie to get his phone out of his pocket and the sleeping infant didn't stir. "Hey."

"Hey, how's fatherhood?" Without giving Frank a chance to answer, Case continued. "You and Trenton are doing a great job getting information we need. With that said, I used another agent's clout to get through to animal control. They're going into the apartment this afternoon to get the scorpion tank out. As soon as that's done, I'll give Withers clearance to go back into the apartment. Trenton wants to go as well, to see what vibes he can pick up."

"Okay. Excellent."

"We also made contact with major chain pet stores in Texas, and I have warrants ready to go for their surveillance videos taken during Christmas week and the week before. I need you to take pics of the kids and text them to me."

"Will do. What about the birth certificates?"

"John's coming into the precinct in a few hours. They're still at the school. I'll bring them to our counterfeit unit. Usually they're for art crimes, but this should be no problem for them. If these are counterfeits, then we're back to square one. Not having exact DOBs will hinder any credible sources."

"I concur."

"If we can't locate the mothers through the National Center for Missing and Exploited Children, we'll have to do a social media blast. One of the requirements to regain custody would be for the mothers to bring in the original birth certificates. The children's names have already been entered into the database, and nothing came up. There was nothing to compare. That raises a big red flag."

"How so?"

"The names the children are using might not be their birth names. And they might not even know. Even in spelling, one letter difference could throw everything off. That's why finding the original birth certificates is crucial."

⌘⌘⌘

As winter raged outside, she needed something to warm her up, both physically and mentally. She needed the warmth of the Florida sun and the emotional warmth from her family. Vicki Trenton pulled a tray of pumpkin-walnut-raisin muffins out of the wall oven in her chef's kitchen, and placed the muffin tin on a trivet on an adjacent counter. Leaning in and down toward the tray, she inhaled deeply. The scent of the tripled amount of cinnamon and double of nutmeg whiffed across her nose and filled the kitchen with a spicy aroma. It was nice. Cooking and baking took her mind off her loneliness. Making friends here in Scarsdale had been hard. Most of the women she met, even those at the community meeting a couple of weeks ago, were high-powered executives. They needed to work along with their husbands to keep up with mortgage payments. She hadn't met any stay-at-home moms.

It was the same on the Upper East Side when she and John lived in his condo. At least in Florida, if she got lonely, she'd be able to go to the range and fire off a hundred or so rounds. Her mind wandered to her guns, all of them. Her Glocks, Smith & Wesson, 357 Mag stainless steel pistol with a six-inch barrel, a Ruger lightweight .38 special, and a 9mm Luger all locked up at her parents' house.

She smiled in knowing that they'd be going down there in April for Frank to track down his parents. Why she and John were sucked into that, she didn't know. She did know that John and Frank had been good friends from way back, even before she'd met John. And she knew her husband. John must have convinced him to do it, the reasoning she wasn't privy to. She knew better than to pressure her husband about details from his cases.

But they'd accomplish two things at once. They'd be there for her dad's retirement party. Finally, after forty years with the sheriff's department, her dad would be retiring from Sun County's highest position, sheriff. The thought gave her chills. Her dad. He'd finally be able to enjoy the rest of his senior years. She often worried about him. Still going out into the field on dangerous cases with her brother, the commander of SWAT, her dad put himself into compromising situations, like becoming active in the hostage situation rescuing Ricky. At least her dad experienced John's negotiation skills up front and personal.

Her gaze wandered around the kitchen. The service they hired cleaned up the space in just a week after the home invasion by Abby Ruthe and her crew in the Scorpio case. Living in a hotel with the three children and an active dog wasn't exactly convenient. She stopped dead in her thoughts. Two houses she'd lived in became crime scenes. Hers in Florida after Barbara Montgomery took her and Ricky hostage in the Gemini case, and just two weeks ago. Was that an omen or what? Things usually happened in threes. She hoped nothing else was in the forecast.

She'd had finally gotten used to the Colonial style house with its huge center hall and three levels. This wasn't to say she didn't miss her home state of Florida. She missed it with all her heart. *Give yourself a break, darlin'.* "Only a month passed since you left Florida," she mumbled to herself.

Looking around the kitchen, she smiled when she saw her son actually reading in the nook. Ricky had come a long way in the year he'd been back with them. Three years for the universe to manifest John's wish was a long time. It was a lifetime, and for Ricky it was a painful three years, filled with foster home after foster home. But he's was doing okay. That's what was important to her, to see Ricky thriving and feeling safe. Lying by his feet, Duke was his best buddy in the entire world. The dog didn't leave his side, even when he went to the bathroom or took a shower, not to mention sleeping in the bed with him at night. Even her neat-freak husband was okay with dog hair in the bed. He'd do anything to foster Ricky's psychological health. Their son had been through more abuse than any child should have to endure.

Vicki sat down on the bench next to Ricky. She rested her palms on her cheeks and elbows on the table, listening to Ricky read aloud. She and John were proud of him.

Though very below the grade level in reading and math for a nine year old, he was trying hard to catch up. She assessed he was at second grade level which was way above what he was when he came back to them a year ago, last February.

Vicki picked up the plastic wrap enveloped New York City newspaper that lay on the edge of the bench. John insisted on getting it daily to keep up with the news. She untwisted the tie and pulled out the paper. After unrolling it, she read the headline as she usually did. *NYPD Calls in FBI Linking Five Similar Unsolved Murders in New York City over a Fifteen-Year Period.*

Oh, God, another case that had John's name written on it, taking more time away from them. She began to read the article. The pictures of the murdered women were in little boxes with their names. Yep, those women sure did look alike. All had blonde ponytails, blue eyes according to the article, toned bodies, and all had their necks slashed. Come to think of it, that described her to a T. Oh, God! What a dreadful thought. Why couldn't she have her guns, again? Farther down in the article, after describing the details, was a drawing of a possible suspect. An eyewitness supposedly saw this man, exiting a bedroom window and jumping down a fire escape. Around forty with shoulder length curly brown hair, medium build, estimated to be about five-ten, large round dark looking eyes, angular chin, and high cheekbones. She studied the drawing and gasped.

I must get my hands on a gun.

∽∾∽∾

As Sam fidgeted on the bench waiting for Benjamin and Melissa to be done with their testing, she kept looking around the office. The school was a lot more modern and newer than her school—by about thirty years, in her estimation. The white ceiling to floor tiled walls gave the perfect backdrop for her to zone out. She was certainly good with a more modern school for her children, comfortable in her new role as adoptive parent. Were the children ready to accept her? She hadn't a clue. She woke herself up. *Not a good time for daydreaming, Sam*, she reprimanded herself. The voice of the paraprofessional from Mrs. Trevor's class talking to Henry as they walked into the office grabbed her attention. The three-year-old ran over to her and stuck out a drawing in front of her.

"Look what I made, Samantha!"

"Wow, Henry. I love it!"

"See? I used pink," he said as he pointed to each color. "Blue, red, and purple."

"Sweetheart, that's the most amazing duck I ever saw."

The little guy pouted. "It's a turtle, not a duck."

Sam tried to hide her laughter. "Come here, sweetheart," she said, hugging him. "It's the most amazing turtle I've ever seen."

Frank looked at the drawing. "I'll say. Hey, Henry. Who wrote your name on the paper?"

He pointed to himself. "Me."

"Can you spell it for me?"

Henry pointed to each letter. "H. E. N. R. I. E."

Frank shot Sam a quizzical look. "You spell it with i.e., not y?" The little guy bobbed his head.

"What, Frank?"

"Brett told me they entered the kids names in the database but nothing came up. He also said spelling counts. With a one-letter difference, there won't be a match. I wonder how Benjamin and Melissa spell their names. We've been assuming it's the traditional way. Oh, and John told me they had unusual spellings, but in the rush, didn't get into specifics."

"However, nothing with Henry Slater Senior was traditional." She looked toward the door at the sounds of Melissa and Benjamin talking to Dr. Cohen. "We'll find out soon enough. Hi, how did you two do?"

"They'll be just fine. Their school was accurate in their

grade placement. They're not happy about it, but they'll adjust. It's lunchtime for their grades. Why don't we do this? Let them start tomorrow. Bring them to the office at eight forty, and I'll bring them to their classes." Dr. Cohen didn't give either Sam or Frank the chance to respond. "Then we're good." He turned and walked back into his office.

Sam and Frank sat for a moment, then Sam smacked her thighs. "Okay, then, let's get outta here and I want to hear everything."

Melissa rolled her eyes.

Sam stared at her, wide eyed. "What's that supposed to mean?"

Melissa pursed her lips. "Let's go. I'm not in the mood." She headed toward the exit.

Frank stopped her, grabbing her arm. "Over here, now." She stood by his knees with her gaze up to the ceiling light. He seemed to do a quick analysis and he compressed his lips before speaking. "You're going to knock off the attitude, and fast." He shot her a stern disciplinary glare that Sam had seen him send Frankie. "Do you understand, young lady?"

Melissa seemed to be immune. She didn't look at Frank eye to eye. For the first time Sam recognized an emotional block. The little girl's eyes went blank, expressionless, as if she'd left the earth plane. She'd had to be used to reprimands by her father. *Is this how she acted, to escape emotion? Wow, I know Frank must be thinking the same thing.*

Frank waved his palm in front of her face. Melissa startled. "Earth to Melissa." She stepped backward. "Where did you go to?"

She blinked rapidly. "Uh, nowhere."

"Look at me," Frank said. "Is this what you did when your Dad reprimanded you? Mentally escaped?"

"What's that?"

"Get your mind to leave the conversation."

"No." Melissa paused. "I'm hungry."

"Me, too." Henry jumped up and down.

Sam had had enough. She got up from the bench and pushed the stroller out of the office. "Let's go, guys. Henry, we'll take you to school tomorrow."

"We'll make lunch at home," Frank said.

"I want to go to school, now!" Henry tried to insist.

"I know you want to, Henry, but by the time we get there, the school will be closed. Nursery school is half a day."

The three-year-old pouted, his lower lip quivering.

"Hey!" Frank demanded. "Don't you start now."

"I'm sitting next to you, Samantha." Henry hugged Sam's leg. "Not you, Uncle Frank."

Frank glared at Sam. She knew exactly what he meant— from his eyes, alone. It was weird. Freaky, almost. When he was pissed off or upset, his dark brown eyes darkened, to almost black. It happened up close and personal in the Aries case when they were in Jen's hospital with FBI Special Agent Brett Case and his team, making the arrests in Jen's murder of those who perpetuated the embezzlement scheme that her murder tried to cover up. Frank was almost at his breaking point then.

She intended to make this right. "The three of you, listen up, right now. When Uncle Frank tells you something, that's it. Case closed. Don't expect me to go against what he said. Mommies and daddies stick together."

Benjamin put his arm around his sister. "That's why Dad said we didn't need a mom. She would only listen a hundred percent to him."

❧❧❧

Frank had prepared tuna salad with chopped hardboiled eggs when he woke up in the morning. He toasted rye bread as Sam and the children sat at the table in the kitchen nook. Sam fed Margie puréed boiled chicken and creamed spinach. The infant loved it. That had to make Sam proud, Frank thought. Sam had made the food and even mastered the baby-food processor.

He especially appreciated that she backed him in the school. He'd show her his gratitude during their alone time in the bedroom tonight, if they'd get any. It was hard enough grabbing time for themselves with Frankie in the house at night, now with five kids? He began to question his sanity. *Knock it off, Frank.* This was so well worth it. He loved his nieces and nephews, and he wouldn't trade Sam and his situation for the world.

After he brought sandwiches and fruit salad to the table and joined them, he needed to get the name spellings correct. "Are you two," he said, pointing to Melissa and Benjamin, "good, so we can have a conversation without any issues?"

Melissa took a bite of her sandwich. "Um, this is good. I never had tuna and egg before."

"Well?"

"Yes, I was hungry. That's why I was cranky. Dad always says that. That we get cranky when we need to eat. Yes, we can have a conversation."

Frank nodded. "Okay, good. Remember Special Agent Case? You met him at the precinct."

"Yes," said Benjamin. "He asked me lots of questions."

"Yes, he did. When you two were in the office, Henry found himself in a pre-K class. He drew a turtle and wrote his name on the paper. We thought he spelled his name with a y, the regular way, but he spelled his name with an i.e. How do you spell your names?"

"How did he find himself in a pre-K class?"

Sam smiled. "A lunchroom lady put him on a class line by mistake. So, Melissa, how do you spell your name?"

"M. Y. L. I. S. S. A. E."

Frank stared at her. "Whoa, that's different. How did that come to be?"

"I don't know. It's My. Liss. Ae," she said with a long a

sound. "But everyone calls me Mel—issa, so I didn't tell you."

"Benjamin, how do you spell your name? I'm almost afraid to ask."

"Why?"

"Well, your Dad certainly did things out of the ordinary."

"B. E. N. G. A. M. I. N. N. With a G, not a J, and two Ns at the end."

"Okay. Dr. Trenton is up at your old school to tell them to get your records sent, so if he sees your schoolwork, are these the spellings you use?"

"Yes, on everything."

Frank's cell rang. After looking at the caller ID he excused himself from the table. He answered on the way to the den. "Hey, John."

"I'm back at the precinct."

"Anything else?"

"Yes, a ton. I noticed on the birth certificates their names weren't spelled the usual way."

"I just found out, literally just a minute ago."

"Okay, tell me what you can about Slater being unusual, out of the box, anything not expected. I'm trying to figure out if he just wants to be different as a creative and an artist, or it has a deeper motivation, like hiding. Or at least making it harder to be found."

"That's a tough call. Everything I've seen was to be manipulative, like the will, wanting me to confront our birth parents before it can be executed. Hold on a minute, Sam would be the best one on this. She went with Brett to Strident. And she spent time with Slater at the apartment. Sam?"

Sam answered from the kitchen. "Yes?"

"Come in to speak to John, please." Frank handed Sam his cell and left for the kitchen.

"Hi, John."

"What did you see from Slater that showed his manipulative behavior?"

"Uh, do you have three hours?"

"No. Ten minutes. Go."

"He wanted absolute obedience from his marital partner, and apparently he told the children that. He used it as the reason they don't need a mommy. They couldn't get away with anything, because both parents would agree."

"So he probably saw a lot of arguing growing up. I'm getting the feeling he was the opposite kind of parent to what he had. That would have to be a conscious effort."

Sam sighed. "So he's pampering, protective, more of a helicopter parent then mine, which I never thought could exist."

"Your story is for another day. I bet mine could match yours item for item. What else?"

"What was on his mind was on his tongue, no matter to whom he was speaking. On the phone and in the family meeting at his apartment, he freaked Frankie out telling him to come to live with us. He really had unrealistic expectations that everyone would kowtow to what he wanted. All the time. That definitely fit with the slave-master relationship. Ah! He told me he'd demand that of the mother of his children." Sam paused. "Hold on a minute. I have to think this through." Another pause. "What updates do you have in finding the mothers? Frank told me about Texas on the box of scorpions."

"Now that we have the correct spellings Agent Case will put the names into the database again. He's getting the surveillance videos, as well. What are you thinking?"

"What if he did have the slave-master relationship with each of their mothers? In my interpretation, that would mean joint custody—no, maybe full custody. If he took the children, he could have told the women that he wanted daddy time. That wouldn't be kidnapping, would it?"

"No, it would not be. And that's what we originally thought happened. But it would be kidnapping if he kept the children for an extended period of time, refusing to bring them back, as with the older three children."

"If the mothers were in the slave role, they'd have to go along with it. If you find him on the tape in the pet store with a woman and Margie, look to see if at any time he took the baby and separated from her. Then look to follow him to the outside. We may have the complete story right there."

"No, Sam. Only when we bring in the mothers will we have the complete story. Speak with you soon." He disconnected.

CHAPTER 9

John re-entered the war room where Lex and Bella downed Italian heroes at a bridge table in the corner. The smells warmed his senses but looking at the crusted bread turned his stomach. He grimaced.

"What's your problem, Trenton?" Withers teased with his mouth full.

"It's not my problem. It's yours. You really need all that bread?"

"Well, excuse you," Bella taunted. "First of all, I think you're hanging around your buddy, Khaos, too much, and second, we don't have a professional caliber chef to go home to like you."

"Okay, I get it."

Before John could continue Special Agent Brett Case entered with two additional members of the task force that John hadn't met, and Case made the introductions. "Kenneth James, Peter Mullen, two of our best techs."

Withers nodded. "Thanks for keeping our Detective Wright safe."

"That's our job," James answered curtly.

John gave him a quizzical look.

"Yeah. These are the agents who set up the mics on Sam and Frank and tracked us in the van to Slater's apartment last week. What have you got for us?"

"Something real fun," Case chided. "Only about four hours work. Finish up and get over here."

Withers stopped mid-bite, looked at his hero woefully,

and dropped it down on the white wrapping paper. Bella ventured to grab another mouthful then did the same.

Sitting around the conference table Case pushed a laptop into the center. James and Mullen took over and set it up.

"Animal Control is at the apartment now. Luckily, I was able to cut their response time by two weeks. As much as I told them to avoid the barriers, and Lex, I did tell them to steer clear of the arts supplies, they told me their boss is the boss—"

"Why bother? They wouldn't care," Mullen said. "We'll just have to deal with it."

"Well I care," John interrupted. "For one, Melissa wanted her dad's art supplies and we also need to check out everything. He has client records in there." He compressed his lips. "Those kids are going to have a hard time, enough. I'd prefer not to add to the disappointment."

"No shit. Going from that pampering private school to public?" Withers let out a deep breath. "Frank and Sam will have their hands full."

"Kids are resilient," Case said then he addressed John. "You have the birth certificates?"

John slipped them out of a folder. "Can you tell by the naked eye if these are the real deal?"

"No way," answered James. "There are over 6000 organizations that dispense birth certificates and over 14,000 different ones circulating out there. This will take some time."

"Okay, pay attention to the name spellings and mother's names. I'm pretty sure that Sara Phipps is not the mother of the older two. The children would know."

"We're paying attention to everything," Case responded. "Every detail will be checked through our info systems. Color, font, stamps, information inserted, dates, and names. This is serious stuff."

Mullen added to the confusion. "We'll also check out those sites online that'll give you a new birth certificate and identity for thirty-nine bucks. Maybe Slater ordered them."

"No shit!" Withers said. "It's that easy?"

"Yes, it's that easy, Detective. If he got them another way, that'll open up a brand new investigation for us," Mullen said. "He could have also used the names of children and parents who were deceased. One more thing, Agent Case, we need to find the children's social security numbers and check them against death certificates."

"That's horrible." Bella said.

"True, Detective," James said. "But unfortunately counterfeiters of children's birth certificates usually take them from deceased children when creating new identities. The new children are the same age as the decedents so social security numbers just transfer."

"Okay, wait a second." John put his pen down. "Thinking Slater has somewhat of an affection for children, more like a tolerance, whether it's an act or not, I really do not think he'd use deceased kids. I think that would be a turn off even for him. He'd have some ethical boundaries on that one. No, I think these children have their own identities. I just got off the phone with Sam. She told me that Slater would demand a slave master relationship with his wife, if he were to get married. He'd demand that of her. He made that clear before a relationship would begin. What if these children's mothers agreed then after giving birth, changed their minds? Their freedoms meant too much to them. And Slater wouldn't deal well with the mind-changing. Striking out in anger over a woman who tells him she doesn't want children and killing her, I'm afraid he might have done the same with these children's moms."

"I hope not," answered Case. We should be getting the Texas tapes, soon. I'm counting on finding Slater, the baby, and a woman in them. If he did indeed kill the bio mom, I can safely assume he did the same to the others."

"Well, that would give Frank and Sam the legal right to adopt them."

Withers got a harsh glare from everyone in the room. "Hey, I'm just saying…"

Special Agent Mullen turned the laptop. "All right,

we're in. Real time." He got a thumbs up from the Animal Control Officer. All of them wore white padded jump suits, helmets with a clear plastic shield in front of their eyes, and thick looking gloves.

As Mullen scanned the room, John and Case got their first look into the organized world of Henry Slater Senior— a neat, large space. As the camera hit it, Withers pointed to the dollhouse that the children knew as a cage. "Take a look at that."

John's brows furrowed. "How in the world could such bright children think that was a cage? Even in books, and he had them read a lot, there were pictures of dollhouses and animal cages. I don't get it. And why would he want to lie about that?" John paused. "Control. He had total control over them. But then, I'd expect them to be introverted and shy."

"It was sicker with him wanting Melissa to be a boy," Bella said.

James and Mullen both did double takes. "Whoa! What?"

"For Slater, it probably isn't as serious as wanting a gender change. My guess, without delving into it, he wanted to avoid the emotionality of girls. He told Frank he didn't feel any emotions. With the boys, he could be straightforward and analytical." He received doubtful looks from all of them. "I know. We need to get into it a lot more. Though the kids did tell Sam and Frank they weren't allowed to show feelings."

They watched two officers lift the drawing table and move it to the other side of the room next to the dollhouse. Its table top contents—rulers, colored pencils, erasers, a stack of multicolored art paper, a compass, a protractor, markers—stayed in place. They carefully placed white tarps over the table and the house. Another thumbs up into the camera. Everyone smiled. Now all attention was on the mahogany wall on the opposite side of the room. An officer typed in the code to open the sliding wood door concealing the scorpion tank. The code worked the first time and the door slid open. As soon as light hit the tank, scorpions rushed for cover under the rocky terrain and sand. The officers flashed lights on the sides of the aquarium to get an idea of how deep the tank went into the wall, and then one of them inserted a ruler.

He held his finger on the edge and held it up for Case's team to see. Twelve-inches deep. They measured the length—seventy-two inches. They could probably pull out the tank and keep the critters alive and well.

An officer pushed in a rolling table to hold the tank after its removal.

"All we have to hope for is that there's no crack in the tank for some of those beauties to escape through," Case said.

John grimaced. "I'd hate to think of that. Where will AC take them?"

"There are several preserves in upstate New York for various species of Arachnida. They'll be safe, and children can learn about them in a protected environment." The officers began to wedge the tank out. "Okay, here we go."

The men pulled each side forward about an inch. They stopped. An officer shone a flashlight into each side.

"Now they're checking for cracks," Case explained. "If there is one, I doubt if any of the scorpions will make their way into the room, but if they do, we're screwed."

Bella seemed to have no patience. "Why can't they just exterminate the damn things?"

"That's not AC's role," Case said. "Their job is to remove illegal creatures and place them safely. Besides, they're immune to all chemicals."

A thumbs up from one of the officers confirmed they were going to be able to do this. Officers pried out the tank, slowly, trying hard not to jolt their charges inside of it. Once on the table, the officers secured the tank with straps connecting to hooks on the table's sides. The camera followed the team as it moved the tank through the room, into the kitchen, into the dining room, into the center hall and out into the hallway.

Case blew out a deep breath. "Okay, we're on. Lex, get Crime Scene back in there and meet them. John, go and do what you do best. I expect all three of you to bring back something we can use to find these children's mothers. The longer Sam and Frank have them, the harder separation will be. It's Sam, I'm concerned about."

౿ఎఴ౩

John, Lex, and Bella arrived at Henry Slater's Upper West Side apartment building at the same time Crime Scene did. The FBI closed off the private elevator that led from the parking garage to the living room. Down to one elevator, it took two trips to get all of them up to the penthouse on the twenty-sixth floor. Crime Scene went in first to make sure the paths were still intact. John waited outside the apartment with Lex and Bella until given the welcome signal, a hand from a lead investigator waving them inside.

John headed right, through the dining room then kitchen, and then into the art room securing the dollhouse. He stood still in front of it, at first just admiring it. He couldn't get over the details. The pink and light blue shingle tiles on the triangular roof peaked about six feet—two inches shorter than he was. The light blue shutters around the open windows on each side of the house and the white door with a puppy-face shaped doorknocker were in perfect proportion to the rest of the house. His Vicki would go crazy seeing this. He peered through the window, seeing the dark pink padded bench on the opposite wall. Walking around to the front, he opened the door, and laughed when he saw the white stove and refrigerator in the back.

"What, Trenton?" Lex, mocked. "What are you seeing in that mind of yours?"

John laughed. "Nothing yet. Slater was some genius,

that's for sure. He must have put an electric socket under the house for the refrigeration. How about giving me a few minutes? And you go check out the art cabinet over there. Maybe pack up some things for Melissa."

"Ah," said Bella. "You could just tell us to get lost."

A crime scene tech called out to them. "Hey, Detectives." He held up a brown rectangular book. "Here's the record book for Slater's customers. Apparently, he wasn't much of a computer guy."

Lex and Bella left John to attend to the dollhouse.

John stared into the space in front of him. The white wall behind the life-sized toy made the perfect backdrop to see the auras around it. He started his diaphragmatic deep breathing as he did before any meditation or intuitive session. Blocking out the voices of the investigators and detectives happened easily because he'd been exposed to their intonations and dialects often. He wasn't expecting anything unusual to interfere with his concentration. He zoned out and let the rods and cones in his eyes do their job—detect the aura of the dollhouse. With the right angle, he saw pinks and blues surrounding it—loving colors, not ominous. He drew his gaze toward the inside, to the bench. There was a gray haze around it—fear. The children were indeed afraid of their father. *What happened on that bench*? John visualized Henry Senior, not specific features, just a gray haze with a muddy dark elephant gray outline. The blue outline of a child sat next to him, but overshadowed by the gray mass. The gray arm of the father held the child tightly. *Okay, control, domineering, possessiveness.* He couldn't make out the specific child of the three, but his gut told him it was Benjamin. He put it out to Max, his spirit guide to come to him. He needed help. The children needed help.

John visualized Max in his white gi coming in front of his third eye. John spoke to him in thought language.

Max, I really need your help, here. You know the story. You're aware of everything. We know Slater didn't do any-

thing physically to abuse the children. Frank examined them at bath time, Miss Monty, Benjamin's teacher said they were well cared for. What should I look for in this house, Max? Guide me to something I wouldn't ordinarily look for. The walls inside the house are covered with what looks like hand painted wallpaper. It all looks smooth.

John felt Max's affirmative jolt in his psychic center—the top of his head on the right side.

Max, are you telling me something is up with the wallpaper?

There was another affirmative jolt. John entered the dollhouse and ran his hands over the walls opposite the bench. Then the walls toward the ceiling. Nothing unusual. His gaze went to the bench again. *Why am I focusing on that bench?* He felt the padding—soft, comfortable. He put his finger under the edge of the seat and tried to lift it. The seat didn't budge. He sat on it, and let his bulky frame sink into the seat. Slater was at least sixty more pounds than he was. The pressure of Slater's body would surely make dents in the cushion. But nothing. Was something under the padding? John got up and focused his gaze through the material. Psychically, he saw a small folded piece of paper—cream-colored paper. John shook his head and snapped himself out of the trance.

Bent over, he got out of the dollhouse and then straightened up. Chills ran through him, and his hands became clammy. This wasn't like him at all. "Lex, get someone over here with scissors."

"What's going on, Doc?" an investigator asked.

"There's something inside the padding."

Lex felt the seat. The investigator did, as well. "John, I don't feel anything."

"Neither did I." John paused. "I saw it. Something cream colored and folded."

After Lex smirked, he told the investigator to go ahead and cut into the padding. John knew Lex from as far back as the Gemini case when John—hooked up in the ICU—heard a message on his cell phone. The phone was off and in Lex's pocket. John even knew the sender of the message. He still heard Bobby Mitchell's voice, as if in real time. John sighed, glad he'd solved Bobby's murder, just two weeks ago in the Scorpio case.

The investigator sliced into the edge of the bench. "Doc, just where did you see this object?"

"Right in the middle, under the padding."

The investigator carefully sliced open the fabric and cut it off around all sides. There was nothing revealed on the surface of the padding or on the underside of the fabric. John lifted up the sponge padding. Right in the center on the frame, they all saw it.

The folded cream-colored paper.

"Well, I'll be," Withers said. "You did it again, Trenton." He lifted the paper and unfolded it. What accosted their gaze, made them all stand still.

Benjamin Slater's original birth certificate and his social security card attached to it with a paper clip.

ᕮᔕᕮᔕ

The newspaper lay on the table. Vicki had taken pictures of the article and suspect and messaged them to her brother, Mark, in Florida. Her cell phone rang less than a minute after she sent the text.

"Where are you?" were the first words her brother said.

"I'm home with the children and Duke. Mark, I'm scared."

"Okay, hold on. Did you call John?"

"No, he's in the field. I don't like to bother him. It's him, isn't it?"

"I can't say for sure, but we can put it into our age progression software. Up in the city, your guys can do it faster. You've got plenty of people to call."

"Not too many people know about my past. And I want to keep it that way." Ricky came into the kitchen and opened the fridge. "Hi, darlin', what are you going to eat, now?"

"I don't know, Mom."

"Mark, did you hear Ricky?"

"Yeah, I got it. Okay, look, you'll have to…never mind, sis. Let me see what I can do."

"Speak to you soon."

Oh God, this can't be happening. The last time I saw you, Jarrett Miller almost eighteen years ago, you were handcuffed and being taken out of the courthouse to prison to serve your sentence. My daddy made sure you spent each day behind bars. Heck, there's no early release in Florida, anyway. And you brought your sorry ass to New York City. All those women you killed. They all look like me, you bastard.

"Oh my God," Vicki whispered with her hand over her mouth.

Did you kill those women to get even with me? I bet you did. Okay, Vicki, time to get tough. Jarrett Miller, you're not killing another woman if I can help it. I'll do what I have to. Even kill again. Just as I did after Barbara Montgomery shot John in the Gemini case. I killed her and didn't think twice about it. I'll do what it takes to protect myself, and my family.

Vicki paced the kitchen. Good thing Ricky took his fruit salad into the den. She called Sam.

Sam answered on the fourth ring. "Hi, Vicki."

"How's motherhood treating you?"

"Oh. My. God. I love it. They definitely keep me on my toes. The two little ones are napping and the rest are studying an issue of Brides Magazine that my mother gave us."

"Deciding on a date?"

"No, not yet. The kids are excited about it, though."

"Do you have a minute to talk?"

"Yes, what's going on? You sound nervous."

Vicki plopped down on the bench in the nook, peeking

into the den every few seconds to make sure Ricky didn't come in. "Yes, Sam, I'm very nervous."

"What about?"

"Have you seen the city paper, today?"

"No, not yet. What happened?"

"A guy, a police sketch, was on the front page. He killed five women in New York City over a fifteen year period."

"And?"

"I recognized him."

"How did you recognize him?"

"Can you get me a gun?"

"What? No, Vicki, I cannot get you a gun. New York isn't a right to carry state. And you won't get licensed for any reason."

"There is a reason."

"Doesn't matter. Vicki, who is this guy?"

"All of the women he killed look like me."

"Vicki, who is he?"

"Jarrett Miller. My first husband."

☙❧

John, Bella, and Lex stood outside the dollhouse, staring at Benjamin's birth certificate as Lex held it between them. John's mind went in a few different directions and he assumed it was the same for Lex and Bella. The spelling of his name was the same, BENGAMINN, as it was on the school's birth certificate and all his schoolwork. His biological mother's name was written as Sarah Phillips. His birthdate, October fifteenth.

"That is significant," John said. "Just a few different letters in the spelling of his mother's name, easy to counterfeit. The states of birth on the first one and this document are the same, Utah. Look at the birthdate. October fifteenth. That makes Benjamin already nine." John paused. "Now I get it."

"Get what?" Bella asked.

"Why Slater pushed for the children to be accelerated in school. They were older than the school knew them to be. They're putting Benjamin into fourth grade. That's age appropriate. I'd make a bet that Melissa and Henry are older, as well. And I'd also venture to guess that their birth certificates are hidden in this apartment, too."

Withers groaned. "Tell me, Trenton, do we have to tear up every piece of upholstered furniture?"

"I sure as hell hope not. I can't force my visions. Benjamin told Frank that he helped his dad build the dollhouse because Melissa was too young. This is just a hunch. What did Melissa do with her dad? Art work."

"She also told Frank she helped him decorate Mike Sheffield's apartment," Withers said. "I hope her birth certificate isn't there."

"No, it's here." John pulled the tarp off the drawing board. He handed all of the stuff on top to an investigator who put it all into a box. Searching around deep sidewalls, John found a latch. He depressed the button and the tabletop popped up. John found two large manila envelopes.

The label on one read *Birth Certificates*. The other label read *Trust*.

"Are you freaking kidding me?" Withers said, looking at the date on the trust. "I don't know the date on the will but this is a couple of months ago. Doesn't a trust usurp a will, unless the trust is revoked?"

"Yes," answered John. "And the trust has to be formerly revoked. Possibly the will we've been looking at isn't official. You know what? Case will have to get some attorneys onboard. What's in the other envelope?"

Bella opened the envelopes and pulled out four birth certificates. Each had a social security card attached with a clip. The one on top was Benjamin's, apparently the one in the bench the original, and this was a photocopy. Next was Melissa's. Her name spelled the way the school had it. Her mother's name was Lisa Brandt. Her birthdate, September thirtieth, and her state of birth was Illinois. Under hers was Henry's with the I.E. spelling. His mother's name Lauren Berkeley, his date of birth, October twentieth, and state of birth, Arizona. The last one was Margie's. Her real first name was Margarita, her mother's name Sonja Santos, her state of birth, Texas, and date, April fourth.

"Take a look at this," John said. "The older three fall under the sign of Libra."

Lex frowned. "What in hell is the meaning of that?"

"I don't know, yet. But I bet it's very significant. Okay, Melissa is already seven. That would explain why she's more mature than a six year old. Henry is well over three, and that accounts for his vocabulary. I bet Slater planned these births. All but Margie's."

"I smell the wood burning, Trenton," Lex taunted.

"I bet Margie wasn't planned. That would have pissed off Slater big time."

"If he was pissed, why did he take the child then?" Bella said. "He would have ignored her, in my opinion."

"That's an excellent question, Bella," John said. "Before we get back, I want to find that rubber dolly. Where's the master? Then I want to see the children's bedroom."

Lex led them through the center hall to the other side of the apartment to the master bedroom.

This is elegant. Frank's a jerk for not wanting to live here, but then again, he hates luxury. Reminds him of the home he was brought up in, and the pain of losing his adoptive parents.

Withers snapped his fingers in front of John's face. "Hey, wake up! Do you want to do the honors?" Lex pointed to under the bed.

John sneered at him. *Doesn't he know by now not to do that to me?* He swallowed hard before bending down. From under the bed, he pulled out the naked life-sized rubber dolly, placing it on top of the bed.

The investigators and the detectives laughed. John shook his head. "I don't know about you, guys, but she doesn't do it for me. Okay, pack her up and see what we get from her."

"What are you looking for, Doc?" an investigator asked.

"I have no idea." John turned and looked around the room. That circular bed was sure his style. The colors, too, burgundy and cream. But just like Khaos, his country girl, Vicki wouldn't go for it, either.

He walked down the narrow hall, stopping to look inside the baby girl's room. He mouthed *wow* then continued into the baby boy's room and through the open doorway into the children's quarters. As soon as he entered, he felt the energy from the bright colors hit him in the face. He jumped back. That was jarring. John walked to the center of the room and stood still. "This is way too much color for a child to absorb. What was Slater thinking? It's like sensory bombardment. How did they ever do their homework in here? Or even better, sleep? I know Ricky couldn't deal with this. And I couldn't stay in here, too long, either."

"My guess is as good as yours," Withers said.

John compressed his lips, not in a rush to analyze the situation. "Okay, hold on a minute. Slater had bad headaches, yes? I remember he told Frank about them, and even Benjamin wants to become a brain surgeon so he could help his father. Maybe Slater needed a distraction from the headaches when he was in here with the children. Staying in here, the color bombardment may have taken his mind off the pain. It may have been good for him, but not for the children." John paused again. "Ask the children if they get headaches."

Withers wrote himself a note on his pad. "Is that hereditary?"

"No, but if he told the children it is, he might have set up this room to provoke them. That's too crazy, even for him. I can't imagine him being one of those parents who sets his children up for pain. No, never. Forget that line of thinking."

"We'll ask them if they get headaches, though."

John looked at his watch. "It's after school now. Call

Sam and Frank to bring the kids up to the precinct. We'll meet them there."

CHAPTER 10

With five children constantly underfoot, Sam couldn't tell Frank about her conversation with Vicki. For sure, she'd have to help her. *Oh my God! What if, what if, Vicki was right? What if this guy killed women to get even with his ex-wife?* Sam had no idea why Vicki would think that at this point. Vicki was a private person. She never got personal with Sam. Come to think of it, aside from Vicki helping Sam with cooking, and assisting a couple of weeks ago in the Scorpio case—when Vicki narrowed down the buffet as the source of the scent on Carrie's hair—they never had girl-time. Even when she, Frank, and Frankie went up to Scarsdale to see the twins, she and Vicki spoke about her relationship problems with Frank, nothing deeper.

Sam's mind wandered. *Why was Vicki keeping her past a secret?* Sam remembered what John said a couple of weeks ago when the team was discussing who'd go into Strident with her. Frank teased him with "maybe you'd teach Vicki something new."

John almost freaked. He filled them in that his wife had been in an abusive relationship for three months. He'd never inflict any pain. This Jarrett Miller was an abusive son-of-a-bitch.

Frank came into the den where Sam sat on the couch and nudged her out of her thoughts. "Hey, John just called. We're needed up at the precinct with the kids."

"Now? It's getting dark already."

"Yeah, now, with Benjamin and Melissa. Kathryn and Walter will watch the other three."

"What other three?" Melissa said as she plopped down next to Sam.

"You and Benjamin are coming into the city with us."

The little girl's jaw dropped. "Oh, no. We all go together. All the time."

"You never went out with your dad alone at times?"

"Nope."

"You went out shopping with me."

"That was different. It was for clothes. And I was excited."

Benjamin was right on her heels. "We stay together. Period."

Frank blew out a deep breath of exasperation. "Give us a break, here. Henry, Margie, and Frankie are staying with Grandma and Grandpa."

Henry came up behind them, yelling. "I go, too!" The three year old stood, stomping his feet.

Sam couldn't help but laugh.

Frank glared at her. "Not funny, princess."

"What, Dad? You can't take them and leave me home." Frankie looked like he was ready to cry. "No, that's not fair."

⌘

Vicki's brother texted John with the article and pictures his sister sent. A photo from Jarrett Miller's arrest caused John to collapse back into the seat. Still in the war room, the team was waiting for Frank and Sam to come up with the kids.

Brett Case saw the despondency on John's face and didn't let it slide. "What's going on?" he asked John who was lost, looking at his phone.

"Another case. A very personal case." John showed Case

his phone. "This guy, wanted in the five murders in the city, is my wife's first husband."

"You're frigging kidding me?" Withers sat up in his seat as Case pointed the phone toward him. "We have a positive ID?"

"Yeah. Vicki called her brother first. I'm sort of bummed about that. He dug up his arrest photo."

"Why her brother and not you?" Nick asked.

John sighed. "Her brother busted the guy. He's the SWAT commander down there and her other brother is a detective."

Withers snickered. "Tell the rest of these guys the more important part."

John sneered back. "Vicki's father is the sheriff of the county. He's retiring in April. She'd been badly abused by this guy over a three-month marriage. He did do prison time, almost two years."

"Okay." Case compressed his lips and nodded. "A positive ID is a great start."

"One other thing," John added. "All of the women he murdered are the spitting image of my wife."

Case got up and swiped the day's paper off a side table. He stared at the pictures of the women. "Have a picture of your wife?" John put his phone onto the table, showing Vicki. "Crap, they sure are."

John got another text. The alert distracted Case's stare on the paper, but he read it instead of giving the phone back to John. "What the hell is this?"

"What?" John asked, grabbing his phone.

Case wide eyed stared at John. "Vicki wants a gun?"

John rolled his eyes. "Yeah. She's quite capable."

"Oh, yeah?" Case challenged. "What do you consider capable?"

"When I met her in Florida, her house was an arsenal."

"Damn it, Trenton," Withers said. "You leave out the most important parts."

John's cheeks puffed and he blew out a deep breath. He

didn't want to rehash the story, but with an FBI agent, he'd had to be complete in his narration. "Vicki is the one who shot and killed Barbara Montgomery in the Gemini case. She'd had taken Vicki and Ricky hostage to lure me in to the house. Barbara shot me and I was incapacitated. Vicki took over."

Case's brows furrowed, obviously not understanding. "How did she have the skill?"

"After her marriage ended, her brothers trained her with guns and in self-defense. The SWAT team was there at the hostage scene, the sniper in place but he couldn't get a clear shot with Ricky in the way, and Barbara had fallen, blocking the door. The only way out was for Vicki to take action, and she did."

"Okay, so I'm assuming your wife can perform under stress." Case tapped his pen on a file in a contemplative moment. "How would she feel about coming in to do a public appeal?"

"Oh, no. I'm not putting Vicki into danger."

"She wouldn't be in danger. We don't know when this unsub will strike next. I know this case. It landed on my desk."

"Why you?" Nick asked.

"The same reason as in the Aries and Scorpio cases. I'm the most experienced on our team in homicide investigations. That's how they select agents for specific cases. We've been handed this a while ago. It was published in the paper now, maybe to intimidate the guy. We need to bring him out. We may wind up having to do something similar to reach the Slater kids' mothers." Case paused. "I need to speak with your wife, John. No ifs, ands, or buts about it."

John knew he had to comply without reservation. This agent was a fine human being. John saw the way he conducted the Slater investigation. "Sure, when?"

"Tomorrow morning. And I expect you to be very clear in telling her that she's not getting a weapon."

Lieutenant Martin opened the door and let the Khaos

clan in. Kid after kid marched in with Sam, and Frank holding Margie, after them. There weren't enough chairs in the room for all of them.

"You wanted to see us, so we're here," Frank said, smiling.

John smiled. "Beautiful kids."

Not knowing John, the three oldest stopped and looked at him.

"I'm Dr. Trenton, and you must be Benjamin." John extended his hand to shake. Benjamin reciprocated timidly. "You helped us a lot, Benjamin."

"Yes, you narrowed down the state Margie was born in," Case added.

Sam unzipped Henry's coat and the others took theirs off and hung them on a coat rack. Officers brought in folding chairs.

Benjamin sat down next to John. "So, what does that mean? The state that she was born in?"

"We're getting videos from the pet stores in Texas. We're hoping to see Margie in a tape. Maybe she'll be with your dad and her mother."

Sadness overcame Benjamin. "So you might find her mother?"

"Yes," responded John, knowing what was running through Benjamin's mind. "And we have news for you, Melissa, and Henry, too."

Benjamin looked up at John eye-to-eye. "You found our moms, too?"

"We found your real birth certificates with your real birthdays and mothers' names."

"Real birthdays?"

"Yes, your birthday is October fifteenth, so you're already nine. Melissa's is September thirtieth, so she's already seven, and Henry's birthday is October twentieth. And Margie—"

Frank jolted in the seat. "They're all under the sign of Libra? What the hell does that mean?"

"Don't know yet, Khaos, and Margie's is April fourth."

"That can't be," Benjamin exclaimed. "We've been lied to? Our whole entire life was a lie? Who was our dad, anyway?" He held back tears. "No, this can't be happening." The nine-year-old ran into Frank's arms.

John shot Frank a serious look. Frank nodded.

"Benjamin."

The boy turned toward John.

"You can cry, it's okay."

"We're not allowed to."

"I figured your dad would tell you that," John continued. "But it's okay. You need to get your feelings out. You're feeling really sad now, aren't you?"

"Yes," Benjamin said with his lips quivering.

Frank hugged him. "We'll work on it. Benjamin, we want you to know it's okay to let out your feelings. It'll take time. I know."

Benjamin buried his head in Frank's chest.

Melissa joined in, hugging Sam on the couch. The adults had a somber, humbling minute. Sam and Frank did their best to console them, patting their backs. Frankie pursed his lips in what John could tell was some jealousy. He understood that. Being an only child himself, he didn't think he'd do as well as Frankie, if four strange kids showed up at his doorstep.

Frankie looked away and scanned the room to take away his focus from Sam and his dad, John assumed. Then he screamed, "Dad, Henry's up there!" He pointed to a bookcase that stood against the wall practically reached the ceiling—twenty feet.

Agent Case, Nick, Withers, and Bella looked up and different obscenities spewed from their mouths.

Frank released Benjamin and went over to the bookcase. He raised his voice. "How did you get up there?"

"I climbed."

"Well, climb yourself down, right now."

"I can't. I'm stuck."

"What do you mean you're stuck?" Frank yelled, "Get me a ladder, fast." He pressed his foot on the first shelf. "If I step on this, the whole thing will collapse."

A janitor brought in a twelve-foot ladder. "This won't work, Doc. Even if you go to the top, you're a foot and a half too short."

"Maybe I can get a look to see what's going on. Henry, I'm coming up."

"No. I stay here."

"No, you're not, bud." Frank climbed up the ladder with Nick, John, and Case holding the sides steady. With Frank's two hundred seventy pound bulk, that would be some feat.

Frank still had his agility, in spite of his size, John acknowledged. *Guess Special Forces training doesn't wain.* John looked up at Frank on the top of the ladder. The landing was narrow. John looked over at Sam who trembled with her lips compressed, holding Melissa tightly in her arms on her lap.

"Frank, should we call ESU?" Case shouted.

"Give me a minute." Frank focused his attention on Henry. "Now where are you stuck?"

Henry lay down on his stomach on top of the bookcase and giggled. He flapped his legs up and down. "Nowhere."

"Henry, you have to come down from there. Swing your legs over, and I'll grab you."

"No!"

"Why not?"

"That mean FBI agent found my mommy. I'm not going."

Silence overtook the room. That would be a problem, and John knew it. Separating kids who'd grown up together and loved each other would be the hardest thing he'd ever have to do.

"No one is going anywhere yet. Now. Let's go. Swing your legs over."

"No." Henry crawled about three feet away from Frank.

"Oh, man. Henry, I can't reach you from there, and you

won't be able to climb down. You can't reach the edge."

"So?"

Lieutenant Martin stormed in, and his gaze took in four children. "Since when did my precinct become a nursery, and why in hell do you need a ladder, Khaos?" He looked around. "Where is Khaos?"

"Up here, Lieutenant."

The lieutenant stood with mouth agape, his gaze following the steps, up to Frank, and then to Henry. "Hey, you get down from there, right now, or I'll haul your behind off to jail!"

Henry gasped and then started coughing.

"I mean it!"

Benjamin jolted out of his seat and rammed into the lieutenant's stomach almost knocking them both over. "You're not taking my brother to jail."

It happened so fast Loo looked dumbfounded. Benjamin flailed his arms, struggled, and kicked. Withers grabbed Benjamin from behind, pulled him off the lieutenant, swung him in the air, flipped him around, and held him tightly. "Stop it. Henry's not going to jail. He's too young."

Frank looked up at the three-year-old. "See what you did? Now, you got your brother in trouble."

Those appeared to be the magic words.

"Hold on, Benjamin. I coming." Henry crawled to the edge, swung his legs over so Frank could grab him. "No. I go down myself."

Frank descended a few steps, positioned Henry on the ladder, and held his waist. Henry came down one step and pushed Frank's hands off him. With Frank behind him, the little guy came down step-by-step twenty feet. It seemed to take forever. John looked at his watch. He needed to get home to Vicki.

Everyone just stared at Henry. When he reached the bottom, Henry looked up at the four huge men staring at him. He burst out laughing.

John shook his head. Clumps of gray dust covered the

kid from head to toes. For sure, the top of the bookcase hadn't been cleaned in years.

Frank got the message. "Henry, look how dirty you got." He spun the kid around so Sam could see.

Henry looked around for Benjamin. "Benjamin, I save you." He ran over to his brother sitting on Withers's lap. Henry hugged Benjamin. "You not going to jail."

"No, Henry, your brother isn't going to jail."

Sam pulled clothes out of a diaper bag. "Come on, Henry, We'll go to the bathroom to get cleaned up."

Frank looked startled.

"I'll always carry extra clothes when they're little. I learned that much from my friends." Sam took Henry by the hand and left the room.

"All right, we have a lot to do here." Agent Case said as they all sat back down at the conference table. "Benjamin, I have questions for you."

Benjamin, still upset, sitting on Withers's lap, sniffled. "I have a question for you, first."

Case softened. "Sure, what is it?"

"If you find our moms, do we have to go with them? What if they live in different places?"

"We'll figure out what to do."

John knew Benjamin saw right through the FBI agent. The boy lowered his head. "I'm not talking to you."

"Why not?"

"You're not telling me the truth."

"Excuse me?"

Benjamin ignored Case and spoke to John. "Dr. Trenton, you'll tell me the truth, right?"

"Yes. I will, Benjamin. When we find your mothers, by law, you have to go with them."

"But—but—but we've been together our whole lives." Benjamin cracked, letting a few tears out, and buried his head in Withers's chest. When Melissa saw the dismal expression on Withers's face, she joined in the whining.

Even Bella and Nick sat still in the solemn moment.

What a situation to have to explain to children.

The door opened amidst the noise of grumbling. DEA Agent Marcus Willtower scanned the room and, from the bewildered expression on his face, he was clueless as to what was going on. "Where's FBI Special Agent Brett Case?"

"Right over here, bro," Frank said. He got up, practically accosted Willtower, and they gave each other military bear hugs. "Back so soon? Still working the Philetano family?"

"No, that and the Aries case were put to bed. Case just screwed us big time, again." His gazed took in the children. "Since when did you start running a daycare—"

"Never mind that," Case interrupted. "I'm Special Agent Case."

He slipped his badge from the pocket of his black bomber jacket and flipped it open. "Marcus Willtower, DEA. That case—" he said, tapping the newspaper, "—the one in front of you, is ours."

"So Drug Enforcement busted into *my* house, again. You know the guy?"

"Yeah, Jarrett Miller," Willtower said. John let out a moan. Willtower noticed and ignored it. "We've been tracking him for ten months. Major arms connections, too. And you had to go ahead and make it public. Now, his contacts will go underground for sure. And who are you?"

"Dr. John Trenton, forensic psychiatrist, and before you ask, Miller was my wife's first husband, eighteen years ago."

Willtower paused for a moment. "Crap. I need to speak with her."

Case had to put it out there. This agent seemed to be big on intra-agency cooperation. "Vicki Trenton is coming in first thing tomorrow morning. She resembles the women Miller killed."

"I'll be here. And who do all these kids belong to?" Willtower said as he looked at them with furrowed brows.

"Right now, me," Frank answered. "Frankie, over there

is mine." Frankie waved. "That's Benjamin, Melissa, and Margie in the stroller. Henry is getting changed. My nieces and nephews."

"Whoa, man. I thought you were an only child."

Frank smirked. "So did I. Found out I have a brother, actually two. You know one."

"Oh, yeah?"

"You were his battalion chief, Carl Glendale."

"No shit!"

"Ooooh," Melissa said. "You said a bad word."

Willtower laughed. "Yeah, well, we use bad words sometimes."

"You said Uncle Frank is your bro? Like brother?" Melissa crinkled her nose.

"Yep."

"How can that be?"

"It can." Willtower looked at Melissa who pursed her lips and turned toward her uncle. "Say what you're thinking about. It's okay."

"How can you and Uncle Frank be brothers? He's white and you're black."

"We're military brothers. From way back in Iraq. Military guys are thicker than blood."

Benjamin got excited. "Were you in the Special Forces military book with the picture of Uncle Frank jumping out of the helicopter?"

Withers straightened in the chair. "Whoa. What?"

e⳥e⳥

The door flung open. Henry ran in yelling, "I'm all cleaned up."

Sam laughed and put the bags on the couch.

"Get over here, now, on my lap," Frank said. "You're not to be trusted."

Henry frowned but climbed up onto Frank's lap.

Willtower laughed. He turned toward Sam. "Well, look who's here. The big-mouthed, rookie detective."

With a snicker, Sam approached him. "Watch it, Agent. What are you doing here?"

"Have you mouthed off to him yet?" Willtower said as he pointed to FBI Special Agent Case.

Sam replied matter-of-factly. "When necessary."

Willtower raised a finger in the air, looked at the newspaper on the table, glanced at Sam, then whisked the newspaper off the table. "Perfect. This one is perfect. You're coming to work with us."

Sam did a double take. "What?"

Case didn't waste a heartbeat. "Oh, no, she's not. I'm going to be getting clearance for Detective Wright to work with the FBI. It's a continuance of a murder case, and so is this one. Murder usurps drugs."

"Looks like we beat you again, Willtower," Withers said loudly from across the room.

As the DEA agent turned toward Withers, Henry yelled, "That man has a pony tail." He looked up at his uncle. "Why that man have a pony tail?"

"It's a braid."

Laughing, Willtower did a fast turn. "And why are you not to be trusted?"

Pouting, Henry said, "I climbed."

"You climbed to where?"

Henry pointed to the top of the bookcase. "Up there."

Willtower looked startled.

"Yep," Frank said. "Up twenty feet."

"Okay, I see a future parkour athlete here."

"Oh, yeah. And a decorator over there." Frank pointed to Melissa. "And a brain surgeon over there," he said, pointing to Benjamin. "And a Mixed Martial Arts champ over there," he said, pointing to his son.

"Not bad, I'm impressed." Willtower sucked his cheeks in. "Okay, Case, we'll be working a joint task-force on this one. I'll see you tomorrow morning, and Detective Wright,

I expect you here, as well." He left the room without saying goodbye.

Sam stared at Case for a moment. "What do you mean you're getting FBI clearance for me?"

"Have a seat, Detective."

Sam sat in the chair the DEA agent vacated. "Your boy-friend—"

"Fiancée," Sam corrected.

"Your fiancée heard this conversation already, and now I believe it to be a viable course of action."

"Special Agent Case, please speak English."

He snickered. "Your skill with Jesus Parvos in the Aries case, and recently going undercover in the Scorpio case, not mentioning specifics for obvious reasons, proved to me you'd be an asset to the bureau. I'd like you to come onboard after we speak with your lieutenant and after your interview with our bureau director."

Sam stared at him with her mouth agape.

"Not on a permanent basis, for that you'd have to go through formal training at Quantico, but on a temporary basis for one or two cases. So what do you say?"

"I don't know what to say. I'm just getting used to motherhood."

"So you mean to tell me you'd want to stay home with five kids all day? Four will be in school. And Frank does it."

"Sam, my in-laws will watch the kids after school, and Margie. As much as you love the kids, I can't see you as a stay-at-home mom after fifteen years working."

"I don't know," John added. "Vicki is doing it."

Frank sneered at him. "Yeah, she's nursing three-month-old twins, and homeschooling. It's different here. And I want to say something else, but I won't."

Benjamin's eyes widened. "I know what you want to say, Uncle Frank." He paused. "You're thinking that if Agent Case and everybody find our moms, we'll have to go back to them and that'll leave only Frankie."

Frank closed his eyes and groaned. "Yes."

"Just how close are you to finding our moms?"

"We're not, Benjamin," John said. "But let's start with this. I want to tell you and Melissa your mom's names and I want you to tell me if you remember anything. Okay?"

"Okay," Melissa and Benjamin said at once.

"Benjamin, you mom's name is Sarah Phillips. Does that mean anything to you?"

"What's mine?" Melissa jumped in before Benjamin could answer.

"Lisa Brandt."

Melissa said the name repeatedly, seemingly concentrating. Sam's heart ached for her precious children.

"No, not yet," said Benjamin.

"Here's what I want you to do. Listening?" The kids bobbed their heads. "If you remember anything, even in the middle of the night—"

Benjamin interrupted. "Like in a dream?"

"Exactly, in a dream. I want you to get up and tell Frank and Sam immediately so they can write it down."

Melissa and Benjamin shot glances at each other.

Sam phrased her words carefully. "What's going on? Benjamin, do you have dreams that tell you things?"

The boy nodded.

Melissa took over. "It wakes him up, and he screams."

"What did your dad do when this happened?"

"It only happened when Dad wasn't home." Benjamin sighed. "Now that he's dead, I hope I won't have them again."

"Okay," John said. "I do want to talk to you about those dreams, okay, Benjamin?" The boy nodded. John continued. "But, I think these kids have had enough for one day."

Sam took a deep breath. "I agree, and tomorrow's a school day." *I hope,* she said to herself.

ⲉⲯⲟⲉⲯⲟ

With the children fed, showered, and tucked into bed, Sam was happy this day was over. They'd been through a lot today. Toward the end of the meeting, Benjamin and Melissa seemed to be accepting the fact that they'd have to go back to their mothers. That was odd to her because up until this point they were so close. The true test would be when it happened. On the drive home, Frank took their minds off the meeting, discussing school, and how they'd love it. The excitement seemed to take their minds of their unknown fate.

She lay in bed waiting for Frank to come out of the shower. They needed to talk about Brett Case's invitation for her to join the bureau, though be it for a couple of cases. Had she been in the same situation as Vicki, nursing her own baby, she'd definitely have given him a flat no. But she had to admit, this offer was quite enticing and would be a feather in her cap on a resume. The shower was still going strong. She guessed Frank needed a longer one, especially after the stunt Henry pulled. He was some character and had to be watched every moment. Her mind went back to the offer—the excitement of working with the FBI, the excitement of being considered an FBI agent. It was beginning to grow on her. She craved excitement. She'd do it.

Frank came out of the shower, naked but towel dried. He slithered into bed next to her. As soon as he bent over to kiss her, they heard it—a scream coming from the boys' bedroom.

Sam slipped on a nightgown, and Frank, briefs, before they ran into Frankie's room. Benjamin was siting up in a cold sweat, shaking and screaming. "I saw my mother!"

Sam comforted him with hugs as Frank grabbed a pad on his son's desk and sat down on the bed. Benjamin stopped crying but it took him a few minutes to stop heaving as he let out short puffs of air into Sam's chest. She rubbed his back and made her breathing synchronize with his until he separated from her, to look up at Frank.

"Okay, Benjamin. We're going to do what Dr. Trenton

told you. Tell me every detail you remember that you saw."

"Okay," Benjamin said, exhaling deeply. "She had short curly hair."

"Color?"

"I think brown. And a big smile, like she was happy to see me."

"Okay. Good. How short?"

Benjamin ran his finger on his jawline. "To here."

"What shape were her eyes? Like mine or Sam's?"

Benjamin studied their eyes. "More round, like Sam's but brown."

"Okay, her nose, straight like Sam's or wider?"

"A little wider."

"Her face, oval like Sam's or rounder, like mine?"

"Rounder, like yours."

"What was she wearing?"

"A doctor's white coat."

"Where was she?"

"I didn't see anything."

"What else about her face?"

Benjamin furrowed his brows, and closed his eyes. He spoke with his eyes closed. "She had a black dot by her eye."

"Which eye?"

Benjamin pointed to the right. "Right on top of the cheek," he said in a voice that seemed to question if he got the exact placement correct.

"Excellent, Benjamin. You're doing great. Did she say anything?" The boy nodded. "What did she say?"

He sniffled. "She said—she's—coming to—get me."

"Excellent, Benjamin. Excellent."

Benjamin finally let the tears loose and lowered his head down on Sam's chest.

Sam could bet nine years of pent up emotions just flooded out. "Oh, baby, I know. It's so hard."

He lifted his head, still with tears flowing. "Uncle Frank,

Samantha, I like you, but if they find my mom, I want to go with her."

At that moment, Sam's heart broke into a million pieces.

CHAPTER 11

The morning was a whirlwind of activity for the Khaos family. Frank's in-laws had come over to babysit Margie, and they'd be there when the big kids were dropped off in the afternoon. After the horrific night Benjamin had with his nightmare, then listening, with Sam, to more details about his mother's description, Frank had serious doubts if the nine-year-old would be able to focus in school. Benjamin insisted on going to his new class. So be it. Frank would never discourage education in any way.

The trip to school was uneventful. The kids had their book bags and notebooks that John Trenton brought them back from Scholars Academy, Henry had his, as well. In the main office, Dr. Cohen greeted them. Frank handed the principal copies of the original birth certificates, both adults satisfied that Benjamin and Melissa would be going into age appropriate grades. Dr. Cohen took the older two, and they left the office.

"We have another stop to make." Frank patted Henry's head. "Let's go, bud. Your school is next."

It was done. They were childless for a few hours. Frank had forgotten what it was like, even though it had only been four days. His in-laws have been the only babysitters Frankie had ever known. But would they be able to handle five kids, yet alone would they want to, yet alone would Frank want to burden them? Probably not, to all of the above. Sam's parents still worked their medical practices, so on their days off, babysitting was improbable. The only thing he'd be content with was for Sam to take a childcare leave, at least until Margie was older. And now, Brett Case had to, of all times, offer her a position with the feds. They hadn't had time to discuss it yet, but driving up into the city would be as good a time as any. He'd never considered himself possessive, but with Sam, the love of his life, he didn't want her in any life-threatening situations. Going under-cover with Slater and having him intimately touch her was more than Frank could bear. Sam was no longer just a colleague and, yeah, he'd have any colleague's back, but Sam—he did not intend to lose her. They walked from the nursery school to his SUV in silence. Opening the car door, he sighed. "Okay, princess, what have you been thinking about Case's offer, and don't give me any BS that you ha-ven't."

Sam fastened the seatbelt. "I want to do it, but I need to know more."

"Whoa! So you mean to tell me you're not jumping in head first?"

She sneered at him. "That's a shocker, isn't it? We have five children to think about now. But I have to face it. When—and in my gut, I know it's *when*, not if—they find the children's mothers, they'll have to go with them. I know the law. Oh, don't we have to find out if Slater and the moms had joint custody first?"

"Sam, we're not talking about that. What are your feel-ings about working with the FBI? I can't say it any clearer than that." He pressed the ignition button and pulled out of the parking spot.

"I think it's every detective's dream."

He glared at her.

"Okay, okay, I'm very excited about the prospect. Let's see what happens in the meeting, and what he wants me to do. Lieutenant Martin would be the one to give me clear-ance."

"What he wants you to do? I think I know exactly what Marcus Willtower would want you to do. He'd want you to go under into places that would draw that Miller guy out, so he'd use you as a target."

She patted his hand. "And Case would have me covered, just like he did last week."

"Yes, but the demands of the FBI and DEA will force you to go further. You got pretty close to being intimate with Slater, and I very well remember Case telling you to go as intimate as need be. It could have been all the way. I'm happy it didn't, but it was too close a call, in my opinion."

"And I remember Case also telling you that you had no voice in the matter. Just because we're engaged now, I don't think he'd change his point of view on that one. Can we just see how it progresses?"

"Yeah. Just remember one thing. Once you say, 'yes,' and you're accepted, there's no going back. If it becomes too hot for you to handle, you're screwed."

೮෩೮෩

"Babe, are you ready?" John called from the bottom of the staircase up to the twin's bedroom.

He had to admit it, he was nervous. And he had no idea how far the FBI or DEA agents would push Vicki for answers about her ex-husband. He'd do what he had to in order to protect her. He buttoned his suit jacket and put on his overcoat.

Vicki came down the stairs holding Alexi, with Ricky behind her carrying Zach. "I'm ready as I'll ever be."

As John slipped Zach out of Ricky's grasp, he acknowledged the apprehension in his wife's eyes, the distant look, like she had the night she left him in New York to return home to Florida, three years ago. It was the same look when he lay on the bed in the ICU after Barbara Montgomery shot him. Doubt. It was unfortunate the kids had to go with them into the city. He'd arrange for Ricky to stay in another room during the interview. It would be the last thing John would want—for Ricky to hear the recount of what his mother went through with her first husband. "You look beautiful, babe."

"Well, darlin,' I don't have too much of a chance to get dressed up, lately. And it's nice, once in a while. Like it?" She twirled for him. "It's from one of the designers Sam buys from."

He smiled at his wife in the aquamarine-colored studded three-piece suit with the moto-style jacket, and skinny jeans. The gold, silver, and hematite-black triangular studs that decorated the outer legs on the jeans, and sleeves of the jacket, sparkled in the sunlight coming in from the bay window. "I love it," he said as he focused on the jeans that accentuated her perfect curves, and round derriere.

She put Alexi into the carrier and put on her coat.

They left the house and settled into the Mercedes. When John saw Ricky with his head set on, he felt free to talk. "Okay, Vick, when Brett Case or Marcus Willtower asks you questions just tell them what they want as briefly as possible. Try not to get rattled—on second thought, yeah, be rattled…maybe—"

"Excuse me? You actually think I'm going to back down? No, darlin', I was raised knowing men higher up in the chain than them. I'm going to do what I have to do to take Jarrett Miller down for the count." She sent John a hard stare. "And I still want my gun, by the way."

"Brett Case was adamant about that."

"How does he know?"

"He was holding my phone when you sent me the text."

Vicki looked at him with mouth agape. "We'll see about that."

"What are you thinking, babe?"

"Don't worry about it, darlin', nothing you can help me with."

⌘

Brett Case was the first to arrive in the Manhattan-North precinct war room. A lot was on his mind, the first being he had no plans on letting Marcus Willtower take over. Hearing about the gutsy DEA agent from the Aries case showed him this dude was a formidable opponent even though, technically, they were on the same side. Having him tight with his military bro, Khaos, would make it harder, especially if Frank wouldn't want Sam to join the FBI. And Vicki Trenton, John's wife, what was this civilian thinking wanting a weapon? He'd never met her but he got the gist of what she was like.

The door opened. Marcus Willtower entered, carrying an attaché and a sour expression on his face.

"Good morning to you, too, Agent," Case said.

"You're not doing this, Case. I've got first-hand experience working with Detective Wright. She went through a rough time with Jesus Parvos. She knows how to talk to sleaze like this. You've gotta show some intra-department cooperation, here."

John Trenton and Vicki entered, pushing the twins' stroller interrupting their conversation. Ricky had been left in an interview room with a female police officer. Both agents looked at Trenton's wife and grinned.

"Sorry, gentlemen, no babysitter," said Vicki.

Oh boy, that Southern accent. Case focused on a file on the table to prevent him from staring.

Vicki took of her coat, looked around the room, and hung it on a rack in the corner then attended to the twins, taking off their blankets and unzipping their snowsuits. She turned toward the men and greeted them with a smile.

Case would keep his manner formal. He realized right away, after looking at this stunner, she'd be high on the manipulator scale. He was skilled in judging body language, and this woman had a presence, one he couldn't deny or disparage—her posture, choice of outfit, everything spewed confidence. Those bright blue eyes and natural blonde hair in a ponytail almost reaching her waist made her a duplicate for the women who Jarrett Miller had killed, and the FBI needed her more than she needed them. "Thank you for coming in, Mrs. Trenton."

"Yes, we do appreciate it. I'm DEA Agent Marcus Willtower. Both agencies have a stake in bringing Miller down."

"As do I," replied Vicki as she looked at her husband.

John sucked in his cheeks then pursed his lips.

Case's brows furrowed. "What, Dr. Trenton?"

"I've already been given instructions to let my wife do the talking."

"Yeah, right," Case said. "Mrs. Trenton, I don't want to bring up some things that might be painful, but I will have to explore your history with the suspect, so we can get an understanding of him."

"We have an understanding," Willtower said. "What we need is his ass behind bars or dead."

"I'd prefer the latter," Vicki said, which gave her stares of surprise from the agents. "Aside from the murders, why is the DEA involved?"

"Jarrett Miller is associated with drug trafficking, mostly pain pills, barbiturates, oxycodone. He has ties to pain clinics in Florida and Kentucky."

"Florida? Wait, wait, wait," Vicki exclaimed. "You still track him going to Florida?"

"Yes, and we know you're originally from Florida. So why are you surprised?" Case asked.

"I thought he was mandated to stay out of the state."

"Yes," Willtower replied. Vicki sat with jaws dropped. Willtower explained. "The provision to stay out of the state was for the length of his parole. Five years. After that, he was free to travel. And we found out about him last spring."

Vicki slumped back in her chair. "And I didn't know."

Willtower shrugged.

"You okay, Mrs. Trenton?" Case asked. Vicki took a deep breath and nodded. Case continued. "Let's start with how you met him and your relationship."

Vicki paused for a moment. "Okay. I'm okay. We met in college, our sophomore year. We were both education majors."

"Where did you go to school?"

"UF at Gainesville."

Case nodded. "When did you marry him?"

"The summer we graduated."

"And then what?"

"Three months later, he went to prison, and we got divorced."

Willtower uncrossed his legs and leaned in toward the table. "We need to know more about that, and not just in a few words." He gave Vicki a hard stare. "Why did he go to prison?"

"Domestic abuse. I'm not re-hashing the particulars, Agent. Use your imagination. It was serious enough for an arrest and indictment. He got the max allowed—one year, eleven months, thirty days. In Florida, there's no early release so he did the full time."

"All right, during the time you knew him through college and during your short marriage, did you ever witness him having any drug involvement? Any drug use?"

"No." Vicki sat with her hands folded on the desk.

Willtower exhaled deeply. "What were his friends like?"

"We dormed in college. His friends were in Sarasota. That's where he's originally from. I never met his high school friends. The four years we hung out with the same groups. We had the same classes. It's a college town."

"Yes, it is. And in a college town, there are drugs." Willtower paused. "Did you ever experiment?"

Vicki laughed. "You're kidding me, right? You know what my father and my brothers do for a living. No. I never experimented."

"Plenty of kids whose parents are in law enforcement get sucked into drugs, so that's no answer," Willtower said. "But, okay. Did he ever go to a pain clinic that you know of?"

"No. But we're talking about a moot point. You should be focusing on his life in prison. He could have made drug contacts in there. And it was eighteen years ago. A lot happens in a person's life. When he got out of prison, he obviously lost his license to teach. Who knows what he did for a living? After he got out, my father and brothers gave him a stern ultimatum to stay out of Florida. I have no idea how they pulled that one off." Vicki paused. "Actually, I do. His grandfather lived in Kentucky. My father had his parole transferred up there because his release was contingent upon someone able to look after him, and none of his relatives lived in Florida at the time. That, at least, got him transferred out of the state. I've had no contact with him from the moment he went to prison."

Case nodded. "Why not from the moment he was arrested?"

Vicki must have caught on. She briefly closed her eyes and swallowed hard. John grabbed her hand. "Do you have to go there, Agent?"

"Yes, and I'll tell you why. He was abusive. We got that. And he was also abusive to the women he killed. I want to hear what he did to you and compare it to what he did to the women. Only then, will we be able to conclude that the abuse was in retaliation for you sending him to prison."

"Does it matter? He killed women. That's all that should concern you."

"I explained why it matters. We study victimology and, in doing that, if we get lucky, we could prevent other women from falling prey to him."

"I don't want to go through an interrogation. If I get you my testimony tapes, will that suffice?"

"No," Willtower said sternly.

"Look, you came in this morning to help us, correct?" Case said.

Vicki nodded.

"Babe, you told me you weren't backing down," John said as he took her hand in his.

"You're right, darlin'. I was just rattled before. Okay—" She inhaled and exhaled deeply. "He hit me in a very sexual way. At first, it was pleasurable. I had no idea what he was doing or what he was leading up to doing. Then it got harder and harder over the months without any sexual activity. He did it when I prepared steak for dinner and he wanted chicken. I was an excellent home chef, even back then. But he wanted to punish me for not obeying his choice. Then he started with a belt. Gently at first, then after a few times, he left welts, despite my screams for him to stop. The last time, I ran out of the house in the middle of the night to my brother, Brian's house. He's a detective now. He called Mark, my twin. Mark took pictures. They were both angry with me that I didn't come to them much earlier on. It was the most embarrassing time of my life, especially since my parents are discreet concerning anything sexual. But the pictures alone worked for the judge. What did he do to the women?"

Case stared at a folder on his desk, contemplating whether to show her or just tell her.

Vicki apparently saw through him. "I've seen crime scene photos before, Agent. I had to explain plenty in the Gemini case. If you don't already know, my home became a crime scene. A bloody one, at that. The bullet that pierced John's shoulder exited and broke tiles in the entry hall. I haven't wanted to go back into it, and we haven't."

"Okay, then." Case opened the folder and placed five folders in front of her showing the backs of the women.

Vicki let her fingers glide over the pictures. "Looks like he used the same width belt. So, did he have a relationship with these women and it led up to this, or did he go straight for the kill?"

"We're interviewing the family of this last victim, Candice Sloan. This murder happened last month. So far, it's been a dead end, but we got the eyewitness account, thus the drawing. Sloan's mother said her daughter was seeing someone but she or her ex-husband never met him. They live in California. From what we were told, the relationship time span was about three months. The main difference was that he never married any of the women."

Vicki nodded. "Good thing for them." She caught herself. "No. Wait. No. I didn't mean that." She shivered. "I'm sorry."

Case sent a sympathetic glance to John. "Mrs. Trenton. No worries. What else can you tell us?"

Vicki sat up straighter in the chair. "Thank you. Um, dead end. Okay. I can understand why. Jarrett was an isolator. He didn't want me to see my friends, nor go out with them, or even talk on the phone. In case you're wondering, this all happened the day after we were married. Before that, our social calendar was booked. Now that I think about it, his plans with me must have been preconceived. No one could do such a three-sixty, naturally." She paused. "Okay, so what do you want me to do—"

"I told you, Case," John interrupted. "I'm not letting Vicki go into any dangerous situation."

Frank opened the door and after a nod from Case, they came in. After smiling, Sam went right to the twins' stroller. She nudged Alexi's cheek and the infant stirred. Sam grinned from ear to ear as Frank rolled his eyes, making himself comfortable at the table.

Sam took the baby out of the stroller and cradled her in her arms. Then she sat, looking around at everyone who just stared at her.

"Hi," Sam said, apparently ready for business.

Case continued the conversation. "Glad you're joining us, Detective. It won't come to that, John. What we'll do, Mrs. Trenton, is set up a media blitz, streaming live to Facebook and the networks. I'll write out a script, and all you'll have to do is read it."

"Adding my own slant, of course."

Case's gazed darted between Willtower and John. He pursed his lips. "Uh, no, verbatim."

"Your goal is to draw him out, correct?"

"Yes, but we want to get him into a controlled environment," Case answered.

"Okay, then you'll have to trust me," Vicki said. "I know how to push his buttons. You'll make it so formal he'll know it's a set-up."

"The mere fact you're putting it out there," Willtower interjected, "he'll know it's a set-up. It's got to be done, but in such a way, his drug connections won't get him into hiding. But then again, he gets the product and sells it directly. And he travels south to get it."

"Okay, but with Jarrett, his needs always came first. So you have to set it up, so that his need to see me is more important than to go underground. Um, hold on a second. Agent Willtower, can you send a message to his drug connections, telling them their source is wanted for murder?"

"He doesn't work like that. He'll go to a pain clinic or an unscrupulous doc for a prescription. Since pharmacies keep data-driven records they know who has filled the script. He'll sell the pills for street cost and give a kickback to the doc."

"That doesn't make sense," Sam jumped in. "Unless, he has other people working for him, too."

"What are you thinking, Sam?" Willtower asked.

"It's not that simple. Even if Miller got the scripts from doctors, the docs give two-hundred-forty pills a month, max. His health insurance might cover the cost. But do you know if he even has a job? The pharmacy might charge him three to four bucks a pill and he could sell them for twenty to thirty bucks each. If we do the math, he can clear forty-eight hundred from each script. Some docs would take up to half, not leaving him with much. But if he has two or more people getting scripts and giving him the supply, he'll make more. And now, unfortunately, people can go directly to the doctors or clinics, themselves, so their need of him is lessening."

"I doubt if he has people working for him, Sam," Vicki said. "He was never a leader. He doesn't have the smarts."

"Explain that, please, Mrs. Trenton, give us an example."

"Give me a minute to think." Vicki paused. "Okay, even with a school project where we had to work in teams at times, he'd never take the lead. Hell, he hardly ever carried through on his part, let alone helped anyone. It was one reason my daddy hated him."

"Really?" Case was surprised. "What were the other reasons?"

"He wasn't motivated. He was just content doing the minimum."

"How did you fall for a man like that?" Sam asked.

"Yeah, right? I was young, infatuated, and stupid. It took three years of therapy for me to get through it. I think part of it was my own doing, wanting to break my parent's hold on me. Do you know if he has any job?"

"We don't think so. He travels too much between Kentucky and Florida."

"How did he cross your radar?" Frank asked.

"A store from a pharma chain contacted us recently because he brought in duplicate scripts. Apparently, he got careless."

Sam repositioned Alexi onto her shoulder. "So is he selling in New York?"

"No, too much competition here. He sticks with Rhode Island, Connecticut, or Delaware. Our forensic tech picked up your article. That's what made me come to the city. We're watching him to eventually flush out any further accomplices."

"Still not good enough," Sam said. "You guys wait too damn long to make the arrests. I've told you that, before."

"Stop the reprimand. I got it the first time. But it's our procedure to make sure all of our arrests stick. And they have. So you'll just have to accept that, Detective," Willtower said, scowling at Sam.

Sam sneered at him. "Yeah, and again, another murder could have been avoided."

"We didn't know he committed any murders."

"Exactly, again," Sam reinforced. "Do you have any info if he bought, or stole, the drugs from the manufacturer?"

"Hey, cut it out! The both of you. We don't have time to rehash old business. Go on," Case told Sam.

Alexi squirmed in Sam's arms, and she handed the infant to Vicki. After she settled back into her seat, Sam clasped her hands on the table. "Many times dealers rip off delivery trucks so they get the boxes straight from the manufacturer, and the drugs never get to the pharmacies. Any cases like that on your desk?"

"Tell me about it, Detective," Willtower responded, smirking. "Yeah, we got plenty, but none Miller was associated with."

"If we stream live onto social media, show his face, then maybe his original sources will be revealed," Sam said. "I doubt if they'll come forward to give him up because that would ruin them, but some cases on your desk might be shaken up. Then you might find a relationship. Even if they're out of the city, news spreads fast online."

"When we do the social media blitz, we're focusing on the murders because they happened here in New York. Stopping his drug business is gravy."

"Okay, agreed," Willtower said.

Case smiled. *Apparently, Sam knocked this guy down a peg or he doesn't want me as an enemy.* Case took out his cell and sent a text. "We'll get the script for you, Mrs. Trenton, in a few minutes."

"We're doing it today?"

"Yes. In the precinct's media room. And while we're waiting, we have another issue to discuss."

"And what might that be, Agent?"

"I think you know, Mrs. Trenton."

"I don't," Willtower said.

"In light of Mr. Miller now being in New York, Mrs. Trenton wants her own weapon."

"I will tell you I'm very proficient handling a variety of weapons."

"So I've heard."

"Then what's the problem?"

"You're not a member of any law enforcement agency," Case said. "Plain and simple. Case closed."

A receptionist brought in a sheet of paper and handed it to Agent Case.

"Thank you." As the receptionist left, he scanned it. "Okay, Mrs. Trenton, have a read, please. Read it aloud, so you can get a feel for it." He handed Vicki the paper.

Vicki let her gaze roll over the paper. She glanced up at the agents without saying a word. "Okay, if this is the way you want it." She began to read. "'This is an open call to a man named Jarrett Miller. I'm sure you remember me. I was your wife eighteen years ago. It seems that there are women with my likeness being murdered in New York and, Jarrett, you've been identified as the prime suspect. The FBI knows you're armed and dangerous. Right now, all they want to do is to talk with you. If you're listening, or if anyone listening knows this man, please call FBI Special Agent Brett Case at two-one-two-five-five-five-eighteen-hundred.'" Vicki put the paper down on the desk. "That's it?" she asked with an incredulous look on her face.

"Yes," Case answered. "Nothing to rile him into more violence."

"This won't *rile* him into coming forward either. One thing Jarrett liked is a little more spontaneity, some liveliness."

"You'll read it as is, Mrs. Trenton." Case paused. "Why don't we take a break, and we'll go live this afternoon? Go for lunch." He turned toward Sam and Frank. "We have the security footage of the Texas pet store."

Sam closed her eyes for a moment. "Catch a glimpse of Slater?"

"The report infers it's more than a glimpse."

"If you don't mind," John said. "I'd like to see it, too."

Case nodded. "Absolutely, Doc. You brought us good stuff."

"You don't mind staying, babe, do you?"

"Not at all. I'll do anything for those children."

Case pressed a button on the intercom and as if on cue, Agents James and Mullen entered with a laptop. They placed it at the edge so everyone could see. It took less than two minutes for them to set it up.

"All right. This is the store in Dallas," Mullen said. "With the baby's pic you sent us, Frank that narrowed the search and made it a lot easier." He zoomed in to the interior of the large pet store chain.

"Good."

Everyone stared at the screen. Mullen continued. "The date in the lower right reads December nineteenth. Henry Slater pushed the stroller with Margie in it through the store entrance. That woman with him has been positively identified as Sonja Santos."

John nodded.

"Yes, Doc, the birth certificates you recently found *are* the valid ones. They're appearing to be an intact couple. And even there, look how he's dressed. A sports jacket to go shopping? What's with his formal attire all the time?"

"It's control," Sam intervened. "He looks and acts the business professional, all the time. It's the never-know-who-you-can-meet attitude. He might be on the hunt for new mothers, you never know. And I'll admit, a woman likes a well-dressed man—"

"Hey, princess, what you see is what you get," Frank hissed.

Sam rolled her eyes. "It's figurative, Frank. And you clean up well when necessary. She's all smiles, that's for sure."

Mullen shook his head. "They're walking through the aisles to the pet food. Here's where they separate. But first, watch this. She takes out a credit card from her wallet and hands it to him. I found that weird because he has plenty of money. And he accepted it. Look how he almost yanked it from her fingers. That shows entitlement."

"Not weird, though. It's planned on his part," John said. "If he's going to buy scorpions, he'd want to use a local address. That came up in our discussion yesterday."

"Yes, it did," Mullen acknowledged. "She grabs a shopping cart and proceeds to the dog food, while he takes the stroller down to the aquarium section. She's putting a large bag of dog food into her wagon. Then we cut to Slater, peering into a scorpion tank. He points to the ones he wanted. A worker scooped those out. That's simple, clear. At the counter, he does fill out the paper work. Yes, we got it. We have the address of Miss Santos. The scorpions are packed in the box."

"That's the box Benjamin said he saw on the kitchen table," Frank said. "So far, so good."

Mullen nodded. "Here comes the separation. Slater puts the box on the rack under the stroller. He proceeds to the store exit, not looking for the mother at all. We go back to Miss Santos. With the dog food in the cart, she wanders aisles. We're assuming she's looking for Slater. When we zoom into her face, worry definitely overcomes the smiles, Sam. She walked around the store for at least twenty minutes. We backtracked to when Slater left the store. The camera caught him putting a smiling, babbling Margie into a car seat in the rear, packing up the stroller and putting it into the trunk, then the scorpion box onto the passenger side floor. He drove away unconcerned. Zooming into his face, a stoic, bland expression."

"It's almost as though he knows he's on camera," John said, "and he didn't want to give anything away. He deliberately kept his body language neutral. If someone *is* kidnapping a child, they'd be anxious, furrowed brows, eyes darting back and forth, looking around. He does none of that. He couldn't care less what he was doing because in his mind, he's doing nothing wrong. He's definitely a pro at deception. That's a practiced skill. I can see how he got the better of Benjamin's teacher, that Miss Monty. She was definitely a pushover for him. Seeing him like this is very helpful. All right, what else?"

"We went back to the mother. Finally, she made a call. It's obviously to Slater. We zoomed in and our translators got her side of the conversation. 'Where are you, honey?' We couldn't get his answers, but we have a warrant out for the phone records. His answers seemed to have left her dumbfounded. The expression on her face is more disbelief—"

"No," Sam said. "It's acceptance. Resignation. Look at her slumped shoulders. You can even see them through her long hair. What else did she say?"

"Very good, Sam. She asked him, 'Where did you go?' He answered. She said, 'What do you mean daddy-daughter time? When are you brining her back?' Then, 'Okay, see you soon.' His responses were quick and to the point, less than five seconds before she resumed speaking. Then, how's this for a motherly response? She sneered and chucked the phone into her bag."

"What?" Vicki exclaimed. "Sneered? Not frowned? Not cried? If that were me, I'd be on the phone to nine-one-one, sobbing. What is wrong with her? And chucked the phone into her bag? I'd be clutching it to my heart. No. Not normal."

"Vicki, it's their relationship," Sam said. "She's complacent. Slater was a dominant in every aspect of his life. Like Jarrett. But you wouldn't go along with that. Me, neither. The children's mothers are probably all like that. They give in to all of his whims. Possibly he acted this way with all of them."

"No, sorry. If it's been a few years, and my husband kept my child or children without me seeing them, I can't even imagine that. Something is very wrong. If a woman is maternal enough to want a child, relationship or not, they'd take action. This woman looks passive, yes, but I don't know. The other children he's had for six, eight years? There's got to be police reports."

"We're looking into everything, Mrs. Trenton. Right now, our team did reach Miss Santos and they're bringing her in," Case said. "That will give us a start. Great job, guys," he said to Mullen and James. Case received a text. He stared at the phone. "Today is our lucky day. The nanny, Locklear Henderson, is on her way back to New York."

৩৩৩

The media room in the precinct had been set up to go live before Vicki and the entourage entered. She looked around. *Pretty up-to-date.* The precincts in Sun County were practically brand new with state-of-the-art technology. Those rooms wowed everyone who entered. This one was far more staunch, even in the wall hangings. Posters of New York City's most wanted hung in plain view. Her gazed scanned them, looking for Jarrett Miller. She stopped when she found him, upper left, as if he was a just-added element. Good enough. At least the bastard was up there for the world to see. *Thank God for the therapy I received.* She'd gotten through her hate, her disgust of him, her fear of him—until seeing the abuser in that article and those hurtful feelings resurfaced. She certainly showed her buried emotions this morning. She'd be depending upon her loving, kind, and thoughtful husband more than ever now. Seeing Jarrett Miller on that poster, her motivation grew stronger to take him down. Apparently, he'd learned nothing in prison. She wondered what really pushed him over the edge to murder women. She never thought he'd have it in him to do that. *Guess eighteen years does make a difference in some-one's life.*

John walked up behind her, startling her out of her reflection. "Ready, babe?"

She turned around and rested her head on his shoulder.

He brought her into an embrace. She looked eye to eye with him. "Yes, darlin', as ready as I'll ever be."

Brett Case stood at the podium. He signaled for Vicki to stand next to him. She did. "I'll start, and then you'll come in front of the mic."

Vicki nodded.

Frank, Sam, and Marcus Willtower sat in the back of the room out of the camera's view.

"I'm FBI Special Agent Brett Case from the New York City office. Over the last fifteen years there have been five unsolved murders, the latest being last month. We have the name of the suspect, and a photo, and this message is to him. Jarrett Miller, we have someone here who wants to speak with you."

Vicki stepped in front of the mic. "I'm Victoria Elizabeth Marin, Jarrett Miller, your wife of three months, eighteen years ago. I'm sure you remember me. I was appalled when I saw the photos of the women you allegedly murdered. I looked at the newspaper in horror, Jarrett. As abusive as you were, it never crossed my mind that you'd ever be able to step to the side of murder. For crying out loud, Jarrett, you even used the same width belt on them as you used on me. Were you trying to get even with me for sending your ass to prison? I really want to find out. For my own satisfaction, actually. No woman should go through this hell and stick it out. Ladies, if you see this man," she said as she held up his picture, "do not fall for his supposed charm. An abuser is an abuser. No matter how cute they disguise themselves. Men like this will not hide their rage. The slightest thought could push them over the edge. Ladies, if you see or know this Jarrett Miller, first run, and then call FBI Agent Brett Case at two-one-two-five-five-five-eighteen-hundred. Right now, there isn't any evidence that this joker-of-a-man even has employment. Keep your eyes open. And, Jarrett Miller, keep looking over your shoulder. I will be coming for you, just like I did eighteen years ago. This time, I have the entire New York City police department with me. Jarrett Miller, you're a goner. Thank you, ladies and gentlemen, for listening." She stepped away from the mic and camera and collapsed into John's arms.

CHAPTER 12

Sam approached Brett Case as soon as he left the podium. He didn't even have the chance to take a seat. "Vicki clobbered your speech, didn't she?" For some reason, she felt in a confrontational mood. Not a great idea, she reconsidered. Why in the world would she attempt to antagonize a fed? She felt Dara's jolt in her mid-section. Yeah, it hit hard. She missed the children. The yearning was there. Whom was she kidding? She'd have to be honest with herself. Did she truly want to work with the feds? Did she feel it? Taste it? Down to her very core? At this moment, she couldn't put her finger on the answer.

Brett hiked a brow. "Yes, she sure did. But she did great. She appealed to the emotions of women. Hopefully, they'll be stirred up enough to keep their eyes open for him." He looked straight into her eyes. "What's up?"

Sam sat next to him at a small round table. "Where do you see my involvement?" She glanced up at Willtower as he joined them. "I'd like to know."

"If we get an account of where he goes, or a spotting, I want to send you in. I'm glad you kept out of the camera's way."

"Didn't take a brain surgeon to figure that one out. I know here my hours are dependent upon the case."

"Same thing with us, but more so. You might be living in a safe house until the conclusion."

Sam gasped.

"That's right, no going home to see the kids, possibly for

a couple of weeks. No friends. No family contact. When you're UC, your life belongs to us. No one will know your real identity. It's a demanding life, Detective. No ifs, ands, or buts about it. We do it for the love of justice and the desire to bring these perps down."

"I get the drill, Agent. What is my next step? How much time do we have?"

"So you're going to jump right into this? No questions?"

"Not reaching for Brownie points, but I trust your judgement. You did right by me in the past."

"Very recent past. And you'll never get Brownie points from me."

"Hold on there," Willtower said. "And I didn't do right by you?" He smirked as he flicked a speck of dust off his shoulder.

Sam didn't have time to take a breath. Agent James interrupted. "Agent Case, Jarrett Miller is on the phone, and he wants to meet Mrs. Trenton."

From the other side of the room, John shot up from his chair. "Like hell, he will."

"Calm down, Doc. That's not happening," Case said.

"Mrs. Trenton did really well," James admitted. "Her live feed has been shared over two hundred times in less than a few minutes. This guy went viral, and it'll continue to spread. You'll be able to bring him in quickly. I'm confident he'll have no state to hide in."

"I do want to speak with him, Agent Case," Vicki said as her husband glared at her. "No, John. I'm here. Safe. He has no intention of coming in. That, I'm sure of. Where is the phone, Agent James?"

After looking around at John and Case who both gave the nod, James turned toward Vicki. "This way." They walked in to another room where a phone, mic, headphones were set up on the table. "Use the headphones and mic, so you don't come across as being on a speakerphone. Let him think you're talking to him one-on-one and personal."

"One thing, Mrs. Trenton," Case said. Vicki looked him

in the eyes. "Stick to the murder cases," he said. "I know you got upset. Don't bring up anything about drugs or Florida. Got it?"

Vicki inhaled deeply and nodded. She put on the headset.

"Ready?"

She nodded again.

"Mr. Miller, Miss Marin is with me. Are you ready to speak with her?"

"Yeah, sure. Put the bitch on."

Vicki crossed her hand over her heart for effect, even though Miller couldn't see her. Sam knew that.

"Oh, my goodness, Jarrett, you never even called me that insulting word when you were beating the living daylights out of me."

John grinned at her display. Vicki knew she was putting it on thick. Just like she did when she was bringing down Barbara Montgomery. Even Brett Case tried to hide his laugh. Vicki scowled at him. Sam controlled herself from bursting out laughing with her hand covering her mouth.

"Ugh, still that naive, Southern farm girl, aren't you, Vicki?"

"I am what I am, Jarrett. What in the world are you doing?"

"What am I doing?"

Vicki deliberately stammered. "Are you—murdering—murdering—women?"

"Now why are you thinking that?"

"For one, all of the women look like me."

"Now don't you have a swelled head? Killing women who look like you? I never thought about it. I just like blondes with blue eyes and ponytails. It's not personal."

Brett Case tapped on the table in front of her. He waved his fingers in what Sam guessed to be a signal to Vicki to continue in that vein. Vicki nodded.

"Jarrett, are you telling me you did murder those women?"

"You're really dense, you know that, Vicki? I know you're probably with those damn cops now, and they're hedging you along. I want to meet you in person. After all, you are my ex-wife."

"That won't be happening, Jarrett, but I'd be willing to speak with you for as long as you want. By the way, what have you been doing over the years?"

"I obviously couldn't teach, now could I?"

"No. That must have been rough. How did you cope being away?"

"Like you give a shit."

"We were married at one time. I have feelings."

John glared at her, and she waved him down, in response, smirking. Frank put a firm hand on John's shoulder, giving the support this time.

"How would you think prison is? It was a blast. Card games, shuffleboard, gourmet meals that made me miss yours. Really miss yours. Solitary confinement for fighting. It was a two-year vacation, Vicki. Plenty of time to think about you." Jarrett lowered his voice. "And plenty of time for me to think about what I'd do to you the next time I see you."

Brett Case gave her a thumbs up. Sam knew what that meant. Getting to his emotions. Bringing up anger. That would make him become careless. Make Jarrett so agitated, he wouldn't think straight.

"I'm sorry that had to happen, Jarrett."

"Yeah, well, Vicki. I had enough of talking to you right now. I gotta crash. I'm beat."

"It's four in the afternoon. You're beat? From what?"

"Some crap I'm taking for a cold. I gotta go to the pharmacy. I'll call ya again, Vicki. Tell those cops not to look for me. I ain't local."

He disconnected.

Vicki sat there, stunned, blowing out a deep breath. She stood up slowly, glanced around to find John, then rushed into his arms.

"You did great, babe." John patted her back and fisted her ponytail, appearing to hold on to it for dear life. "She's done," he said to Brett Case. "I won't allow this anymore."

Vicki lifted her head from her husband's shoulder. "No, John. I'll be done when Jarrett is behind bars or dead himself."

"You're a civilian. No one can coerce you into doing this."

"John Trenton—don't tell me what I can and cannot do. You very well know I can handle myself." She stood there in seeming defiance with her hands on her waist, looking around at everyone's faces—scowls, smiles, red cheeks. "Sorry, but this moron got to me, and I'm stopping him!"

Brett Case approached her. "You're not going to do exactly that. No face-to-face meetings for you. When we get a handle on where he is—"

"We found him, Agent Case," Mullen said. "Got his active ping. In Delaware. So he's not an immediate threat. He used his own phone. Guess he's not tech savvy. He didn't even bother to redirect or use anything to transfer the signal. I sent a team to pick him up and the signal is on the move with him. We can't say he won't figure it out and dump the phone, though."

"That's the beauty of social media in action," Case said. "We've gotten a ninety percent increase in arrest rate since we've been going live. And it works fast. No one wants these perps on the streets. Good work, everyone. All right. Everyone go home. Sam and Frank, I need a word with you first." He exited and returned to the war room.

When Sam and Frank entered, Case gestured for them to take a seat. "I want your opinion on this, Frank. A solid one, not an emotional one. We're brining in Margie's mother and, hopefully, she'll give us leads to the others. I want the both of you in on these interviews, also with the nanny. Now, do you think Sam can handle it?"

Sam shook her head in disbelief. "You're asking him if I

can handle it? I'm shocked you even think that. Yes, I can handle it. Don't do that to me again."

"Okay. I needed to hear that so I pushed your buttons. On the other hand, being so maternal, are you going to go off on the mom for being lax in letting Margie be taken?"

"I might not be able to help being judgmental internally, but I'll keep it to myself. Rest assured. Have you decided if we're going to hand back the children as we meet their moms, or are we doing it all at once?"

"What do you think, Frank?"

"All right. I know you discussed this with John, and we did, too. It'll be frightening for the kids to go home one-at-a-time. They'll be worried about the *if and when* for them. I say, let's get all the mothers together, let them meet. They are all related somewhat. The kids have to have a chance to say their good-byes." Frank glanced up at Sam who had become teary-eyed. He clutched her hand.

Noticing that gesture, Case shot Sam a hard glare then nodded to Frank.

She sniffled. "Look, I know it has to be done, and it's the inevitable. But as much as I know it, it'll hurt. I'll admit it. We both love the children, and I also understand how tormented their mothers are not knowing where their babies are. For those women, I'll be strong. I promise. I think we should have a party for them. And I want to make sure the mothers allow them to be in contact with each other, see each other on vacations. I don't want this to be an ending for them but a new beginning." Her nerves couldn't bear anymore. Tears started. Sam turned away and nestled her head in Frank's shoulder.

Frank embraced her and looked up at Case with a solemn expression. "Yeah, she could handle it," he mouthed.

℘℘℘

As soon as Sam and Frank opened the front door, four children vying for attention, surrounded them for hugs. Sam beamed. She embraced each one in her arms as Frank struggled to get past her through the entry hall.

"How was your first day at school? I want to hear every detail." She led them to the couch oblivious to Kathryn and Walter who stood staring at her with jaws dropping. As she sat on the couch, she looked up at the grandparents. "Thank you so much for doing this. I hope you're not too exhausted."

Those words seemed to be the acknowledgment the seniors wanted—and needed. "They're a pleasure to watch. We're fine, but now we're going home. They're all fed, homework done, and now they're all yours," Kathryn said as she handed Margie over to Frank. They grabbed their coats and ran out the door.

Sam puffed out a breath. "So tell me, everything. Have enough to eat? Where's your homework? I need to see it all—"

"Hey, Sam," Frank reprimanded. "Stop. Breathe. There's no urgency."

Melissa looked at her, startled. "Sheesh. Are you always going to be this nuts?"

Sam glared at her.

"We're used to being with adults, and Dad never got like this."

"Okay, so how did your dad do it? I can probably learn from him."

"I think you could," Benjamin said. "Everything is okay in school. Our teachers are nice."

"Yeah," Melissa added. "My teacher, Mr. Bannon, likes to play music and he sings. I never sang before, ever, and I didn't know how, but he's showing me."

"You never sang?" Frank asked.

"No. Dad hated music. It gave him headaches," Melissa said. "So he'd never play any songs in the house."

"What about in school?"

"We had a choice. Music or art class. And Dad insisted we take art. And there was a separate music class, so we didn't have music in my class with Miss Monty."

"Don't worry about us in school." Benjamin stared at Sam. "How did it go with finding Margie's mom? And tell us the truth, please."

Sam embraced him. "Benjamin, you are so beyond your years. Yes, we saw your dad in a video with Margie and her mom in Texas. Agent Case is bringing her to New York and we'll meet with her."

"When?"

"She'll be here in a few days."

"Will Margie have to go back to her mom right away?" Melissa asked with a sullen look on her face.

Frank decided to bite the bullet. "No. We decided that none of you are going back to your moms one-by-one. Everyone is going to meet."

"And we're going to have a big party," Sam said, smiling.

"A party? We never had a party," Melissa said. "What for?"

"We're going to celebrate," Sam said, choking up, "a new beginning for all of us and for you." She sniffled. "But that's not happening right away because we have no idea where your moms are yet."

"Uncle Frank, did you tell Agent Case and Dr. John the description I gave you of my mom," Benjamin asked.

"Yes, I gave them the paper that I wrote the notes on. The FBI has a program that can match a drawing to a real person. And now that we have your mom's name, Agent Case should be able to find her. It's not immediate, and it might take a while. But I promise you, Benjamin, I'll tell you the truth as soon as we know. Okay?"

"Okay."

Sam glanced at her watch. "Yikes. It's after nine. Time for baths and bed."

Amidst groans, Sam and Frank led the children upstairs.

⁐☙⁐

Jarrett Miller, taking a long drag on a cigarette, tossed his overnight bag onto the back seat in his Toyota. For the first time he was happy he hadn't pimped up his drug-mobile as many of the competition. Flash was not his style—no flashing decals, standard tires and rims, no specialized plates. Low key—his rationale for avoiding capture over the last ten years of his budding career. And now of all times, his ex came into the picture. *How in fucking hell did that happen?* Something in him snapped. Seeing that first blonde bitch triggered his memories of her—Victoria Elizabeth Marin.

Oh, how she fought her parents in marrying me. They wouldn't even make a wedding. Imagine that. She wanted to give it to them real good. So we eloped. They didn't talk to her for the three months of the marriage. Ah, what the fuck? How the hell did they find me? I haven't been back in Manhattan in over a month since the last one. I think, Jarrett, you better damn well get the New York paper. You sure as hell can't trust what you see or not see on Facebook. Good thing I trashed the phone, and pretty much demolished it, after I spoke with the bitch. The feds are probably on their way to Delaware. Too bad, I'm a hundred miles north now. Next stop, I'm coming for ya, my darling ex-wife. I thought doing those other women would take my mind off you. And it did. Why in hell did you have to go live on Facebook today?

Jarrett ran his hand over his baldhead as he lowered into the driver's seat. He'd certainly have to get used to missing his curls. His hair—his pride and joy. Guess he expected he'd have to change his look eventually. He did, in prison. The first thing they did was shave off his hair after pumping him full of vaccinations. Yeah, right. As if he was carrying cooties or something.

It was getting real late. Before he started to drive, he realized something. For sure, some of his cronies saw the live feed. He slammed the steering wheel with his fist. He'd better junk this car, too. Anyone who'd be looking for him would recognize his jalopy. *Okay, time to get rid of it.*

He drove off the highway, one he'd driven on many times going up to New York, and continued onto the road that had become his piss-stop. No one was around so he'd use it to take a leak or a dump.

Hold on a second, there, man. I'm a college-educated man. Use your smarts, Jarrett. There's enough of me in this heap of junk to help those damn cops. Can't get rid of the car here. Yep. I'm using my smarts. Oh, Vicki, you're going to regret your gorgeous sorry ass you sent me to prison. Oh, man, and what a gorgeous ass it was. I wonder what you look like now under that expensive outfit. The cops used your maiden name. Did you ever get married or did I ruin it for you for life? If ya did get married, and you and those pigs hid that little fact from me, I have some news for your hubby. I'll get him, too. With your taste in men, I'm assuming he'd look like me. Yeah, I'd use a knife on him first then I'll slit your gorgeous throat.

Jarrett drove the car back down toward the highway. He got on, going north, and drove twenty miles before getting off at a rest stop. *What in hell am I doing here? I need gas, that's why I'm here. And to ditch this pile of junk. Okay, choices, Jarrett, choices.* His mind rattled off scenarios. He could pull in at a pump, ignite the car, and blow up everyone. And everything around him. Nah. That would bring too much attention. Maybe he'd grab his bag, jump into a car while a woman was pumping gas, and drive off. That'd been done before. Nah, women were getting smarter. But he would have to steal a car. He pulled into a spot far enough away from the building entrance. Before leaving the car, he pulled packets of oxycodone from the center console and stuffed them into his duffle. He'd didn't intend to leave a few thousand bucks of street value behind.

He observed every car on his walk to the building. The area was lit up and he knew he'd be taking a risk. Maybe some dumbass left the engine running. Dumb them. No one was truly safe with him. The only thing his customers could count on was quality product. Beyond that, there was no loyalty from him.

He tilted his head toward the sound of a purring engine. He looked inside the old model Ford, checking for a baby seat and children's bags. Nothing. This was going to turn out to be his lucky day. No one was walking toward the car. He slipped his fingers around the door handle and gave a slight tug. Opening the door, he slipped into the driver's seat. Keys hung from the ignition. He shifted the car into reverse, pulled out, and headed toward the north exit.

CHAPTER 13

Five Days Later:

S am's body shuddered in fear when she opened the Manhattan-North precinct door. She'd known this day would come—the first in breaking apart her world. One down, three to go at any given point in time. Would it be days? Weeks? Knowing Brett Case, he'd want it fast. She also knew that the infallible agent had no confidence in her to be able to stand up to the stress of having to return *her* children—*yes, that's right, they are now my children*— to their biological mothers. What would possess the women to accept that Henry Slater could walk off with their children? The children they bore in their womb for nine months and then nursed for eight months. No, something was very wrong. Not all of the women were like Sonja Santos. She was sure of that. She was also well aware that many children were kidnapped and they were not reunited with their families, though they were alive and well. *Okay, Sam, you have to get to the bottom of this, no matter the emotional pain it's going to cause you. You've always been an advocate for the child, and you've proven that as a classroom teacher and as a cop in juvie. Now it's time for you to fight the grown-ups some more.*

Sam marched down the hall, not even feeling her shoes squish on the wet carpet. Frank lagged behind her, and she understood his deliberate move. He was letting her process the situation in her own way as he always did. And, oh boy, did she need to process this. How would she approach Margie's mother? Like the patient woman, she was not? Go on a tirade? Nope, not her style either. She never went on a tirade with a parent of a child in her class, even when she knew they were being destructive to the child's health, mental or otherwise. No, she'd bring in her calm, professional manner as she did when she sat behind the teacher's desk— same desk, different location, and with a big difference in authority. The question being, would Margie's mother be open and honest about her relationship with Henry Slater Senior?

Frank knocked on the door to the war room and heard voices telling them to enter. He opened the door slowly. Sam stood at the entrance and let her gaze scan the room. Brett Case, Lex Withers, and Bella Richards sat at the conference table. Where was Sonja Santos? Frank nudged Sam in with his palm on her back. After hanging up their coats, Sam and Frank sat around the table.

"Miss Santos will be here in a few minutes. The team just picked her up at the hotel," Case said, staring at Sam. "How are you this morning, Sam?"

"I'm okay, thank you. The kids love school, and their dad had trained them well regarding doing their homework. Frank's in-laws told us they were wonderful. That alleviates a lot of stress for us. At least I can work with a clear head. How are we going to proceed?"

"And you mean what?"

"Who's going to do the questioning? Lead the interview?"

"I will," Case answered. "I'm not going to stop anyone from interjecting, but I want to stay on track, so no going off on tangents, please. The goal of the meeting is to: one, determine the relationship between Ms. Santos and Slater; two, try to get any information we can which will lead to finding the three other children's mothers; three, what she can tell us about his businesses, finances, child support. Anyone else have ideas of what we need?"

Sam raised her hand.

"You're not in a classroom, Detective, what?"

"The other three children's birthdays fall under the sign of Libra. Margie's birthdate of April fourth does not. I'm getting the feeling that she wasn't planned. Since Slater was so controlling down to the minutest detail, how did he let that happen? I see Miss Santos to be as much of a manipulator as he was. Was it her who pushed to conceive? I'm just wondering."

"How does that make a difference, Sam?" Bella said. "Pregnant is pregnant."

"Hold on, Bella." Withers paused. "Look at Melissa's teacher. Slater wanted it more than her…well, almost more. They went the surrogate way with in vitro. Her baby is being born in May. Not Libra, either. The bigger question is why Slater is having children now, not under the sign, when the first three seemed conceived according to the calendar. And the old fashioned way."

"We're not sure of the conception method of the older three yet, so we can't speak to your last point," Frank said. "Nor of Margie, but that we'll find out soon."

"I just want to make a point, as a father," Case said. "No one is going to jump on this woman for anything she says. No judgements. We're here to fact find. Personal feelings are out of the equation. We're conducting the parent interviews strictly in police fashion. We're not going to allow our personal viewpoints to color this, because if we do, we'll never reach our goals. And for the children's sakes, we need to find their mothers fast. Agreed?"

Words of agreement flowed from everyone's lips. Case got a text. "Okay, good, Miss Santos is being escorted down the hall."

Lieutenant Martin opened the door and escorted Miss Santos into the room. The woman stood frozen, her nervousness obvious to Sam and probably everyone else. Sam assessed her as if she was analyzing a science experiment—cold, calculated, so unlike her. Miss Santos was conservatively dressed, not in the elaborate style that Sam knew Slater would prefer. Her skin tone and straight dark brown hair that flowed down her back indicated some Mexican ethnicity. Margie was darker skinned than the other children. The woman's dark oval brown eyes—also like Margie—seemed to be full of worry, and sincerity. Sam would give her a chance.

"Have a seat, Miss Santos," Case said, as he pulled the chair out for her. "I'm FBI Special Agent Brett Case, and these are detectives Sam Wright, Lex Withers, Bella Richards, and Dr. Frank Khaos. We're happy we found you."

"I'm happy you did, too." Her eyes darted between the people at the table. "Where's my baby?"

"Margie is safe and sound, Miss Santos. She's with Dr. Khaos and Detective Wright in a loving home."

The woman crossed her heart and said a silent prayer. "Thank you. When can I take my baby home?"

"It will be some time before that. Margie is one of Henry Slater's four children whose mothers we are looking for—"

"Four children? Impossible. Henry told me Margie is his first. What is going on here?"

"We have a lot to tell you, and even more to ask you."

She took in a deep breath. "What do you need to know?"

"Let's start with Henry Slater. When and where did you meet him?"

She compressed her lips, and her gaze darted to the floor. She took a moment to brave it, Sam assumed. "Look, I have a stressful job, and I need a break once in a while."

"That doesn't answer my question. But what do you do?"

"I'm the PR director for a major clothing store chain. I have a PhD in Business Administration."

"Okay, good. That fits Slater's profile."

"Meaning what?"

"He chooses highly educated women to be the mothers of his children."

"I don't know whether to be flattered or offended by

that. What did this man do, aside from stealing our child? For the FBI to be involved, it must be more than a parent-child issue."

Case stared right into her eyes. "Yes. It is. Henry Slater murdered seventeen women over a nine year period."

After closing her slackened jaw, she snapped back. "Impossible. Henry is a kind, gentle man. I never met a man who was so giving, so in tune with a woman's needs on every level. I wanted for nothing. Where is he? He will answer your questions, I'm sure."

"Henry Slater is deceased, by his own hand, after his capture. He preferred suicide rather than spending the rest of his life on death row."

Miss Santos collapsed into the chair. A couple of silent minutes passed. She barely looked up. "So the man I was so deeply in love with was a monster in disguise?"

"Yes, and he left four beautiful children in the wake. Where did you meet?"

Miss Santos swallowed hard. "At a club in Texas."

"Okay, that fits. He met his victims in sex clubs, as well. Tell us about your relationship and how Margie came into the world."

"We met three years ago," she said, straightening her posture. "By the third time we played in the club, I knew I loved him. Surprisingly, he asked me for my number, though frowned upon by the club's owner, but it was mutually agreeable. We started to date whenever he returned to Texas, about once a month. We didn't speak much on the phone in between, and he hated social media. He saw me smile at children in carriages as their parents walked by. He smiled, too. We both loved the idea of having children, and my clock was ticking. I'm forty-four now. I asked him how serious he was about our relationship because I didn't want to waste time being with a man who didn't want to go anywhere with *us*. We started talking about it, and he said that he wanted children, too, but not yet. I lied to him about being on birth control. So he felt safe after a while about not using a condom. He'd always use one, and he prided himself on that. One night we got carried away, and Margie was conceived."

"Whoa, I have to butt in here," Frank said. "You lied to him about being on birth control? How did he accept that? Knowing Slater, you would have signed your death warrant."

"He was indeed angered. It wasn't so much that I was pregnant but when. He had this weird notion that he wanted the baby to be born under the sign of Libra, and Margie is an Aries."

"Now, we're getting somewhere," Frank said. "What's his obsession with Libra, because the three older children fall under this sign?"

"Do you want the list?"

"Absolutely."

"Henry was a green personality if you ever studied personality types. We do all the time in business. We need to know how to speak to clients with their needs primary, and reach them on an emotional level. With that said, he researched everything, even in his daily life. In his infinite wisdom, he concluded Libra's are the most gentle, peaceful sign. It's the sign of balance, a balanced heart, a balanced life, inside and out. Librans like to live in harmony. They're tactful, but indecisive, loving, romantic. They also think of themselves and make themselves of primary importance. He'd give me lessons on astrology and make me Google all of the horoscopes. What it means in relation to his life, I have no idea. Well, I do, actually. His was a life of turmoil. Bad relationships with his parents, stress—they treated him abominably like they didn't want him—no siblings—"

Frank raised his finger in the air, interrupting her. "Major revelation, here. I'm Henry Slater's biological brother."

Miss Santos gasped. "Oh, my Lord! I saw a resemblance and, in my nervousness, it totally went over my head. Did Henry know?"

"Yes. It was discovered through familial DNA a month

ago. I have custody of the children with my fiancée here, Samantha."

"We love the children, Miss Santos, and we are prepared to adopt them if we don't find their mothers, so we need your help there, too," Sam added.

"I will do anything to help you."

"Okay, good, we appreciate that," Case said. "We all saw the pet store tape and were able to analyze your conversation, so tell us in your own words how Slater came to take custody of Margie."

She blew out a deep breath, her discomfort obvious to Sam. "From the moment Henry found out I was pregnant, he showered me with love, kindness, and everything a new mom wants. He made sure I went to the doctor for my checkups and he always came with me. He followed the doctor's word on everything since I am classified as high-risk because of my age. He was the doting daddy-to-be. I didn't want to know the gender, but obsessive-compulsive Henry did, so we found out."

"You always went to his way?" Sam asked.

Miss Santos must have picked up that Sam understood. "Yes. That was our relationship. I'm guessing you're familiar, Detective. Yes, we had a master-slave relationship. Henry gave me whatever I wanted. All I had to do was appreciate him. It was nice after a career of clawing up the corporate ladder, fighting tooth and nail, so to speak, to accomplish my position. It's nice to relax and let someone else be in control. I had no stress with Henry. I was on an open-ended childcare leave. How many of you can say you have a stress-free relationship?"

"Let's stay on track," Case said. "How did he leave the store with Margie? Let me rephrase. We saw the tape. Why did you let him leave?"

"So now I'm being judged, Agent?" Miss Santos looked up at the faces giving her their full attention. "I guess you all can't help it. So I'll set the record straight. Henry and I had joint custody. And he paid for everything for Margie.

For every bit of her clothing, her room furniture, her toys which were always educational. She had loads of books. What I did complain to him about was that he didn't see her often enough. He wholeheartedly agreed. His response was that since I was nursing and he was such a big proponent of that, he didn't want to take her for weekends yet. A few weeks before he took her, we agreed to start her on the bottle so he could feed her when she visited with him and I still pumped.

"So when he came to Texas that last time, I knew she'd be going with him. What I didn't expect was for him to take her without a formal goodbye. I did speak to him later when he returned to New York, and he explained why he did it that way." She took a breath. "He didn't want to stress Margie out by showing her the separation. He felt that was the best way. He took away my stress, too, by the way. It may not be obvious, but I would have had a meltdown handing her over. Henry knew me very well. His prime motivation was to reduce stress in my life."

Sam nudged Frank's arm. "Hope you're taking notes," she chided.

"Okay," Case said. "You had no idea about the existence of the other children?"

"Correct."

"On their birth certificates which we recently found in his apartment, all of the children were born in different states. Did Slater explain anything to you about his work-related travel?

"Yes, that might surprise you. As I said, he was the stress-reliever so he told me where he was at all times."

"Do you have any of this documented?"

"A woman in my field documents everything. Part of my paranoia, I guess. But Henry taught me how to trust." She slipped her hand into a pouch on the outside of her designer tote. Sam noticed it was a Prada. She pulled out her smartphone, swiped to the notes app, and let her finger slide to a page. She opened it, showing it to Agent Case. "Here is his schedule for the next three months…well, from Christmas on."

"That might not do us any good now. Do you have his past travel records? For the two years you've known him?"

"No. Henry only started to give them to me a few months before Margie was conceived." She took the phone back and scrolled more of the notes. "Here, these start exactly sixteen month ago. It was his way of showing me he was committed to our relationship."

"Um, we've already established that the murder this past January was the first he carried through on in over a year," Frank said. "We're still profiling him and we need to speak to the other mothers, but I'd venture to guess that during the times he was in a loving relationship with a new baby on the way and or an infant, he curtailed his murder spree. Did he ever flat-out ask you if you wanted children?"

"Yes," she said excitedly. "On our very first date. He was so happy I wanted children."

"We're getting a good picture, Miss Santos, but so far nothing has been revealed about the other children's mothers," Case said, puffing out a breath. "As a father of four with one on the way, I'm asking you from experience. My wife recycles and reuses clothes from the older children for the younger ones. Did he ever send you care packages with items that'd had been used? Books, like you said, clothing?"

"No. Never. Everything was brand new."

Sam wanted to see the schedule on the phone. *Would Brett let her interfere?* She'd risk it. "Miss Santos, may I please see the document Henry sent to you?" She glanced up at Brett. He nodded.

"Sure," Miss Santos said, handing Sam the phone.

Sam bit her lip as she scanned the document. She shook her head repeatedly. "I'm sorry to tell you this, Miss Santos, none of these places are accurate."

"What do you mean?"

"After analyzing the data on Mr. Slater's computer, our

forensic scientists discovered that Mr. Slater never visited the states in this document. He never went to Nebraska, Oklahoma, North Dakota, or Washington State. He lied to you about everything."

"That bastard!"

CHAPTER 14

John and Vicki Trenton lay snuggled in each other's arms in their bedroom. Finally, some peace and quiet with the woman he worshiped and put on a pedestal. This was their silent time. Their needed private time when Ricky and the twins were in bed, asleep, hopefully for the night, but with the almost-four-month-old twins, it was still hit or miss. He perched his chin on top of her head as he thanked his blessings for having Vicki in his life. He stared around the room that was coming together to resemble the bedroom they both loved in his Manhattan condo. The only thing missing was the twenty-four karat framed ceiling mirror from his swinging bachelor days. No need for that now since Vicki is the only woman who'd ever be lying in his bed. This was their bed. Always the *we,* the, *us.* He didn't even think in terms of *I* anymore. Vicki's performance a few days ago at the precinct and on the phone with Jarrett Miller certainly lived up to his expectations. The shy, country-girl he met in the Florida Emergency Room had become a woman to be reckoned with—a woman who would send Jarrett Miller into the hell in which he belonged. John had no doubt about that.

He moved his arm to lie across her stomach. "What are you thinking about, babe?"

She caressed his arm in her hand. "Nothing really. Just enjoying feeling safe here with you." She turned and gazed into his loving eyes. "I'm a little scared. More for Ricky and the twins. He's been through enough in his nine short years, and I have no intention of allowing the twins to play catch-up."

John hugged her. "Babe, with the power of social media, he'll be apprehended fast, believe me. The FBI has a quick record for that now. No one escapes, even when crossing state lines disguised. I can't be more proud of you. And now, I want more of you." He rolled over on top of her, caressing her cheeks in his hands. "I love you so much."

Their lips met. The passion he and Vicki shared the day after he met her in Florida hadn't waned. He melted into her warm, loving body, caressing her face, moving his hands down her neck, her decollate, her warm milk-filled breasts. He squeezed and his hand became moist with her life-giving-force for their children. He smiled and suckled, Vicki moaning in delight. He loved the taste of her, the scent of her, still with her favorite fragrance—gardenia. He reveled in the love from his beautiful wife as her body pulsated beneath him. She cascaded her hands down his back to the small of his back, one of his sensitive areas. He groaned. He understood her signals, all right. John slid off her and lay on his side as he cascaded his fingers down her mid-section, down past her belly and thatch, finally sliding over her wet sex. He moved his fingers within her cavity as Vicki squirmed, impassioned by his loving touch. He'd never be rough with her, never been more than she could handle, though in his bachelor days he did it all, never missing his playboy life now. She gasped then moaned as he toyed with the spot, getting her more ready for him.

John slipped on a condom though he would have been happier to go longer and relish her body more. Since having the twins, their lovemaking had to take on a different path—shorter time but much more often. He slipped into her with ease. They were meant for each other in every way. He started slowly as he always did and built up momentum as they both became engorged with lust. He pumped harder.

"John," she gasped, huffing shallow breaths with her lips

apart. She couldn't stop whispering the sounds of mounting tension, just as he wanted.

She riveted stronger. She moaned, holding in a scream not to awaken the infants. John pulsated within her, he felt himself giving way as Vicki emerged with release. He always waited for her to climax first, held himself back, and he knew she loved him for it. He collapsed on top of her, releasing himself from her. Relaxed, sweaty, hot, and satisfied, it didn't take too long for them to hear it.

Zach's crying through the intercom.

ↄↄↄ

Quiet, peaceful, everyone sleeping—or so it seemed.

Benjamin's screams during another nightmare pierced through the dark. Frank jolted up in bed, just as he did in the military when bombs went off around him. Within fifteen seconds, he was alert, with pants on, and out the bedroom door. By the time he had gotten into the room, Frankie was on the bed with his cousin who knelt over bent knees, curled up, crying. Uncontrollable crying. Sam ran into the room with a robe wrapped around her.

Frank embraced him, and Benjamin collapsed into his uncle's chest. "Tell me," Frank said as he sat down on the bed.

In between sobs, Benjamin could barely get the words out. "It—wasn't—my mom—this time."

"Then who?"

"A monster."

"What was the monster doing?" Sam asked, sitting down on Frankie's bed.

Frank would let Sam take over. She was the one who was a whiz with dream interpretation. One of her dreams in the Aries case helped the department to solve it. She definitely knew what she was doing.

"It was over me, swallowing me whole, all of me in its

mouth, at the same time. I felt like I couldn't breathe." He looked up at Sam with pitiful eyes.

"Okay, bud, you can breathe. Give me some deep breaths," Frank said, rubbing his back.

Sam bit her lip, Frank guessed, in an attempt to stay calm—and neutral. "What did the monster look like?"

"A brown blob. It didn't have a shape that I know, and it didn't look human either."

Sam sat on the edge of the bed. "Tell me."

Before he could answer, Melissa ran in. "Benjamin, still?"

He cried, looking up at his sister. "Melissa, it was the same dream. The same one I had when Dad went away." He looked toward Sam. "Sam, is Dad still killing in Heaven?"

"I don't think that's possible, Benjamin. This may be hard to understand, okay, so listen carefully. In a dream the bad part is usually coming from the dreamer so it's not someone else. It wouldn't be your dad. This dream happens over and over again?"

The boy nodded and sniffled.

"The monster is swallowing you up, or is it covering you?"

"No, I'm in its mouth. I said that."

"I wanted to be sure. Is the monster preventing you from talking?"

He looked up at her excitedly. "Breathing, at first. But when I tried to yell, it pulled me out of its mouth, and then it pushed something that looked like a hand *over* my mouth."

"Breathing first?"

"Yes, in the beginning. Then like this." Benjamin put his palm sideways over his mouth.

"Do you still smell that stuff?" Melissa asked.

Frank's brows furrowed. "What smell?"

"Yes. The monster has a bad cleaning smell. It makes me choke."

"Like ammonia?" Frank asked, remembering that Slater washed his victims down with it.

"Yes, that's it. Dad was afraid of germs, and he cleaned the whole house with it. When I went into my bathroom right after he cleaned with it, I couldn't breathe."

Melissa perked up. "Benjamin! I just thought of something."

"What?"

"You had the nightmares the days Dad cleaned the whole house."

"No. I had the bad dreams when Dad went away for the night."

"That was the same day, Benjamin. He always cleaned the house before he left."

Frank and Sam shot each other quick looks. What Benjamin and Melissa just told them proved that Henry Slater did pre-meditate his murders. They didn't happen on a whim. Frank choked back an expletive.

Did he clean the house so they couldn't find his DNA after his capture? He knew exactly what he was doing and where he'd find his victims. This would change the son-of-a-bitch's profile, but not that much—after the fact. Did the scent of ammonia trigger the headaches that for some reason the murders relieved? Was he trying to bring on the headaches as an excuse to murder? Or was the organic damage to his brain responsible for this? I have a lot more work on this one.

"You told us a lot, Benjamin," Sam said, "that could help us, but there's more to the dreams. Okay. I'm taking this from the first day we met at the precinct. You told me that your dad wouldn't let you voice your opinions, and it was his way all the time. Do you remember telling us that?"

"Yes, and you remembered it, too?"

"I remember everything, sweetheart."

"And we never cried before coming here either."

"Crying and letting out your emotions is a good thing. In a dream when something or someone is preventing you from speaking, the dreamer, in this case, you, wants to say things. What do you want to say that you couldn't say to your dad? It has to be really important."

Frank placed his palm on the boy's shoulder. "Listen, Benjamin." Benjamin looked up at his uncle. Frank nodded. "We want you to know that you can tell us anything. Ask Frankie. He never gets punished or yelled at for expressing his feelings or opinions. You're safe in this house. Understand? So what are some things that you're holding onto?"

"That you want to say, but don't," Sam explained.

The nine-year-old sniffled but with easier breathing. "For one, I wanted to tell Dad not to use that cleaning stuff."

Frank chuckled. "What else?"

"I wanted to tell him to see a doctor for his headaches."

"What else?"

Benjamin and Melissa glanced at each other.

"Tell them, Benjamin," Melissa said.

"I knew something was not right when Dad brought Margie home because she was older already. You know I can tell things and Dr. John can do the same thing. Then Melissa and I talked about it. Henry was about Margie's age, too, so we began to think that Dad stole the babies. But we didn't know what to do. If I asked Dad if he stole babies, then he could get rid of them, too. I was afraid he'd get rid of me and Melissa, and we love each other. We decided to speak to Locklear."

Sam leaned toward the boy. "What happened?"

"We told her what we thought," Benjamin said.

"Okay, let's go slowly," Frank said. "How long ago did you speak with her?"

"It was like, in January. After Dad went away. After he used the bad-smelling stuff. But she wasn't of any help. She got mad at us for bringing it up."

"What exactly did you tell her?" Frank asked.

"That we thought Dad stole Margie and Henry—"

"And us," Melissa interrupted.

"From our moms."

"How did she react? Do you remember what she looked like in her face?" Sam asked.

"Yes!" Melissa exclaimed. "She got so red in the face, and she started shaking. She dropped a coffee cup, and it broke into a lot of pieces on the floor. She has wood floors."

Frank and Sam shot each other another look. "Then what did she say?" Frank asked.

"That we were both wrong, and that we should never ever talk such foolishness again, if we know what's good for us," Melissa said in a mocking tone, probably imitating the nanny.

"Yes, Locklear used those same words," Benjamin said. "Now I remember."

"Then what?" Frank asked.

"Then she called her friend, Chantal."

"Yeah, Sam. You remember?" Melissa asked. "I told you about Chantal. She and Locklear were talking when Dad came in and he got mad."

"Yes, I do remember, and we'll be sure to talk to Chantal and Locklear."

Crap! He and John, as well as the team, thought a child-kidnapping ring might be part of this scenario. *If Locklear and Chantal are part of it, Slater sure kept his sources close.* They'd find out in the morning. The FBI was bringing in Locklear Henderson.

"Anything else?" Sam asked.

Benjamin compressed his lips.

"Come on, Benjamin, tell them. Uncle Frank and Aunt Samantha are the only two people we can trust. Bad things are happening around us, and we don't know when they'll stop."

"Whoa," Frank said, astonished. "We can't leave it like this. What bad things?"

Benjamin nodded in affirmation to his sister's comment. "Yeah, okay. One thing I know for sure."

"What, sweetheart?"

"My teacher, Melissa's teacher, Miss Monty," Benjamin said, "is having a baby, and I know our dad is the father."

Sam shook her head, almost involuntarily. "How do you know things like this?"

"I took a good guess. And I talk to it. It's a boy."

"What does he say?"

"He knows his mommy doesn't want him. That got me thinking that our moms don't want us either. Do they? Do you think my mom—wants—me?" he said, bursting into tears.

Frank noticed that Sam did what she could not to burst out in tears, too, holding Melissa in her arms. Frankie collapsed into him. Frank knew his son couldn't handle this either.

"What if she was having the baby and then Dad was going to steal him, too? Now Dad's dead, so what's going to happen? Miss Monty doesn't want him, so will you, Sam and Uncle Frank, adopt him, so we can all be together? I talk to him almost every day, and he wants to come live with us, too. Can he, Uncle Frank?"

Oh, man! It was not as if he hadn't thought of this very issue. *Would Sam want to adopt a newborn with the possible sacrifice of her having her own?* Frank had to tell him. "We met with Margie's mom today, and she wants her. So I'm taking a really good guess that your moms want you, too. And Miss Monty isn't due until the end of May. Let's see what happens, okay?"

"Margie's leaving?" Melissa whimpered, looking up at her uncle.

"We're going to wait until we have all your moms together, okay? I promised you that."

CHAPTER 15

S am felt overwhelmed—very unusual. With her compartmentalized mind, nothing overwhelmed her. She'd been able to categorize every aspect of the Aries case. Even as more data flooded into her on Frank's wife murder case. She certainly unraveled Dingo Withers' and his wife Lisa's plan—right down to the embezzlement scheme that Jen's murder intended to cover up. And she knew how she processed the info on Slater's serial kills along with his motives. So what was overwhelming her now?

Even her spirit guide, Dara, hadn't been giving her as many signals. Dara was well enough aware of all of her inner thoughts. Since the Scorpio case and her love for Frank and his son Frankie—whom she wanted to call her own— her maternal instincts rose within her and spiraled out of control into the galaxy. It hit her. Dara was forcing her to come to terms with her own decisions about her relationship with the children—her love for them along with her feelings about sending them back to their mothers. Spirit guides did that. They didn't make themselves available for situations of the ego—not being there to stroke it. When they did make their presence known, they helped their person become in tune with their unconscious and bring up unknown realities.

Sam knew that. That was why Dara didn't come forward. Sam knew exactly how she felt on the issue about having the children she loved more-than-life-itself return to their moms, after being their guardian—a devastatingly slow death.

Frank didn't rush her, standing behind her, as she stood outside the war room door in the Manhattan-North Precinct. Very well aware of his presence, she bent her arm and placed her hand upon his as his clutched her shoulder. Sam turned and rested her head on his chest. She gazed into his eyes and nodded. She was ready.

She opened the door to see Brett Case, and John Trenton waiting for them, sitting around the conference table. She stared at them then her gaze wandered to the empty chairs. Where were the other members of the team—Lex Withers and Bella Richards? *Uh, oh, what's going on?*

"Come in, make yourselves comfortable. This will be a long interview."

Sam and Frank hung up their jackets on the coat rack in the corner and joined them.

"I want to say that the both of you are doing great eliciting info from the kids," Case said. "And with kids their age, it's hard."

"Well, they're mature for their ages, and with Benjamin being so aware, he's been on-target. He's truly a psi-kid," Frank said.

"Care to explain that?"

John smiled. "Children who are spiritually aware. Children who can see deeply into others. Psychic intuition."

Case stared at John wide-eyed. "Okay. I'll take it. Actually, that can turn out to be very useful."

"Slater did one thing right," Sam said. "He raised smart, articulate children. Can't take that away from him. Where's Lex and Bella?"

"When they come back from Locklear's apartment, they're going to go through the databases checking for info on the nanny and her friend Chantal. Based on what Frank told me about what you gathered last night on Benjamin and Melissa's fears, the warrant we had covered us. We got her address where she was visiting her sister, but now crime scene will tear the apartment up, looking for any evidence of the child-kidnapping ring. If they find anything, Sam, you're on."

"What do you mean?"

"The nanny will be here soon. She was out of the apartment before our unit went in, so she's unsuspecting. We're going to pump her but good, and we can hold her as a material witness. Withers will text me the moment they find any evidence confirming what we suspect. Here's what I laid out. You and I will be going UC as a couple." Case looked at Frank. "Calm it, Khaos. Sam's safe. And she has to go through an interview in order to be approved for the assignment. I have no doubt that it will fly. She'd proven herself on more than one occasion."

Sam smiled.

"We'll be putting in an application to adopt a child, a toddler, a child who's speaking just a little. Maybe the child could tell us something. As soon as we get any info for the possibility, and it could take a few days to set up, I'll have my department get together papers, right down to our marriage license, doctor's reports that we couldn't conceive after several years, and a few in vitro attempts. They'll make up a residence—which Sam and I will be living in— of course names, and even birth certificates for us, credit cards, drivers' licenses, social security cards, work histories, passports, lists of friends and family who can vouch for our acceptability as future parents, as well as work colleagues."

"All that in a few days?"

"A lot is already compiled." Case looked toward Frank and Sam. "I don't want the two of you to take this the wrong way. It's purely procedure. During the interview, you two are to stay out of the questioning. John will be taking over when need be, Frank. Your love for the children and your becoming more attached by the minute may increase your angst about this, and that might take us off track. Especial since your bond is now stronger than it was in the beginning."

Sam became despondent, and she knew Frank did, as well. "What if I put two-and-two together and come up with something relevant?"

"We do not— and I repeat, do not—want to give Locklear Henderson any clues of what we're suspecting. So, no putting two-and-two together in her presence. Save that for us at our private meeting right after. Can you recall all of your thoughts, after the fact?"

"Yes, I know what you mean. I remember my brain's ramblings."

"Very good, and it's been called that, by the way."

After a slacked jaw response, and everyone laughing, Sam retorted, "Thanks, Special Agent Case."

"You can thank me when we rescue additional kidnapped children. Right now, yours are safe. That's more than I could say for any kids in transit."

Lieutenant Martin opened the door with a staunch look on his face. "Got news. Locklear Henderson ditched the escort." He pulled out a chair and sat down next to Sam.

Case punched the table with a clenched fist. "How in hell did that happen?"

"We figured she'd be easier to bring in, mainly because of her love for the children, or so we thought. We sent two rookies right out of the Academy."

"Where are they now?"

"Sulking in the office after I reamed into them. Detective Valatutti is interviewing them and taking their reports. Bottom line, she complained about lower back issues and a bad hip, so they let her walk slowly. The officers got a little impatient with her pace so they edged forward and wound up in front of her. She saw an opening and darted in between cars on the four-lane avenue. No hip or lower back issues. We have a unit looking. She couldn't get far. One thing she disguised, she dresses more matronly than her age, obviously. They thought she was mid-sixties." He addressed Sam and Frank. "Did the children ever tell you how old the nanny is?"

"No, and we never thought to ask."

"All right. I don't think she'll go back to her apartment so, Agent Case, text Withers for them to check out her wardrobe and possible disguises. Where are the children now?"

"In school," Sam said, relieved.

"Tonight, get any information you can on Locklear Henderson."

The door opened and three uniformed police officers escorted a handcuffed Locklear Henderson into the room as she spewed obscenities at them.

Um, this is the way a so called she's-a-really-good-nanny-as-per-Melissa, speaks? Wonder what the elegant Mr. Slater would think about that. Wow! What a different impression I had of this woman. My feelings of love toward these children are sure clouding my judgment, and that's not a good thing.

The officers struggled to contain her but finally plastered her into a seat. "Of all places, she slipped into a crowded donut shop. We heard the rookies screaming, and we were standing right inside in line for coffee. Easiest arrest of my career yet."

Locklear pulled out of the cop's hold.

"Knock it off and I'll let go of you."

She sat handcuffed with her hands behind her back. "Take these off me," she said with a hint of an Irish accent.

"No," replied Agent Case. "Not with the way you're behaving."

The woman huffed out an unintelligible word.

"I'm FBI Special Agent Brett Case, that's Dr. John Trenton, Detective Samantha Wright, and Dr. Frank Khaos to your right."

The woman nodded after each introduction.

"Why did you run? And what did you think we wanted with you?" He nodded to the officer who took his leave

"I'm very shy." She kept her gaze straight ahead, going in between the people at the table.

Sam looked at the woman wearing a frumpy white blouse with lace around the collar and a long striped skirt that reached about mid-calf. Navy socks and moccasins adorned her feet. No jewelry. Sam looked her up and down, focusing on the poor quality wig on her head—curly and not attractive to her long oval face.

John sucked in his cheeks. "Shy? About what?" He leaned back into the chair and crossed his right leg over his left.

She ignored him. "Why was I brought back from my vacation with my sister?"

"What did the consulate tell you?" Case asked.

"That there was something wrong with the children I watch. I got very worried and packed immediately. They told me there was nothing else they could tell me."

"Yes, packed immediately, after the consulate finally found you." Case turned toward the team. "Miss Henderson wasn't staying at the address on her papers." He shot the nanny a hard stare. "How do you feel about the children?"

"I love them with all my heart. That's why I came back as soon as possible. Where are they?"

"They're safe," Case said. "How long have you been their nanny?"

Sam knew the routine. Ask simple questions to make the suspect comfortable. Ask questions that could be verified and would prove to be truthful on the part of the interviewee—the easy stuff. Build rapport—police interrogation one-oh-one. Yep, Sam knew it all and she was confident Agent Case had it down pat. Now she'd wait to see it play out, right before her eyes. She'd wait for the sizzle when the questions became harder. There would be shifts in body language and body responses that revealed the true character. Yep, Sam prepared herself for the routine.

"Since Mr. Slater came to New York three years ago."

"How did you meet?"

"Through an agency."

"Which one?"

Brett Case sure had patience. He didn't push. He went as slowly as needed. Sam was taking mental notes. She could learn a lot from him, aware she needed to slow herself down. She wanted it fast, like in the Aries case, with Calinda who was having an affair with Steven Larcon and his son Adam at the same time. Maybe Calinda wouldn't have bolted out of the office so fast if Sam had taken more time. Technically, she was still a rookie with a lot to learn.

Focus, Sam, focus, don't let your mind wander to an old case now. Stay in the moment.

"Deacon Agency."

Case jotted it down. "Where is it?"

Locklear hesitated. "Lower East Side."

"And you were working there?"

"As a temp. Then Mr. Slater came in. He interviewed over thirty-five women. He asked me to come to his apartment to meet the children. I fell in love with them."

"If I take the cuffs off you now, will you remain cooperative?"

"Yes, yes," she said as she turned her back toward him.

Agent Case removed the cuffs.

"Clasp your hands on the desk."

She followed the directions.

"How many children were there when you started?"

"Benjamin and Melissa. Henry came two weeks after I started."

"Okay, think back, please. What reason did he give you for Henry to all of a sudden show up?"

"He told me Henry's mother was ill, ovarian cancer, and he was taking custody of his son."

"Did he tell you what happened that made him a single dad to Benjamin and Melissa?"

"No. He laid out…how do you say it?…ground rules. He said I'm never to ask him personal questions. He told me about Henry willingly and then also about Margie. He probably didn't want me to be nosy."

"What did he tell you about Margie?"

"He wanted another child so he adopted."

"And you believed him?"

She let out an exasperated breath. "I can't believe this is happening. Where is Mr. Slater?"

"Mr. Slater is deceased."

Locklear paled. She crossed her hands over her chest then drew a cross over her heart as she mumbled a prayer. Her eyes looked frenzied. Her pupils looked almost as if they shrank. This was a real panic response. "Oh, my God, no. No. How did that happen?"

"We have to talk about other things first. How much did he pay you?"

"Eight hundred dollars a week," Locklear answered, trembling.

"How did you come to live in his apartment building?"

"He told me he owned the building, and it was important for me to be close by because of his job travel, so he insisted I move into his building. I'm a woman alone so it wasn't a problem and my apartment is so beautiful," she said, her voice sounding nostalgic.

"What did Mr. Slater tell you about his travel?"

"He didn't tell me exactly where he'd be, but he told me he'd call me a few times a day. On my house phone, not cell."

"Why do you think that is?"

"He wanted me to stay in the apartment all of the time. He told me, if he called and I didn't answer, I'd be fired immediately. So I stayed with the children at home."

"Did he give you any reason why he wanted the children in the apartment all of the time?"

"I don't understand. Mr. Slater cooked all of our meals and brought the food for me to heat up. He's a wonderful father. A wonderful man." Her gaze darted between the people around the table. "Why are you asking me all this?"

This time, Case ignored her. "How often did Mr. Slater go away and leave the children with you?"

"I'm getting very nervous."

"Just answer the questions, and you'll be fine."

"Okay. Okay. He left on business trips for four days at a time, yes, yes, four days, but maybe twice a month."

"Did he ever go away just for overnight?"

"A few months ago."

"Remember when?"

She looked up at the ceiling as if mentally calculating. "Mid-January, no, the second week, I think."

The night he killed my best friend, Carrie. So where did he go after the murder?

"Do you know where he stays when he goes away for the night?"

"No. He doesn't tell me. He may even be in his apartment for all I know."

"You said he paid you eight-hundred dollars a week. Is that on-the-books or off?"

Locklear's voice lowered. "What do you mean?"

"Are you an American Citizen?"

"Yes, of course. I came here when I was ten."

"How old are you?"

"Fifty-eight."

Case shot her a penetrating stare. "So you know exactly what I mean."

"I—pay—taxes."

"Okay. Good. Mr. Slater was a businessman. And he was very professional. I'm assuming he gave you a W-Two? For your taxes?"

"Yes, yes. He did."

"Perfect. We'll need to see that." Case jotted a note down and did some math. "Okay, thirty-two hundred a month, times twelve. That's thirty-eight thousand, four hundred dollars a year. How much is your rent?"

Locklear smiled. "Mr. Slater didn't charge me rent."

Case chuckled. "Why did I already figure that one out?"

he said snidely. "Why did he pay your rent?"

"It was on his insistence that I move into the building. He paid for everything for me. He decorated the apartment, mainly for the children. He paid for all of my food. He paid my medical insurance and even any doctor co-pays and deductibles."

"Nice boss. So were you able to save a lot of your income?"

"Some, but not a lot."

"Why not?"

"I'm helping my niece by paying her tuition for her masters degree in education."

"How much helping?"

"I love my niece so much."

"How much helping?"

"She's straight As."

"That's all well and good. How much?"

"Twenty thousand a year. The last two years."

"That doesn't leave you much for going out or spending on yourself."

"I don't go out. Mr. Slater has me on call one hundred percent of the time."

"So essentially, you don't have a life of your own."

Sadness overcame her. "No, I don't."

"How do you feel about that?"

"I love the children, and he's such a good father. It's my job to obey my boss."

Interesting choice of words—obey, Sam thought.

"Did Mr. Slater want you to *obey* him all of the time?"

"Yes. That's the word he uses."

"We need to see your bank accounts. How many do you have?"

Locklear cringed. She stared at Agent Case as if she was about to lose it. Sam actually could see her blood boil through her skin. What? She never had that ability before. The haze around the nanny's energy field acted as a barrier. Keeping her eyes firmly peeled on her, Sam was able to penetrate that barrier with her psychic vision. Her intuition was crystallizing. Now she could see through people when she steadied her focus. She looked at John Trenton. He acknowledged her with a nod. He saw it, too. When would Brett Case allow John to jump in? Vicki's husband sure had control to step back and let someone else handle the questioning. But then again, FBI Special Agent Brett Case had been clear on his expectations. Case's gaze darted between Sam and John. He had to have caught on. He confirmed it.

"Dr. Trenton, do you have something to say?"

John leaned forward. "I do," he said, smiling. "Miss Henderson, you've gotten very nervous. I see that. What's going on?"

She stammered, obviously searching for an excuse. "I'm a very private person. I'm not used to answering so many questions in front of people."

"We're doing this for the children," John said. "The children you said you loved with all your heart."

"Yes, yes. But why do you need to see my bank account?"

"We're investigating everyone closely involved with Henry Slater," Case added. "It's strictly police procedure."

"I don't have it."

John's brows furrowed. "You aren't in possession of your own bank account? Is it in a passbook, online?"

"Mr. Slater keeps everything for me."

"How do you pay your bills?"

"I told you. Mr. Slater does."

Not to interrupt the conversation, Frank jotted down a note and slipped it to Sam. She took it down to her lap and held it there.

"What about when you paid your niece's tuition?" John asked.

"That was automatically paid through my checking account."

"We'll need to see that, too," Case said.

"No," Locklear said, strongly. "I am putting my foot

down there. You are getting too personal, and I don't like it."

"What are you afraid that we'll find?" John asked.

She shook her head. "Nothing—nothing."

Sam peeked at the paper in her lap. *Slater told you the same thing about how he'd control your finances.* She sneered.

"Detective Wright, do you want to say something?"

Sam looked at Case, startled. "Actually, I do."

"I was waiting for that," John said, giving her the approval to take away the lead from him.

"Miss Henderson, the children are living with Dr. Khaos," Sam said, pointing her finger toward Frank, "and me, and we both love them so much. You know how smart they are."

"Yes, they are very, very smart."

"Melissa and Benjamin already know what they want to be when they grow up, and Henry, he's such a hoot." *Hoot?* Sam surprised herself, letting that word spurt out of her mouth. "And Margie is the sweetest baby, ever."

"Yes, they are."

"Melissa and Benjamin love to talk, and I love, love, love to talk with them. Want to hear something funny?"

Locklear looked at Sam as if she was from different world. "Okay."

Good, thought Sam. *I'll put on more perky.* "Melissa in her seven-year-old wisdom is planning Dr. Khaos and my wedding."

"You two are getting married?" Locklear asked sadly.

"Yes, and she wants to be the decorator, and she even doesn't want my parents or Dr. Khaos's parents involved. How cute is that? So tell me, please, what fun things did you do with them that I can do? We're still getting to know them."

Case shot her a glare.

Yes, Brett, I know I got off the bank accounts. I'm getting there. Let me find my own way.

"Pretty much, it was all schoolwork. We did watch educational movies."

"So the children didn't have any exciting activities? Yes, I know. They told me they never went to a restaurant even."

"No. We never went out." Her gaze landed on her lap.

Um, this woman is slow or being deliberate, Sam thought. "They told me sometimes they'd go to their Uncle Mike's apartment."

"I don't know what they did with their father."

Pick it up a notch, Sam. "They also told me about your friend, Chantel."

Locklear bolted up from the seat—too fast for Case to grab her. Frank and he got up and pushed her back into the seat. "Whoa, where are you going?" Frank reprimanded.

"I'm not talking anymore."

"Miss Henderson," Sam said. "I feel so bad. What did I say to offend you? Why is the mention of Chantal a problem?"

"Er—er—er—nothing."

"Okay, I'm going to get to something else. Do you know that Benjamin is capable of making great inferences?"

"What's that?"

"He can put two-and-two together, and he senses things. Did you see that?"

"Uh, no."

"You must have seen that he has nightmares?"

"No, never. He must be lying."

"When he wakes everyone up in the middle of the night, screaming, and he tells us what's in the nightmare, he's not lying, so what do you expect us to make of that? Of you not being forthcoming with us?" Sam stared straight into her eyes.

"I don't know what you're talking about," Locklear rebutted as she crossed her arms across her chest.

"I'll make this analogy. You know the children better than us at this point, so it makes more sense they'd be more open to you than us, correct?" Sam asked. Locklear nodded.

Sam continued. "If you're not telling us the truth about the children, I can assume you're not telling us the truth about your bank accounts, and yes, I'm assuming there's more than one. Nor will you tell us the truth about Chantal, or even how you got your job."

Locklear lost it. "I'm not telling you damn people anything!"

Sam smiled. She liked that reaction. She'd push until Locklear flat-out asked for an attorney. "How about if I tell you that your boss, none other than Henry Slater, was a serial murderer? And he killed seventeen women in different states while you were taking care of his children, therefore you afforded him the opportunity to do it."

"Murder? He didn't have anything to do with murder. What are you trying to put over on me?"

"It's true. His last victim, Carolyn Baines, was my best friend. That was his second week in January nighttime getaway. So, in your knowledge, what did he have something to do with? I have the distinct feeling you know."

Case got a text from Withers. He read it, pursed his lips trying to conceal a grin.

He passed the phone to Sam with the text showing on the screen. She glanced at it. *We found a bank account with a balance of three-hundred sixty-thousand dollars.* "Detective Wright, please continue," Case said.

"I don't know what you're talking about," Locklear said.

"There's an expression, 'from the mouths of babes.' Have you heard of it?"

"Yes."

"So you'll definitely know what I'm talking about. Here's what the children have told us. Listening? Because this is important."

Locklear nodded.

"Now, I want you to think about it because your future depends upon it."

"Are you threatening me?"

"That you understand, but not Benjamin's nightmares?"

Sam said, shaking her head. "I have a feeling you'll understand this. Benjamin and Melissa both told us that they told
you that they feared Henry and Margie were stolen from
their mothers, and they believed they were, too."

Locklear paled to the point Sam felt the older woman
was going to pass out.

Sam continued. "But in your dismissal of the seriousness
of this, you told them 'not to talk such foolishness again.'
And, Miss Henderson, I believe those were the exact words
you said, judging from your attitude, persona, and word
choices. How am I doing so far?"

Locklear slumped into her chair.

Sam didn't let up. "Miss Henderson, we are on a search
for the children's biological mothers. Nothing more. Nothing less. We need to know what you know."

"What do you already know?" she answered smugly.

"Fair enough. We know Henry Slater took Margie from
her mother. He and the mother had joint custody. We spoke
with her, and Margie is going back when we find the others.
Therefore, Mr. Slater lied to you. Margie was not adopted
as you said. Or did *you* lie?"

Locklear looked down at a brown square on her skirt.
Okay, she lied.

"I just wanted to protect Mr. Slater. I never knew how
the children came to him."

"Okay. But do you know how you came to have three-
hundred sixty thousand dollars in your bank account?"

"*What*?"

"It was found by our investigators," Case said, "as they
were searching your apartment. They're still there. Now is
the time for you to come forward and tell us the truth."

"Why should I?"

"Because you're looking at life in prison if what we suspect becomes a reality." Case continued to stare at Locklear
with such a stern glare, Sam quivered.

CHAPTER 16

Locklear Henderson's apartment—the bland, inexpensive version of Henry Slater's taste in decorating—bustled with a four-man crime scene team—photographer, packer of evidence, and two men who dug deep, tearing apart her drawers and what they'd consider to be personal hiding places. With this not being a murder scene, Detectives Lex Withers and Bella Richards felt out of place and followed the *diggers* around, getting glares and shaken heads every time they made eye contact.

"Sorry about our intrusion, but we need to be here for as long as it takes." Withers walked into the bedroom with monotone light green walls. A double bed, and light green-painted wood night tables and a dresser were the only pieces of furniture. *Not even a mirror?* He shook his head, not expecting this from Slater.

"We found the bank account statement, but I'm guessing there's more," Jack Hampton, a crime scene investigator said. "With Henry Slater dead, Henderson might come clean, fast."

"Not necessarily," Withers said. "This might be bigger than just her and Slater if she has other affiliations, and if that's the case, she'll need protection. That'll depend on her role."

With his back toward the detective, Jack continued to purge the contents of Henderson's underwear drawer. He held up a pair of full briefs. "What are we specifically looking for?"

"Don't make fun of her," Withers said, smirking. "What are we looking for? Any ties to anyone. I know, vague. We need people. Look for a ledger, a computer, anything to show this woman had any contact with the outside world. Slater kept her an isolate. It would make sense that he took away her ability to communicate with anyone. Maybe we'll get lucky and find something out of the profile. I'm going into the kitchen. At least, it's a little brighter in there. Bella, stay with Jack. Women's clothing is more your speed than mine."

"Okay, good. Look into every canister on her counters," Bella said.

"Canisters? Why?" Lex asked.

"It has been shown that women hide things in them," Jack said. "Yeah, I know. Weird."

Withers turned away from the investigator and his partner. He bit his lips as the memory flooded him. His brother hid embezzlement money in the canisters in his kitchen, and the gun he used to kill Frank Khaos's wife in a metal box in the cabinet above the refrigerator. His brother, Dingo Withers, once NYPD's lead homicide detective was now serving life behind bars for the crimes he committed in the Aries case—four months since his arrest and the wound still burned like alcohol on a fresh cut. Lex looked down at the tile floor as he made his way into the kitchen, still untouched by Crime Scene.

Sure enough, the galley style kitchen—in green and yellows—had canisters lined up along the entire length of the counter facing the outer side—looking into the living room. With a gloved hand, Withers opened the first—brown sugar, filled to capacity. *Who has completely filled canisters?* He poured out the sugar slowly into the sink. Almost at the bottom, he heard a clinking sound against the ceramic sides. "Packaging, in here, now!"

Russ Medo ran in with the manila packing bag and tape. "Detective?"

Withers pointed into the sink. The sugar slipped into the

drain and plugged it, but what clanked was shiny and visible.

"Looks like a bank safety deposit box key." Before he touched it, Medo took pics on his camera from every angle, including the inside of the canister, then he pulled it out of the sink, slipped it into the manila envelope, sealed it with tape, and wrote his and Withers's names on it, the date, time, and where it was found. They both signed off on it.

"Stay with me here. I'm going through all of these." Withers mentally counted the canisters—seven. *Who has seven canisters?* He opened the second. Some kind of flour. He knew Slater only used gluten-free, but this didn't feel like gluten free flour or look like it. This was pure white. Gluten-free, as he learned from Frank Khaos, was a little darker. This was real flour. *Was Locklear Henderson going against Slater's orders or did she have guests up here against his knowledge whom she baked for?* This time he tilted the canister and with his gloved fingers scooped out about a tablespoon at a time, spreading it between his fingers before it landed in the sink, and at the bottom, another clanking sound. This time, it was a smaller key. He picked it up and dusted most of the flour off it. "What kind of a key is this?"

"Honestly? It looks like a gun case key."

"A gun case key? So she'd dig into this flour to get the key if she wanted to use a gun? That's a lot of work to do in an emergency." Withers went to the entrance of the living room. "Hey, Hampton, look for gun cases. We might get her on gun possession at the very least."

"Sure thing, Detective. I'll go through her clothes closet and shoe boxes."

"Go through everything." Withers took the lid off the third canister—whole-wheat flour. Again, he scooped it into the other side of the double sink with his fingers. A set of car keys fell out and landed on a peak of flour. "Looks like Locklear Henderson got around a lot more than Henry Slater knew." He read the tag on the electronic key. "Lexus.

Nice car. And the kids don't know about it? I know how she did it. Slater told her he'd call on the house phone and she'd better be home. I bet she call forwarded the house phone to her cell. He'd never be the wiser." He made a call for a unit to check the garage for her car.

Medo packed the car key. "If she didn't want Slater to know, maybe she didn't park in the building's garage. She's apparently a lot more cunning than she came across at the interview."

"She sure is." Withers opened the lid to the fourth canister—cornmeal—filled to the very top again. Withers changed his gloves. He dug his hand into the canister as cornmeal poured out onto the counter, grimacing when he felt something. He pulled out a passport, along with much of the canister's contents. "Now, we're getting somewhere." Withers opened the cover. "Whoa! It's her, with the name of Charlotte Baluch. Different wig. Which one is the alias?"

"And are there more?"

"I bet there are a few more, at least," Withers said. "Wait a minute, hold on a second. She pours all of this crap out, gets the item, and pours it all back? That would make a mess."

Medo turned and opened a walk-in pantry almost the size of a small bedroom. He walked in to the back with shelving. "Hey, Detective?"

Withers joined him and looked around. "My wife would sure love this. What have you got?"

Medo pointed.

"That's sure a lot of flour, sugar, and cornmeal bags. So she dumps it each time. And maybe the car key is a spare." He left the pantry and yelled again to Hampton. "Hey, Jack! Look for a set of car keys to a Lexus." Withers went back to the canisters. He took off the lid to the fifth, and moved it toward him—pasta rounds. He grabbed paper towel off the roller that stood close to the edge and lined the counter with it. He dumped the pasta onto the paper and the men hit pay dirt. A USB device fell out on top of the pasta. "We're moving forward here. She told them at the interview she knew nothing about computers. Yeah, right. I think we need a larger team up here. This will turn out to be a week-long project, without the murder, I hope. At least we won't get blood stained." He put in the call.

There'd be about an hour wait to assemble another team. Withers asked for John Trenton, too. Maybe the doc could shorten their time and at least come up with some on-the-spot-analysis. Withers wasn't one not to defer to the experts, and he'd gotten to know how John's and Sam's brains worked. To him, Sam was out of the question. She was in too deep emotionally. But John Trenton, now *he* was an asset.

Okay, two more canisters to go, Withers thought. He pulled the sixth one forward. Crap, it was heavy. He removed the lid. Coins. Locklear used this one as a container—quarters, dimes, nickels, pennies. "She must have a few hundred bucks in this eight-quart canister. Where in hell do I pour out this? Got a box?"

"Be right back," Medo said as he walked away.

While he waited, Withers pulled the seventh canister over to him. This one was too light. He opened the lid. It was empty...except for a dead baby scorpion, lying on the bottom. At first, he jolted back then he peered into the jar. With his hands on the outside, he shuffled the scorpling back and forth. It remained lifeless. When Medo returned with the box, Withers titled the canister toward him. Medo had the same reaction then laughed.

"What's so funny?"

"Not funny. Weird. Did the nanny find this amongst the kids' things and plan to tell Slater? Or did he bring it in inadvertently? I was on the team in his apartment, and we found none loose. That man was careful."

"We'll ask her. This she'll be honest with—I hope."

"Hold on, Detective. I just got a thought. This creature looks like it's been dead a while—see, it's browning on its edges and shriveling? Its tail's extended too. Our guys will be able to tell its approximate time of demise. What if the three-hundred sixty thousand was deposited at the same time? Granted, we don't know if it was one deposit or multiple, but what if—what if—Henderson was blackmailing Slater?"

Withers nodded. "Okay, let's run with that. Would Slater tolerate it or would he kill her?"

"If she's the only one qualified and available for his children, like she said, twenty-four-seven, he might go along with it. Especially if he didn't want to spend the time to find someone else and train her."

"Okay." Withers put his finger up to make a point. "We'll keep that option open."

Medo placed the box on the granite counter top. Withers poured out all of the coins. Toward the bottom, two pre-paid cell phones fell out. Withers tapped the recent calls icon. The phones were both used days before her trip to Ireland and Slater's suicide. "This will turn out to be a successful day yet."

Withers stared at the cupboards behind him. He opened the doors with the tip of his index finger—cans of food. He didn't think the nanny would be careless enough to keep open cans out of the fridge, so he made the assumption that these were brought in from the store. "Hey, Medo, just in case, it's rare though, have the new team check all these cans. I'm not leaving anything to chance or the obvious."

"No problem, Detective."

Withers opened up the other cabinets—mostly dishes and fine China, at that. *Finally, something I'd expect from Slater*, he thought. The cabinets were high, taller than what Locklear Henderson could reach wearing flats, and they were filled with dishes. Maybe she stood on one of those old-fashioned stepstools. He looked around—none. Was something behind the plates on the top shelf? The first thing he noticed was that those dishes protruded more to the front than the ones of the same size on the lower shelves. He was tall enough. Carefully, Withers took down the stacks of light green plates and placed them on the counter. He noticed the shine. Everything was surely immaculate. He peered into the back of the cleared-off shelf. He bellowed laughter.

"What, Detective?"

He pulled the object out with his index finger in the trigger pull. "Look at what we have here. A nine-millimeter Ruger. And not even stored properly. One count weapons possession, a felony, and counting. Oh, and look at this," he said with a mocking tone. "The serial number, a poor attempt at filing it off. It can either belong to Henderson, or maybe even her good friend, Chantal." He slipped the gun into a manila bag and Medo proceeded to file it. "I'm far from done in this room, alone." Withers continued to open up the top cabinet drawers. His luck had run out. Then he tackled the bottom cabinets—pots and pans, storage containers, kitchen appliances, the usual. "Have the team look in here, too."

Medo nodded.

Withers joined investigator Jack Hampton and his partner in the bedroom. They were clearly doing their jobs. Every bit of Locklear Henderson's clothing was in piles on the bed. He grimaced. "All matronly? That doesn't fit with what we found in the kitchen. I'll fill you in, later."

"All drawers, the same," Bella said.

"Wild hunch here. Check the doors or inside the closets to see if there's a connecting closet. It wouldn't be to another apartment. She couldn't hide that from Slater. I'm recalling that Barbara Montgomery used a connecting closet which did lead to another apartment in the Gemini case. That's where she hid the weapons she used to annihilate Trenton's initial NYPD team."

Hampton gave him a shocked look.

"Yeah. It was gruesome. But that's how Bella and I were called in. In these Upper West Side buildings, it's a possibility."

"Yeah, well, Slater had hidden rooms," Jack said.

"True. And he designed this one, too. Maybe he didn't share that info with the nanny and she discovered it on her own. There's a lot more to her than this persona she's showing us and wants to lead us to believe."

"From how Slater designed his apartment, I know what to look for as to where the release buttons are," Jack said. "I'm counting on him being consistent."

"Good enough," Withers said as the doorbell rang.

John Trenton and the second crime scene team had arrived.

ↄ৹ↄ

He did it. Jarrett Miller slipped into New York City without delays, except for the bumper-to-bumper traffic coming out of the Holland Tunnel. Yeah, he did ditch the car he picked up at the first rest stop, but another one was as easy to attain at the last one. He'd made sure it didn't have New York plates, and this one even had one of those toll transponders. *Oh crap!* He'd be tracked for sure. Waiting to move, he used his fingernail to nudge off the transponder on his front window. Damn, it didn't budge. "What did they use for this shit? Crazy Glue?" He opened the center console and stuck his hand in, looking for a pen. His hand touched something familiar. He lifted it up, took a quick glance, and dropped it back into the console. "Fuck me now!" he said out loud, glad the window was closed. A Glock. "What in hell am I going to do with a Glock?" he said, again out loud. He dug under the gun, and pulled out a sticker-remover, the kind with the hidden blade. The one that was supposed to be hidden. "Ow!" he exclaimed as he removed a bloody hand. The blade struck across four fingers. It stung like hell, and he bled. He stared at his hand as the horns beeped behind him. Dripping blood. He was certainly used to the sight of blood. Just not his own.

He always thought about why knives were his weapon of

choice. He loved blood. Everything about it—the color of purple in the veins, the oxygenated red blood as it hit the air, its thickness, its energy. For some reason he got a thrill—almost orgasmic—when he watched the women bleed out. Yeah, he'd made sure he stuck around. He wanted to witness their last bit of energy sapping from their once alive and beautiful bodies. They should be thankful, those funeral directors. They wouldn't have to spend the time with the embalming process. Jarrett bellowed laughter, at his own thought. Actually, it was a diversion from focusing on his screaming-in-pain hand. Did he at least have a rag? He couldn't get to duffle in the back seat.

He drove to the nearest intersection on the West Side in Manhattan when the traffic moved. He wound up on First Avenue and East Twentieth Street. Good enough. He knew Vicki Marin-whatever-the-heck-her-name-was-now was in the Upper West Side of Manhattan. That's where the precinct was when she made that Facebook live. *Yeah, Jarrett, you're on the ball man. You notice everything.* Yeah, they could move her, but he was on a mission. He parked the car, took out a T-shirt from his duffle bag, and wrapped it around his right hand. Exiting the car, he left the gun and his blood as evidence—all because he couldn't get his mind off her.

ℯ♋ℯↄ

John Trenton stared at the manila envelopes on the kitchen counter as Lex Withers gave him a recount of what had been discovered so far. Brett Case arrested Locklear Henderson on weapons possession without a permit, especially since she couldn't produce one, nor did she try to convince them she was licensed. Withers went on to tell him another scenario, a what-if about a nanny-cam.

John reined in his thoughts for a moment. "Did you find one?"

"No, that's the thing. Since Slater was a control-nut, I'd think he'd have one. We looked all over at the usual spots, but found nothing. That struck me as extremely unusual. What do you think?"

"All right. Let's just see how this flows. From what you found, this Locklear is a lot more assertive than she led them to believe in the meeting. She knew she had Slater where she wanted him, being the best caregiver to the children. Maybe she flat-out told him, if he got a nanny-cam, she'd quit. I think he needed her more than she needed him. Besides, the children would have told him if anything untoward was going on. He'd want to hear that from them, I'm sure. I'll call Frank and ask if Slater asked the children what happened when they were at the nanny. I make a bet he did. The children wouldn't know, though, what Locklear was doing when they were in school. I wonder if Benjamin got any vibes about her. Okay, at least we know where to focus our questions to the children."

Medo called from another room. "Hey, Detective, Doc, we found something!"

John and Withers rushed into the living room where the other investigators gathered, all staring into another once-concealed room—now a closet. In it, on-trend, in-style corporate women's clothing, belonging to Locklear Henderson hung on racks. John walked in and Jack showed him a tag—the price and size were still hanging from the sleeve.

"A six-hundred dollar suit," John said. "Size fourteen. That about right?"

"From the description Agent Case gave me, yes," Withers answered.

"Let's see if there's any evidence to where Miss Henderson wears these clothes." Jack opened a dresser drawer from the built-ins on the surrounding walls. "This is the kind of closet we see in celebrity homes. Did Slater know about this or did our nanny hide this, too?"

John shook his head. "I'm guessing he didn't know. This woman has more than one income stream." John paused in deep breathing. He felt Max's jolt go through his right side. *Yes, Slater did know. I'll wait until I have more evidence before I add another dimension to this case.*

Withers noticed John's concentration. "Let's get outta here and let Doc do some of his magic. Find us something good, John."

Withers left the closet with the rest of the team.

John appreciated that—Withers's trust. He stood in a humbling moment. The detective, who once thought he was a total nutcase in the Gemini case, came through in the Scorpio situation, solving the murder of Bobby Mitchell— the murder that was a cover-up for a book pirating operation. The detective had stood by him, with all of his rambling and profiling, and it worked. Now after finding the children's birth certificates, John made it a priority to help find the children's mothers. He'd always been an advocate of the child. Usually, he got them when they progressed into schizophrenia and they became his forensic patients, unable to stand trial because of their mental state. Now he had the opportunity to save precious, innocent lives not yet tainted by gruesome acts, and he hoped they never would be. *Get it together, John. Stop with the self-analysis and get to work.*

He stood still, quieted the over-active-mind state, did some diaphragmatic breathing, and focused. He put out a message to the universe to keep Max with him, unsure if his spirit guide stuck around. He'd even stopped to think at times that after forty-five years of Max being with him since he was three, that maybe it was time for Max to move on and attach himself to a different, younger soul. The thought saddened him. He would approach Max about that when he'd have the time to go into that deep of a meditation. Now wasn't the time for it either. His body tingled as the energy from deep breathing ran through him.

Find me a link to Henry's, Benjamin's, and Melissa's mothers.

He walked to the wall opposite to where he stood, and opened the full-length folding closet door—shelves, sweaters neatly folded. He needed more than the obvious. He ran his fingers around the perimeter of the closet, slipped his hand into the back of each shelf looking for hidden objects—nothing. He stepped back and his gaze traveled from sweater to sweater—left to right—pausing, staring.

One baby-blue cashmere sweater caught his eye. He picked it up with his gloved hands and unfolded it. *Beautiful quality*, he thought. There had to be more to it because this sweater drew him in and not just because he loved the color blue. Spreading it out, he placed it on a cushioned bench, probably the one Locklear sat on to get dressed.

He focused. A cloudy vision began to appear—a newborn that the nanny was holding close on her shoulder. A middle-aged hand surrounded by a pink aura—pink energy—patted the baby's back. Okay, loving energy. Locklear held a baby when she wore this. Looks a lot younger than Margie, and she wouldn't have worn this particular sweater with the Slater kids anyway. This was a different child. Who? John snapped himself out of the vision. He went to the living room entrance. "Packaging, in here now."

Investigator Medo was there almost instantly. "Yeah, Doc?"

"Package this and get the DNA for the newborn Locklear Henderson was holding when she wore this sweater. If not DNA, a baby's fingerprint or footprint for identification would do. If I'm right, this could lead us to the people we were hoping not to need to find."

CHAPTER 17

Frank had the list of questions that arose from the meeting with Locklear Henderson. His in-laws had directions to keep the children up and luckily, there would be a day off from school for them tomorrow—staff development training. They'd be getting home late since traffic from Manhattan was slow, even after rush hour. His mind reeled. *Will Benjamin and Melissa be of any help? How in the world would they know what their nanny did when she wasn't with them?* Then the realization hit. Melissa said bad things were happening around them, but the children didn't go into details, except for telling about a nightmare and about Miss Monty's baby who Benjamin communicated with. *Was that all?* Frank seriously began to doubt it. Phrasing questions was his job—his skill. He'd use it tonight.

Two inquisitive minds accosted them as soon as he and Sam opened the door. "Whoa! Slow down. Can we at least take our coats off?"

"No," Benjamin said hastily. "Did you meet Locklear? Does she miss us?" He trailed his uncle from the coat closet into the den and plopped down on the couch next to Frank.

Melissa followed suit without any prompting from her brother. "When can we see her?"

Frank smiled and responded thoughtfully. "I know you miss her, and yes, Locklear misses you with all her heart. That's why she came back from her vacation as soon as she was called."

"But?" Benjamin asked. "I know there's a *but* in there, Uncle Frank."

"Yeah, there's a big *but*," Frank replied as he rustled Benjamin's hair. "Sam and I have a lot of question for you, and we need you to be honest, and also to remember correctly. Okay?"

"What's going on?" Benjamin asked.

Frank's in-laws smiled, knowing this was official business. They literally tiptoed to get their coats, and waved to Sam and Frank as they left the house.

"Remember, Melissa, when you told us 'bad things are going on,'?" Sam asked, "and you both didn't know what to do?"

Melissa nodded.

"Well, there are things going on, and we don't know how bad things are, yet, and we need your help in finding your mothers. So tell us, did Locklear ever tell you how old she is?"

"No, but she's old." Benjamin crinkled his nose. "Oh, she's about Mrs. Sulley's age. Our principal's wife."

Sam crinkled her nose, doubtful. "I think she's younger than Mrs. Sulley. Locklear told us she's fifty-eight, though from her style of dress, she may look older."

"Tell me about it," Melissa said. "It's weird because Dad always liked to get dressed up. But, I heard him tell Locklear he wants her to dress like an old lady."

Sam laughed. "Why?"

"Yeah," Benjamin interjected. "He said something like 'people will believe she's a real nanny.' Isn't she a real nanny? She was our nanny."

Melissa raised her index finger into the air, making a point. "That's what I meant when I said, "bad things are happening around us." That was one of the bad things."

"Yeah, what would Dad want Locklear to hide?" Benjamin asked. "I mean, that scared us."

"We're trying to get to the bottom of it," Sam said. "What other bad things?"

"Okay, okay, here's one." Melissa perked up. "We were sitting on the couch, getting ready to leave to meet the school bus, and Locklear needed to sign a note for school. She dug into her bag and had to take out stuff to find a pen. She accidentally took out car keys. And we were like, *car keys*? Why do you have car keys? We don't go in a car, ever. We're not allowed. And we never ever went in a car until we came here."

"This is very important," Frank said. "What exactly did Locklear say to you? Think. We need it word-for-word."

Melissa sat back with a determined expression. She compressed her lips and closed her eyes. Sam looked at her adoringly. Melissa took a few deep breaths, and then sat up. "I'm ready. I'm good at remembering things. First, she acted all nervous. The keys dropped onto the floor, and her fingers shook, like this," she said, demonstrating with her own fingers, "when she lifted them up. I asked her why she was shaking, and she told me that she had too much coffee in the morning. I didn't understand. It was seven in the morning. How early did she get up? And I didn't smell any coffee, in the apartment or on her breath. Then I asked her if they were car keys. I couldn't believe what she told me next."

"Which was?" asked Frank.

"You're really serious, aren't you, Uncle Frank?"

"Very."

"So something bad is going on," Melissa said.

"Yes. Tell us what Locklear said."

Melissa swallowed. "She wanted us to go along with a game she was playing with Dad."

Frank hiked his brows.

"I'll tell you before you ask. The game was not to tell him she has her own car, and she goes places with her friends. I asked her what places, and she said she needed to make extra money. Then I asked her 'why.' She said Dad pays for everything but she's helping her niece through school. We could understand that, so we said, 'okay.'"

"Did she say what her job is?"

"That's where the *something bad* comes in," Benjamin said. "She told us, and this is word-for-word, she 'works with people to get babies new mommies and daddies because their real mommies and daddies don't want them.' Then she must have felt bad about what she said when she saw my face. I was shocked, because when we asked her if *we* were stolen from our moms, she got angry. I guess she doesn't remember because she's old. She said, 'oh, it's not that at all, I was teasing,' but she was so nervous she couldn't say the words right. I think it was the truth and it just slipped out of her mouth, like without knowing that was going to happen. That night I had a bad dream again. Mommies and daddies want their babies, right?" Tears welled in his eyes. "Now I know our moms didn't want us. Why would Locklear tell us that in the first place? That was so mean, and she was never mean to us before. Why did she say that?" Benjamin said as he collapsed into Frank's chest.

"Oh, man." Frank patted his back, hugging him. "That sure was mean. When did she say that?"

Benjamin looked up at Frank with reddened eyes, sniffling. "Like, last year."

"This school year?"

"Yes, in October. Yes. Margie wasn't with us yet. I think Locklear was mad at Dad when she said it."

"Mad, how?"

"He had to go on a business trip, and she told him that she had something planned, and he told her to change her plans."

"You heard that in person?" Sam asked.

"No, she was on the phone with him," Benjamin said. "And it was that morning with the car keys. He gave me an envelope to give her, and when she read the letter inside, she called him. She hung up and her face looked so mad. Then she had to sign the note for us for school, so she started throwing stuff out of her bag."

"Changing her plans really got to her, uh?" Sam said.

"How did she act after that? I mean, how long did she stay mad?"

"Not a long time, at all." Melissa jumped in, obviously—to Sam—because she wanted to tell her part. "She was all happy the next day. But I know why. I'll tell you before you ask, again. Dad gave her money for changing her plans for him. He always did things like that, because he knows Locklear is a really good nanny. I don't know how much money, though."

"Do you know if Locklear ever goes away for more than a day?"

"No, never. She's there to pick us up or take us to the bus. Now Margie is with her, too."

"And Henry, too," Benjamin blurted out.

"So she's got six, seven hours, max?" Sam asked.

Melissa nodded.

"Does Henry go to school all day?"

Melissa looked up toward the ceiling as if mentally figuring it out. "Uh, no. Monday, Wednesday, he goes full days. Tuesday, Thursday, Friday, he goes from nine to twelve. He hates those days. He wants to go to school all the time, like us."

Sam swooned. "I'm so glad Henry likes school. And that was very nice of your dad to give Locklear money when he needed her to change her plans."

Frank stuck to business. "Do you have any idea where Locklear does that job? Ever see her go out dressed up, like in a business suit?"

"Like the kind Sam wears?" Melissa asked. "Uh, no! I saw her closet. Ugh, all old-lady clothes. Even her pocketbook is canvas. Those things I notice, remember?"

"Yes, I remember," Sam said, laughing. "You know your dad liked to hide rooms. Do you know of any hidden rooms in Locklear's apartment? Um, did you ever see her look toward the baseboards at all and then turn her attention away quick?"

"Oh, not exactly that!" Benjamin blurted out. "But she's got a big pantry…yeah, I think that's what it's called…in the kitchen, and I saw the same buttons from our kitchen on the baseboard."

"Does Locklear know you saw it?"

"I think so because she told me to get out of there because there's nothing in there I want. It went out of my mind after that."

Frank let out a deep breath. "All right, listen carefully, Benjamin. What I'm going to ask you to do is a stretch. It's okay if you can't do it. Okay?"

The boy nodded.

"I'm asking you because Dr. John can do this and you have the same skills. See if you can try. I want you to focus on that door, in the pantry, the one with the knobs on the baseboard. If you can focus on it, do you think you can tell what's on the other side of that door? Is it a closet or a full room? Do you see anything in it?"

The nine-year-old stared at his uncle. "I never did that before, Uncle Frank. That may be too hard."

"Sometimes, we don't know we can do something until we try. Want to give it a go? I'll understand it you don't want to."

"I do because we want to find our moms." Benjamin leaned back on the couch. He squeezed his eyelids shut and rolled his lips tight. "The knobs are a light blue. I saw them. It's weird because the door is light green. Everything in Locklear's apartment is light green. That's her favorite color. Maybe they're blue so she can find them easy. She is old." He sat in silence. After a long two minutes, he jolted. "Uncle Frank! I did it! I see babies in that room. Not real babies, but pictures!"

✺✺✺

Sam and Frank couldn't wait to get into the precinct.

They'd left the house at five a.m. to beat rush hour, arriving in the Manhattan-North precinct in less than an hour. Swinging the door to the war room open, Sam found Special Agent Brett Case sitting at the conference table, chomping on a breakfast sandwich, large fries, and an extra-large coffee.

Sam sniffed. "Oh God, I haven't eaten that in years," she said, taking her seat.

"Once in a while it won't kill you."

"Once in a while becomes a habit," Frank touted.

"What have you got?"

The kids did come through," Sam said. She caught Brett up on everything, referring to notes she'd written to make sure she didn't forget anything, despite her photographic memory.

"He saw pictures of babies in the adjoining room. Any descriptions?"

"No, he shut down after that."

"Lex and Bella are still at Henderson's apartment. Give me a sec." Brett pulled out his phone and sent Withers a text. "I'm sure he'll appreciate that." After a short chuckle, he continued. "Okay, here's what we have. Crime Scene and the detectives found a lot at the apartment."

Sam sat with mouth agape, listening to the new profile of Locklear Henderson. Wow! She'd misread this woman, but good. Then again, when someone takes on a new persona to lie to the public and everyone around them, they believe their lies and become that person. "Okay, so how long will it take to find a baby footprint—" The thought provoked a smile. "—and the identification?"

"Footprint, if we're lucky could be today. DNA not for a while, but all hospitals retain newborn's records. If we get the name, we'll be able to track down the biological parents, and that'll be the start to what we need."

"The age of the baby will help, too, right?"

"Absolutely."

Sam's mind turned inward. She visualized a possible

scenario and nodded, seemingly to herself.

Brett promptly interrupted her. "Out loud, Sam, tell us what you're thinking."

Startled, Sam's jump almost pushed the chair backward and down to the floor. Frank's swift reaction prevented her from a hard landing. She looked toward him, almost unaware of what she'd done. "Oh, that wasn't good. I'm trying to put all this together in my mind. Lex found the set of keys. Did they find the car?"

"Yes, and as we expected it wasn't in the apartment building lot. It was parked in an outdoor lot three blocks away. A little inconvenient but Henderson coped with that. Tell me what you're thinking."

"We know she's between fifty-eight and mid-sixties, correct?"

Brett nodded.

"A little younger than my parents, so I'm judging from them. My mother insists on using the navigation system even if they're somewhat familiar with where they're going. How about looking at the nav system and seeing her stored previous destinations? I know because my service guy told me the nav system is directed through a satellite. Yes, I asked. I was curious as to how it worked. Anyway, he also told me that the system records the dates and times. We can check if any of the dates and times are approximate with the baby's age, and we'd be able to tell where Locklear was at the time. If we discover where the infant was taken from and compare it to her locations, then we'll know she's the kidnapper. It adds something to what we have against her. And if she does indeed do what she told Benjamin, and I'd be heartbroken to find that out, maybe she was instrumental in Benjamin and Melissa's kidnapping, too. And Henry's. The only thing we really know for sure is that Slater, himself, took Margie. And the USB could possibly have the pictures that Benjamin saw, and even more info on it." Sam paused. "Oh, and," she said, excitedly. "Locklear Henderson—if, in-fact, she's involved in a child-kidnapping ring—

has been doing this a long time. So why now is she becoming careless? To store items in canisters? That's uncreative at the least. No. She knew Slater was dead. One of her sources told her. She had the weekend to pack, and she left when the children returned to the apartment. She *knew* what she was sending the children into, that dirty-dog. She deliberately set things up, knowing we'd apprehend her. Who knows? Maybe she wanted to end this. Did she ask for a deal? When can I get ahold of her again? Oh, my blood is boiling. She set us up, Brett." Sam sat lips compressed tightly with her arms across her chest.

"Yes, we'll examine the nav system for sure, and I got it all, Sam, and it makes sense, but we're not jumping in, yet. We take our time in order to insure everything against her will stick. The bureau wants no losses on a technicality. We arrested her on illegal gun possession charges last night. We haven't put a classification or degree on it yet because it may or may not turn out to be part of a bigger case, though it's going in that direction. With a stern judge, even though it could be a misdemeanor, she could get one-year jail time. That might not be enough for her to call for a deal. I want to pile it on, when everything falls into place. She doesn't impress me as a hardened criminal who'd cope well behind bars. She's maternal and soft. John thinks she held that infant on the blue cashmere sweater in a loving way. I think she'll break-down fairly quickly."

"Has she asked for an attorney?" Sam asked.

"Believe it or not, when she was arrested right in the holding cell, she didn't say a word. She was nervous to the point the female officer thought she'd pass out. The officer had her sit down, got her water, tissues. In the report, the officer wrote that Henderson's pupils' dilated—she looked frenzied as if she didn't realize what happened or where she was. It was as if she'd had a memory lapse."

Sam sneered.

"Yes, it could be an act, Sam. Give me some credit. They were ready to call an ambulance. The officer asked her if she'd like to call an attorney. All she got in response was, 'Yes, yes.'"

"If she's involved in something like a kidnapping ring, she's a lot more sophisticated," Sam rebutted. "I don't buy that poor-me, scared-me attitude at all."

"Agreed. We'll have a lot on the USB device," Case added. "Agent Mullen will be here soon, and I'm sure we'll have a few hours work. Other agents are on the footprint ID and contacting the biological parents of the baby held on the sweater. Hopefully, we can reunite this infant with them as soon as possible. And what would be even luckier is if this happened in New York. With Henderson's work schedule tied so tightly to Slater, I doubt if she had time to travel far. What would be even better is if Withers would find a picture of the same baby in the room off the pantry."

"Again, the nav system will tell us all her locations—"

The door swung open and Agent Mullen leaned against the door to roll in the laptop. "Beat you to it, Detective," he said, smiling. "The end of Locklear Henderson and the kidnapping ring is coming to a quick collapse." He set up the laptop on the corner of the table, sat down, and took the remote out of his attaché. "From the photos Detective Withers sent in, we've got a bunch of possible kids in transit and the Slater kids aren't on these documents, so we're not a hundred percent where we want to be yet. Ready to see this?"

"So does that mean Sam will be going under with you, Brett, sooner than later?" Frank asked.

"Definitely," Case said. "Get ready to be a single dad for a few days."

Sam tossed Frank a sad look.

"Ready?" Mullen asked again, ignoring the sentiments.

"Go ahead," Frank said, sounding to Sam as if this meeting wasn't on his mind.

"First, the nav system led us to Prospect Park in Brooklyn, Chelsea Park, Central Park, all during school hours when Henderson didn't have the Slater children. The dates and times of arrival and exiting the parks are noted in the written report." He distributed the reports around the table. "There isn't a time of day that the parks aren't crowded, but it lessens in the children's area late afternoon. The USB held videos and pictures of children who were the targets even before their abduction. And not every child in the pictures was kidnapped. Some they might have decided against taking or the most opportune moment to carry through hasn't arisen yet. We will make contact with all of the parents and put them on warning. Yes, we did find exact matches of children in the pictures and videos. Someone in their organization filmed children first, which is what kidnappers do, then they assess the danger, the parent's schedule, who else is around, and they go back. Henderson seemed involved in every part of this operation, though we need specifics verified from her. These videos were within the past six months. Interestingly, she wore a cashmere sweater in all of the kidnappings. Their softness, maybe. Her presence is a constant." He pulled up a Prospect Park scene on the laptop. "Focus right there at the monkey bars, dead center. It's two-thirty in the afternoon; the less-crowded time because parents leave the park to pick up school-age children. The swings are to the right, the slides to the left. There's a young mom, mid-twenties, pushing a four-year-old boy. Look behind her to the left. That carriage. It's for an infant. We have that same family three times. Now this is where we nail her."

"Look who we have here," Sam said, "and she's wearing that baby-blue cashmere sweater. Wait! So someone was filming her!"

"Yes, Sam," Brett said. "It's their system of checks-and-balances. Henderson may not have been the organizer, or even the one to hand over the children to the adoptive parents, but she may have been the selecting person. I'm beginning to believe in that wanting-to-end-it-story. With Slater dead, and her now being unemployed, she'd have the freedom to leave the country. She also had to know, we'd be interviewing the children—the extremely verbal, bright children. Her end was near. What else?"

Mullen continued. "Watch her. The play area emptied. The four-year-old decides to make a run for it. The mom checks the sleeping infant then darts off after the boy. Locklear slips over, lifts the infant, and watch this, she runs to the nearest exit, but the exit is out of this camera's view."

"Oh, my God!" Sam exclaimed. "No hip and back issues there. Could it have been any easier? What happened next?"

"We don't have that on film, but there was a police report. The local precinct is gathering the file and will be sending it over. The baby was two weeks old at-the-time. This happened in October."

"That poor mom," Sam said with her heart bleeding. "He's five months old now. Benjamin told us about a strange happening in October. The only way to find out where the baby went is to ask Locklear. Ooh! This was before Margie came to them. So, if Locklear is *still* doing this, who's watching Margie?" Sam smacked her thigh. "I bet a lot of people are involved. And we'll find more USBs."

"We'll find out," Case said.

"Yes, Sam. Benjamin was correct," Mullen confirmed. "Mid-September she was scouting Central Park, but there were no reported kidnappings."

"We got her, Sam," Case said. "Now we have a lot to put on the table. Great work, Mullen."

"Don't thank me. It's the advances of technology."

"Sam, I think the feminine persuasion would help now." Brett sounded like he had an idea. "Feel like taking a road trip?"

"To where?" Sam said suspiciously.

"To meet with Miss Locklear Henderson. Since this is a federal case, she's detained in Manhattan, though no ties to terrorism. Her luck, but she brought it on herself."

"That's the same jail where Leonardo Philetano, AriellaRose's street pharmacist and boyfriend from the Aries case was placed," Sam said.

"Actually, no. He was at the Manhattan all-male detention center. Though now, Philetano is in an upstate prison, I'm guessing the first of many. And I'll give you a gift."

"What's that?"

"I'll place Locklear Henderson right into your lap. She's all yours."

Sam smiled from ear to ear.

"And what do you want me to do?" Frank asked.

"Go home. Prepare the kids that Aunt Samantha won't be home for a few days. Sam, go back to your own house. I want to avoid emotions changing your mind. Pack for a few days. Do you have any want-to-be-mother clothes?"

Sam laughed. "Excuse me?"

"We're going under as a married couple who'd been trying to conceive for several years. I already told you what the bureau will have for us. So, corporate-casual like you wear, without the bling. You're a fifth-grade teacher."

"And that I was. And I wore the bling."

"That fits your happy, assertive persona, not a married woman who's been trying for years to conceive. The more conservative the attire, the better."

"What happened to my needing clearance by the department and bureau?"

"Because you *were* a teacher for ten years before joining the NYPD, and you spent five years in juvie, your cover was easier than usual to set up. And your record in the past few cases proved you're capable, so Lieutenant Rojas, who knows you well, signed off on the paperwork. You'll just have to agree and sign, as well."

It really is happening, Sam thought.

"We'll need some time anyway to make sure Locklear's attorney is available for later on, and I'll have to get clearance for us to see her."

"Speaking of her attorney," Sam said. "If he's connected to this ring, won't that nix our chances of going under as a couple? We'd be made in less than a second."

"Believe it or not, Locklear *is* playing that poor-old-lady card. She went with Legal Aid, and right now it's a misde-meanor weapons charge."

Sam grinned.

"Yes, Detective. I like surprises as much as you do. You'll need to change. Don't wear any shade of blue or green. Put on a sports bra, nothing with wires. No jewelry, including your pendants." Sam sneered at him. He raised his palm toward her. "Don't get on your high-horse. I know you know the dress code on the inside—in the back of your mind. I have to bring it to consciousness. One small thing against their rules, and we don't get in. They don't bend for us. Clear?"

"Clear."

"No metal on any clothing, no decoration. A cotton tank top under your pants suit jacket. No metal in shoes either. Sneakers with laces with plastic tips. Wear full briefs in case they ask you to lower your slacks."

Frank raised a brow.

"Knock it off, Frank, you've been there. No spandex, no skinny jeans. I've never seen you do it, but no chewing gum—"

"I get it, Brett. Really, I do. I've been to Rikers."

"More strict here, and we want it that way."

Agent Mullen pushed the door open again. In his gloved hand, he carried the manila envelope securing the USB. "I have a surprise. Locklear Henderson's prints are not on this device."

"Then whose are?"

"None other than our decedent, Henry Slater. And only his."

"All right, have a seat," Brett said contemplatively. "We have to work this through. Any time-frame?"

"Hard to tell," Mullen said. "But they're fresh. The pasta in the jar didn't interfere. Interestingly, the gun-box and safety deposit box keys did have Henderson's prints, as well as the car key-fob. As for Slater, he knew you were close. If he was going down, he wanted to take everyone with him."

"Could it be he wanted to cleanse his conscience?" Sam asked.

"No, not Slater," Frank said. "He was egotistical. I didn't see any remorse, even when he wrote out the confessions. He actually told us there's no emotion. For him, it was monetary. He paid the families off. Look at Barbara Montgomery from the Gemini case. She wanted to take everyone with her, too, and she went after Trenton's wife and Ricky. No, Slater is more like Montgomery. They both had a soft spot for kids. Slater is doing this to end something he can no longer control. He was probably active, if not the spearhead of this kidnapping ring. He wanted the glory. In light of this, it's a good thing you didn't want me to go UC, Brett. I'm sure they'd seen Slater. Now, did Slater plant this device to get even because Henderson was blackmailing him?"

"Whatever it is, this new-found information will cause her to roll real fast," Case said.

CHAPTER 18

S am couldn't believe that, even with Brett Case's influence, they had to wait forty-eight hours to see Locklear Henderson. Court time took up the Legal Aids attorney's day. The dusk wind rushed the mid-February frigid air through her as Sam and Brett walked down the block to the facility. He forgot to tell her a couple of details she remembered—to wear one layer of clothing under her jacket, and no pockets. That last one was a challenge with her wardrobe. But she found a pair of boot-cut pull-on cotton jeans without pockets and bling. *Who said having so much clothing was a negative?* They'd left their overcoats in the car, and she wore a long sleeved T-shirt under her blazer. Nonetheless, she shuddered.

Greeted by armed guards at the front entrance, who stood stoic with frowns, didn't do anything for Sam at-the-moment. She shot through their intimidating glares—and their stature compared to hers—by merely showing her badge, accompanied by the same frown. She could have sworn she received a snicker as the guard opened the door for her and Brett Case. One foot into the facility, they slipped their weapons into a lock-box, hung their jackets on a hook for scanning and putting into a closet, walked through a scanner with their arms above their heads, and then were escorted to a room with a sign on the door, *Legal Consultation Room.* Agent Case carried the evidence bag with the USB in plain sight. Sam and Case peered through the bulletproof plexi-glass on the top third of the steel door.

Sans wig, Locklear Henderson with short, cropped gray hair—and an ashen complexion to match—sat at the conference table, looking forlorn and definitely her age. Not a spot of makeup covered her liver spots on the sides of her face, or deep lines above her lips. Two nights behind bars certainly had its effect. *How would she cope with a long prison sentence?* Sam didn't give it more than a moment's thought. She couldn't have cared less.

The youngish attorney sat back in the chair with her arms across her chest, papers on the desk, apparently done with explaining the process to her client. Case nodded and the guard opened the door, permitting the detective's and agent's entrance. Then the attorney sat up straight while Locklear remained slumped in the chair.

"Sorry to interrupt your afternoon, Miss Henderson, but we have a lot to talk to you about," Case said.

"I'm Constance Contrell, Miss Henderson's attorney. Why am I here? You know we're overloaded, and we only see clients at courthouse for their indictment. How did you pull this one off?"

Brett Case placed the evidence bag on the table then made the introductions. Sam noticed Locklear's gaze darting toward and away from the clear plastic front. She assumed from Brett's snicker, he did too. "This is an FBI investigation, and our director sent orders to your office."

"When am I being released?" the detainee asked. "I can afford the bail."

"It's too soon for that," the attorney replied, patting Locklear's hand. She addressed Sam and Brett. "You have the weapon, so it's out of any harm's way. With Miss Henderson's impeccable record, I'm sure we can negotiate you dropping the charges."

Sam smiled. "Sorry to disappoint you, but new evidence has arisen, and before you jump down our throats, there was no time to get a hold of you, nor opportunity, plus our crime scene investigators are still at Miss Henderson's apartment collecting data." She paused for it to sink in.

The attorney shot a suspicious glare toward her client. "Miss Henderson, are you aware of what they might be talking about?"

"I haven't the slightest idea."

"I'll enlighten you, Miss Henderson. We found your Lexus."

Hearing the last word, Locklear jumped up from the seat, and as she shouted, "No!" she attacked Sam, trying to pummel her face with both fists. Agent Case thwarted the attempt, throwing his body across Sam—hard to do in the tight space between them and the desk—making himself the target as Henderson's fists landed on his back. The guards burst in and pulled a struggling Miss Henderson away, handcuffing her. They held her against the back wall.

"You okay, Detective?"

"Yes, Agent," Sam replied, recuperating from the warmth of the FBI agent's chest across her breasts. "Yes, thank you. We can add 'assaulting a police officer and federal agent' to the accruing list. Sit her down, please. That unfortunate incident cannot delay this."

The guards shackled Locklear Henderson's feet to the legs of the chair, and her hands to the bar on the table in front of her.

"So what if you found my car? Yes, I have a car. I had to hide things from that controlling bastard. He didn't want me to have a life."

"Um, so now your faithful boss who rewarded you with extra money when you had to change your vacation plans is a *bastard*?"

Locklear's eyes widened. She obviously realized where that bit of information came from.

"Where did you go? You had to be home for the children after school."

The lawyer intervened. "Don't say a word until we have time to talk. They already know. Police tactics one-oh-one. Right, Detective? Police ask questions they already know the answers to."

Sam smiled. This attorney was sharper than she gave her credit for. "Okay, yes. You're correct. I'll tell you what we have. In the search of Miss Henderson's apartment we found in addition to the weapon, a couple of keys—one to the gun case and the other to a safety-deposit box."

Locklear's gaze darted to her attorney who sat with her lips parted.

"In addition to the matronly clothing in your bedroom closet, we found another hidden closet. You know about Mr. Slater loving his hidden rooms, I'm sure. There was a dead scorpion in a kitchen canister. We're working on finding out how that creature wound up on your kitchen counter preserved for humanity to see at some point in time."

The attorney's face contorted into a ghastly expression.

Sam sucked her cheeks in. "Oh, the additional closet. Gorgeous business style clothes for you. Many suits. Expensive ones at that. We also have a damn good idea where you went to wearing those clothes."

"Really? Impossible."

"No. Very possible. The navigation system matched your destinations, including time and place, with this." Sam held up the manila envelope containing the USB device.

Locklear was shocked. "That's not mine! I swear!"

"Then why was it found in one of the canisters containing pasta rounds on your kitchen counter?" Sam fell silent, crossing her arms across her chest.

Locklear became frantic. She tried to pull her hands loose, to no avail. She jumped barely an inch off her chair. "Please, Miss Contrell, that's not mine."

"Then whose is it?"

"What's on it, Detective?"

"What do you think can be on it, Miss Henderson?" Brett Case asked. His intonation must have sent a message to the attorney.

"I must, bound by law to protect Miss Henderson's rights, end this interview in order for me to have time to speak with my client privately."

Sam and Case nodded.

"Okay. We'll give you thirty minutes, right now. We'll be in the waiting area. You'll be pleased we forced you into coming up here today." Case turned to the door, called in the guards, explained the situation, and he and Sam were escorted out, with both of them smiling on the inside.

❧❧❧

Jarrett Miller waited until after dark before he took refuge in a shady motel on Tenth Avenue in Manhattan. The girls on the streets paid him no attention, and he ignored the ruckus they caused with their clients inside the rooms. Even if a john was beating up his girl, Jarrett dismissed it. He wasn't a do-gooder and turned his focus to some needles in the corner of the room that stuck out from the curled carpet edges. He grimaced, glad he wasn't a user. He just supplied these fine folks what they needed to stay happy. Yeah, he was a gem of a guy, he thought, laughing out loud.

Nothing would distract him from his goal—finding Victoria Elizabeth Marin. He hadn't stopped thinking of her, more so since he heard her smooth Southern voice on the phone. Knowing better than to think she was speaking to only him, Jarrett put the police presence out of his mind. He took the SIM card out of his jacket pocket and inserted it into his smartphone. Yeah, right, *his* smartphone, he thought. It was a bonus find in the first car he stole. He removed the card in case the cops tracked it. What the heck? He planned to use the phone only for a minute.

He pulled up Safari and wrote Victoria Elizabeth Marin into the search bar. Maybe at the very least he'd find her Facebook page. He stared at the screen, his face heating up then flaming. There she was all right. All gussied up on date with a Dr. John Trenton going to a children's hospital charity event. Whoa! That was his Vicki? With a New York City doctor? He looked at the date, 2013. Clicking on all ten of the links on the page, he saw his Vicki at different functions and locations throughout Manhattan. Then he read a current article. *Dr. John Trenton, formerly New York City's most eligible bachelor, with his beautiful wife, Victoria, was seen today with their children, nine-year-old Ricky and three-month-old twins, Alexi and Zach, at The Stage Deli in New York City.*

When was this? Crap! Crap! Fuck it! Five days ago. Five days ago, his ex was having the time of her life with a new family. A nine-year-old? Must be from that creep's first marriage. "That family should have been mine!" he screamed at the screen.

Okay, Vicki, the stakes have risen. I'm taking your children down with me, too. They'd be my easiest kills yet.

ↁↂↁ

Sam and Brett sat opposite Locklear Henderson, still shackled and handcuffed, and her attorney at the table. Sam stared at the woman who'd had aged fifteen years in thirty minutes, her eyes being the dead give-away—redness, profuse tears, the dark circles under her eyes became puffy.

"Okay. I hope your attorney advised you to cooperate."

Contrell put her pen down and addressed Sam. "We want to know what's in it for us."

"Too premature for that," Sam said. "What do you think is on the USB?"

"Pictures and videos of my client in uncompromising situations."

Sam stopped dead. She was a newbie attorney after all. "Okay, please be specific."

"Henry Slater was an evil man. What he did and forced Miss Henderson to do was unconscionable."

Sam brows furrowed. "Again, you need to be specific. In legal situations, we cannot assume we're on the same page."

Locklear nodded to her attorney.

Constance Contrell blushed.

Sam crossed her legs. *That's an inappropriate reaction to this situation.*

Miss Contrell swallowed. "He made Miss Henderson bathe him in the tub, with her being naked, and you can imagine how embarrassing that is for an older woman. And he filmed it."

Sam did all she could do to prevent it. Her stomach ached. She looked at Brett and the both of them burst out laughing at the shock of the unexpected. It took her a few moments to compose herself. "Seriously? Really? Seriously? That's what you got out of a thirty-minute conference? Oh my God. And you believed her? Even *after* we told you about the closet with expensive business clothing? What you should have done, Miss Contrell, is ask to view the videos on this device for yourself, because what your client told you and what's on this, are two very different things. In fact, Agent Case, can we view this together? In all honesty, I want to cut through this bullshit as quickly as possible. And I know you, as well as me, are not in the mood for such foolishness, the expression Miss Henderson likes to use."

"No. I don't want to see it. He made me do it."

"Your attorney needs to see this so she can give you her best possible representation," Sam said. "Who made you do it?"

"Henry Slater. He told me if I ever did anything to upset him, he'd hand it over to the police. I never thought he'd plant it in my apartment. How dare he?"

"How dare he? How dare you wear a blue cashmere sweater, stake out Prospect Park looking for a two-week-old infant for you to kidnap and hand over to new parents?"

Miss Contrell gasped, placing her hand over her chest.

"Yes, Miss Contrell, your client was involved in a kidnapping scheme spanning many years." Sam glanced toward Brett. He nodded, giving her the clearance to make the arrest. The guards entered, Sam declared the arrest, read Locklear her Miranda rights, and got up to leave with Brett, leaving the envelope on the table. "This is a copy for you, Miss Contrell. We have the original. Please review this with the higher-ups in your office. Miss Henderson will need qualified representation." Sam handed the attorney her card. "When your client is ready to tell you to whom these kidnapped children were handed over, we need to be notified immediately. With these charges, her flight-risk ability, as well as possible damage to the case by contacting other involved parties, we will be insisting on no bail. A possible sentence with all of these counts accrued could be life in prison without any chance of parole. I'm sure your client would like to avoid that."

The attorney sat with jaws dropping as guards escorted Sam and Brett out.

As the door shut behind them, Brett whispered to her. "Expect a call soon."

CHAPTER 19

Two Weeks Later:

Sam wheeled her suitcase up the driveway to the house, walking side-by-side with Brett Case as they were beginning their new life together as husband and wifey. *Yikes, husband and wifey?* He used that term driving up here. She'd become Brett's wife before Frank's. That wasn't supposed to happen. Maybe she'd get some good marital tips. Brett was Frank's age, had four kids and one on the way, and he was happily married for over eighteen years. Okay, she'd use this as a learning experience.

John Trenton had found a fully furnished rental for them a block away from his home in Scarsdale, New York. Though his house was massive and striking, this one was smaller, a three bedroom, with almost the same square footage as hers in Brooklyn—nineteen-hundred. She didn't realize that Scarsdale had smaller properties. If the inside of the impeccable Tudor mimicked the outside, she'd like living here. The multi-shaded bricks brought a smile to her face. She loved color and when she approached the doorway, Sam couldn't help but run her hands over the textured surface. *Really nice.*

Brett had to notice her quietness. "Nervous?"

Sam smiled. "No, just admiring the brick work. We have Tudors like this in Marine Park."

He opened the door, and the inside furnishings didn't disappoint—contemporary furnishing with straight lines and no glass. Everything showed these adoptive-parents-to-be knew what childproofing meant. To the world, they were Mr. and Mrs. Anthony Freeman—she, Amanda, a fifth-grade teacher at a private Manhattan school, and he an English professor. An *English professor? Him? Brett? Maybe in a past life.* She wondered how the FBI created these profiles. Never mind, she thought. That was way above her pay scale.

On the plush, leather beige couch, Brett spread his arms our over the top. "Have a seat."

Sam's only choice was to sit in front of his arms. She sat forward so as not to touch him. Doubt began to set in. Why was she being so tense? So unsure of herself? This wasn't the Sam she liked to be. Her gaze darted to the brick fireplace on the wall across from them to the wood slatted fan on the ceiling, and back to the red rug under the coffee table.

Brett pushed her back and his left arm fell onto her shoulder. "Knock it off, Sam. You can do this. If not for the bureau, do it for the Slater kids. I know it's the first time you're going UC in this capacity, but I won't cater to your insecurities. I'm not tolerating it."

Sam swallowed hard. She appreciated how dedicated to his job this man was, and she had to live up to his expectations. "You're right. I can do this. Tell me what's happening. You were pretty quiet on the drive up."

"From now on, we talk to each other with our cover-names. You address me as Tony. I might call you Manda, but to everyone else you're Amanda. We bought this house in cash, seven-hundred thousand from my family's inheritance. We couldn't afford it on either one of our salaries. Previously, we lived in Queens, also a family hand-me-down, and we moved here to reduce your stress. You're on leave, in case they bring up your traveling into Manhattan for work. Maybe that was interfering with our ability to conceive. We're going to a community meeting tonight, and we'll be with John and Vicki. They're in on it."

Sam smiled.

"No smiles. We're not having any contact with their kids. So no twin-cuddle-time for you." Sam frowned. He sneered. "If we're lucky, you'll have another toddler to bring home to Frank and the kids, while we take this group down. The bureau is confident any child will be safe with you. We can go in for two children. A newborn will be the second, but we have to play that as it comes. John agreed to go in, and we can possibly use Vicki if there's another child in transit. Now, ready to go up and unpack?"

"Sure."

As they were walking up the stairs to the bedroom, He dropped another bomb with his back facing her. "We're in the same bedroom, the master."

Sam stopped on the sixth step. "Excuse me?"

From the landing, Brett turned toward her. "Are you kidding me? Yes, same bedroom, same bed. We're a happily married couple. They, and I don't know yet who *the they* are, but before an agency will let us adopt, they'll be coming to check us out, talk to neighbors, and they'll do whatever it takes to find us to be a set-up. Nothing can be at risk."

"Okay, I get it. The reality just set in. That's all. I can play the happily married *wifey*."

As she passed him in the hall, he swatted her behind. Sam turned abruptly toward him.

"Don't say a word, because in public we need to be affectionate. Handholding, maybe kissing. In the house, we can keep it professional. But get used to seeing me walking around as scantily dressed as I was in Strident."

Sam laughed. "Um, Strident. We certainly learned a lot to take Henry Slater down in that sex club. And some more things, too."

"I'm not shy, at least when my kids aren't around."

In the bedroom, Sam plopped her suitcase on the bed. She loved the country cottage furnishings. The light blue and cream floral wallpaper and cream-colored furniture coordinated with the style of the house better than the main floor. The fabric canopy over the bed had just the right amount of frills not to make it too girly.

"Speaking about not having the kids around," Sam said, as she opened the dresser drawer to put in her tops, "how do you do it—with your wife? The-not-having-kids-around issue has hampered Frank and me. We haven't had that time. When it was just Frankie, Frank's in-laws had him a lot, especially when he was working."

"Yours are much closer together in age than mine. And morning sex is great, when they're off to school. Steph is a stay-at-home mom, and I can go into work later. That works for us."

"Well, so far, we're both working, even on my supposed weeks off. I don't know if I can be that stay-at-home mom. Did Steph work before the kids?"

"She was a full-partner in a criminal law practice. It was hard to give up. But Steph's an only child, and she wanted more children. I don't think she misses working. You know what? When the time comes, you ought to talk with her."

"Thank you. Maybe I will," Sam responded as she went to explore the master bath. A blue and white tiled room matching the fabrics in the master continued the calmness and serenity that Sam needed right now. She wasn't happy with herself that Brett was so sharp and in tune to her anxiety. This man would be judging her and her future career with the bureau and the NYPD. *Come on, Sam, put on the act, just like you did with Henry Slater. You were never the wimp. Why now?* She had a lot to think about, but the ringing of Brett's cell interrupted. His silence forced her back into the bedroom.

With a broad smile, he grabbed his coat off the chair in the corner of the room. "Locklear Henderson wants a deal, and she's ready to tell us everything. Seven a.m. tomorrow." He glanced at his watch. "Let's go, honey. Our first gig as a married couple."

As he grinned from ear to ear, Sam felt as if her stomach sank six feet underground.

❦

Brett drove the FBI issued Mercedes sedan around the circular driveway in front of the community center and followed the arrows to the parking area. Pulling into a spot, Brett sat still for a moment, observing Sam. She'd changed for the occasion and in the chambray denim skinny jeans with a floral embroidered pattern up the outer sides of her legs with a matching moto-jacket, she definitely fit the persona of a Scarsdale woman. Her highlighted blonde hair flowing down to her mid-back cinched the deal. Looks could be deceiving, though. He doubted if Sam had the same perspective on life and values as their current region, though many of these women were New York City escapees, too. Sam was a Brooklyn woman, through and through. Hopefully, her assertiveness wouldn't alienate too many of the women. He smiled inwardly. Oh, yeah. She'd definitely do that. Actually, the thought of hearing the exchanges she might have excited him. He looked forward to it.

Looking out of the car window, watching the adults flow into the center entrance, Brett realized he'd never seen so many blondes in one place before. All that didn't matter. His concern was if Sam could pull this off. She did great going solo with Jesus Parvos in the Aries case, and again with Henry Slater just last month in the Scorpio situation. But could she work as a partner? A married partner? He knew how his wife felt about it. This wasn't his first time going UC with a female and having to live with her under the guise of marriage. His wife knew what she was getting into, but did Frank? One thing though, their trust of each other, rather Frank's trust of Sam, would be tested now. Sam glanced at Brett, apparently knowing that he was assessing her.

"I'm ready. So you can stop wondering about me. I'll be the social butterfly, if that's what you want."

Brett chuckled. "Okay let's go, honey."

Exiting the car, Brett came around the passenger side, and grabbed onto Sam's hand. Apparently, she'd gotten into character because she laid her head on his shoulder for a moment before they proceeded on the walkway to the entrance of this one-hundred-thousand-square-foot building. To his surprise, Sam's palm wasn't sweaty. *Okay, she's less nervous than I'd assumed she'd b*e.

John and Vicki should be inside by now and they'd be their liaison to the neighborhood. Brett liked having an inside-man, in this case an *inside couple*, who'd add credibility. Opening the door, he stared. The sight of the decor in the lobby had that wow-factor with the pastel and green-blue leather studded couches and club chairs, gray marble tables, and historical artwork covering the walls. Seating in various arrangements filled the lobby as individual rooms lined the perimeter. Brett's gazed scanned the gold plated signs on the walls looking for The Flower Room.

❧❦❧

As soon as they entered through the open double doors, Sam spotted John and Vicki toward the back of the room, sitting at a round table with three other couples. Vicki stood up and waved. Sam smiled and rushed over to Vicki with Brett following as the dutiful husband. The women embraced. Brett and John shook hands, as Brett noticed the jealous glares from the other women toward Sam, and lust-filled grins from their husbands. Sam noticed, too, and she poked her "husband" to snap him out of it.

Vicki made the introductions with smiles and handshakes. "So how did the move go?"

"It's tiring, but we're all set," Sam said as she unbuttoned her blazer before taking her seat.

One of the women, dressed-to-the-nines with imitation diamond rings and earrings that she was pushing off as real, moved her hand on the table toward Sam. The raised princess-cut-ten-karat cubic zirconia, that Sam knew Brett could identify as a fake in a millisecond, reflected in the light from the ostentatious chandelier above the table. "Amanda, I just love your outfit. It can't possibly be a real Meghan-what's-her-name? Oh why can't I think of it? She was murdered in November if I remember correctly."

"Yes, Erika. This is a real Meghan Mason." For added effect, she mimicked the woman's obnoxious tone. "I don't do copies. I can tell in a heartbeat if something's not the original." She patted her husband's hand. "Right, sweetheart?" She stared at the woman. "Tony says I'm notorious."

"She certainly is."

Erika squirmed and apparently wanted to pass over that comment. She didn't miss a beat before she spoke again. "Have you read about her murder? Oh, my God, honestly, it was like out of a mystery novel. Killed by a crazy lunatic girl who also killed her family, that is, except for her twin." She grimaced in disgust. "What a bizarre world that fashion industry is."

Sam had to hold it in. "Well, from the little that I did read, she was a very disturbed woman."

"Disturbed or not, I'm glad we moved out of the city. The police even named the murder The Aries case. Would you believe that? Thank God we don't hear of anything like that here."

Vicki leaned toward Erika. . "Did you forget our house was broken into four weeks ago? Things do happen here. Don't kid yourself."

"Well, I certainly hope that doesn't happen on our block." Erika turned her attention back to Amanda. "Anyway, with that woman—"

"What woman?" Sam asked.

"Now I remember. That Larcon woman, in that case.

What else do you know about it, since you were near there? We don't get the city papers. I just want to forget the chaos. By the way, I have a few Steven Larcon gowns."

"Much to the chagrin of my wallet," responded her timid husband.

"No, as much as I love fashion, I try to stay away from gossip like that." Sam looked at Brett. She wanted to avoid this conversation.

"Well, Amanda is very considerate of my wallet," Brett said as he patted her hand. "What is this meeting about, John? I never did ask."

John laughed. "No, you didn't. And I didn't say. I just wanted to get you two involved in the community. It's about financing a new swimming pool for the high school. That should peak your interest, right?"

"No, darlin', not financing," Vicki said. "That was done. This is to vote on the color for the tiles. Some people are arguing that it should *not* be the school colors."

A swimming pool? A meeting about a high school swimming pool? The colors? Oh, God. Suburbia isn't for me. Sam swallowed and put on a solemn expression. "So those of us without children will be contributing to this?"

Erika sat up straight in her chair. To Sam, it looked like she was contemplating how she'd hammer-home a message. "Oh, darling, you don't have children?"

The sledgehammer hit Sam hard. "Not yet. We're planning on adopting."

Erika quivered in her chair. "No, offense, John, Vicki, but I'd find that awfully hard. Those children bring so many problems with them. Just like your Ricky."

Sam revolted. "Excuse me? Those children deserve a loving home and parents who want them more than anything in the entire world. And Ricky is a wonderful little boy."

"Erika, that was uncalled for," Vicki said. "You mean to tell me your children are perfect?"

"Absolutely. Jeremy is on the honor role, and his class

president. He wanted to run for VP, but we convinced him to run for the top position. Why settle for second best? And Suzie,…well she's still finding herself, but she's thirteen, and Sol here says to have patience. She certainly is trying on me, though, but if I just give in, it saves me the tantrum, and I can stay sane. Anyway, so as long as she gets her A's and B's, we're happy."

"So you mean to tell me," Sam asked, "that you give into her every whim?"

"Just about," Erika delivered with a smile that quickly faded.

"Then how do her teachers feel about that?"

"W—What do you mean?"

"I've been teaching for sixteen years now, and children who are so pampered at home tend not to get along with others in school. It's the world-revolves-around-me syndrome." Sam paused a moment to let that sink in.

"Oh, no worries about that, Amanda," Sol said. "That won't happen in our house. My wife has claim to that one. Suzie is second fiddle to her. Right, sweetheart?"

Everyone around the table laughed—except for the wife.

"I'd much rather talk about something else, anyway. Children bore me. So what made you two, move here?" Erika asked. "Vicki told us you lived in Queens." She shuddered. "I couldn't imagine. It's so dreadfully overcrowded."

"Exactly. One of the reasons we moved. We were ready for more suburban living, and John and Vicki love it here. And I wanted to…relax," Sam said, almost choking the last word out.

"Now, I get it. Relax as in able to conceive?"

Brett put hand into his pocket and pulled out his cell phone. After a quick glance, he leaned in toward Sam's ear. "We have to go."

Sam pushed her chair away from the table.

"Sorry to interrupt folks, but I have to cover for an early class."

After the "ah, no's, goodbyes," Sam sprinted to the exit. Brett followed her just as fast.

∽∾∽

Locklear Henderson pivoted into every conceivable position, twisting and turning her body on the clumpy mattress in her six-by-seven-foot one-person cell. She landed flat on her back, staring at the pebbled, peeling, white-brick ceiling. She tugged at the undersized prison garb, loosening it from her back. It was obviously made for a smaller-busted younger woman, one whose breasts didn't sag almost to her waist. Ugh, what an ugly shade of green. That was the least of her worries now. The four walls caved in on her. She closed her eyes in fear of what the rest of her life in this room, or a room like this, would bring. The vision wasn't a pretty one—abuse by the guards, other inmates, no freedoms. Her life as she knew it was over, two weeks ago. Would a woman her age receive special privileges? Yes, probably she would. How many Caucasian women in their late fifties were incarcerated in a federal prison? Not many, she'd bet her bank account on it. At the very least, they wouldn't keep her with the general population. Or would they?

Some attorney she had. After looking at the videos, Constance Contrell had the audacity to advise her to tell the truth—what she knew about Henry Slater and how he came to have custody of his children—not to mention the little boy she kidnapped while she was wearing her blue cashmere sweater. Little did the almighty Miss Contrell—or anyone else—realize that sweater was worn with many of the kidnappings, so how would the authorities figure out even with DNA testing which baby was which? They couldn't, unless they went back years. For sure, the DNAs would blend. What the heck? She had no idea of the technology they used.

She knew what she was getting into when she signed up for this deal eleven years ago in California. Meeting Chantal Robinson changed her life for the better, or so she thought at the time. A chance for travel, huge amounts of money, and minimal risks as Chantal put it. After all, they were saving unwanted children from a life in the foster care system, taking children from teen girls who were unprepared to be mothers. Willing participants. Simple and quick, the transactions accomplished in one day with the girls being given five thousand dollars at the hand-over, and a couple of days later the baby being transferred to awaiting anxiously thrilled parents in a pretend-legal adoption for sixty grand. Well, it was sort of legal. A real attorney drew up the contracts and was present at the signing. A private adoption—legal. So private, the attorney failed to tell the loving parents the adoption wouldn't be registered with the state—not legal. No parent quipped at the fee. After all, matching the baby's ethnicity and age to the parent's requests took planning.

She'd been the scout, searching out the teen candidates. Local churches and soup kitchens never lacked in the supply of homeless, pregnant teens. If she was lucky, the girls had already given birth. That was good, too. Awaiting parents wanted children of various ages, not only newborns. No one would question the girl if she told people she'd placed her baby for adoption. They'd praise her for thinking of her baby's future. It was legal, according to the girls, and they had paperwork. All was good. Locklear was proud of herself, especially in the beginning, the first few years, actually.

All she'd had to do was to confirm the girls weren't drug addicts and they didn't have families to turn to. Easy-peasy. The girls gave birth in the comfort of a hospital on the state's dime, gave the social services an address where they'd be living, not mentioning that it was courtesy of their agency. The teen mom left the hospital with the baby and, as soon as they got to the apartment, the transfer occurred.

In cash. Clean. Simple. Their compensation could at least get the girls off the streets for a while, and Locklear hoped it would give them a new start. For a few years, all was good.

Yes, she needed to move after a while. It wasn't that the supply of babies dwindled, the agency didn't want anyone getting onto her. They paid for everything—her move, apartment, furniture, expenses of daily living.

Little she did realize the agency would be expanding their searches to kidnapping babies from hospital nurseries, parks, and even further to snatching babies right out of their cribs in their homes, taking them from their loving parents. After moving through ten states, and more than thirty baby-exchanges, Locklear found herself in Utah.

I hate Utah. No. I hate Henry Slater. It's your fault. You changed the owners of the agency. You came in to the picture and asked them to take Benjamin away from his mother. The powers-that-be didn't even question you, you bastard. Your son was eight months old. I don't even know the lame brain excuse you gave them. Yes, money does talk. You came in with a hundred grand. And who was I to question it? My commission for that deal was twenty-grand, the most I ever received, that is, until you wanted Melissa and Henry. All I had to do was case-out the houses, writing up the schedules for when the mothers would be out working or whatever. Then the team would send in someone to ring the bell to distract the babysitter with some nonsense about an impending brownout, saying he'd needed to check the outside wiring. Plotted to the minute, it worked every time. I was pissed you got Margie on your own. I could have used another twenty grand.

Oh well, I just had to go with it. No, I didn't. I planned my revenge on you. I had the perfect plan. I took quite a bit, holding it over your head that you wanted Melissa to be a boy. How dare you? That little girl was dying on the inside. All I had to do was threaten to turn you in. You just smiled and handed me the cash. I lost count already. Those feds found one account. That was the tip of the iceberg. I have enough cash for whatever bail they set. Yes, I'll be getting out of here very soon.

Locklear, what kind of a person did you become? A hardened criminal, that's what.

She exhaled deeply, rolled over into a fetal position, and fell asleep. The sound of the heavy locks opening at six a.m. woke her with a jolt. The hefty female guard grabbed her arm to wake her. Locklear turned arrogantly as if awoken from her beauty sleep.

"Get dressed. Your attorney is coming with the cops."

CHAPTER 20

Sam paced in the legal consultation room, waiting for Locklear Henderson. Seeing Brett Case relaxing and slumped in his chair behind the cold metal table made her skin crawl. The man's confidence unnerved her. Rubbing her arms with her hands did nothing to calm the nervous energy swirling though her. Last night was the first time she'd spent a night in bed with a man with whom she wasn't involved in a relationship. A restless sleeper, she'd must have bumped his legs about twenty times until she fell asleep.

Frank would push her over when her legs landed over his, or he'd compress her legs between his. This character, Brett Case, let her legs stay where they landed, without so much as moan of annoyance. He was probably thinking that this detective was more of a nuisance than he bargained for. Then again, he got even this morning. He had no qualms about coming into the bathroom when she was in the shower, and then again when she was putting on her makeup. Glad it was a double-sink master-bath, Sam and he just caught glimpses of each other through the corners of their eyes, with Brett trying to conceal a snicker as he shaved.

The nerve of him to remain quiet and not address the sleeping situation. He should have at least given her the courtesy of explaining why she couldn't settle down. She'd forgotten to pack her nighttime supplements, the ones with calcium and magnesium to help ease her self-diagnosed restless-leg syndrome. Maybe he'd let her go back to her house to get more of what she needed today. Slim chance of that.

The heavy click of the bolt snapping the inner lock on the door brought Sam back to the table, and Brett to assuming a formal posture. Constance Contrell, eyes peeled to the ground following her client and a guard, looked to Sam as if she'd been through the ringer and back, probably by her colleagues in her office. Inadvertently that law practice caught the case of the decade, one that would take enough money if the case went to trial to increase taxes. This would be that case where they'd beg their client to take a deal— any deal offered by the DA. Too early for that. Today's agenda would attempt to get Locklear to tell them what she knew. Specifics. They'd be after specifics.

As they sat at the table, Miss Contrell demonstrated right off the bat she was in over her head. "My office looked at the videos several times. We know the evidence is jarring to say the least."

"Jarring?" Sam pushed. "Look, let's make this simple. It's clear. Your client was caught red-handed. The man who took the video or who had access, is dead. Please, for the sake of the children, Miss Henderson, you and only you can make this right. You said you loved the children, do you, or do you like your bank account more?"

Locklear waved a dismissive hand. "I'm not their mother. I don't know what a mother feels. To answer your question, I like my bank account more."

Contrell closed her eyes.

"Don't fade out on us, Miss Contrell," Sam said punitively. Sam cringed, not done yet. "You're not a mother. I'm not a biological mother either. But I'll tell you, from the moment I laid eyes on the Slater children, my heart, my very open heart, enveloped them. Every ounce of my being fell in love. Just as if I bore them in my womb. The love I felt then could not be surpassed by any biological mother, and the love I feel now, after five weeks, knowing I'll have to return them to their bio mothers, is making my heart break. But it's because of this love, I'll go to any lengths I have to, to convince you to tell us what you know."

"Let's lay it on the table, Miss Henderson," Brett said. "I'll lay it down in simple legal terms since you're a hardened unemotional woman. I agree with Detective Wright. We're not going to stop. And believe me, my office has the resources to dig as deep as we need to, with or without you. So here's what it looks like legally, in years, of behind bars for you. This is an estimate, of course, until the DA compiles all of the charges. Felony kidnapping, fifteen years in New York State. In other states, it may vary. Now, that's for one kidnapping. My people are going through the videos as we speak, and they'll be counting all of the kidnappings and missing children's reports."

"Ooh," Sam exclaimed. "You've heard the term 'mushroom effect,' yes?" She didn't wait for Locklear to respond. "One thing leads to another, maybe another USB device will surface."

A guard entered and handed Brett a sheet of paper. He read it and a broad smile replaced the serious frown lines. He looked up and nodded to the guard who then left the room. "Well, well, well."

Locklear accosted him. "What is it?"

Brett handed Sam the paper. She figured it was a stall tactic to increase Locklear's anxiety. When Sam read the note, she gasped and whispered a silent "Thank God," facing the ceiling.

"What is it?" Locklear screamed.

"The infant you kidnapped from Prospect Park in October, remember him? He was two-weeks old. He's almost six months now. We identified him. Tyler Whyte. The FBI is interviewing his birth parents. His biological parents who desperately want him back."

"So what?"

"Wait. There's more," Sam said. "There was a paper trail. Crime Scene found his picture and pictures of prospective parents in the room on the other side of your pantry. All they have to do is track down the couple that has Tyler now, and we'll reunite him with his birth parents in a few days. Then I'm sure the adoptive parents will tell us where they had the transaction." *Transaction?* The word made Sam's skin crawl. "You know what, Agent Case? Our need for Miss Henderson is lessening. So we may not even need to present any kind of a deal."

"What does that mean?"

"You're fifty-eight, so you'll never be able to wear any of the designer suits in your hidden closet ever again."

"No. Wait. You wouldn't put a woman my age in prison."

"Where did you hear that?" Brett said. "From someone on another planet?"

"No. No. You can't find a paper trail. I didn't keep any such thing in that room." Locklear slumped in the chair after finishing her sentence.

Sam controlled a smile. "Then where? We're searching every bit of your apartment. We'll find it. Just let me know to which charity you want those gorgeous suits donated."

Locklear gasped then clutched her hand to her heart. "I can't breathe. I have a heart condition."

"Why did you fail to mention that? Or at the very least, tell a guard on your floor," Brett said. "They have a medical unit." He signaled to the door for a guard to enter. "We can't take a chance. Miss Henderson needs a wheelchair to take her to the infirmary. Make sure a doctor is on call."

While the guard took care of Brett's request, Brett focused on Locklear. "Before your breathing gets too tight from holding all of that in, why don't you answer Detective Wright's question?"

"The records are kept at the agency that handles the adoptions."

Another guard entered the room with a wheelchair and a paramedic carrying a bag of medical equipment. The guard helped a heaving Locklear into the wheelchair.

The paramedic checked her with a stethoscope. "She's not faking it. We have to move fast."

Sam didn't care. Professional or not, she was going to get the information she wanted. "Locklear, this might be the last thing you get to do. Make thing right." Sam raced down the hall, holding the armrest of the wheelchair.

"I—told—you. The—Deacon—Agency."

"Okay, good. Now how did you get three-hundred-sixty thousand in your accounts? We know Slater put the money in. We found the deposits. Were you blackmailing him for something?"

"Yes," Locklear said as her eyes rolled back and her face paled.

"Detective, enough," the paramedic demanded. He wheeled Locklear into an elevator.

I'm not letting up now. Sam followed them into the elevator, and she shook Locklear's arm. She was still with them. "Locklear, please. Tell me. I know you can hear me. Tell me, and we'll leave you to rest and get medical attention."

Locklear gasped out the words. "That—bastard—wanted Melissa—to be—a boy."

⁂

In the war room in the Manhattan-North precinct, Frank Khaos slumped in the swivel chair as John Trenton and Nick Valatutti stared at him in apparent sympathy, his gaze fixated at the file-cluttered table. Frank compressed his lips, holding in the rage building inside of him. He knew it was the inevitable. He was fighting the inevitable in his mind every day for over six weeks. Yeah, right. He put the blame on Sam. She'd be the one to fall apart, not him, the Special Forces warrior who put fallen soldiers back together in Iraq. Not him, the third degree Black Belt in BJJ who whipped everyone's butt in the cage. He was certainly getting his own butt whipped right now from the hearts of four children who deserved more than the hand they'd been dealt. "Okay. Thanks guys for handling those calls. Three out four mothers are coming in. I got that. Melissa's mother is out of the country. Don't know how long that will take. Brett's team knows what they're doing, so I'm guessing fairly quickly." He chucked the pen he swirled between his fingers onto a folder.

John stared through him. "So what's the problem?"

"Problem?" Frank responded snidely. "Okay, problem one. Sam's going to fall apart."

"Not Sam, you."

"No. Sam. She was born to be a mother."

"So, work on it," Nick said.

That earned the detective a dirty look. "When we have time. Okay, it's me. We love the kids. Frankie loves having brothers and sisters. He's pretty much an easy-going kid, but now even more so."

"We all knew from the beginning, and it was made clear to you and Sam, that our goal was to reunite the children with their mothers," John said. "From day one, it was made clear. You're talking BS, pal."

Frank's cheeks puffed out before he emitted a distressed breath. "Yeah. You're right. Time for some self-analysis. Look, I can't help thinking about my own mother. Did she place me the moment I was born? And why wasn't I adopted immediately, like Carl? I know. I know. I was with a foster family for four years. Why didn't they adopt me? Were they only in it for the money?"

"Whoa, whoa, whoa. Since when are you into pity-parties?" Nick said. "We've both known you a long time. Never did we hear you say that."

"Yeah. I haven't thought about in years. All right. Last night, Frankie came home with assignments for his spring break. It's four weeks out, but for those kids who'll be away—and it dawned on me, that's us—his teacher wanted to give them a head start. Yeah, John, I remembered what you got me into. I'll be confronting my bio parents in four weeks. That sucks."

"Mind catching me up?" Nick asked.

Frank frowned, not wanting to rehash one of most aggravating situations of the Scorpio case but he had to for the sake of this one. "In our meeting with Henry Slater a few minutes before he offed himself, he told me I had to deliver a message from him to our birth parents in order for the will to be carried out. They're somewhere in Crystal River, Florida, not far from John's parents. Now we find a trust. I'm sure provisions for his children will turn up somewhere, and my concern to have them set for life mandates that I carry through on his wishes."

"Listen to me," Nick said. "You've turned out damn good and successful. They did you a favor, and you've probably had a better life than you would have had with your first foster family. One thing the world didn't need was another Henry Slater."

"Yeah, you're right. And this guy," he said, pointing to John, "wanted me to thank them for giving me up. That's not happening."

The phone on the desk rang. "Detective Valatutti here."

"Brett Case."

"Hold on, I'm putting you on speaker. John and Frank are here."

"Henderson went into respiratory arrest when it got too hot for her to handle. She'll be all right, but the infirmary doc made us leave. I need you, Richards, and Withers to get what you can on the Deacon Agency. That's where the adoptions contract meetings took place. Look for the record of Tyler Whyte, the two-week old. If we can reunite him with his parents, we've done good. Sam and I will get into the agency, but not till I know what we're getting ourselves into. Another thing, John, the rubber dolly you found under the bed? Just Slater's DNA but when the lab guys cut it open, knowing Slater's penchant for hiding things, bingo. They found stock certificates and bank papers for each of his four children, the stocks from each of the casinos that Foods Unlimited, his business, supplied. Apparently, he was a legitimate partner and received fifty percent of the monies the restaurants brought in, in addition to what he got as a vendor. He must have inserted the papers into the doll as he took custody of each child. The dates coincided with their eighth-month birthdays. He planned their abductions from the moment they were born."

"Talk about control. He proved that again. And fifty percent?" Frank said. "That's high, don't you think?"

"Very high. They must have been appreciative of the man's talent. Or he blackmailed them into it."

"Hey," Nick said. "One case at a time."

"Who knows what will come up? Our white collar crime unit will deal with all of that. Slater's percentage will stop, of course, from his DOD, but what accrued will stick. The kids' bank papers are in high five digits, Benjamin the highest, Margie the least, which makes sense. When the kids are twenty-five, they're to be given their bank account with some stipulations. Frank, are you sitting down?"

"Yes, what bomb are you going to drop on me now?"

"Very perceptive. Just as Slater appointed your brother, Carl Glendale to be the executor of the other will, Slater appointed you as the one to hold onto his children's papers. You're to hand their monies over to them at twenty-five, the stipulations being that they've achieved at least a masters degree, and they're settled in a reputable career."

"Whoa. I have to carry through on his wishes with that, too?"

"Right. What's wrong with him having high aspirations for his children?"

"Knowing Slater's controlling nature, did he go as far as naming the careers?" Frank said.

"What are you thinking?" Nick said.

"First, tell me if he mentioned careers."

"He did, and it's uncanny how on target he was with his children's interests. He's was spot-on with Melissa. She wants to be an interior decorator and designer. He saw that and encouraged her. For Benjamin, and we know his verbal skills, he wanted him to go into some sort of counseling, or become a lawyer."

"Too bad on that one. Benjamin wants to be a brain surgeon. Granted, he'll have to be sort of a counselor with patients. What about the little guy?"

Brett laughed. "He wants him involved in a sports team, coach. That fits in with his climbing ability."

"Oh, man." Frank sat up in the chair. "Sam got me looking into that astrology stuff. All of those careers and it fits me, too, are Libran. The mediator, counselor, the arts, referee, lawyer, are all careers that bring people together. Slater did his research, chose the calmest-known sign. Sonja Santos told us this, too. Now he's controlling them through their adult life. To tell you the truth, I sort of like that I'm in control of the finances. That will be the binder keeping them in our lives. Yeah, I do like that. And it'll be motivation for Frankie. I'll go along with the masters but reputable career choice is totally up to them. That's the least of our worries now. How did Sam make out as your wife?"

"Not comfortable at all. Especially in bed. She couldn't get herself still. She blamed it on not having her night time vitamins."

Frank laughed. "Yeah, they do help."

"Well, I didn't want to get as close as you get, so I tolerated the bumping feet. To tell you the truth, I can't wait to get back to my wife. Nick, how did the calls go?"

"Benjamin's mother and her husband are coming in from Utah. They'll be here next week. She put me in touch with the PD and the detective who took all of the reports in Benjamin's kidnapping, and who apparently investigated. The babysitter skipped after the kidnapping. She didn't even wait until the mother returned home, so all investigative leads led to her being the kidnapper. The decomposed body of the girl, a twenty-year-old in college, was found one month later in The Red Desert in south central Wyoming.

That was some feat. It's over ninety-three-hundred square miles. Some oil diggers discovered her body feasted on by the wildlife. The case went dead after that."

"What was the COD?" Brett asked.

"Gunshot to the head," Nick said. "Execution style. Bullet went through the brain, and they cleaned up and took the evidence."

"So it wasn't Slater," Frank said. "Not his style."

"Not Slater at all," Nick said. "He was back in Florida, doting on his first born. And even though it looked like a mob hit, that was ruled out. And Lisa Brandt is still in Italy, closing some deals."

"That's telling," Brett said.

"Don't go yet," John said. "We need some clarification."

"Sure," Brett said.

"You and Sam are going into Deacon. Give us a timeline. Meeting the parents first? Sending the children home? What?"

"Okay, here's what's happening. I actually wanted to go into Deacon first and take it down, but in discussion with the home office, our original timeline didn't make sense. There are teams looking into adoption agencies in all of the states in which Henderson lived. That'll take time and we don't want to give them a heads up, obviously. So, we're meeting the Slater children's mothers first. We'll press them as much as we can. Chances are they know nothing about the agency. It's actually two different cases. These children went directly to their father. The agency was involved in their kidnapping, period. Frank and Sam will still keep the children until we get all the mothers together, as we discussed. Nick, your team will do online searches, find reviews, satisfied, dissatisfied parents. Contact them. Find out what the parents were told about the origins of their children. The excuses. That's major because when Sam and I go in, we can be in-sync, and the agency will view us as potential parents. We also might be able to match the parents who wrote reviews to the children's DNA on that blue sweater and the pics from the room in Henderson's apartment. We're looking for matching dates. And listen to this. The Deacon Agency is in Brooklyn, not Manhattan as Henderson told us. Another lie. So, here's the end result, Frank, you and Sam will probably have a toddler and newborn added to your crew, before the Slater children leave. Can your house handle seven kids?"

Frank's jaws dropped, and he didn't have a chance to answer.

"Don't answer. It's a rhetorical question. You'll make room. What we'll do is have UCs track any activity from the agency, especially Chantal Robinson whom we didn't bring in yet. She's got a tail, and she's been going into Deacon, the office in a building on Livingston Street. We do not know if they're leery now because they haven't had contact with Locklear Henderson. We couldn't get any specific info from her, yet. There's a lot of what ifs. And we're on a time crunch here."

"How so?" Frank said.

"In four weeks, April tenth, right, you're all going down to Florida to confront your parents. I didn't forget. So before that time, the Slater children have to go back with their moms, and the Deacon Agency has to be taken down. We're charging Henderson, and we'll add more charges as we go. Our trafficking units throughout the US will take over reuniting children over the past eleven years with their biological parents."

Frank fidgeted in the seat. "Where are you guys now?"

"I'm home. Vicki and Sam went to a Women's Newcomers Club. That should be fun. Sam, I should say, Amanda, wasn't thrilled with the idea. A couple of those women ticked her off big time the other night. We have no control over anyone from Deacon going in for references, so she's on orders to play nice."

"That's one thing I'll check on," Nick said, "if adoptive parents gave references and to what extent they were checked. On the other hand, Deacon may be cautious and not bother. A legit adoption agency would definitely do that, but this one? They'd be skimpy at best."

"Let's hope. I gotta run." Brett disconnected.

Frank stared at the phone. "Seven kids? He expects us to have seven kids?" He laughed out-loud. "Oh, man! Maybe that'll change Sam's mind about wanting her own."

John shot Frank his signature look and Frank got it. "That'll take you off the hook, won't it?"

Frank blew out a breath and swiped his hands down his face. "Freudian slip. But they're always on-target, aren't they?"

John nodded.

"No. I really do want a child with Sam. I love her more than anything."

"That's the first time I heard you say that," John said. "Now you need to tell Sam."

CHAPTER 21

A bizarre silence loomed over them as they searched on Google for the Deacon Agency. Sitting in his chair, Nick rotated his shoulders in an unsuccessful attempt to shake off the heavy energy, as the March snowstorm pounding against the precinct's windows did nothing to lighten the mood. The sky, dark and dismal, forced the detectives to use all of the overhead lighting in the war room, contrary to their preference of allowing the natural sunlight to peek through the blinds.

They were getting close to having to return the Slater children and take down the agency that precipitated their kidnappings. As a parent, his heart pained. Yes, he'd trained himself not to become emotionally involved in a case. He recalled seeing Steven Larcon's chopped body in Chelsea Park in the Aries conundrum last November which left him unaffected, as did interrogating the less-than-innocent adult children of the decedent. But this situation was different. Young children were different. He understood why Brett Case didn't want Frank or Sam involved this far into the investigation. Frank's emotional state earlier this morning showed him the shrink couldn't handle this, objectively, especially not knowing what they were going to find, if anything. Lex and Bella had to feel the same. They were the first to meet the Slater children and fall under the spell of their charm. Nonetheless, Case assigned them here today.

Nick stared at the computer screen—the same one Lex and Bella had in front of them. A search of the Deacon

Agency in Brooklyn, New York, yielded a mere ten hits in five seconds. Folders of forensic evidence collected from Locklear Henderson's apartment and children's identification from the pictures found lay next to his laptop on the table.

The detectives separated out the information into categories.

"All right. Let's do this," Nick said, taking the lead. "Links. We're looking for links. Here's a list of the kidnapped kids and the dates," he said, lifting the pile and then slapping it down on the table. "We have their parents' names and police reports. An FBI team contacted them to let them know an investigation is re-opening or ongoing, whatever the case was. Let's see if we can find names, any names, hopefully of the adoptive parents."

The first article showed a photo of the storefront of the agency off Atlantic Avenue. He studied the calligraphy in the font. Gothic looking. He didn't click on the article. The next item showed a stone building on Livingston Street, a formal, forty-story business building that housed over thirty corporations. The agency supposedly had an office inside the building. A stenciled sign on the glass front door showed the exact font. "Let's think about this. The first two listings. Brett said Robinson went into the building on Livingston. Let's start there."

"The real agency that does legit adoptions, if there is such a thing here, or a front?" Bella said. "Robinson could suspect a tail, and she'd do anything to throw us off. Though, the office inside here could be the legal adoption office. I'm sure the owner of the building checked them out before renting space. Their credibility is on the line. Which one should our guys go into? Hey, wait a minute. Brett and Sam need an appointment. They can't be accepted as a walk-in. Did they make any contact yet?"

"No. Not yet. They're still setting up their covers," Nick said as he clicked on the second link, showing the Deacon office-space in the building. "Look at this."

Bella and Lex clicked. Lex's eyes widened, and he curved his lips in approval.

Nick leaned forward and, with a bent elbow on the table, gently pounded his lips with his fist then pointed to the details on the screen. "Yeah, right? This is upscale. Those chandeliers alone are worth more than my house. Beige leather seating arrangements. But look at them. Without a scratch. No discoloration. How can that be? Burgundy carpeting and accents. Mirrors covering each wall. All this gives a definite persona of credibility. But it's really hard to judge."

"Sure does," Lex said, hesitating before he continued. "In Henry Slater style. The carpeting did it for me. So is—was—he a partner in this business, too, or just the decorator?"

Nick sat back in a contemplative moment. "Knowing Slater, and that this agency facilitated the kidnapping of his own children, I'd conclude he's a partner. Do they know he's deceased?"

"Let's think it through," Lex said. "Case didn't bring in Chantal Robinson yet. She had to know Henderson was going to Ireland for three weeks. For all she could know, the nanny could have extended her stay. Why would she interrupt her vacation? Deacon would think the same thing. We know Slater has one in the oven with Miss Monty, and it's not his pattern to have more than one at a time, so there may not be a need for them to contact him." Lex bellowed a laugh.

Bella looked at him from the corner of her eye. "What's so funny?"

Lex continued to laugh. "I just got the mother-load of an idea."

Nick was as amused as a rancid pickle. "So are you going to spill it, or what?"

Lex unbuttoned his sports jacket.

"Ah," said Nick. "Get ready for a long-winded story now."

"Never long-winded. You're confusing me with your partner. What if? What if Frank goes into Deacon?"

"Brett and Sam are going in."

"Hear me out. That could happen. But also, Frank could go in and, hopefully, we could find the person Slater dealt with in the kidnappings. He meets with that person, who'd definitely see the resemblance, and go nuts. Frank could tell him that he spoke with his brother, Henry, and he, Frank wants the agency to help him in the same way. Frank can go in to a long story about how the mother of his child is a dysfunctional woman, a horrible mother, and he wants the child. The courts don't see that so he has to take matters into his own hands—"

"Nope," Nick interrupted. "That's flawed. They had to know Slater was an only child. But wait a minute." Now Nick bellowed laughter. "What if, we do use Frank? But not as a real person?"

"Excuse me," Bella said.

"Hold on. I need John on this." Nick tapped the keys on the console phone.

"John Trenton, here."

"Hey, John, it's Nick. Lex and Bella are here."

"Hi, guys. What's up?"

"We're working on getting info on the Deacon Agency before Brett and Sam go in."

"Okay."

"We're toying around with an idea to use Frank."

"He can't go in. They'd recognize something is up in a heartbeat."

"We got that."

"So what's your idea?"

"There was something in the Gemini paperwork."

"How did you get to that?"

"I pulled it up when Sam and I first met Lex and Bella, a couple of months ago in the Scorpio case."

"They came onboard toward the end of Gemini."

"I realize that. But there was something about a cinematographer making holograms. What was that about?"

"Ah, Clancy Davis," John said. "He was the partner of Barbara Montgomery, and he made holograms to taunt, and cause the mental breakdown of Morgan Reynolds, Barbara's target. Barbara was big on sensory bombardment." John paused. "That's how my team was wiped out."

"Now, I remember," Bella said. "We watched that DVD. Clancy created the hologram to intimidate Reynolds and snuck up the fire escape at his apartment to play it on his walls. He made Morgan do some weird stuff. It creeped me out. Nick, you want to do something that gross?"

"No," John said, answering for Nick. "That may not work. We'd keep the style of a hologram with a montage of moving pictures, hazy backgrounds, weird positions, and stranger music, but the point would be to gain information. What were you thinking, Nick?"

"How about if we use Frank to pose for these pictures, dressed like Henry Slater? I'm sure one of Brett's techs could do it. And we play it when Brett and Sam go in, but they'd have to pretend they don't see it. Only the person interviewing them would."

"No," John said emphatically. "That would scuttle Brett's plan to get two children, who they have marked for kidnapping already. We saw a female toddler being stalked in the video, and they were also tracking a pregnant woman who looked like she was ready to give birth within a few weeks. This was probably the last thing Slater filmed before his suicide."

"That's right!" Nick said. "He told us this morning, he and Sam would be getting two kids, a toddler and newborn. I was working another part of the case. I didn't see that feed. If the children were already targeted, why doesn't the FBI contact the parents and tell them? The kidnappings could be avoided altogether."

"That's the question of a decade," John agreed. "You know what? Call Brett and conference us both in. I'll hold. But I have an idea how to use the hologram."

Brett answered on the third ring. "Hey, guys."

"You're being conferenced with John. We're working on the Deacon search."

"And?"

John sounded impatient. "You have kids already targeted. Why can't the kidnappings be prevented?"

"Fair question. That's not how we operate. Then we could catch the kidnappers in the act. That would end it. Period, without a link to the agency and there's no guarantees. We have an operation in place, and it's on a need-to-know basis."

"And we're not need-to-know?" Lex said snidely. "Come on, Case, thought you'd give us more credit than that."

"Need-to-know, Withers, whether you like it or not. You're doing a search? How many items came up?"

Nick startled at the question. "Only ten."

"That's it? Ten? Then it's totally a scam operation. A legit adoption agency would come up closer to a hundred. I'll bet whatever locations you find are fronts. They might have a legit brick and mortar location, but nothing goes on within the walls. Look for scam reports, negative reviews."

Nick's intonation changed. "We're going to do that."

"Anything else?" Case said, ignoring Nick's tone.

"Yes," John said. "We were tossing around the idea of using Frank in a created hologram to taunt the owner of the agency. Have him dressed up like Slater. When Clancy Davis used it on their target in the Gemini case, it weakened the guy. Maybe we can set the dialog in the video to ask certain questions, to which the owner will succumb. But he'd appear in the office when the guy was alone. Like the ghost of Slater."

"A ghost? A ghost doing an interrogation? Yeah, right. I'm seriously not in the mood for this. Don't go off the deep end now. Time is crucial, and we need every minute for planning. Slater's kids' mothers are starting to come in next week. Get me something I can use." Brett disconnected.

"Whoa," John said. "The true colors of FBI Special Agent Brett Case just came flying through."

"Oh, yeah," Nick replied. "Guess the FBI does think they're superior to us. Let's prove him wrong. Okay, John, we'll talk later. All right, back to this." Nick scrolled down the first page, articles about the adoption process and how the Deacon Agency could help want-to-be parents. Nick went on to the second page. A broad smile appeared on his face. He clicked on the first article.

Lex beat him to it. "Look what we have here. Testimonials from satisfied parents. No. No. No. This is too easy. I get the front thing, and what Brett said about a legit agency. Most perspective parents would go through a state-approved agency. We'll check these out, but I bet ninety-nine percent of these, if not all, are bogus." Lex scrolled down the list of parents that also showed headshots. "Now, I know they're bogus. Look at the fifth photo."

Bella leaned in toward the screen. "The woman with the short Afro? Hell, yeah. That's none other than Chantal Robinson. We just wasted an hour."

"Maybe not," Nick said, scrolling through the list. "Only seven. That's a small amount of so-called testimonials. These could be employees and I use that term loosely. We have their pics, let's start by looking up their rap sheets, and I bet they have them."

It didn't take long for the detectives to find rap sheets for the seven of Deacon's employees/satisfied parents. Mae King, three misdemeanor charges for shop lifting and a felony conviction for less than one ounce of cannabis that was dismissed; Milton Carey, three counts rental lease fraud; Catherine Spelling, three counts possession of oxycodone without a prescription over a two-year period; Geraldine Salmon, car theft when she was fifteen; Dallas Kayman, five counts real estate fraud—skipping with renters' security, first and last month's rent; Paula Ranger, possession of oxycodone without a prescription; and lastly, Chantal Robinson, stealing from homeowners while on babysitting assignments, three civil law suits that were still pending in different states.

"All nonsense stuff that would have gone under the radar if they weren't caught," Lex said.

Nick laughed. "Spoken like a true homicide detective."

Lex pulled a folder toward him. "Hold on. Let's check Robinson's cases against Henderson's known addresses." He thumbed through. "Okay, exact match. So their history is longer-term than New York."

Nick nodded. "At least we have something on them. I'll fax these pics to Case. As with Robinson, I'm sure he doesn't want them brought in, but he and Sam will at least have a visual of creeps they might come across. He might want to add a tail on all of them, too."

Lex picked up the folder of the kidnapped children and laid them out in front of him. He just stared.

"What are you thinking?" Nick said, leaning forward.

"Okay. Okay," Lex said. "Hear me out. Adoptive parents are so excited about their children they might post their pictures all over social media. The bio parents would post pics of their missing children, so why haven't they met? If my kid was kidnapped, and I saw a likeness of him on Facebook, I'd sure as hell take action. But, like with the Slater kids, Slater never even took pictures of them, yet alone posted publicly. I'm guessing the agency told these parents not to, under any circumstances, post pics of their children. And wouldn't that raise a red flag to the adoptive parents?"

"Adrenaline," Nick said. "In the excitement of the moment, they wouldn't think of it. Holding their baby in their arms, their laps, paying the sixty grand, the joy they're feeling would stop any common sense. And after the fact, if they did think that request was bizarre, would they want to risk losing the child they'd bonded to? I'm guessing not. A social media blitz of the missing children might attract the adoptive parents unless, the adoptive parents have less-than-noble backgrounds themselves."

"Doubt that one," Bella said. "People into crap, the last thing they'd need is a kid holding them down."

Nick nodded. "True."

He forwarded the pics of the employees to Case who responded in less than ten seconds with *Thanks*. Another text from Case came thirty seconds later. *Have u found adoptive parents?*

Nick turned his phone toward Lex and Bella, who both sneered. Nick started to write a text back, *we think it's likely that the agency told the parents not to post the pics on social media, like Slater didn't so finding the pics of the parents with the children is unlikely—*

Before he hit send, Bella interrupted him. "Tell him we're going to look at adoptive parents' forums and message boards."

Nick smiled in response.

"Yeah, my cousin adopted and she got a lot of support on those boards. Recently, too. Her son just hit six months." Bella sent a text to her cousin.

Nick widened his gaze, but he gave her a thumbs up and returned to the text, adding what Bella told him.

After Nick clicked Send, Brett responded with *Now you're thinking.*

Bella sat up straight. "Wow! That was fast. My cousin must have been holding her phone."

"What did you ask her?" Nick asked.

"For links to the message boards she participated in before the adoption."

Nick's posture intensified. "Have you met her son?"

"Not yet. We're not that close."

Nick paused in a pensive moment. "What's the baby's name?"

"They named him Calister, Calister Hendrick. Why?"

"Did you see the video? We don't have the reports yet."

"No, we missed it, but John, Frank, and Sam watched part of it with Brett," Bella said. "The FBI took possession pretty quick. Where are you going with this, Nick?"

"Six months? Adoption in New York City?"

Bella nodded.

"This may or may not be far-fetched, but ask her what agency dealt with the adoption."

Bella slumped in the chair. "Are you freaking kidding me? You think that my cousin's son could be that kidnapped two-week-old, Tyler Whyte?"

"Stranger coincidences could happen, Bella," Lex said. "We got Tyler's name from Brett, but is he included in the paperwork?"

Nick scanned page by page of the children's identification from the pictures found in Locklear's apartment. "He's not in this packet. Before I text Brett, ask your cousin the name of the adoptive agency."

Still slumped in the seat, Bella sent a text. When she read the response, she compressed her lips, closed her eyes, and mouthed, "Oh, no."

The detectives sat in a solemn moment before Nick text Brett. *What is the race of Tyler Whyte?*

Again there was a quick response. *Both parents are African American. Why?*

Nick text, *Bella's cousins are his adoptive parents from the Deacon Agency.*

⌘⌘⌘

That was a call he didn't want to get—a situation he'd be dealing with fourfold, soon. Frank raced down the front steps of his house and couldn't get into his Explorer fast enough. The meet-time approached for when he was meeting Bella and Lex at her cousin's house. He had to wait for his in-laws to get home from their veterans' meeting. The need for babysitters wore him down. He loved the idea of Sam being a stay-at-home mom. *Would she go for it? Yeah, if she was nursing her own newborn. She said it herself.* Yeah, he had to get a move on it. But he'd leave that self-analysis for another time. Today would be more pressing. *How do you tell adoptive parents that the son they love with their hearts and soul had been kidnapped from his birth parents?* If Benjamin and Melissa could understand it, so could Bella's cousins. Henderson told Brett that each child carried a sixty-thousand dollar price tag. Hopefully, these parents wouldn't miss the money, and the chance of them getting any back was no-chance-in-hell. Money was the least of it.

The trip to Bedford Avenue would take him less than ten minutes. He knew the area well. Upscale with money. He and Jen looked there for houses when they were house hunting. But they preferred a more modern look, rather than historic.

Bella and Lex had found a parking spot in front of her cousins' Colonial style house on Bedford Avenue in Brooklyn, a couple of blocks away from Brooklyn College. Having luck, Frank parked behind them. As they got out of the car, he watched Bella's gaze scan the historic block with houses maintained in the early 1920s tradition. Flawless, refurbished, keeping the era's integrity, these huge homes on the tree lined block—now barren in winter—had that wow factor. For sure, if the Deacon Agency sent reps to inspect her cousins' home, they'd be impressed, Frank thought. And raise the adoption fees.

With the driver's side door open, and with him looking over the door, Lex was too busy looking at the houses to pay attention to his partner, yet alone to Frank exiting his SUV. "What do your cousins do to afford this neighborhood?" Lex asked. "These houses go for in the three millions."

"A lot higher than that," Frank said, coming up behind him.

"Right," Bella said, glancing away for the moment. "Shawna is a stay-at-home mom. She's on leave from her husband's orthopedic practice. Travis is a surgeon."

"No wonder," Lex scoffed. "Frank, this'll be the hardest notification you'd ever had to do."

"For sure. How in hell do you tell adoptive parents that their child is a kidnap victim? And worse yet, the baby has to go back to his parents today." He exhaled a prolonged breath. "Let's do this. They know we're coming?"

"I called Shawna and asked if I could visit because I haven't met the baby. She sounded suspicious, especially since I asked her about the message boards and forum. And she knows I'm not necessarily a children person. But she said to come on over."

The trio hurried up the six steps to the porch that spanned the entire perimeter of the house. Frank looked up at the towering attic, and he walked to the front edge of the porch while they waited for someone to answer the door. "This house must be close to seven-thousand square feet. And I thought mine was big." When he heard the door open, he returned to the detectives. Bella's cousin, holding her cute baby boy, greeted them. The smiling infant had curly brown hair, chubby cheeks, and round brown eyes.

Bella made the introductions, but right away, Shawna knew something was up, and she didn't waste words. "Come on in, and Bella, you better be straight with me." She led them into a sitting room. The decor fit the era, wood carved furniture—rose-toned upholstery with shades of blue, and florals. "Please, sit."

The detectives sat in club chairs, while Frank sat next to Shawna on a longer couch. The baby babbled, and Frank put his hands out toward him. "Want to come?"

Calister smiled and jumped into Frank's arms.

"Oh, man. I love this age," Frank said, hugging him.

"Dr. Khaos, what kind of a doctor are you?" Shawna asked, pursing her lips.

"I'm a psychiatrist."

"Listen to me. I'm very upfront with my patients, no matter what their diagnosis is. I've learned to become bulletproof as they say. For Bella to text me, and now appear with another detective and you, something is up. Tell me. No small talk. No niceties. Just truth."

Whoa, this woman is hard-nosed, Frank thought. But no, she's a new mother. He'd go gently. "Mrs. Hendrick—"

Shawna sneered at Bella, knowing her cousin didn't tell her team everything. "Dr. Hendrick. I'm an orthopedic surgeon, as is my husband."

Frank compressed his lips, holding back a sarcastic smile. "Dr. Hendrick. How did you find the Deacon Agency?"

"I told you, no small talk."

"We need to know this information. Just go with it. Please."

"I met two women on a message board. Mae King and Chantal Robinson."

Lex readied to take notes. "We know their names."

Frank nodded. "What did they tell you?"

"They knew of a private, credible agency that could help us adopt. They'd be expensive but they'd help with everything. What is wrong?" Shawna began to stammer. "They—sent—me—papers—documents."

Here comes the hard part, Frank thought. This bulletproof woman was not a bulletproof mom. He glanced toward Bella who got the message, and she got up to sit next to her cousin. "We'll need to see the documents." Forcing the baby on her, he reached over Dr. Hendrick and handed Bella the baby. "Here, Detective, meet your little cousin." He grinned at Bella's intimidation.

Bella came through. The baby smiled, showing his two bottom teeth just piercing the gum-line. Bella held him and immediately Frank saw her facial expression soften. Bella returned the smile and ran her finger down the baby's arm. He giggled. "Wow, so soft." She took him into her arms and hugged him.

Frank reached out and held Shawna's hand. "Dr. Hendrick, if what we suspect is right and you've had Calister since he's two-weeks, correct?"

She nodded.

"If what we're thinking is correct, your son was kidnapped from his biological parents."

A long minute of silence passed. The sophisticated doctor was dumbfounded. "I must call my husband." She paused, trembling. "I—I—can't. He's in surgery."

"We understand, Doctor. You'll have a few hours to tell your husband," Frank said. "There's a plan in place to take this agency down, and arrest all those responsible."

"When? When will we have to return our baby to his natural parents?" Breaking down, she cried her words out. "No—it—can't—be. What if you're wrong?"

"We'll need your permission to take Calister's footprint and DNA."

Bella handed her a tissue from her bag.

"Yes," Shawna said as she wiped her eyes.

"I know how hard this is for you."

"How can you possibly know? We've been trying to conceive for nine years."

"I'm a parent. And I understand the love when you bring a child home. And suddenly things change."

"How would you know that?"

"I'm in the same position as you with having to return four children to their mothers."

"Four?"

"Yes. Please, don't be insulted. Our situation is different, but the same thing is happening. My fiancée and I have custody of my nieces and nephews," Frank explained cognizant not to tell her too much of the case. "My brother is deceased, and the Deacon Agency kidnapped his children for him from their mothers." *Yeah, there is no easier way to say it. She's a medical professional so she'll understand confidentiality.* "What I just told you is not to go further."

"Definitely. I understand. I can't imagine. How old are the children?"

"Nine, seven, three, and ten months."

"Oh my God! How many children has this agency kidnapped?"

"The FBI is investigating in ten states. The Deacon Agency has been in New York a few years."

Shawna patted her son's back as he slept contentedly on Bella's shoulder. "Oh, my God! As much as my heart is breaking, I took an oath to do no harm." Teary-eyed, she turned toward the detectives. "How I can help?"

"Thank you," Frank said. "We need to know step-by-step what the process was from the contact to handing Calister over to you and your husband."

"I can tell you everything. Do you have a couple of hours?"

"We have as long as it takes," Frank said.

CHAPTER 22

One Week Later:

Having to take time off in the Scorpio case, because his wife had a health scare hanging over both their heads, reinforced how much Nick loved his job. It had been the longest two weeks of his life. And the loneliest, in spite of the daily calls from Sam checking up on him. She'd become the baby sister he never had. He'd never let her know that, though. To Sam, he was probably the same hardened partner she met on the stoop of the house in Sheepshead Bay in November—the day the Aries case began—her first day in the rank—when they were called in for the domestic disturbance. Now he'd become her protector whether she wanted it or not. Whether she acknowledged it or not. Yes, on the job, they were equals, and he'd trust her with his life. She'd proven her competence to him—more than once. On the personal side, he'd hammer Frank until he'd do right by her. Frank wouldn't be here either today.

Brett Case wanted full objectivity, no personal involvement. Pure police work. The FBI agent didn't even want John to be in on the interviews—no one with a soft spot for the children because they had developed emotional bonds. They were interviewing in the war room, mainly because it had the largest conference table and seating,

Nick flipped through the documentation they had on the Slater kids' mothers, looking specifically at the reports they had on Sarah Phillips, Benjamin's mother who'd be coming in shortly.

Lex and Bella came into the room, Lex carrying a fast-food breakfast for everyone, including Mrs. Phillips, and Bella, a tray of coffees. "I guess you expected our hands to be full," Lex said as he used his shoulder and back to push the door shut.

"Nah, just wanted the air. Have you read this file?"

"Yeah," Lex said, sitting down, "including the description Benjamin gave Sam and Frank of his mother he saw in his nightmare." He slid the bags of breakfast and coffee tray to the opposite end of the table.

Lieutenant Martin opened the door and escorted Sarah Phillips into the room. Nick just stared at the nervous woman whose gaze darted back and forth between the detectives. It was uncanny how accurate Benjamin's description of his mother was, especially on the black dot on the top of her right cheek. The white coat he indicated in his dream had to be in a hospital setting. Dr. Phillips—according to the files—had a background in pharmaceutical research and now headed a hospital pharmacy.

Nick was the first to speak. "Glad you were able to arrange a flight, Dr. Phillips." He made the introductions. "Please, have a seat. I thought you were coming in with your husband."

"We're separated," she said, smirking. "It wasn't worth marrying him." She sat, without taking off her coat, and wrapped her arms around her bag as it rested on her lap. "The only information I have is from a phone call, saying it was about my son Benjamin. Have—you found—him?"

"Yes. He's—"

She broke down crying. "Is—he—dead?"

"No. He's alive and well."

"Oh, my God!" she said, moving her hands to her heart, throwing the bag on her lap out of balance, toppling it to the floor. The contents poured out from the unzipped tote. Bella bent down to help her, bumping heads. Sarah gasped. She sat up and composed herself, leaving much of the bag's contents on the floor. "How can that be? The police found our babysitter, shot, and they had no other leads. It's been over eight years. The police even spoke to Henry Slater, his father, and they even gave him a polygraph. Nothing. He was traveling all over the country with his casino restaurant business and his decorating business. Where is Henry? Have you spoken with him? Are you sure it's my Benjamin?"

Nick didn't want to interrupt her rambling. The woman needed to vent. It was interesting she gave them information about Henry Slater without prompting. *Another woman who is protective of him.* He just imagined what it would be like for his wife to go through something like this. Dr. Phillips went on for a couple of minutes. When she paused to breathe, he had the chance to continue. "Dr. Phillips, since you mentioned him, when was the last time you spoke with Henry Slater?"

"The end of January. And that's strange because we speak every couple of weeks."

"Hold on," Bella said. "You still have a relationship with him?"

"Yes. We're desperately in love."

Nick compressed his lips to avoid laughing. "Then why didn't you marry him and not the man you did?"

"His traveling. I couldn't deal with it. I wanted a spouse I can do things with—dinner, shows, traveling for pleasure. He'd never take me on his business trips. And then again, I'm not a free-agent. There are times I work a double shift."

"There's a reason for his behavior," Nick said. "And we'll get to it. But first, what kept your relationship going? There didn't seem to be anything in common."

"Wait a minute. I thought you called me about our son. Why is the conversation going to Henry?"

"Oh, we'll get to your son, but please, we need to make sense of this. What kept your relationship going?"

She shrugged. "Sex. Sex kept our relationship alive.

Henry is the perfect partner. Now where's my son?"

"I hate to burst your bubble," Lex said. "Henry Slater was the perfect partner, could have been the perfect partner, except for the fact that he murdered seventeen women. I'm guessing that's the reason he wouldn't take you on his trips. But there's a lot more."

"No, can't be. Where is he?"

Lex sounded happy to relay the news. "Mr. Slater is deceased, by his own doing."

Dr. Phillips sat stunned. Her eyes glazed over. She barely got the word out. "When?'

"January twenty-ninth."

"Oh no!" She sat almost catatonic for a couple of minutes.

"Dr. Phillips?"

She startled but came back to the present. "Yes. Okay. My son. What does Henry have to do with Benjamin?"

"The people who *kidnapped*—" Nick said, stressing the word. "—Benjamin did so to hand him over to his father."

Again, Dr. Phillips sat stunned, but she fired back quickly. "Can't be. The police investigated him completely."

"He was a proficient liar. Did you know he now has three children younger than Benjamin?"

"He told me Benjamin was his only child."

Bella leaned forward. "He told that to the mother of his youngest child, too, and I'm guessing to the others, as well."

"I can't deal with anymore. I'm ready to have my own nervous breakdown. Don't tell me anything else. I don't even want to know who he murdered, if that's even possible." She sat back and crossed her arms across her chest in a defiant move, Nick guessed, to stop a further inquisition.

Nick questioned this woman's ability to care for her son. "Dr. Phillips—"

"No. Just bring me my son so we can go home."

Bella glanced at the bags of food and cups of coffee. Pulling them toward her, she said, "Dr. Phillips, here, you must be hungry. I know I am, and you haven't eaten yet."

Dr. Phillips sighed and picked up the cup of coffee. "Thank you, Detective. No, I haven't." She unwrapped the egg-on-croissant sandwich. "I get very cranky when my blood sugar drops. I'm stable, but I do test several times a day. It's my profession that makes me so cautious."

"We understand," Bella said after she swallowed. "This is very stressful."

"Are you a mother?"

Bella smiled. "No, not yet."

With taking a few deep breaths, and after eating, Dr. Phillips seemed to calm down. "Please, continue. I'm sorry for my outburst. How is Benjamin and if Henry is de— deceased, who's taking care of him?"

Hold back on information, or not? Nick thought. "It's a long story. We found out that Henry has two brothers placed for adoption at birth. One of the brothers is our forensic psychiatrist, who was more than happy to take the guardianship of his nieces and nephews, and permanently, if we didn't find the children's biological mothers."

Dr. Phillips smiled. "You found out through familial DNA." The detectives nodded. "I'm a pharma researcher which includes blood study," she continued. "How does your psychiatrist feel about being blood related to a serial killer? No, don't answer that. It's none of my business. But Benjamin is and the jury is still out whether serial killers have a genetic or organic component. Which is it for Henry?"

"Dr. Khaos—"

She sat with jaws dropped. "Frank Khaos, the husband of Jennifer?"

Nick did the same. "Yes. You know them?"

"Yes. I was a resident when Jen was in her nursing school internship at the hospital in Brooklyn, and Frank was in medical school. We became friends. When I got the position in Utah, I moved there. I was horrified when I found out through a mutual friend that Jen was murdered. Did you solve her murder? The last I heard, you hadn't."

"Yes, it was solved in November by my partner, who is now Dr. Khaos's fiancée. The children are living with them."

Bella straightened up. "Wait a minute. Frank knew the name of Benjamin's mother. Why didn't he say anything?"

"No. No. No. I never met the infamous Dr. Khaos. Jen and I never got together outside of the hospital. She told me he was the loner type. Not exactly anti-social, just not the type for chitchat."

"I believe that. From what I know, he and Jen didn't discuss work-related business at home," Nick said.

"Yes. That's true. Back to my question, environmental or genetic for Henry, or don't you know yet?"

"Dr. Khaos, in speaking with Henry, was told the cause was from a head trauma in childhood. Do you know if Henry experienced headaches when you were together? And what was your history with him?"

"Headaches, yes. But, please tell me about my son. You keep going off to questions about his father."

Nick exhaled deeply. "It's an ongoing case. We have no choice. Benjamin is doing great. He's exceptionally bright. He's healthy and well cared for, and his father was very protective of him and his siblings."

Dr. Phillips scoffed. "Protective? It's what I'd expect."

"Was he protective with you?"

She exhaled deeply. "Henry wanted me to be a stay-at-home mom. And for the eight months when I nursed, I was. I loved my job and it was a hardship to give it up. Financially, too. But Henry paid for everything and, along with that, came directives on what I could and could not do. At first, I thought he was being the doting partner, then dad. But even long-distance, he controlled everything I did. I wanted my own money to be in charge of me. To tell you the truth and I know it's horrible of me, and I spent two years in psychotherapy after Benjamin's kidnapping, but after a while, I was happier and more content being a single woman alone."

Nick tossed her a hard stare. "Are you telling us you'd rather not have your son back?"

"No. No. Not now. I'm settled in my career now. I could re-work my hours to when he's in school. Tell me about Benjamin, please."

"Was his pregnancy planned?"

"Yes! Henry wanted to wait until January for us to try to conceive. We were very surprised when I became pregnant the first time. Why do you ask?"

"He seems to have wanted the children—"

Sarah jumped in. "To be born under the sign of Libra, yes. I know. Very weird. I know nothing about that astrology crap, nor do I care to. And I have no idea why Henry cared, either. Unless something can be scientifically proven, I don't believe in it."

"I'll be blunt," Nick said. "With Benjamin, you'd better start."

"How do you mean?"

"He's very perceptive. You can call it intuitive, maybe even psychic. Nowadays, he's called a psi-child."

"Oh, give me a break. All of that is garbage."

"Well, I'll tell you this. Benjamin told Dr. Khaos and Detective Wright from a nightmare he had, that his mother is coming for him." She looked startled. "And he even described you down to your, white lab coat, and black birth mark on your upper right cheek."

She startled then touched her cheek as if checking it for herself. Her hand swiped a curl behind her ear. "I do wear a white lab coat at work."

"Another thing," Lex said. Sarah turned her attention to him. "He can tell if you're lying to him. So I wouldn't go nuts and tell him you've been looking for him non-stop."

"Which is what normal mothers would do," Sarah said snidely. "Is that what you're saying, Detective?"

Lex tilted his head in response.

"I'll deal with it. So when can I take Benjamin back with me?"

Nick's gaze went onto the folder on the desk in front of him, before he looked up at her. "We're waiting for two mothers to come in. We want to have a group reunion so the children don't feel singularly picked out. They've become very attached to each other, being raised together over the years. Their father saw to that. There's no competition between them, no favorites. This will be harder for them than for you mothers. So maybe, a couple of weeks."

✿✿✿

Making sure Bella's cousin, Shawna Hendrick, and Chantal Robinson were active in the forum chat, Sam clicked away at the keyboard. Shawna had agreed to help them take down the agency. Her position as an MD would certainly make her recommendation a reliable source, or so Chantal thought when Shawna approached her about being a spokesperson. In less than five minutes—while the detectives and Frank were still in Shawna's house—her profile went up on the website in the testimonial section. It surprised Sam that Chantal didn't have to go to someone in the agency for approval. Either she headed the group, or the head honcho kept him or herself deep within a bubble.

Sam created a profile for a new forum member using her identity the FBI set up, with her name Amanda Freeman, and handle of MommyAmanda17NewYork. What a time they had finding a handle not used throughout social media, or on forums. Agent James told her he was ready to pull his hair out of his head. The thought made her chuckle. She and Brett would follow the directions Shawna gave them with slight variations not to make Chantal and Mae suspicious.

Sam read the conversation as it scrolled the screen. Chantal couldn't have been more obvious if she tried. The head honcho must have laid it on her to get another set of perspective parents. With the success of getting Shawna and her husband, the renowned Travis Hendrick—who had a reputation amongst the best—to bite, then they could get anyone.

Shawna, I'm so exited to see you in the forum today, girlfriend. Chantal put it on. *How's our baby boy?*

Chantal, he's a pure delight. My husband and I can't thank you enough.

Anytime. I'm surprised you even have a moment.

He's napping. Not sleeping through the night, though. LOL.

Do you miss working?

I don't. We tried so long, that I was more than ready.

Glad to hear that. Welcome MommyAmanda17NewYork. Just jump right in.

Sam knew how these forums worked. She couldn't say she'd been lurking a while, because Chantal had access to the stats. Sam had to play the newbie. *Hey, gals. Thanks for the welcome.*

Hi, Amanda, are you seventeen?

No. LOL. That's for a year.

Oh, what brings you here? Chantal asked.

My husband and I want to adopt, and it's so hard finding a credible agency that some of our friends suggested going into forums and message boards for advice.

Yes. You can get a wealth of information from parents who've accomplished it.

That's what I did, Amanda, Shawna wrote.

I'd like to hear how, Shawna, seriously. My husband and I are so ready. And very frustrated at the same time. Actually, I found your name in an internet search.

On our agency website? Chantal asked.

Is it Deacon? Shawna asked.

Yes, exactly. Under Shawna's profile, this forum was listed as a resource, and her work credentials really impressed us.

What do you do, Amanda? Chantal asked.

I'm a fifth grade teacher and my husband is a college professor, English. Do you have a brochure or something?

We don't send those out lightly. It's not easy, mind you. We have strict requirements and our perspective parents undergo a rigorous process.

I would hope so! Sam put on the excitement. *What would you need us to send in first?*

"*Definitely your employment histories and payroll stubs.*"

Understood. We have those handy. We've been longing to adopt for years.

We'll look at that first, and if we feel there's a chance this will work, I'll forward the brochure. It explains our fees. You know, it's for our attorneys and legwork, making sure we fulfill your needs too. And more importantly, this is a group decision. A panel convenes and goes through everything a couple submits. The decision to move forward has to be unanimous.

Thank you! That's much appreciated.

I wouldn't get too excited, too fast, Chantal said. *Financial status of the parents is closely scrutinized. I doubt if educators like you and your husband make enough to qualify. But nonetheless, it's worth you trying. If we feel there's a great fit between you and a child who needs a home, we may be a little flexible for the child's sake.*

We'd appreciate that, Sam wrote. She turned toward Brett sitting next to her. "Maybe the bureau needed to give us different careers." She typed again. *I'll send the documents.*

A notice came up on the scene. *Chantal left the chat.*

⃝

Two more mothers to go. All in one day. *When Brett Case gets on it, things move fast.* The detectives barely had time for a quick lunch. Sarah Phillips had turned out to be a piece of work. After Dr. Phillips left, Nick doubted her ability to handle Benjamin, and would she even want to try?

Before Nick had time to think anything through, Lieutenant Martin opened the door, and to the surprise of the three detectives, escorted the mothers of Melissa and Henry into the room.

The detectives didn't know which woman to focus on first. Nick could easily guess that in a bright pink cowboy hat and pink boots, with flaming red hair under the hat that cascaded down her back, this woman was Lauren Berkeley, Henry's mom. Her western pink and red plaid shirt was tucked neatly into indigo jeans. This woman was the stereotypical Arizona ranch hand, but in this case, the ranch owner. The second woman in a navy corporate pants suit had to be Melissa's mom, Lisa Brandt, the partner in a top Illinois law firm. Neither woman seemed pleased to be there from their sneers when Lieutenant Martin introduced the detectives.

Nick glanced at Bella. She caught on. "Ladies, please have a seat. Did you have time to talk?"

The women sat next to each other across from the detectives. Cowgirl was the first to speak. "Actually, we did. At the breakfast buffet at the hotel. This one, here, looked at me like I was from another dimension."

"Well, you're in Manhattan, for Pete's sake. You could at least dress the part."

"Well, excuse you, you high fallutin' lawyer. But I'll tell ya, that breakfast didn't hold a candle to our meals at home. No barbecue, no biscuits. All that gluten-free, sugar-free crap."

"Well, some us watch what we eat," Lisa said.

"Look at me, baby, does it look like I don't?" Lauren said, shaking her head.

Bella got the message from Nick that she'd better end that nonsense. "Okay, doesn't pay to ask you how your stay was, then. You're both in one piece so I'm assuming there wasn't a bar fight."

"Very funny, Detective. We did talk civilly if that's what you mean," Lisa said. "We both got a call from a FBI Special Agent Brett Case to come to New York about our children. I had to fly back from Italy. Have you found them?"

"Yes. Melissa and Henry are together, well and safe."

Both women crossed their hearts and said a silent prayer of "Thank you."

"Tell them the best part," Lauren said.

Nick looked at his partners as if finding their children wasn't.

Lauren continued in spite of the glares. "I'm sure they know, and that's why we're here. No, I'll tell them, and I'll use more colorful language than you." She sneered at the suited woman and then the detectives. "We were both fucked-over by one Henry Slater. I swore Henry took his son, but the police in Arizona didn't believe me. I'll bet my ranch on it, all five-thousand acres. I'll also bet Henry paid off the chief of police. Stranger things have happened."

Nick opened the file in front of him. "Yeah. Stranger things have happened. This case gets stranger by the moment. Do you have any proof of that?"

"No documents, if that's that you mean. Henry is three and a half. A couple of months after the kidnapping, the chief retired to the Cayman Islands, and all case files went poof, gone. No one took it further, and before you ask, I didn't either."

"Why not?" Nick said.

"Okay. Henry had full custody, anyway. He insisted on it, even though Henry was with me only, for eight months. And in my gut, I knew Henry had him. So does he?"

"Yes, he did. But before we get into more, Ms. Brandt, what's your story?"

"We had joint custody of Melissa. I told Henry I was getting bored staying home. He actually became irate with me. At the time of Melissa's abduction, the nanny was with her and I was abroad finalizing a corporate merger with our American and Italian partners. I fell in love with Italy and wanted to stay there. The police called me to tell me. I was shocked. Henry had my phone number and a few days later

in a brief call, he told me that he had Melissa. I was so relieved. Henry was in Miami and when I called him a few
months later, he'd disconnected his number. I tried to track
him through his business, no numbers forwarded. I was still
in Italy, so I couldn't take care of Melissa anyway—"

Sending her partners looks of disdain, Bella's nerves
stirred. "Unless you took her abroad with you."

Lisa exhaled deeply as if this detective would never understand. "She'd still have a nanny, which isn't the worst
thing. I still have to be available to entertain—" She
stopped after glares from the detectives.

Even cowgirl looked at her strangely. "And you were
judging me? That's a laugh," Lauren said.

"Not entertain that way. A lot of meetings were after
work hours."

"Wait a second," Lex said. "Did you call the police to
tell them Melissa's father had her?"

Lisa let out an exasperated sigh. "Yes. I did. They asked
me if I was okay with it, and I said, yes. I don't know what
they did after that."

"That's very suspicious to me," Nick said. He turned toward Lex. "Get in touch with their PD."

Lisa sucked in her cheeks. "What difference would it
make?"

"For one," Nick said impatiently, "other children could
have been saved."

"Henry told me Melissa was his only child."

Lauren perked up. "That's what he told me. So where
are our children now?"

"I was wondering how long it would take you to ask,"
Nick said. "Melissa and Henry are safe with Slater's two
other children, Benjamin who's nine, and Margie, who's ten
months. Henry Slater was the father of all of them."

"Was?" Lauren asked.

Lex leaned forward. "He's deceased."

Lauren clapped her hands together. "Woo hoo! Someone
knocked off that mother-fucker!"

Lex sat shaking his head. "No. He offed himself."

"No way!" Lisa said. "That man was an ego maniac. He thought he was better than God himself."

"And in line with that mentality," Nick said, "goes not being able to cope being behind bars for the rest of his life."

The women stared at Nick, startled.

"He murdered seventeen women."

"No, not possible," Lauren said. "An ego maniac, but a pampering one."

"Well, you four mothers lucked out," Bella said snidely. "Now the question remains, with your schedules, will you be able to care for your children?"

Their voices trampled each other's. "Yes, of course."

"Okay, good," Nick said. "We'll tell you about your children, then."

Lauren crossed her legs and leaned back in her seat, tapping the leg of the table with the pointed toe of her boot. "What's there to tell? Henry is three."

"And Melissa is seven. They'll be easy. When can we have them?"

"Have them?" Lex sneered. "As if they're property?"

"Look, Detective," Lisa spouted. "I have to get back to work."

"That's too bad," Nick said. "You'll be here at least another week or two until we can get everyone together. You two might as well become friends because you're attached for life."

CHAPTER 23

Two Weeks Later:

At their kitchen table in their Scarsdale home, Sam and Brett sat looking at the twenty-page document that Sam downloaded from Chantal's email. Sam squinted, not being able to read a good portion of the tiny print. The rest was in legalese. Frustrated, she pushed the stapled packet of paper away from her so hard it slid across the shiny marble table and landed on the floor. Even with Brett's punitive stare as he got up to retrieve the documents, Sam stood, ignoring the non-verbal reprimand and leaned against the window sill, parting the blinds to look out into the backyard. Though dark, not being able to see a thing, she still didn't like the suburbs. This was way too much property for her. One half acre of greenery, though now it was covered with snow. She let out an anxious sigh, thinking about how content she was in Brooklyn at her house or Frank's where concrete ruled. She longed to be back there with the children. Too bad quitting this assignment wouldn't bode well for her, not that it didn't cross her mind several times an hour. Never again. Her career with the FBI was over after this case. The thought of having to play *wifey* to a man other than Frank made her stomach curl. Not only that, she wanted to be the best step-mom a kid could ever have to Frankie—more than a step-mom, his real mom.

Brett brought her out of her reflection. "Hey, Amanda!"

She didn't respond.

"Sam!"

She jolted. "Oh, okay. Chantal sure sent the brochure and the documents fast. How are we supposed to get through this? I can understand why so many parents got sucked in," she said as she sat down. "I bet people just signed away without reading a thing."

"How many people do you know who actually read a contract thoroughly? I bet, none. Not even for a mortgage, insurance policy, or a loan. Yet alone for an adoption, which is overwhelming, to say the least. It's deliberately confusing. This looks like a legal contract, and I've seen legitimate adoption ones. But look here." He pointed to a section on the twentieth page. "In a legal adoption contract, it usually has a clause that the biological parents have a documented amount of time to change their minds and void the contract. It would at least have the biological parent's names, unless it's a closed adoption, which I bet this is. But this contract doesn't have anything noting it's closed. And, read this, Amanda."

Sam brought the document closer to her. "'Under no circumstances will this contract between the Deacon Agency and the perspective parents be voided.'" Sam shook her head. "I can guess what that means."

"Yep. If the child is a behavioral problem, has an illness or disability, even though concealed, the agency wouldn't re-home him or her. Not like in foster care."

"If my child had a disability, I wouldn't do that."

"Sorry to say it, Amanda, a lot of people do. You'd better get used to responding to that name, think deeper. It's more than health. It's genealogy, ethnicity, criminal past of the biological parents, where they obtained the child, whatever. That's the most important one."

"Obtained the child? Like a property?"

Brett let out a frustrated sigh. "Amanda, you need to save the maternal instinct for our meetings with them. There you can go all gaga. Right now, you need to think like a cop. Yes, to these people a child is a property to be exchanged to the highest bidder."

She closed her eyes. "Got it."

"Did Frank ever see his adoption papers?"

"He never mentioned it. And if *any* adoptive parents had a reason to return their kid, it was them. His behavior was intolerable to anyone other than Theresa and Peter, but that was so long ago. However, his brother, Carl, found his in a safety deposit box when his adoptive dad went into a nursing home. I think he was told it was a closed adoption, but their parents legally placed him at birth."

"All right, just let's sign these babies."

Sam glared at him.

"I'll motorize them and send them back electronically." Brett took off the cap of the notary stamp and pressed it on the line. "There we go. Notarized and signed in the presence of Glenn Farmington."

Sam laughed. "You have many identities, Tony Freeman."

It was done. Not a minute later, Brett's cell rang. "Hey, Nick."

"The meetings with the mothers are—"

"Hold on." He put the phone on speaker. "I want Sam to hear. Are the women ready to take custody of their children?"

"Yeah, so they say. They've been cleared through the courts, had background checks, and met with judges."

"I sense some hesitancy. What do you three think?"

"Honestly? Henry Slater must have known it, and in all honesty, again, he did his children a favor. He was a much better parent than these women would be. He was overprotective, yeah, for obvious reasons, and he chose professional and educated women on purpose. And yes, he wanted women who wanted children—at first. But they were also career women. These four didn't learn how to balance the two. Each only had her child eight months, and there are reasons the cases went cold. You already know our impressions from the initial meetings but more from the courts just came in. I'll send you the reports rather than rehash it here. You've got to read it to believe it."

Sam smiled from ear to ear.

"What, Sam?" Brett coaxed her to continue.

"If the mothers aren't fit, can Frank and I retain custody?" She bit her lip.

Brett glared at her. "No. It doesn't work that way. Okay, just tell me, were any of them druggies, or impress you to be abusive?"

"No, nothing like that. They're family-court approved. Sorry, Sam, it's the law. If biological parents come forward, the children have to go with them. I know. It sucks. It's us against the system. But because Slater assigned Frank to be in charge of their accounts, and he's their uncle, you'll still have contact with the children. What's next?"

"Things are going to be moving fast from here. We expect to have a meeting with the owner of the agency soon. The bureau already gave me cash for two children. We're going into the first meeting with it."

"Okay, that's what Shawna told Frank," Nick said. "Flashing the green got them the baby faster."

"The agency actually wanted it noted in the documents how fast we could obtain the legal fees. I wrote that we already have it in cash."

"That should do it."

"For now," Brett said, "tell Frank to prepare the children. Tell them we met with their moms, and they're all so excited that they're safe and sound, and that we'll all be getting together very soon."

"Make you a bet Benjamin will see right through that."

"It's the chance we have to take." After a ding, Brett looked at his phone. "Bingo. Got to go. Keep me posted." After disconnecting, he looked at Sam. "We're meeting them tomorrow late afternoon to see if we're a fit."

Sam took a deep breath. "Okay." *But I already have the children I want.*

☙❧☙❧

On the drive home to Brooklyn from his MMA training gym in Harlem, Frank listened to the basketball game on the radio. Bumper-to-bumper traffic dominated the two-hour drive. He used it to his benefit though. This was his time. Reflection time. So many thoughts rumbled through his mind, he couldn't concentrate on one particular situation. Sam not being home with him and the children was number one. Nick and the team meeting with the children's mothers and him not being included gave him the energy to knock the hell out of the heavy bag in the gym. He was dying inside to meet the women who were taking his nieces and nephews away from him and Sam. At least she was occupied with Brett Case. He, on the other hand, had nothing to keep his mind occupied except bombardment by the children as soon as he walked in the door every evening. Anxiety riddled them. Their teachers sent home notes, for Frankie included. Concentration faltered, classwork incomplete, restless behavior, going on since Sam wasn't there. Knowing they'd be leaving soon added to their insecurities. All they wanted to do was sleep in the bed with him at night. He shocked even himself that he allowed it. Frankie joined them, too. They fell asleep hugging each other for dear life. Oh, man. He hugged too, grateful he was able to be there for these children. No one was there to hug him when he was their age.

Nick's incoming call through the Bluetooth interrupted the game. "Tell me straight."

"Prepare the kids. And yourself. Sam and Brett are going in to meet with the agency director tomorrow and no, they don't have a name. Now I can't tell you for sure when the reunions will take place. How are you doing?"

"After this call? Like a volcano ready to explode."

"Sam has to finish with Brett. Do you want John to help you out?"

"No. This is a…family thing." He disconnected before saying goodbye. First call, Jen's parents who were with the children now. He had to do it fast—before overthinking made him stall and turn into a basket case. "Mom—"

Kathryn must have heard it in his voice. "Frank, what's wrong?"

"Can you and Dad stay late tonight? It's time to tell them."

"Yes, of course."

"Thank you," he said, disconnecting, not sure if his mother-in-law heard him. Sam's mother picked up the phone so fast it was as if she was holding the handset. "Marilyn—"

"Frank, when?"

"Yes. It's happening. We're telling the children tonight. I'm on my way home. Can you and George come over? I want to—tell—them—as a family," he said, rushing the last three words out.

"Yes, we'll be there."

He heard her voice tremble. So did his. He swallowed the tears. "Thank—you." He disconnected, letting tears flow. He hadn't been this emotional since having to tell Frankie his mommy wasn't coming home, and then again at Jen's funeral. Damn! He didn't want these feelings.

Okay, Frank, calm down. Come on, you're a psychiatrist. You'll figure this out. It was a good thing Nick didn't tell him about their mothers. Frank didn't need to know. This way, he wouldn't have to lie. He could honestly say he didn't know anything. He took deep, diaphragmatic breaths, like John Trenton had reinforced, on the spot, at Jen's funeral. It worked for a while, until Jen's casket was lowered into the ground. Then he lost it. Breathing or no breathing, he knew he was going to lose it again tonight. How could he not? And with Sam not being there? He braked fast, nearly hitting the truck in front of him. His mind stopped just as fast. No way would he go it alone. The grandparents would be there. Not the same thing. He needed Sam. The children needed Sam. Brett answered on the second ring. Frank didn't give him a chance to say a word. "I'm telling the children tonight, and I need Sam there."

"No way."

"No, Case. She's as much a part of this as I am."

"She's UC now. We can't risk it."

"No one is going to see her."

"We have an application in. There are many people involved. We don't know for sure who's tailing us."

"Don't you have surveillance teams out?"

"We have quite a bit of manpower out. We're in for the evening."

Frank made the quick decision not to question Brett about the *manpower*. Especially knowing the attitude he delivered to Nick and Lex earlier. "I'm not accepting that. Disguise her. I don't care what you do. I expect Sam at my house."

"You're telling me what to do? Do I have to remind you Khaos—"

Frank braked again. "I don't give a flying fuck what you have to remind me of, Case. And I don't care if you bring me up on insubordination charges, for that matter either."

"You wouldn't want that, believe me. Don't push it."

"Listen to me, and you listen good, Agent. This is the department psychiatrist talking. And I'm using my clout here. You people call me in for my psychological opinion. Here it is. The kids already feel abandoned by Sam from the mere fact she hasn't seen them in over two weeks. As bright as they are, it's just reinforcing them not to trust women, just as Slater told them. That mommies aren't reliable. How do you think that's going to affect their return to their mothers? Don't even respond. The kids need her when we tell them. Sam needs to cry just as the children will. Like all of us will. And you can't deprive Sam, either."

"Are you done ranting yet?"

"Only if I made a dent in your thinking."

"All right. I have an idea."

❦

The Trenton crew arrived at Tony and Amanda's house, following the directions they were given. Vicki wore a long winter coat, with the hood covering her hair and part of her face, and knee-high boots. The twins bundled in their carrier were fast asleep, and Ricky, who refused to wear a hat or gloves, came in rubbing his hands together with teeth chattering.

Brett looked at John and sneered at Ricky while shaking his head.

John understood the sneer. "We're in learning-by-doing mode."

"Oh yeah, you're way too soft." Brett shot Ricky a glare.

"Okay, okay. I'll wear gloves going home. Sheesh."

Brett looked out into the front yard. Pitch blackness. Streetlights reflected on mounds of snow. The FBI Jeep was parked down the block. No other cars were in sight except for John's in the driveway. "Okay, Sam, are you ready?"

She inhaled and exhaled deeply. "Yes."

"Let's do this."

Vicki took off her boots, and Sam put them on, covering her jeans. Sam put on Vicki's coat and lifted the hood. Brett fluffed the hood to make up for the women's two-inch height difference. From a distance, no one would be able to tell Sam wasn't Vicki when she left the house with John. It would be less than five steps to the passenger side of John's car, so Brett had hopes this would go off without a hitch. As John embraced Sam, he led her out of the house and his stature protected her view. He opened the car door and she slipped in. John ran around to the driver side, got in, and started the engine.

Brett stood inside by the open doorway. "Have a great time. The kids will be fine."

The driver in the Jeep followed John's Mercedes down the block. Brett closed the door and leaned against it.

Vicki took the infants out of their carrier and put them onto the blanket Ricky laid on the floor. "Agent Case, what's the matter?"

"It's Brett. I wanted to protect Sam, but I also needed to listen to our forensic psychiatrist. Frank was right. The kids needed her. I'm concerned she'll come back tonight so whacked out, she won't be fit for tomorrow. I shouldn't be worrying. We have all of our bases covered."

Vicki got a Facebook notification. She stared at her phone. "Oh no, oh no, oh no. I told Erika not to do that. That woman!"

"What did you tell her not to do?"

"At our girl's night out, she took pictures of Sam, as Amanda, and I told her not to post anything up on her Facebook. What does she go ahead and do? Here, look."

Brett's eyes bulged when he saw Sam holding a huge margarita between her hands and winking into the camera. It was playful, but not the conservative image she needed for a perspective mom. At first, he chuckled then his expression turned to a frown quickly. "What was she thinking?" He closed his eyes and slammed his fist on the table. "We do not have all the bases covered. Did Sam ever mention to you if she has a Facebook page?"

"Yes. We're friends."

"What's her page?"

"S. E. E. Wright."

"That's good. At the academy, we stress not to have one, at least not to use your full name. Shorten it, misspell it. Does Sam have a lot of friends?"

"I do know she keeps in touch with her former colleagues who are good friends. Even more so after their friend Carrie's murder. That affected them deeply. As much as she loves the twins and Ricky, she only took one picture with Alexi."

Brett closed his eyes. "Yeah, she used that one to show Henry Slater when they met up at the casino during the last case. Crap. She did take a selfie with Melissa, and then with the other kids and sent it to me because we needed photo IDs. But those weren't uploaded to social media. Let me play with this. Do you know if she has another account?" Vicki shook her head. Brett went into his Facebook. "Hold on. Her middle name is Emilee." He typed "Samantha Wright into the search bar. He frowned. "There are several hundred Samantha Wright's." He typed in Samantha Emilee Wright. None. "Okay, if she has another account even from as far back as when she was teaching, she's one of the hundreds. They may or not find her. Just a minute."

"Why don't you text her?"

"Wait a minute. Facebook has a tag-a-friend feature on pictures. All right, here. Sam is in the photo with you and other women. I can't do the tag, but you can put the pic on your page."

Vicki reposted the group pic onto her page and tapped on it. Faces of all the women appeared squared, and she tapped on them. Names appeared for each. Vicki found Sam's Facebook page, S.EEE.Wright, even though Amanda Freeman's page was supposed to show. She turned the phone toward Brett. Vicki was able to see the threads.

When Brett tried to access the page, he couldn't. "Okay, very good. It's not public. Only friends can see it."

"She also has it set up that only she can post on her page."

"All right, excellent. So if Erika tries to post the pic on her page, it won't be allowed, unless—"

"No, Sam didn't exchanges pages with her. But wasn't Sam in the newspaper with Frank when you busted the embezzlement scam in November? I remember reading it. John told me he was called in to debrief her after her first shooting."

Brett collapsed in his chair. "Yup! She sure was, and so was I. If these guys do their research, we're sunk. Hold on," he said, smiling at Vicki. "You know what? Nowhere on the application documents did it require a copy of a photo ID or a current picture. That's very odd. Just goes to show us they don't give a damn about where the perspective parents come from. That's very telling, come to think of it." He paused and tapped a pencil on the table. "Okay, Sam didn't have an avatar in the forum—you know what?" He blew out a deep breath. "Worrying about Sam blocked my thinking about this completely. She's Amanda Freeman in all of the social media we set up. She doesn't have any pictures, so if Erika tried to share it, it would be under the new profiles."

"No. You're not safe. I just posted a pic of *Amanda*," she said, stressing the name. "But Facebook recognized her as S. E. E. Wright. They did a visual ID. And I don't know if she plays those games which give the apps access to your photos and contacts."

"Damn it. That's right. You're right. Maybe to play it safe—"

Vicki seemed to have gotten the message. "I know John agreed to this, but we've been in the papers, too, and throughout social media. Speaking about social media, the situation we discussed a few weeks ago—" Vicki tilted her head toward Ricky who'd dozed off on the blanket next to Alexi. "—have any progress report?"

Brett compressed his lips before he responded in a whisper. "Don't worry, we'll find him."

Ricky stirred. Vicki changed the subject. "What you have to do is disguise Sam and yourself. No two ways about it. And I know the perfect disguise for Sam." She sat back with a sly look on her face.

೧ೂ೧ೂ

Their cars were parked—both sets of grandparents. They'd grown as much attached to the children as he and Sam had. Living a few minutes away and seeing them almost every day wouldn't make this separation any easier. "Okay, Frank," he mumbled to himself, clutching the steering wheel, "get out of the car and do it." He glanced at the rear view mirror. No sign of Sam. It would take another hour for Sam to get there, if—and it was a big if—Brett let her come. Then again, as the department psychiatrist, he had more clout than the detectives. Crap. How long should he wait? Should he text Sam? *What if Brett didn't tell her I wanted her here?* He couldn't do anything to sabotage Brett and Sam's relationship. *Not now when they're UC together.* Under Cover. His fiancée and another man, in the same bed. He pounded the steering wheel with his fist. Not again. Never again. He wouldn't allow it. Then again, with hot-headed Sam, would his opinion matter? Would Sam wanting to go into the FBI break apart their relationship? He had to do it. Time was of the essence. As if on cue, he received a text. *I'll be there in thirty minutes. John's driving me in.* Relief, tremendous relief flooded him. He blew out a pro-longed breath. So his being an MD did have clout with the almighty FBI. Good to know. He shut off the engine. Exiting the car, he looked up into the den window. Aged fingers separated the blinds. A female right hand. Either Kathryn or Marilyn. From the distance, he couldn't tell. He didn't see Kathryn's military ring she wore every day. Okay, it was Sam's mom.

He closed the car door. The beep of the car alarm triggered the house door opening and four children without coats ran down the ten steps to meet him. With arms wrapped around him, he couldn't give a reprimand about the coats. "In the house, now."

As Frank ushered them up the steps, Henry tripped. Frank caught him before his face hit the concrete. One busted lip prevented.

Getting into the front hallway, Frank saw the worried gazes from the four grandparents. They certainly weren't good actors. Before he had a chance to take off his coat, Benjamin accosted him. "You met with our moms, and we're going with them, aren't we?"

☙❧

In Brownsville, Brooklyn, the neighbors had no idea that two of the residents in their low-income apartment building headed a kidnapping ring that was in its third year of operation throughout New York City. Not that any one of them would care. They were too busy holding their heads above water, and most of them were under the sea of poverty, criminality, drug trafficking, and gang wars. Little did anyone realize Chantal Robinson and Mae King had enough money to buy this thirty-story building ten times over. Their creative bookkeeping kept them eligible for the government subsidy to reside in the building. Most of their monies were in bogus accounts and with Locklear Henderson. *After all, she has a legitimate job, a wonderful boss, so who would suspect her?* Chantal thought. *Come to think of it, is Locklear still in Ireland? She was due back already.*

Mae swiped her hair off her face and flipped through the adoption application Tony and Amanda Freeman sent. "Looks like everything is in order. They initialed everything in the right places." She smiled. "And they already have the money."

Chantal's brows furrowed. "You didn't hear from Locky, did you?"

"No, but she should be back. We should call her. The two children we have are in our safe house on Long Island. They're really cute kids. Just what the Freemans ordered. All we have to make sure is that they're decent people." After a glare from Chantal, she recanted. "For appearance's sake. You know that."

While Chantal looked at her reflection in the full-length mirror, she called Locklear from her cell phone. She sensed the nervousness in her own eyes. From what, she couldn't pinpoint yet. Little did she realize, FBI Agent James was listening in from the so-called safe house on Long Island, with a two-year old girl holding a teddy bear on his lap, while the newborn boy slept in a blue bassinet. The call went straight to voicemail. Chantal didn't leave a message. "That's strange. Her phone is never off. It's strictly against the rules."

"Call her sister. Maybe she's still in flight."

Chantal scanned her phonebook then clicked the number for Sae Henderson. Chantal didn't think of the time difference. It was nine p.m. here but two a.m. in Ireland. Consideration of others was not one of Chantal's traits. Her heartbeat pounded faster with each ring. The landline rang four times before a groggy Sae answered the phone. "Sae, this is Chantal, Locky's friend. Is she still with you?"

Agent James sat up on the couch and handed the girl to her mother, signaling to her to leave the room. He had to protect these mothers from any more emotional stress.

"No. Locky had to go home early. She didn't contact you?"

"No. Why?"

"She got a call from some FBI Agent—"

"FBI Agent?" Chantal's face heated up. Their end couldn't be near. She wouldn't allow it.

"Yes, telling her something was wrong with the children she nannies. No, the consulate called, for the FBI."

"Sounds like an excuse to me. What was the agent's name? Do you know?"

"I overheard the conversation."

"His name. His name, Sae," Chantal demanded.

"I think it was Brett…something…like what the police work on a case. Case, that's it. But I don't remember if that's his last name or if the consulate said this agent needed Locky for a case."

"When was this?"

"Last month."

"Damn it," Chantal screamed before she hung up. She pulled her laptop over to her and opened the lid. It seemed like it took forever to boot up. "Fucking shit. This isn't what we needed. She's home for weeks and she didn't contact us!" Pounding the table with her fist didn't make the connection go faster. Finally, the home screen lit up. She took chance. In the URL bar, she typed in *FBI Special Agent Brett Case*. "This is a long shot, a very long shot. He's got to be from the New York office." Articles from the FBI came up, but only one picture. "Well, here he is. I thought they keep their agents in secret. This is from November." Her gaze scanned the article. "Apparently, he and a team arrested those responsible for a hospital embezzlement scheme. They're bringing out four people."

Mae pointed down the page. "Look at this part." She read out-loud. "The murder of the wife of NYPD Forensic Psychiatrist Dr. Frank Khaos—" She stopped dead. "Oh, my God! He looks just like—"

"What the hell is going on?" Chantal screamed.

CHAPTER 24

"Now what are we going to do?" Chantal said, standing, pushing the wooden chair back away from her with the back of her knees. "Something is definitely up. That shrink is a double for Mr. Slater."

"Don't get nuts right away. That was in November. Four months ago, already. That case has nothing to do with us."

"I'll give Mr. Slater a call. If he has a brother who works with the cops, he would have told us, wouldn't he? No, he told us he was an only child. That's why he wanted four children."

Mae's eyes widened. "Wait a minute. Yes. That's it! He didn't tell us the truth. That's why he moved to New York! His brother would cover for him. No one's gotten suspicious of us. We're beyond reproach. Yes, definitely. He has a cop in his pocket."

Chantal turned away to avoid listening to Mae's rambling.

"Where are you going? If the FBI has Locky, it's about something else. She'd never talk. Sae said it's about the children. Uh oh. Then it does involve Mr. Slater. He has to have them. He doesn't allow anyone else to babysit them. He arranged to stay local when Locky was away. Okay, relax. Something happened to Mr. Slater. That has nothing to do with us."

"Shut up and let me think." Chantal peered into her own reflection on the full-length mirror attached to the wall outside the bedroom door. Damn, she didn't like what she saw.

Her face heated up. Her hair frizzed more than usual from her body-heat. She put up her hands to cool her cheeks. Cold hands, hot face. She knew something was very wrong. She turned back abruptly. "Okay, Google Henry Slater and I'll call him."

"If you're calling him, why am I searching, again?"

"You know he never answers, and I have to leave a message. And see if there's any news articles about an accident or something. If there is, with an adoption meeting tomorrow afternoon, it'll fall on us." Chantal dialed and the phone went to voicemail. "Hello, Mr. Slater, sir. It's Chantal. We're just checking to—" She put her hand over the mouthpiece and whispered to Mae, "I can't tell him about the agent." She went back to the call. "Oh, Mr. Slater, sir, there's static on the line. I faded out. I just wanted to know if you'll come to the adoption meeting tomorrow. There's big bucks coming in. Daryl Williams is out of town. And you're his fill-in. If I don't hear from you, Mae and I will do it. All the papers are in order. I know it's last minute, and thank God, you never had to fill in before, but I know how much you love kids, and this is a double adoption so…anyway call me back, please. Thank you, Mr. Slater, sir." She disconnected.

ꞔꞩꞔꞩ

FBI Special Agent Mullen sat stoic behind his desk in the New York City field office with Henry Slater's phone on his desk. After a moment, a huge smile crossed his face.

ꞔꞩꞔꞩ

Chantal approached Mae, looking at the computer screen. "Find anything?"

"Nothing recent. No articles, accidents, nothing."

"If we don't hear from him, it's you and me. Let's go

back to that article again. The one with Brett Case."

Mae backtracked to the article. She pulled up a closer photo of Frank Khaos and a blonde pony-tailed woman next to him. "Isn't she a pretty one, clutching him around his waist? Detective, Samantha Wright."

"This might be our last adoption, if Mr. Slater doesn't call us back," Chantal said. "Fuck. We don't have any of the backup we had in Utah. Capping the babysitter was a bad move. The last thing we need is a murder rap connected to us. Here, Daryl doesn't give us any protection. Him, with his non-violence philosophy. I don't know which is better."

"We had no idea that hit was going to happen. That was all Mr. Slater's idea. He was the one who ordered it, probably with his own people, and we're not privy to any of that. I doubt if he'd do anything to get his own hands dirty."

"Well, I have no intention of us getting caught so I just decided. We'll have our own backup." She opened the desk drawer and pulled out a revolver.

୧୬୧୬

In the Manhattan-North precinct war room, Nick, Lex, and Bella, answered a conference call from Agents Mullen and James who signed in from different locations. Empty coffee cups decorated the desk, along with candy bar wrappers, and sandwich parchment paper. At ten p.m. they were in a double shift—their orders from Lieutenant Martin until this case was over.

Exhausted, Nick croaked out the words. "What's happening?"

"Okay," James said. "A lot. Right now, I'm babysitting with the children's mothers. The kids are finally asleep. Did you hear from Case?"

"No," the detectives answered at once. Nick continued. "He apparently wants us in the dark. You're babysitting?"

"Yeah. This ring is non-violent, which is a good thing for us."

"And?" Lex jumped in impatiently. "What does that mean exactly?"

Mullen continued. "A unit made contact with the parents of the children who were on the watch list in the videos. That you know. A couple of days ago, agents took up residence in the houses around each family so they'd be ready. This evening everything was executed. Two teams."

"Hold on," Bella said. "Heck, Case told us there's a lot of manpower out, but how many agents are there working this?"

"Total? About sixteen. The photos of the people you sent with their rap sheets were the ones doing the kidnapping. Lucky us. They only took the children when babysitters were in the house. Agents became the babysitters. We knew the kids would be safe because there are buyers for them. When the little girl and newborn boy were taken from their bedroom windows, we moved in. There were two kidnappings going on at the same time from different sections of Brooklyn. The kidnappers are in custody and so are the children. No one was harmed. One woman at the kidnapping of the little girl, Geraldine Salmon, couldn't stop talking. She was scared shitless. She was shocked seeing so many of us. We believe they'll cooperate. The most important thing to find out was where they planned to take the children. That woman spilled it when told she was looking at life."

"That's where I came in," James said. "I'm at a house on Long Island with the children and their mothers."

"All right," Nick said, relieved. "Do you know if Frank told the kids yet? When I spoke to him, he was anxious."

"Haven't a clue," Mullen said, "but we have to talk about this first. I have Slater's phone, and Chantal Robinson left a message for him to call her back. Now we all know that's not happening. A Daryl Williams is the owner of the agency, and he won't be doing the adoption meeting tomorrow. We have a team out looking for him. Chantal and Mae King will take over."

"Another call," James said, "went to Sae Henderson and she told the women about Brett Case having the consulate call her sister. These women aren't stupid so I'm betting they looked him up, found pictures of him, and maybe of Sam and Frank, too. We can't take a chance. I texted Brett, and told him both he and Sam need to disguise themselves. Brett told me they're working on it. Their meeting with the agency is five p.m. tomorrow afternoon, and Brett gave us the location. That was very careless of Robinson and King. In most of these illegal adoptions, the adoptive parents are kept in the dark until the last minute to avoid things like this. Right away, Brett knew the women were nervous not having communication with Locklear Henderson. And we'll have the suite wired by then. Oh, Nick, what you mentioned about Frank. Somehow, Frank convinced Brett to let Sam go to the house tonight so they can tell the children together. Dr. Trenton drove her to Brooklyn."

Nick blew out another breath of relief. "Okay, good. What else?"

"All right," Mullen said. "In jest, Brett told us the idea that you three and Dr. Trenton came up with."

Nick laughed out the words. "The hologram?"

"Yep. We want to do it."

∽∾∽∾

With all of the children questioning him, Frank delayed until Sam got there. It was the longest half-hour of his life, talking about school and what Grandma and Grandpa did with them today. Everything went in his ear and out the atmosphere. He wasn't even concerned about the bad note Frankie brought home. His attention focused only on the front door.

In the past, Frank was shy about being affectionately

demonstrative in public, in front of the in-laws, and now even Sam's parents. Not tonight. Tonight, the moment Sam opened the door, he embraced her in the most passionate kiss of their relationship. His body fired up before contact, hoping it was the same for Sam. They didn't come up for air. After the kids spewed sounds of disgust, they actually tried to tug the two lovebirds apart. Little Henry squished between them and pushed on Frank's thighs. He grunted, giving it his all, and pounded Frank with his fist when his uncle didn't budge.

Melissa and Frankie grabbed onto Sam and tugged her arms away from Frank's body. Benjamin pulled on Frank's T-shirt from behind until it stretched out to fit two of him. Frank and Sam finally gave in, and he was more annoyed by the interrupted embrace than bothered by his stretched-out shirt. Oh, well. The shirt would shrink back to shape in the dryer.

While Sam and Frank were reuniting, John excused himself to go sit in the den. Frank appreciated that but he knew John well enough to know that if he fell apart, John would be on it in less than a heartbeat. Frank plopped down on the carpet in the center of the living room with his arm around Sam in desperation. With Sam and Frank both sitting with their legs crisscrossed, it was time for the family meeting. In the same positions, the children sat around them, all of them, minus Margie who was in her crib upstairs. Two sets of grim grandparents sat on the couch and love seat around them, holding hands.

"Tell us the truth," Benjamin said with Frank knowing he understood it already.

"We'll definitely tell you the truth," Frank said, clutching Sam's hand, trying to sound clinical. "Sam and I weren't there. Detectives Valatutti, Withers, and Richards met with your moms."

"Even Dr. John wasn't there," Sam added.

For affirmation, Benjamin looked up toward John sitting in the den. John nodded.

"Why weren't you there?" Melissa whimpered. "Then you can't tell us everything."

Frank smiled. "Agent Case wanted it that way, and he's in charge."

"He's in charge?" Benjamin said. "It's our lives and—"

"Hold on there a second. You're children and, unfortunately, what you want can't be held up in court yet. But Agent Case felt it was better that way because we're too emotionally involved, and it would be upsetting for us, too. Look at it this way, Sam and I will meet your moms at the same time you do."

"What if we don't like them?" Melissa said, crossing her arms across her chest. "You didn't meet them so we don't have anything to go by. That's not right."

"Something to go by. Okay, I understand," Frank said. "Detective Valatutti told me they're nice, and they have good jobs so they can take care of you."

"Take care of us?" Benjamin said, squirming. He stared straight into Frank's eyes. "You're forgetting something important."

"What's that, sweetheart?" Sam said.

"That," Benjamin said, pouting.

Sam sniffled, and tilted her head. "What's…that?"

"You and Uncle Frank love us, and I wasn't exactly sure what *love* was until we came here. Dad never ever said he loved us, but he had a good job and took care of us. And now that we know what Dad did—we don't want to be just taken care of anymore."

"That's right," Melissa said as tears started to flow. "We—don't—want—to go—to strangers." She slid over to Sam and settled herself in the space between Sam's legs.

Sam held her tightly. "Oh, baby. I know. It's hard. We were strangers to you, too, eight weeks ago." She rested her chin on top of Melissa's head. "It's going to be a major adjustment for all of us."

"And—and—I—" Frankie stammered, "—got used to having brothers and sisters." He let the tears flow. He got up from the floor, running onto Grandpa George's lap, crying. "I don't want to be an only child again! You're not thinking of us, Dad. How can you let this happen?"

Frank's gaze went from Frankie to Benjamin to Melissa and finally to Henry before he spoke a word. "I know." He swallowed hard. "It's the law, guys. You've been with us on the condition that when your biological moms were found that you have to go back with them."

"But we'll be separated," Melissa cried, running to Benjamin, and they wrapped their arms around each other.

"And we're in different parts of the United States," Benjamin cried the words out.

"It's not like you're never going to see each other again. We'll make sure of that. We'll see each other on holidays, and special occasions," Sam said, sniffling back her tears.

Melissa got up, crying. "No! No! No!" Running up the stairs, everyone heard her scream, "Now we won't be able to plan the wedding!" The slamming bedroom door rattled its wood frame.

☙❧

His patience wore thin and he expected a text by now. Brett texted John. *Where the hell are you two?*

The answer came quickly, but it wasn't what he wanted. *Sam and Frank are calming meltdowns. It'll take a while.*

Brett tossed the phone down next to him on the couch and slouched down, resting his head on the back cushion.

"On their way back?" Vicki asked as she nursed Zach.

"Not yet. The kids aren't taking it too well."

"Aren't taking what too well?" Ricky asked.

"Well, you haven't met them yet, but Aunt Sam and Uncle Frank are taking care of some children until their moms come for them."

"Why aren't they with their moms now?"

"It's a long story, Ricky," Brett said.

Ricky plopped down next to him on the couch. "So tell me."

Brett didn't expect the inquisition and glanced up toward Vicki.

The nine-year-old wouldn't give up. "Agent Case, I've gone through a lot myself, so I'll understand."

"He sure has."

"Oh yeah? What have you gone through?"

"Mom, he doesn't know?"

"No, sweetheart. You can tell him if you want to," Vicki said as she switched breasts.

"Well, you know I was adopted, right?"

Brett looked at him warmly. "That, I do know."

"Do you know how?"

"Actually, I don't."

"Okay, it's a long story, too."

Brett leaned back on the couch and smiled at the nine-year-old.

"I met Dad the same night the two of them met in Florida. Mom used to be my kindergarten teacher."

"Really? Where did you meet your dad?"

"In the hospital. Grandpa Sam had a car accident and Dad was there. And Grandpa Brian was in the hospital because he didn't feel well. And Mom was there. And I was there with my old mommy because I was having an asthma attack."

Brett curled his lips. "And?"

"Dad—my dad now, John—he helped me stop my asthma attack, and then he spoke to my old mommy and convinced her to leave my old daddy because he was doing bad things to me. I was five then. Now, I'm nine."

Brett rubbed his forehead. This long story would be another horrific one that he'd heard many times. He was a firm believer in allowing children to vent, so he prepared to hear more. "And then what happened?"

"Daddy, my old daddy, got mad and he took me and

Mommy and held us in a house and wouldn't let us go. He had guns. Uncle Mark—"

"Who?"

Vicki smiled. "My twin brother. He's the commander of SWAT. I mentioned him in our meeting."

"Ah," Brett said. "Go on."

"Yeah. Uncle Mark and Grandpa Brian were there and John came. And John talked my daddy into letting me go. Then I told John that Mommy was doing bad things to me, too, so John and Grandpa Brian put them in jail." He blew out a deep breath.

Brett compressed his lips, not knowing how to respond. He picked up his cell as a distraction.

"There's a lot more, Agent Case."

"Oh, yeah?"

"Yes! I wanted to go live with Vicki and John then, but some mean old lady wouldn't let me go, and I didn't come back to John and Vicki until I was eight. I was in different foster homes—"

The door opening interrupted Ricky's story, and for Brett, it couldn't have happened at a better time. Seeing children go through traumas like this constantly reinforced his *why* for his career. It was a major *why* for many of the agents he knew. As soon as John took off his coat, Ricky jumped off the couch and ran into his arms.

"Don't get too comfortable, you two, we have to go home," Vicki said as she started to prepare the twins.

In paying attention to John embracing his son, Brett didn't notice that Sam had left the room. After glancing around, it caught his attention. "Where's Sam?"

John pointed to the bathroom. "She's taking it hard. It's not like her to be silent on a drive. And not like my usual self, I let her be. It's something she and Frank have to work out."

"He better get on it soon," Vicki said as the Trenton clan left.

∞

Fidgeting, Sam sat with dye in her hair, and foils interspersed amongst the color. The steamer set to twenty-five minutes was supposed to allow the color to absorb into the hair more effectively to show the varying shades. Bored out of her mind, though knowing the drill, having highlighted her hair for years, Sam couldn't wait for today to be over. The tears and crying from last night reverberated in her brain. She barely slept five minutes at a time before waking up from a nightmare. That was unlike her. She'd remember her dreams—good or bad—but last night left her with nothing to analyze. She sat still, focused on her breathing, and tried to quiet her mind. No go. The jazz glaring from the speakers threw off her concentration. *Okay*, she thought. She'd better focus on the adoption hearing in a few hours.

The takedown of the adoption agency would be the pinnacle of her career so far—her fairly short, but productive career as a detective. She looked around the salon, focused on the walls with photos in yellow marble frames of models in different cuts. For the case, Sam agreed to change her color. In no way would she compromise the length.

And she had been contemplating this color for months anyway. She'd driven her colorist in Manhattan crazy about it, changing her mind every time. Hunter—the native Staten Island gal—knew her like a book. Sam would only go to the most skilled stylist in a salon, and that was Hunter. This woman was the most talented with long, highlights. And her blowouts, not to be surpassed. Sam would cringe, hearing horror stories other clients would tell Hunter as she waited her turn. Hair was such a precious commodity for a woman. A bad color or cut could make a woman want to hide in a closet for months, yet alone, the cost to correct a mistake. Luckily, for Sam, she'd never gone through this. Knowing that kind of a day could happen, she prayed today wasn't it.

This salon in Scarsdale certainly was fancier in decor

than the salon in Manhattan, and that one was upscale. She'd dropped three hundred bucks for her color, cut, and style. She expected it to cost more here. But Brett gave her the cash for this bill. She couldn't help but think Brett felt bad about not covering them online well enough. Then again, could it ever be foolproof? There'd always be a glitch somewhere. The good guys would hope it wouldn't be detected. Then again, would Brett *feel* about anything? She'd never met such an even tempered man.

Sam's gaze went to the yellow-green marble counters that matched the tile floors. The seating was a beautiful shade of butter yellow. She'd like it here. It was pleasant. Cheerful. She only hoped this stylist would be as skilled as Hunter whom she wouldn't trade for the world. But she was undercover, which meant she couldn't travel into Manhattan.

Vicki's friend, Erika, recommended this guy, Freedom. One thing Sam would give her was that her hair was a vibrant shade of auburn, and Erika told her, he's great with reds. So here she was—in a salon, trusting a new colorist with a new color—a color that had to come out right the first time because she was going undercover in exactly four hours. Not only did she have to present a well-put-together appearance, she didn't want to focus on an iffy hair job. That would be the first thing a woman would notice. She put her hand to her heart in a silent prayer, clutching the sugilite and moldavite pendant she wore under her T-shirt. Oh, crap! She'd forgotten to take it off before her color-job. *Red dye on a fourteen-karat chain? Okay another causality of the job.*

Freedom raised the steamer. He unwrapped a foil on top of her head. "You're cooked, Amanda."

Amanda? Oh gosh, she couldn't wait to go back to Sam. Simple. One syllable. She smiled.

"Over here." He led her to the sink.

Sam made herself comfortable, as comfortable as she could under the circumstances. She scooted her butt as far back into the seat as possible. As the warm water poured, Freedom removed the foils. With Hunter, she constantly asked her if the color looked right. This time she fell silent. Apparently, Freedom was good at reading people, and he didn't rush conversation. Her nerves must have frozen her. As she sat leaned back, stretching her midriff—her solar plexus, the emotions center—the pressure forced a release. Out of her control, tears began to drip.

Freedom noticed before she did. "Amanda, what's wrong? You can't be that scared of me."

Sam laughed, wiping her eye with the edge of the towel wrapped around her neck. "No, I'm not. Today's going to be a rough day." She paused to get into Amanda mode. "We're adopting two children today. Well, not rough, but emotional."

"That's so freaking awesome. Congratulations!" He continued to wash her hair. "Well, why doesn't the mommy-to-be just relax and let me give her scalp a great massage?"

Mommy-to-be. Mommy-to-be. Yeah, I'm going to be a mommy-to-be, for an hour or two, tops.

At first she and Frank thought they'd be having the two children for a while, but since Brett's team got the parents on board, she would just be a babysitter.

All well and good. Having two more children with the others and having to hand them over wouldn't be great for the Slater kids to see. My children. All four of them going back with their moms. Oh, God, Dara, please do something. I love these children more than life itself. And Frankie, too. God only knows when Frank and I will have any of our own children.

Freedom's massage must have opened up all of her chakras. The tears flowed. Sam gasped.

"Amanda, there's a lot more to it than that, hon," he said as he lifted her head and wrapped her hair. He handed her towel.

"Thank you." She blew out a deep breath. No way could she tell him anything and break her cover. "It's been an emotional roller coaster ride for us. I can't believe the day is finally here."

"Well, it is. Right now, you have to focus on your fabulous color and cut. How short did you say you wanted it, chin-length?" he said, smiling as he led her to the chair.

"Funny man," she said, laughing. "Just a trim. But you know what? How about bangs? I haven't had them in years."

"Bangs could work. Accentuate your blue eyes. Wispy or thick and straight across?"

"Oh, I don't know. What do you think?"

"Let me play with it." He ran his fingers through her hair. "What do you think of the color so far?"

"I can never tell when it's wet. It'll be a big change for me. I'll probably need to change my make-up palette for sure."

"Most likely."

He blew her hair out first and as it became dry, Sam sat with her mouth agape. "Oh, my God, Freedom, I love it! I'm so glad, I made the change. I hope my—husband likes it." *Crap, I almost said fiancé.* She fluffed her mane. "I can really see the highlights."

"Yes, we can. Just sit without turning your head." He held up the scissors.

Sam laughed. "How do you describe the color?"

"It started as Intense Copper Fire and with the added blonde highlights, it's now Crimson."

❧❧❧

Frank had never been there. Even with the debriefing in the Aries case, when Special Agent Case took down the embezzlement scheme, that meeting took place at the precinct. He had no idea why Agents Mullen and James asked him to come into FBI headquarters this morning. His mind wasn't on this. Rather, he was obsessed with how Sam was doing after last night. He hadn't slept a wink. Not like him. Soon, his life would be much emptier. No way in hell, could he at forty-four and Sam at thirty-seven, have four children to fill the void and give Frankie siblings. But he'd sure as hell throw away the condoms, and if Sam wasn't ready, he'd prick pinholes in them. He looked up toward the sky.

Mom, do something to help us out here. I don't exactly know what to ask you, so you'll have to figure it out.

Before opening the front door, he showed his credentials to a guard. Next, he was escorted to a sign-in counter where he had to turn in his cell phone and give up his weapon before going through a body scanner. A quick but thorough procedure and he was escorted to the technology lab.

Agent Mullen greeted him with a smile. "Ready, Doc?"

"Ready for what?"

The agent handed him an outfit on a hanger—a sports jacket, polo, and slacks from Henry Slater's closet. "Are you ready to become Henry Slater's ghost?"

CHAPTER 25

Livingston Street in Downtown Brooklyn bustled at rush hour as office workers kept the turnstile capsules spinning in the building Brett and Sam tried to enter. The crowd on the inside exceeded a hundred people that multiplied by the minute. Sam recalled the same kind of mass exodus in her teaching days when she had to go into the Department of Education Building a few doors down the block. After school hours, her usual wait to enter was fifteen minutes. It was a good thing she and Brett had time to spare. Shivering, not cognizant if the dropping temperatures or her nerves were the cause, she pulled her coat sleeves over her hands and brought her arms close to her body. She flinched, not feeling her weapon in her waist holster. Come to think of it, Brett wasn't carrying either. Just the suitcase filled with money—one-hundred-twenty thousand in small denomination bills. Visitors had to walk through a scanner once they'd entered the building. *Um, but what about the Deacon Agency employees?* They were known to be non-violent, but she wouldn't count on anything.

The lines into the building began to inch forward. They made it to the customer service desk to be registered and then directed to the elevator to the fourteenth floor. Sam watched her reflection in the shiny brown marble floor and moved her gaze up to the glass mirror on the wall next to the elevator door. What she saw shocked her. A redhead. She was actually a redhead. Wait until Hunter saw this, but

Sam knew she couldn't send her a pic just yet. What would Frank think? *Oh, my God,* she thought. He loved her blonde hair. And the kids? Would she want them to remember her as a changed woman? What the heck. She'd be Sam again tonight. That was the most important thing. And she couldn't wait.

Sam and Brett entered the elevator along with ten other people, pushing them to the back. "Fourteen, please," Sam said, standing on tiptoes.

One man dressed in a corporate suit pushed past another man to press the button. He smiled at the man. "It's my turn." After he hit fourteen, he backed up into Sam.

It's my turn? That's the FBI secret code of the day. Brett arranged backup. To make it clear, the agent backed up into me. Very cool.

Sam crossed her arms in front of her. The ride to the fourteenth floor took forever. She and Brett squeezed out of the door with Corporate Suit following them. Headed to Room 1436, Sam checked the wall and followed the arrow. As she looked around at the gray marble patterned wallpaper, nervousness overtook her. Not watching where she was walking, she caught her stiletto on a frayed loop on the Berber carpet, flying forward. Brett did a quick save, grabbing her, and broke her fall with her knee hitting the carpet, and Corporate Suit swiped against her. Sam gasped and froze in enough time to see it. Corporate Suit slipped a wrapped cough drop into Brett's suit pocket and then disappeared into the office adjoining 1436.

Chantal Robinson opened the door as the perspective parents reached it. "Hello, come in. I'm Chantal Robinson, the vice president of the Deacon Agency."

"Thank you so much, Miss Robinson. We're thrilled to be here." Sam was all smiles walking into the office as her gaze took in at the burgundy leather couches, mauve club chairs. The cherry wood conference table sparkled with its high-polished finish. Knickknacks covered the coffee table and end tables with pictures of happy parents and children.

Sam focused on one. Shawna, Travis, and baby Calister. She picked it up and held it within her palms. "This is so precious. I recognize Shawna from your website. Look, sweetheart, how happy they are."

"You'll be just as happy today. Come sit down." Chantal walked to her desk that matched the conference table.

Sam turned and paid attention. Chantal wore a straight-lined olive green knee-length skirt, a matching blazer, and mint green blouse. The jacket looked loose enough to conceal a weapon and Sam bet right there and then she had one. Dara confirmed the thought with a jolt to Sam's stomach. Sam sat in a club chair opposite the desk, and Brett placed the attaché in between them before he sat in the other chair.

"I love the decor in here. It's absolutely spectacular," Sam said, sounding like a giddy schoolgirl as she looked up at the tree-like glass chandelier above the conference table.

Brett became comfortable, crossing his legs. He took Sam's hand in his, probably to signal to her to calm down. "Was our paperwork satisfactory?"

"Yes, I'm glad you asked." Chantal clasped her hands on the desk. "Mr. and Mrs. Freeman, we have some concerns."

Now it was Brett's turn to put it on. He did a double take. "Concerns? What kind of concerns? I can assure you we have the money you requested. To the penny."

"Yes. Yes. That's fine, Mr. Freeman. We must…for the children's sake, ask you some more questions. There are two children involved."

He nodded and he must have forced himself to mellow. "Of course."

"Mrs. Freeman, you're a fifth grade teacher, correct?"

"Yes," Sam said, smiling.

Chantal scanned the application. "So let me ask you, after fifteen years devoted to teaching, how are you going to feel being a stay-at-home mother?"

"Miss Robinson, I am so ready to be a stay-at-home mom. I've—we've—been planning for a child for several years now. Please believe me." Sam crossed her palms and rested them over her heart. "We want this from the very bottom of our hearts. Every time we see a baby in a stroller, or a toddler, our hearts hurt. We'll be the best parents ever. I can assure you of that."

"You sound very sincere."

"I am being sincere," Sam said, hoping Frank would be seeing this somehow.

"Mr. Freeman, another concern, is of a financial nature."

"And?"

"How will you, as the only income earner in the family support Amanda and the children?"

Sam smiled, knowing Brett was the only income earner in his family now.

"Believe me. I'm excellent with budgeting and finance, and we have a family inheritance to back us, besides saving for years. No worries."

"Well, we do worry. But I like the two of you." Chantal pressed the intercom on her desk phone. "Mae, come in and join us."

Mae King, also dressed in a conservative straight lines skirt entered the room with a smile on her face and a camera in her hands. "Hello, Mr. and Mrs. Freeman. I'm Mae King. The second VP. It's a pleasure to meet you."

"The pleasure is all ours," Sam said, extending her hand to shake.

Mae took Sam's hand in hers. "So how is the meeting going?"

Chantal shot Mae a glance. "We're good, but we're discussing some issues."

"Is there anything else?" Brett said.

"Actually, yes. I'll get to the point. We don't have any pictures of you. We checked your social media accounts as per our protocol. We research our parents thoroughly. And I'm sure you can respect that. You each have no profile pictures. And that's a big concern for us, especially for you, Mrs. Freeman. It's odd for a teacher, not to have pictures of the children in her class. We saw pictures of friends in your

photos, trips you've taken, but you're not in any of the pictures yourself. How come?"

"I'm very camera shy."

"Why? You're a beautiful woman."

"Ah, thank you. But I'm a teacher in a private school,
and they have a confidentiality policy. They will not allow
us to post pictures of the children. And they actually want
us out of social media, to be honest with you."

"Well, *we* need to have a picture of you to upload to our
website. So please, go sit over there on the couch. The both
of you."

"Sure," Sam said, getting up and walking without her
usual swagger.

Brett followed, blowing out a breath. Sam noticed.

ојој

In office 1438, the FBI task force watched and listened
to the exchange. In addition to four agents, Frank, Lex, Bella, and John focused on the conversation, given instructions
to spot anything unusual. Agent Mullen readied the computer to project Frank's hologram onto the wall opposite the
desk if needed.

Frank paced, wanting this to be over. His mind rambled.
What the heck was he nervous about? He heard Sam profess
how ready she was to become a stay-at-home mom. That
was definitely a message to him. Sam knew he'd witness
this. The condoms were definitely gone. No need to prick
holes. He laughed at the thought. He wouldn't have done
that anyway. He wouldn't do anything behind Sam's back.
This adoption ring was supposedly non-violent, but then
again, a babysitter was murdered. Who knew? One thing he
was confident of, when someone went undercover, their life
was on the line, no matter how much experience they had.
He was so preoccupied it took him a few minutes to notice
Sam was now a redhead. Whoa! He jumped back, and a

huge smile crossed his face. When he saw her back in November for the Aries case, all cleaned up and in a suit, the only two words he could think of was stunning, spectacular. Wow! She was even more spectacular as a redhead with bangs. Definitely made her blue eyes pop. He loved it. Yeah, he'd love Sam, no matter what she looked like.

They watched Mae take individual pictures of Sam and Brett. And they listened. The audio and visual came through clearly.

"We're going to upload these to our website and our private Facebook group," Mae said.

"I didn't know you had a Facebook group," Sam said. "As long as it's private. I can't go against my school's rules."

"It's a private group, only for our parents."

"Why is that? Why is it private?" Brett asked. He coughed, pulled the cough drop from his pocket, removed the wrapper, and popped it into his mouth.

"Get ready, Mullen," Corporate Suit said. "That's a signal something is wrong. I don't exactly know what, yet. Possibly about the Facebook group. Brett knows though. Anyone?" He looked around at blank faces. All, but one.

"Well, Mr. Freeman, a lot of our parents preferred it to remain confidential. Sometimes an adoptive parent doesn't want to tell their children until they're adults. We want to protect the children, so no nosy neighbors leak it to their children, and—I'm sure you understand where I'm going with this."

John moaned. "I sure do. Vicki and Brett were talking about Facebook last night."

"Go ahead," Corporate Suit said.

"Vicki's friend uploaded a picture of Amanda to her page, but the facial recognition IDd her as S. E. E. E. Wright. But she was blonde."

Frank bolted. "Listen, Gabe," he said, calling Suit by his first name, "I'm going in if it gets ugly."

"You're doing no such thing, Frank," Gabe said. "We'll

start the sting, and you'll read the script, just like we practiced this morning, probably adjusting it to the scenario. We need the money to exchange hands and the children to arrive and be given to Brett and Sam. The kids are on their way. No matter what happened in the conversation, Chantal plans to release the kids to the Freemans. Let's watch this play out."

Chantal uploaded the newly taken photos of Sam and Brett to the Facebook group. "There, you're members."

Sam jumped up excitedly and rushed over to see the computer screen. "So does that mean we're getting the children? We're becoming parents! Oh, Chantal, this is the happiest day of our lives. Oh, Mae, you can't believe how happy you two have made us!" Sam hugged Chantal hard and then glanced toward Brett. "Where are the—our children?"

"There," Frank said. "Sam's glance toward Brett. She felt Chantal is carrying."

"You are quite the excitable one, aren't you, Mrs. Freeman?" Chantal said and laughed. "Have a seat on the couch. The children will be here shortly." She tapped the keyboard.

They couldn't see what Chantal typed. That was a nerve wracking few seconds. Chantal's expression changed to grim. Pursed lips. Then her eyes widened, and she mouthed 'oh shit' to Mae who peered at the screen, over her shoulder.

They were made.

As Chantal stood, lifting her hand to her chest, there was a knock at the door.

∽∾∽

Staying in character, though she wanted to rush the arrest, knowing she couldn't just yet, Sam clapped her hands and put them under a chin into a prayer position. "They're here? Our children are here?"

She jumped up and down in front of the club chair.

Chantal looked anxious to Sam. She was biting her lip. A woman with a gun, and anxious. That was a dangerous combination. Chantal opened the door.

A security guard held a two-year-old girl's hand, and in his other, a baby carrier.

"You're not the usual deliverer," Chantel said.

"Just filling in," he said, handing the baby carrier to Chantal. "Two beautiful kids for new wonderful parents."

Chantal brought the children in. Her lips quivered while her gaze darted between Mae and Brett then back to Mae.

Sam didn't waste time and knelt down in front of the bewildered little girl. "What's your name, sweetheart?"

Brett handed Chantal the attaché with the money and picked up the carrier. He took the baby out and embraced him over his shoulder, patting the tiny boy's back, watching Chantal and Mae counting their stash.

"Emma."

"Emma. That's a beautiful name. You're so precious. Come here, sweetheart," Sam said as she attempted to take the toddler into her arms.

Emma pushed Sam away. "No."

"Oh, why, sweetheart?"

Emma looked around, extending her lower lip. She whined the words out. "Mommy."

Sam embraced her. This had to be painful and confusing for the tot, but Sam had to do it. "I'm your mommy, and he's your daddy, and Michael," she said, pointing to the newborn, "is your baby brother."

Emma crinkled her nose in disagreement then vehement-ly shook her head. "No. Baby brother home." She put hands on her hip and wiggled, giving Sam a defiant look.

Sam melted in love before she stood up and glared at Chantal then at Mae. *Play the cop or disgruntled new mom?* It didn't matter. A womanly response would be the same. "Miss Robinson, Miss King, where did you find these children? I read in the contract that we're not supposed to ask, but—"

"Wouldn't you like to know—Detective Samantha Wright, and FBI Agent Brett Case?" she said with a quaking voice, pulling out her weapon from her skirt band and aiming it at Sam. "Thanks to Facebook and newspaper articles, we know who you are. Red suits you, but him? Blond to black doesn't work." She laughed deviously. "See? Even cops can't hide."

Mae pulled out her revolver from her back waist holster, looking more confident than Chantal.

Sam and Brett shot glances toward each other. "We're not armed," Brett said.

"Good. Sit down with the child, Detective. And you stay put, Agent Case."

Brett nodded at Sam to listen. Two women with weapons pointed at them while the *adoptive parents* held children in their arms weren't good odds. Sam trusted Brett and grabbed Emma. Before she could sit with her, an image of Henry Slater appeared on the wall, along with Frank's voice emanating through it. "Well, well, well, you have to resort to using a gun, Chantal? I'm disappointed in both of you."

Sam pushed Emma behind her as she sat in the chair, and turned toward the hologram. It was Henry Slater all right—in a navy sports jacket, dress slacks, and maroon polo. She almost laughed. Frank sure must be uncomfortable. Emma didn't waste time grabbing onto Sam's hair, and she played with it, making Sam wince.

"Where in the hell are you, Mr. Slater? We've been trying to reach you for days."

"I'm not local. I'm projecting to you through Skype."

"Skype? Where?" Mae looked at the computer screen. "There's nothing on here."

Sam didn't think. She had to dig it in. "He's in either Heaven or Hell, not sure which."

Brett glared at her. *Oh my God!* She could ruin their sting.

"What—do you—mean, Detective?" Chantal stammered out the words.

"I'm Henry Slater's ghost. Want to know why?" Frank said as the hologram flipped to the other side of the room. He scratched his neck then put his hands into his slack's pockets.

"Why? Why are you doing this, Mr. Slater, sir?" Chantal was confused and rattled.

"What am I doing? I came back from the dead to visit. You have called me, haven't you?"

"What? You're dead?" Mae said, backing up to the wall.

The hologram moved to Chantal's desk with Frank sitting on it. "Yes, Mae, I'm dead." His hands moved out to each side

"I don't believe this," Chantal said, turning and holding the gun on the hologram.

"Well, for one, you better believe it. I came clean to the cops with what I've done. They know you've helped me get three of my four children, who'll now be going back to their mothers."

"You told them everything, you traitor! How could you? After all we've done together over the last nine years. After all the money you made?" Chantal jumped forward toward the hologram, falling through it face down onto the desk. She shimmied up and leaned on her side on top of the desk before she sat up. "What the hell is going on here? This can't be real!"

Distracting Chantal's aim, the hologram shot to sitting on the couch by the window. "I wouldn't do that if I were you. Listen to me, it's over." Frank crossed his legs.

"How is it over?"

"Seriously," Sam said. "You don't get it?"

"Why don't you explain it, Detective?" Chantal said. "And I want to hear it from her!"

Emma pushed on Sam's back. "You squishing me." She wiggled to slip to the front of the chair and sat, dangling her legs.

"Oh my goodness, sweetheart, look at the pink socks with the lace." Sam leaned over the toddler to protect her if Chantal fired. "Chantal, let's be adults here. Why don't we let Emma and the baby leave?"

"Don't even think it, Detective. They're our assurance we'll walk out of here."

"Seriously?" Sam paused. *The team is next door*! She had to confirm. "Henry, can you tell them? Can you tell them what you did?"

"I sure can, princess."

Yes! Only Frank calls me "princess."

"By the way, princess, I love the red."

"What the hell is going on?" Mae screamed. "Henry, how do you know that detective?"

Chantal's jaws dropped. "Wait a minute! We saw you in the newspaper, Detective with a forensic psychiatrist! Yes! A Frank Khaos. That's it. He's a double for Henry Slater. Yes, Mae. Didn't we say that?"

"Yes. We did."

"So that's who you are!" Chantal marched to the couch and swiped her gun through Henry's head in the hologram, falling face down onto the couch.

Frank bellowed laughter. "How can you possibly not know I'm not really in here?"

There was no way Sam could get up with Emma's hands entangled in her hair. Brett sat, holding the newborn on his shoulder. He'd need at least one hand free but the baby's head wouldn't have support. Right now, any move from either of them would be deadly. Chantal and Mae appeared too nervous to control themselves. She'd have to trust.

Frank's voice came through again. This time by the door. "Now that you know who we are, we need to have a conversation."

Chantel and Mae, both with trembling hands pointed their guns toward the voice then back again toward Sam and Brett.

"Why don't you drop your weapons and then sit on the couch."

"No. For what?" Mae yelled.

"Well," Frank said, "for one, your friend Locklear Henderson is locked up and she's talking to get the best deal possible. If she gives us what we need, you two will get nothing. Oh and by the way, the rest of your kidnapping crew is in custody as well."

Mae and Chantal exchanged glances, dropping their weapons to the floor.

CHAPTER 26

oming home with Sam made Frank's day. His weeks, actually. Knowing he and Sam were on the same page about wanting a child and ASAP, he knew his praying every day to his mother worked. He also gave his mom another task. But fighting the system. Crap. Libra. The Scales of Justice. Balance. It was a lot more than the kids and he being born under the sign. Where was the justice system now?

The kids belonged with him and Sam. There was nothing in the world that could stop them from going with their mothers next week. Having them spread all over the country aggravated him to no end. Though he was in charge of their trusts, and he'd be involved in their lives, how often would he and Sam see them? With their tight work schedules and Frankie having school vacations that were different from the rest of the country, chances of family get-togethers were slim. He embraced Sam close to his torso, going up the ten steps to his front door.

He heard the children in a mix of crying and fighting with each other. That was new. The arguing. For the first time in their lives, they were revealing their emotions. He'd have to stop that for now. Going off angry at each other would not bind them together. Just the opposite. Unconsciously, maybe that was what they were doing. When he opened the front door, everything quieted and the herd ran to them, lassoing Sam in their grasps for dear life.

It took a moment for them to realize Sam looked different. Even the two sets of grandparents sat stunned. Melissa was the first to acknowledge it. "Sam! What did you do?"

Sam laughed and hugged her, the girl's head on her midsection.

Melissa looked up at her with her mouth agape. "Turn around. I want to see. Grandma, turn on the light, please."

After Henry and Benjamin let go, Sam spun around, giving an actress spiel, running her fingers through her tresses, allowing her hair to flow up and out. Frank loved the blonde highlights heightened by the extra light that sparkled through the red. Very cool. A keeper. Sam was a keeper. She and Frankie would be his priority after the kids left, even though he'd have to work with Brett and John with their upcoming trip to Florida.

Maybe Sam could take a few days off to settle back in. *Yeah, right. Fat chance.* Debriefings and writing reports would dominate her week.

"I love it, Sam!" the seven-year old exclaimed. "Why did you do it?"

Sam sat on the couch, tossing the throw pillows onto the floor. "Well, I needed to disguise myself for a case."

Benjamin plopped down next to her. "What case?"

Sam hugged him. "Remember we talked about you being kidnapped from your moms?"

Benjamin nodded. "Yes."

"It was why I was working with the FBI for the past weeks. Uncle Frank couldn't tell you much because I was undercover. That means no one knew my real identity. These people also kidnapped other children, and I went undercover with Agent Case to stop them. And you know what?"

"What?"

"We did. And I feel really good about it."

"Why?"

"Because, we stopped other children from being kidnapped."

Benjamin looked up and away for a moment. "Are the

children who were kidnapped going back to their moms, too? Like us?"

Sam sat in a solemn moment, compressing her lips. "Yes. The FBI has teams all over the country looking for the children."

"That isn't fair," Benjamin said, sniffling.

"How isn't it fair?" Frank said, kneeling one knee on the floor in front of him, knowing what was about to happen.

"Look at us. We were kidnapped and we have a new family. We don't want to go back." He got teary-eyed. "So, Sam you're happy that the other kids are going back to their moms. So are you happy that we are, too?"

"Then you don't really love us!" Melissa screamed.

"Hey," Frank raised his voice and then let out a deep breath. "I know how much this hurts. It hurts us, too. We're seeing it first hand from both sides of the law. The kidnapped children's parents want them back from the bottom of their hearts. And I'm sure yours do, too."

Melissa cried, collapsing into Frank's arms. She picked her head up. "What if we tell our moms we don't want to go?"

"The thing is, you have no choice," Sam said. "Let's try to make the best of this. We'll arrange to see each other as much as we can. Okay?" She patted Melissa's back. "Come on. We've had this conversation, a lot. Let's make sure you're all packed, baby."

With her head still on Frank's shoulder, Melissa whimpered the words out. "We're all packed already. And Grandma said you'll mail boxes with our stuff and my art supplies."

"You know. Sometimes in life," Grandpa Walter said, "things don't work out the way we want." The kids turned toward him. "We never expected our daughter, Frankie's mother, to be murdered. We waited and waited for over two years for someone to find her murderer until Sam found the man who killed her. We just had to step back and hope and pray that it would all work out."

Frankie burst into tears. "Grandpa! Why did you have to bring up such a bad memory?"

"Frankie, we all have memories," Grandpa Walter said.

"Hey, champ," Frank said. "Listen up. Remember the day you got suspended?"

Frankie nodded, sniffling.

"It was the same day Sam and I met. Do you remember what you told me when I described Sam to you?"

He swallowed. "I think so."

"What did you say, sweetheart?" Sam said.

Frankie looked surprised. "Dad, you never told her?"

"No, I didn't." Frank said, smiling. "Why don't you tell everyone?"

"I was upset that Dad didn't have a girlfriend, and I did. But I got an idea." He looked up to the ceiling. "Yeah. This is it. I said to Dad, 'Maybe Mom sent Sam down from heaven for us.'"

Grandma Marilyn put her hands to heart and hugged her husband George. Tears ran down her cheeks.

Sam's mouth formed an O. "Oh, my goodness, Frankie. That was so sweet!" She grabbed onto Frank's arm with both hands.

"Well, I really think she did," Frankie said. "You found out who killed Mom."

"I got an idea, Frankie!" Melissa bounced up and down on the couch. "Do you think your mom can do something for us?"

"I don't know. I'll ask her. And she listens to me."

"How so?" Frank asked.

"I never told you, but I asked Mom to send me a brother and sister. It took a long time, but she sent me four!"

Grandpa Walter wrapped his arms around Frankie who sat on his lap. "That's what I meant, Frankie. We have to sit back and wait for our wishes to come true. As long as we're asking someone in heaven."

Frank closed his eyes. *That's for sure.*

Melissa and Benjamin looked shocked.

"Now I definitely know your mom can help us," Melissa said.

"Oh yeah? How," Frankie asked.

"I think it'll work best if I keep it a secret. Her name was Jennifer, right?"

"Yup," Frankie replied.

"Sounds good," Frank said. "It's getting late. Let the grandmas and grandpas go home, and we need to get to bed too. And Sam probably hasn't slept in a week."

"You're right on that one." Sam got up and hugged her parents and then Frank's in-laws.

The kids followed, hugging everyone. The four grandparents became tearful.

"You're all coming to our good-bye party, right?" Melissa asked.

"We sure are," came from the mouths of the four grandparents.

The two couples left and Frank watched the grandmas break down crying going down the steps. Frank had to hold himself back from doing the same. He was never the one who felt grown men don't cry. He'd cry plenty tonight.

❧❦❧

Sam watched Frank twist and turn in bed, moaning—so unlike him. He usually found a position and lay in it. She, on-the-other-hand, was on automatic in bed. And she even took her nighttime vitamins. Tonight she lay still. "Praying to someone in heaven," as Grandpa Walter said. She always did. Usually praying to Dara worked. Tonight she needed to bring out the big guns. Theresa. Frank's adoptive mom— the mom whom Sam felt loved her dearly and whose hands she felt around her between the ropes when Henry Slater bound her. The mom whose warmth took away her fear when held captive by that psychopath. Yes. Tonight she'd needed Theresa big-time. Sam quieted her mind and body with deep breathing to get her into the alpha state, inhaling through her nose, exhaling through her mouth. In thought language, she told herself to flex and relax her toes, visualizing the earth's energy around them. Bringing the energy up to her ankles, calves, thighs, pelvic area, stomach, midriff, heart, throat, forehead, and the top of her head, she continued the deep breathing, feeling the tingling go through her. She knew not to rush it, though clear consciousness came more easily now, the more experience she had. She reached the calm state, sensing she'd be open to universal messages.

Theresa, I know you can hear me. You've been protecting me since Frank and I met, and I felt you for the first time when I was with Henry Slater.

She felt the chills of energy hit her from head to toes. Theresa was indeed listening.

I know for sure you've watched over Frank. This is a horrible time for him. For us. We love these children with all our hearts. But yet, we're messengers of the law. I would never say this out loud. I'd lose my career and wind up in prison to boot. Please, I need you to work on this. The children are leaving with their mothers next week. We can't stop this. But can you, will you? No, I'm not supposed to beg the universe. I'm asking that you work on this to find ways to bring the Slater children back to us. That's all I'm asking. I don't care how you do it. We want the children back without bringing harm to anyone. Thank you from the bottom of my heart, Theresa. I know you'll do it.

ᕱᗧᕲ

The kids met in Frankie and Benjamin's room before settling into bed. Henry squeezed between his sister and brother.

"Move over," Frankie said. "The more brains on this, the better."

Melissa and Benjamin shrugged but did it.

Henry gave them dirty looks.

Melissa sighed. "Okay. So how do we do this talk-to-someone-in-heaven thing?"

"It's easy. My dad taught me when I needed to calm down after Mom died. Let's do it together. Then she'll really listen."

"Okay, tell us what to do. Henry, close your eyes." Melissa poked Benjamin. "Listen, if anyone can reach Jennifer, you can, Benjamin."

"But Jennifer doesn't know me."

"Yes. She does," Frankie said. "She knows all of you. I told her when you first came. This is what we do. Start breathing heavy and blow out deep breaths."

Melissa and Benjamin started, with Henry following. Melissa's cheeks puffed out and her face reddened.

"Hold it. That's too deep. Don't turn red. Breathe normal. I might have to ask Sam how to do this."

Melissa shook her head. "No. Don't. We can't let them know. What do we say?"

"Just talk normal from your heart. And use her name. Tell my mom what you want."

"I got an idea," Benjamin said. "Let's do this on our own. So she'll get us talking to her separately. With us sending different—talking to her with different words, she'll listen."

Melissa and Frankie nodded.

"Deal. Do it as soon as we get into bed." Melissa took Henry's hand and left the bedroom with him.

Frankie scrambled under the covers, lying on his back, pulling the blanket up to his neck. He took a few deep breaths with Benjamin watching him. Frankie moved his mouth in prayer. Benjamin followed his lead, watching his *brother*. "I can't hear you, Frankie."

"Shush. You broke my concentration. You're not supposed to hear me. Sam says it's talking in *thought-language*."

"Okay. Now I get it." Benjamin looked toward the ceiling.

The boys' room fell silent.

CHAPTER 27

One Week Later:

John and Vicki, both their hands full carrying balloons and wrapped presents, entered the party-decorated war room of Manhattan-North. Without the obligatory greeting, Lex and Bella helped them unload. The deli down the block delivered four different kinds of sandwiches, salads, bottled drinks, plus foods that Frank and John would eat. Nick placed the weighted balloons on the tables that were arranged in a L-shape. The room had an unsettling silence. John didn't like it.

John looked at his wife, and they both connected. Today would be the hardest day of his career, and he was sure it would be for everyone else, too. There was no way to circumvent the law. The mothers were deemed fit through the interviews. They showed up with the original birth certificates. All of them had the means to support the children. Maybe, just maybe, his spirit guide, Max, would step up to the plate and do something. What, he didn't know. Then again, it took the universe three years to send Ricky back to them. At least it happened. He stood still and observed the other solemn faces. "Where's Brett?"

Nick uncovered the sandwich tray and put the plastic into the garbage. "Since when do you do small-talk?"

Yeah, he got the message. That was all anyone could possibly do now. "Just trying to figure out how long we have until the inevitable."

"The team is picking up the mothers." Nick checked his watch. "They'll be here in a few. Sam and Frank are on their way."

Vicki tossed her handbag onto the couch. She turned abruptly to the brooding herd. "Listen, y'all. You can't allow the children to see y'all like this. Whether you like it or not, you have to put on a happy face as the song goes. They'll have a new life and, hopefully, they'll move on. Kids are resilient. More so than adults."

Lex sucked in his cheeks. "You haven't met their mothers. Charm school graduates, they're not."

"Doesn't matter, Detective. I bet when they get reunited with their children, hearts will flood open and melt."

Brett Case opened the door and ushered in the four mothers with Agents James and Mullen following. "All right, everyone, here are the Slater moms. Make yourselves comfortable, ladies."

The women looked around and walked toward those who they were familiar with—the detectives—but with solemn expressions on their faces.

Cowgirl was the first to speak, giving John the up and down. "So who might you be, sugar? You weren't at our meeting." She strutted up next to him with her boot heels clacking on the linoleum floor.

Vicki used the same strut to reach John and locked her arm in his. "He's my husband, darlin'. Tell me, whose mother are you?"

"Ah, taken, and respected. Okay. I'm Henry's mother. Lauren Berkeley." She extended her hand.

Vicki reciprocated. "I'm Vicki, Vicki Trenton, and my husband is the team's forensic psychiatrist."

From the other side of the room, Sarah Phillips startled. "You're not Frank Khaos. Not from pictures Jennifer showed me."

"No, I'm not. There are several forensic psychiatrists in New York City."

"Where is he?" Sarah asked, looking around. "I really

want to get this over with." She sat on a chair by the wall and crossed her arms over her chest. "I have no idea why you went through all this trouble. I'm not in a partying mood."

"It's for the children," Vicki said. "They're very nervous about this, and angry." She clutched onto John's forearm. "It's a day late, but we're also celebrating Margie's first birthday."

Sonja Santos brought her fisted hands to her heart. "Thank you, Mrs. Trenton, for remembering my baby's birthday. I nearly forgot it's passed. April fourth. How could I possibly have done that?" She started to weep.

Vicki approached her and wrapped her arms around her shoulders. "Sonja, it's Vicki. The stress of this affected everyone. Your baby is very much loved."

Lauren smirked. "Listen. Stop making such a big production over this. They're little kids. They don't even know what's happening yet."

Nick shook his head in disbelief. "They certainly do know what's happening. These kids are exceptionally bright and verbal. They'll cut through your BS, fast. Listen to me. It's going to be a hard adjustment for them, especially for Melissa and Benjamin who've been together for seven years. Miss Santos, you'll have an easier time with Margie. It's only been four and a half months. But the rest of you, expect to work hard. And your love better be genuine."

The women's reactions were head shaking, rolled eyes, shifting body positions, and spewed arrogance. John had to put the nail in deep. "You're going to have to get close to them here," he said. "Sit with them while eating. Talk about what they like and don't like. Seriously, develop a positive relationship here, or we'll have all-out tantrums to deal with. They're leaving loving homes, and two sets of grandparents, plus, the camaraderie and love for each other."

"All right," Melissa's mother said. "I think we get it. We're not imbeciles."

"Okay. Good. We don't think you're imbeciles either.

We want them to have each other's phone numbers so they can keep in touch." The moms nodded. "And you'll have ours in case something comes up. We also have folders for you with their medical and school records. You'll sign some papers acknowledging receipt of the documents and that you're taking custody of your children. Dr. Khaos will also sign papers that he's releasing guardianship. An attorney and rep from Child Protective Services will be here to bear witness. Any questions?" John observed four solemn faces. "Good. I'm glad it's sinking in that today is a life-changer."

Frank opened the door and all gazes landed in his direction. Sam carried Margie in her arms and entered the room first. Henry, Melissa, and Benjamin had to be prodded in by the grandparents. The kids, clinging to each other, stood still by the back wall, and the mothers seemed equally as frozen.

Frankie clung to his grandparents as they led him to the couch by the opposite wall. Grandma Kathryn handed him a tissue as he buried his head in his grandpa's chest.

Sonja Santos was the first to react. She raced over to Sam and put her arms out to take Margie. Despite coaxing, the infant clung to Sam, and Sam rubbed her back. Sonja became weepy as did Sam. Everyone in the room remained quiet and watched them. To John, time stood still. Even his psychiatrist brain couldn't figure this one out.

Sonja tickled the baby and the little one laughed. "Want to come?" Her hands were on the baby's torso.

"Go ahead, Margie," Sam said. "Go—to—your—mommy. Do you want to show Mommy how you walk?"

Sonja gasped.

"Yes, she does, don't you?" Sam said, addressing the infant. "She just started walking two days ago."

As soon as the little one went to her mother, Sam turned, covered her face with her hand, and raced to Frank. He held her tightly as she concealed her face on his chest. He wrapped loving arms around her.

Sonja, hugging her daughter, went over to them. "I can't

thank you enough for taking care of my baby, Detective, Dr. Khaos. I'll be forever grateful."

Frank compressed his lips probably in an effort not to break down himself, John thought. "Just remember we're her aunt and uncle, and we expect to see her."

"Definitely. That's a promise." She took Margie to sit with her by the couch.

All right, that's a true love, John said to himself.

John couldn't believe he had to say it, but he did. "Why don't you mothers go to meet your children?" He stared at the women who didn't budge for a few moments. He approached Sarah Phillips. "Dr. Khaos is over there if you want to speak with him."

She sneered at John. "On second thought, with all that I'm going through today, I think I'll pass." She walked away from him, fast.

Yeah, John said to himself as his gaze followed her.

Cowgirl walked over to Henry and kneeled in front of him. "Hi, Henry, I'm your mommy, Lauren."

He scrunched his nose. "Why are you wearing a cowboy hat?"

"Well, why don't we sit over there, and we'll talk about it over lunch?" She went to take his hand. The little guy leaned against Melissa. She prodded him to go. He sniffled, but took his mother's hand.

Lisa Brandt, Melissa's mom, and Sarah Phillips, Benjamin's mother approached their children at the same time.

"Hi, Melissa. You are so beautiful."

Melissa smirked. "Thank you." She scanned her mother's outfit. "And that's a pretty suit. Sam has outfits like that."

"I'm glad you like it. Let's go get some lunch, okay? And you can tell me about all the things you like."

"Okay." Begrudgingly, she released Benjamin's hand.

"Hi, Benjamin, I'm your mom, Sarah."

"So what do you want me to call you? Mom or Sarah?"

Sarah rolled her eyes. "Mom, of course. Want some lunch?"

Benjamin stared at her for a moment, looked around the room at everyone watching him, and then ran to Frank, grabbing him around his thighs. "She doesn't want me."

"Whoa, whoa, whoa, bud." Frank knelt down. "You've got to give her a chance. This is a big adjustment for both of you."

Sarah knelt by them. "Benjamin, I love you. When I found out you were alive and well, I nearly lost it. We'll make this work, Benjamin, I promise. Come here, baby."

"No."

"Hey, Benjamin, your mom is a doctor," Frank said, sounding clinical on purpose. "I bet she knows a lot about the brain."

"I sure do."

"That's great because Benjamin loves studying the brain."

"You do?"

The saddened nine-year-old nodded. Sniffling, he said. "I want to be a brain surgeon."

"That' so wonderful. Come here. We'll talk all about it."

Benjamin let go of Frank and slipped into her embrace. Crying, he rested his head on his mom's shoulder.

John came over and mouthed to her, "It'll take him time."

The next two hours dragged. John observed stilted conversation between the mothers and their children with very little laughter, but at least no tantrums or tears. Frank stayed with him, being the quietest John had ever seen him. Vicki had taken Sam to talk to her with Bella. John knew calming Sam down was no easy feat. But she wasn't hysterical, at least. Jittery, yes. Hysterical, no. The team kept in the background. John knew that was deliberate. Lex and Nick probably experienced their own tortured emotions. The FBI team? He didn't venture to guess. They were hardened in training and sticklers for the law.

Come to think of it, Libra is kicking all of our butts.

John pulled Frank back from going to find Sam. "No, Frank, deal with it at home. You're too close. You have to keep it professional here. Let the women do it. And you have to stay strong for your son."

"You're right, pal."

"By the way, Sarah Phillips doesn't want to speak to you, either."

"Good. Let's keep it that way." Frank looked toward Sam, who had composed herself, then to the team. "They're closing the folders, I guess I'm on."

Brett came toward them. "It's time. The social worker came in the back entrance. Ladies, I need you to come with me, please."

Sonja handed Margie over to Grandma Marilyn and waited for the others. One-by-one the mothers lay kisses on their children' cheeks and went over to the conference table in the corner.

Frank and Sam followed them. The children huddled together and ran to their grandparents and Frankie. John tossed an eye signal to Vicki and they both went over and pulled chairs in front of the couch.

"Hey, guys."

"Dr. John, this isn't going to work," Melissa said, shaking her head.

"And you made that decision how?"

Melissa put her hands out to the sides. "She doesn't like colors. She only wears black and white. How can that be?"

"Excuse me?" John had to keep himself from laughing.

"It's not funny, Dr. John," Benjamin said, reprimanding him. "This is serious. You know how much Melissa likes art."

"Yes, I do know. But you can't make a decision on whether or not you like someone based on their color choices. That's not fair to your mom."

"Life's not fair," Frankie said to everyone's stares. "That's what Dad says."

"Okay, exactly," Grandpa Walter said. "Look, we all have to adjust to this."

"Oh, Grandpa. We did what you said last night."

"Frankie!" Benjamin and Melissa said at once.

"What did I say?"

They couldn't ignore the sounds of the chairs moving away from the table. The FBI team, Frank, Sam, and the mothers adjourned the meeting. Everyone had their gaze peeled on Frank as he went behind one of the tables. "Come on, guys, we're done. Time to have some cake—to celebrate." He choked out the words.

Frankie ran to him. "Dad, you're letting us have sugar?"

"Yes, champ. Today is a special day. And we have to sing 'Happy Birthday' to Margie."

The team, FBI agents, the children, their mothers, John, and Vicki stood around the vanilla butter cream frosted sheet cake. After Sam read the inscription—*To A New Beginning*—she clutched onto Frank, causing her to lose it. After her first audible sob, Brett, closest to her, wrapped his arms around her and took her out of the room. John could tell Frank's heart was breaking as well by the way he held the knife. Shaky. John relieved his cutting duty that he knew Frank appreciated. Without acknowledging anyone, Frank nodded and darted out of the room.

The kids tried. They tried to keep a stiff upper lip. They trembled. Their small, fisted hands lay close to their bodies. John recognized the tension in their auras. He had no idea how long the solitude would last. This was an eruption in the making. Not even conscious of what he was doing, he sliced the cake and Vicki handed out the plates. The moms coaxed the kids back to their places on the couch. The kids were so stiff, they could hardly walk.

On the way, Henry's piece of cake slipped off his plate onto the floor.

John saw red in his mother's aura—anger, impatience— not good for this little kid. She refrained from giving a reprimand. Just the opposite. A saccharine sweet smile overtook her face. "Don't worry about it, baby. We'll get a new piece." She picked up the fallen cake with a stiffened posture. John saw Benjamin watching as well. He'd bet the nine year old suspected trouble from Henry's mom. John would have to agree.

The team ate their cake in silence. Even sugar-phobic John had a piece, acknowledging his own uneasiness. After a few minutes, Frank brought Sam back in, composed, along with Brett. Frank pushed a plate with a piece of cake into her hands. She accepted it and nibbled, but she couldn't let her eyes meet the children's.

For a few minutes, the atmosphere was peaceful. A stiff silence. Stagnant. Then it happened.

Four limo drivers entered the room. Brett put his plate down. He stood still, taking a few deep breaths. "Okay, folks, it's time. Our drivers are here to take you to your flights."

All John heard were gasps, even from the team, and then the screams of the children. "Noooo!"

"Hey," Brett yelled without a wavering tone. "This is not the end. You all have each other's phone numbers and your uncle and aunt will be seeing you. No doubt. And you have wonderful homes to go to. Right, Mothers?" He definitely sent a powerful message. At that moment, John gained a new respect for this man.

The women's voices trampled each other.

"Yes, of course."

"It'll be wonderful."

"That's what I expect. Nothing less. Your luggage is outside. We labeled it. Moms, you have your plane tickets in your folders. Please check."

The women fumbled with the folders, John suspected as a nervous reaction to Brett's sternness.

"All right, give each other hugs, keep your chins up."

The kids rushed Sam and Frank. They held on for dear life. The mothers stood still. Only Sonja, embracing Margie seemed to John to be loving and confident. Cowgirl smirked and turned away. Sarah Phillips, judging from her pale gray jagged aura might have been in need of some of her own pharmaceuticals. *Yeah, Nick was right. We'll have to keep an eye on that one. Yes! That's why she didn't want to speak to Frank. Didn't want to get too close.* And Melissa's mother. Her aura projected a brighter yellow and green. Business oriented. But a mom? John doubted it. And he couldn't do a damn thing about it. About any of them. But he sure as heck would have Frank check up on the kids frequently.

Brett walked over to Sam and whispered to her, "You better keep it together, Detective. That's an order."

Sam stared at him but it must have been her wake-up call. John got it. FBI Agent Brett Case had to be the bad guy here. So much for the glamorous job.

"Okay, let's go," Sam said, sniffling. "We'll see each other soon."

While the detectives and the FBI team stayed in the back of the room, Sam and Frank inched out of the room to where the drivers had put the luggage—with the kids still firmly holding onto them.

John observed the moms who trailed behind them. Their auras reflected uncertainty, hesitancy, and torn emotions. Everything, but joy.

⌒⌒⌒

Tucking his son into his bed brought an onslaught of Frankie's tears along with it. The eight-year-old kept staring at the empty bed against the opposite wall his cousin occupied for the past nine weeks. He'd even fluffed up the plaid blanket to make it appear a body lay under it. Frank noticed the sloppy attempt and ignored it. Blocking his son's view of the bed, Frank lay down next to him with his huge frame extending over the sides and footboard of the twin bed, and he brought Frankie, still sobbing into his arms.

Frankie buried his head into his father's chest. "Dad, I'm going to be so alone."

Frank clamped his lips shut in pain, himself. He took a moment. "No, you're not, champ. Sam and I are with you."

"It's not the same thing. You don't get it. I finally had brothers and sisters."

Frank rubbed his son's back, looking out the window. There was nothing to see but streetlights through the shades. Words didn't come easy. Again. This kid sure went through a lot the past three years. "You know. I think you need to talk with Ricky."

"Ricky? Why?"

"Because he's been through emotional traumas, too. And he's doing great now."

"Okay." Frankie sniffled before he got the word out. "When?"

"You'll be with him for a full week in Florida. There's plenty of time to talk then."

"Yeah, I almost forgot. When are we leaving?"

"Next week. John and Vicki with their kids and Duke are driving down in a few days. John didn't want Duke in the luggage compartment. And we're going on Friday. Your teacher already knows you'll be missing a day of school, and a few days after vacation if we need it."

"Why would we need it?"

"Well, I have to carry through on the will that your Uncle Henry left, and we don't know how long it'll take to find my birth parents. We don't know where they are. So you'll be staying with Vicki and John's parents while John, Sam, and I work with the police there."

"Why can't the police find them before you get there?"

"That's a very good question, champ. I have to personally hand over the documents, so they know it's the real deal. And it'll take time for them to verify it. Understand?"

"Yes. Dad, what's Florida like?"

Frank smiled. "I know it's warmer. But I've never been there, and neither has Sam, so it'll be a new adventure for all of us. And that's a good thing. It'll take our minds off what happened today and give our hearts time to heal."

"My heart will never heal," Frankie said, shaking his head.

"Oh, man. It will. And when we come back, you'll call your cousins and tell them all about Florida. Okay? And you can talk to them as much as you want."

"Okay."

"Come on, champ. You really need to get to sleep." Frank struggled to get out of the bed without falling off, making Frankie laugh. He bent over his son and held him tightly, kissing the top of his head. "Get some sleep."

Frankie rolled over onto his side, and Frank pulled the blanket up over his son's shoulders.

CHAPTER 28

Sam came out of the shower, a towel wrapped around her, water dripping from her hair down her cheeks, mixing with tears. She'd never thought her heart could be hurting so much. Her children were gone. She plopped down on the bed not caring how soaked the comforter got.

She gazed at her reflection in the mirror above the dresser, and in a moment of awareness, she realized her hair was bleeding. Bleeding onto her face, the light blue towel, and upon pivoting her body around, she realized the comforter was getting new abstract artwork. Crap. She'd forgotten Freedom told her reds bleed the first few washes. Without wasting another moment, another stain, she whisked the towel from around her and carelessly wrapped up her hair, tucking in the end. For sure, Frank wouldn't be a happy camper. Then again, after today, she was sure he'd be in a pampering mood. And if there was one thing she needed, it was to be pampered.

She didn't notice Frank watching her as she tried to dab up the stain on the comforter with tissues, startling when she heard the door open all the way.

After closing the door behind him and locking it, he snuck up behind her and wrapped his arms around her bare waist. "Got your *friend*?"

She twisted around in his embrace, laughing, as the tip of the towel dislodged. "No, not for another couple of weeks. It's hair dye. Worse to get out. I'm sorry." She put on the puppy-dog look, wanting sympathy as the towel un-wrapped and fell down her face onto the carpet.

He grimaced at the dye-stained towel. "No problem. We needed a new comforter—and a towel—anyway." With his fingertips on each of her shoulders, he pushed her onto the bed. "We might as well stain the rest of it."

Sam landed on her back, horizontally across the com-forter. She perched up on her forearms. "Frank, I have to dry my hair."

Standing over her, he unfastened his belt and unbuttoned his jeans. "Why? Remember in November? In the gym?" He winked, salivating as he pulled his T-shirt up and off, dropping it to the floor. "In the cage? You had wet hair then. Best sex we've ever had." He yanked off his jeans and briefs and lay down next to her.

She gasped. "It was in your secret place, not the cage, and you're comparing our sex to when we had just met? It's gotten even better, and you know it."

Growling, he moved on top of her, holding her hands above her head, resting his head next to her cheek. He whispered into her ear, "We have to talk, princess."

Sam sighed. "Frank, I thought you wanted to play."

"I do. But I want to make sure we're on the same page, here." He kissed her neck with his moist kisses and ran his lips across her shoulder.

Sam shuddered. "Your touch feels so good on me. I've missed that." She became alert. "What page?"

"Did you mean what you told Chantal about being ready to be a stay-at-home mom?" He let his fingertips cascade down her body.

Sam exhaled deeply.

"Sam, look at me."

She looked at him eye-to-eye. "Yes. I meant every word." She brought her arms down to around his neck.

"So, no more undercover work with the FBI?"

"No more FBI, ever again."

"No matter how much Brett demands it?"

"No matter how much anyone demands it. Satisfied?"

"Not yet, princess, but I will be," he said, giving her his seductive wink. "One more thing—"

"Come on, Frank. I need you. Stop with the being clinical."

"One more thing." He kissed the tip of her nose. "Are you ready to go natural?"

"Natural?" She rolled her eyes. "Oh, God."

"Yeah, primitive. No contraception."

"I know what it means." She laughed the words out then placed her hands on both sides of his face. "Yes! Yes, Frank. I want to have a baby more than anything else right now. And I want to have her with you."

A huge smile crossed his face. "Her? How do you know we'll have a *her*?"

"Her, him, whatever God gives us, I'll be happy."

"Then let's do it. No more talking."

Frank lay on top of her, their lips melding into each other's. Through his positive energy, Sam felt his warmth, his sincerity, his passion and commitment. She'd wanted to hear his commitment to them becoming parents for a long time now. *Knock off the thinking, Sam. Go with it.* She moaned as he moved his hands down her body, squeezing her breasts then tickling her. She writhed under him.

He slid off to the side and, through her smile, he must have realized she was in la-la land. "What's the matter?" He kissed her cheeks then slowly brought his lips down her breasts, and kept them steady on her belly, pecking at her.

She exhaled deeply. "Nothing's the matter."

"Don't BS me. Having second thoughts?" As he spoke, she felt his breath on her stomach and midsection as he moved his head up.

"About what?"

They were now eye-to eye. "Becoming a mom."

Sam ran her palm up and down his forearm. "No. What if it doesn't happen?"

"Hey, you're a perfectly healthy woman. And don't give me the age bull."

"Not only me. You'll be forty-five. Are you positive you want to start with diapers again?"

"I'm well aware of how old I am. Didn't you hear me when I said I want a child as much as you do? And have you been wearing blindfolds the past two months?"

"What? No!"

"I beg to differ. Had your eyes been open, you'd remember I changed more of Margie's diapers than you."

Sam laughed. "You kept count? Yes. I believe you did. Okay. I'm convinced."

"Convinced?"

"Yes, Shrink Khaos, take—me—now."

"You—got—it, princess."

Frank pulled her over him, and Sam moaned, laying on top of him resting her head on his pecs. What comfortable pillows she'd have for the rest of her life. His hands caressed her bottom, squeezing intermittently with gentle spanks. That was what usually got her going. Not tonight. No matter how hard she tried, she couldn't get into the mood. Her usually free flowing energy was blocked. She felt stiff, frigid. Definitely from the stress and heartbreak. She knew it. She understood it. Would Frank? What kind of wife would she make? This man, the man who she loved with all heart would be so disappointed in her. And she loved sex. This never happened. And she'd never say "No" to her partner. *Okay, Sam, go with it. You must please Frank, she thought. He's the most important person in your life.*

ෲෲ

He felt her stillness, the lack of chills and energy that normally ran through her. Yes, Sam was a normal woman who'd just gone through trauma whether she'd admit it or not. With so much on her mind, and her heart laden with sadness, no woman would be aroused during sex. He'd think less of her if she were aroused. Only a cold potato would be able to perform after what she went through these past weeks. He'd become hard the moment he saw her bending over the bed. Sam's flatness now made him the same. "Sam, it's okay—"

"Okay, for what?"

"Sam, we don't have to."

"Yes. We do. I want it so bad. I need it so bad."

"Your body is telling me different."

"Come here," Sam said, inching up his body so their eyes met. "I just need more playing. Women need more than men."

"Now who's being clinical?"

"You'll just have to work harder than usual," she said, tossing him a wink. "Up for the challenge?"

"I think I can manage it." He flipped Sam over onto the bed." He went down on her, her scent driving him nuts. Lavender, she bathed in it. He toyed with her thatch, and bringing his tongue down, he tasted her dryness, like a board.

Oh, man. This isn't going to happen tonight. Why can't she just accept it?

"Frank," she moaned, pushing his head down as her signal to stay there.

He let himself go wild, already hard, sucking her, taking her folds in his teeth, gently tugging, then more with his tongue swirling from her clit to her cavity. He growled softly not to awaken Frankie. She started to tingle under him. He felt the lust, the energy. He inserted two fingers into her and tapped her spot, making her slippery and wet.

"Oh, my God, Frank, now, go in me now."

He turned her onto her side, her arms above her head, holding onto the headboard, and he moved her legs into a fetal position as he cuddled behind her. Sam moved her tush closer into him. He raised her left thigh putting it over his hip as he went into her from behind. Dry. She dried up, preventing him from going in deep. He'd never force it, risking hurting her. She feigned moaning. No way in hell could she disguise this. She'd open just enough for him to get in past his head. It was the first time they've felt each other raw. Oh, man. He'd love that feeling. Her smoothness. Her softness. Not covered by a sheath. But not tonight. She was so damn dry. He pumped, with his arms wrapped around her torso, his fingers playing with her clit at the same time. Shallow pumps. He loved her so much. Her mere touch aroused him. As he bounced toward and away from her spot, he felt her juices beginning to flow. He'd had to admit it, he needed to release. How much longer could he wait? Not long. He felt himself getting hotter, sweatier, then he squirt inside of her with fast short pumps while taking quick breaths. He stayed inside her, waiting. Sam let out a quiet moan, moving her body from side to side.

She faked it. The love of my life faked it. And she did a lousy job of it to boot.

And it was okay. He rolled Sam over onto her back. He lifted her legs up above her head.

She laughed. "Frank, what are you doing?"

"You're a bad girl. You faked it."

"I'm sorry. I never did before. I just couldn't get into it tonight. What are you doing?"

"Hey, give yourself a break. You've been through hell. I'd be more upset if you were in the mood. Keep your legs up."

Her laughing at least decreased her tension. He felt her relax. "Why?" She put her hands onto her stomach.

"You know I came inside of you, right?"

He seemed to have brought her to awareness. "Yes. You did," she said.

"This is an old fashioned way to get the sperm to travel up."

"Seriously?"

"Your parents are both MDs and they never talked to you about it?"

She burst out laughing. "You're kidding me, right? My parents talk about how *to get* pregnant? Never. So you're not mad at me?"

He lowered her legs and brought her into his arms, holding her like the vulnerable woman she was now. And that was fine with him. "I could never be mad at you, princess."

"I love you," she said, holding onto him, looking over his shoulder, and then seeing the comforter. "We made a mess. Let me get up and I'll clean up. And you can change the bedding." Sam attempted to sit up. She put her hands up to her head before she fell onto Frank. "Whoa. I'm dizzy all of a sudden."

"Hold on. You are getting pale." He helped her sit up and bent her head down. "From what?"

"I'm positive it's stress. And I know I haven't eaten anything but the cake." She lifted her head and shook her body. "Whew. It's better now." She swung her legs over the bed and took some deep breaths. A little wobbly, but she managed to stand. Sam stayed still for a few moments. "I'm okay now."

Frank exhaled deeply. "I'll bring you up a banana with almond butter. And then we'll both get some sleep."

☙❧

Florida? I can't believe I'm actually going on a vacation. It's more like a work-vacation unless Frank's okay with me staying on the beach while he carries through on the Scorpio case. Hell, no. I wouldn't let him finish it without me. He needs me with him. Facing his birth parents will probably be the hardest thing he'll ever have to do. Damn you, Henry Slater Senior. You were the bastard of all bastards.

Sam paused in a pensive moment.

No, burying Jen was the hardest think that Frank ever had to do. Now what in hell do I pack?

At her own house in the Madison section of Brooklyn, Sam took a good hard look at the clothes in her walk-in closet in her master bedroom. "Okay. Vicki told me she lives in T-shirts or tank tops, shorts, and flip-flops all year round. That's not exactly me. And I'm sure I'll still need professional clothes. Right? Yes. Definitely." She took her time focusing on her lighter spring corporate casual suits. "Okay, I'd better get this show on the road. We'll be there…um at least seven days, ugh, fourteen outfits? My suitcase will be over the limit." Sam pulled out three solid pants suits, figuring she'd mix and match different blouses and tops. After the third suit lay across her arm, a wave of dizziness flowed through her, the same dizziness she felt the other night in bed with Frank. She wobbled and grabbed onto the top bar in the closet. "Damn it. I hope I'm not coming down with something." Again, the weakness passed in less than a minute. "Whew, at least it passed fast."

She brought the clothes over to her bed and lay them down. Queasiness in her stomach unsettled her. "Oh, no. Please don't let me come down with something." She said a prayer looking up to the ceiling. "Thank you, Lieutenant Martin, for giving me the time off."

Relax, Sam, relax. You've got to shake this.

She started her deep breathing to get into a meditative state, focusing on the earthy dark red energy at the bottom of her feet. Bringing it up through her, Sam's body tingled in her usually receptive way. The energy crept slowly and remained red in color until she felt it swirl around her pelvic area and turn into a baby-girl-pink. She jolted, knowing the color should have still been red. She remained focused, still not comprehending what happened. She'd learned to trust the universal energies and to go with it.

With concentration, she tried to pull the energy up to her navel, and then it would have gone up to her stomach. But no. The energy stayed pink where it lay, totally bringing

Sam out of the meditation. *What the hell happened? Pink? Was it telling me to give sex a rest because I didn't climax last time? Pink is a very healing and loving color. Yes, that's it. I need to love myself enough to forgive myself. Yes. I will.*

Sam left the clothes on the bed and picked up her cell phone, deciding to check her Facebook. Scrolling down her feed, she came across an interesting post. On the pink heart background, a woman wrote, *Ladies, how long after you conceived did you feel you were pregnant? Not with a test. With your intuition.* Wow. That got her interest. Eighty-five women responded, and she read every response. If anyone was intuitive, it was she. She couldn't believe so many women responded that they knew immediately. And they had dizziness. There was a reason she came across this post.

Oh, my God! Am I pregnant? And with a girl?

Tears of unexpected joy flowed.

Dara, tell me. Am I pregnant?

Sam stilled her mind, wondering if Dara would even respond now that she had called upon Theresa. But she did. Sam felt Dara's affirmative twitch in her stomach, as well as twitching coming through from her pelvis.

Oh, my God. I am *pregnant.*

She collapsed onto the bed, bursting into tears.

CHAPTER 29

One Week Later:

It was Frankie's first time flying, and he entertained himself watching some martial arts cartoon on Frank's tablet until he dozed off leaning against Sam. He'd even pulled up the four-inch lace border on her swing top to use as a blanket. Why she needed a cardigan that had a fifty-four inch sweep was beyond him, but what the heck? She was the fashionista. Frank laughed inwardly. She actually knew the dimensions when he asked her. And he loved her in soft-blues. His bride-to-be sat the entire time with her palms on her lower stomach. What was that about? He wouldn't venture to guess. After a while, it dawned on him. Could she be pregnant? Was Sam aware of it? She didn't have the pregnancy glow yet, yet alone any baby-bump. She was rather pale, despite makeup, especially during turbulence when she held her stomach tighter. Large swing on her cardigan? Maternity clothes? Already? Nah, it was too soon to tell. He dismissed the thought. For a moment. But he couldn't let it go.

He did know she wanted a girl, letting it slip the other night, and he didn't need her to do that. She lit up every time she picked up Alexi, or Margie, or had girl-talk with Melissa. He smiled at the recollection and stared at Sam sitting on the aisle seat, pensive as if she was in her own little world. That look. Her face void of expression but serene. She wanted a girl, all right. So did he. That was why he put her into that position. And with shallow penetration, that was the way the studies said to plan for a girl. He wouldn't mock it. It worked for him and Jen. She was three months pregnant with a girl when gunned down. The conversation from the people shuffling down the aisle to exit brought him back from the past heartache.

They landed in Tampa International Airport.

Frank with a duffle over his shoulder, Sam wheeling her carry-on by her side, and Frankie pulling his from behind, walked up the ramp from the plane to the lounge area. As soon as they reached it, Sam raced into the ladies' room opposite them. Frank's gaze took in the crowds, suntanned, in lighter clothing, and even in the air-conditioned terminal, he felt himself becoming too hot in his T-shirt and long jeans. He should have listened to John when he told him April in Florida was hot. He pushed his leather jacket through the handles of his duffle. He'd have to carry it until they picked up their luggage. In their first time traveling together, he'd certainly learn a lot about his future bride.

Sam came out of the ladies' room, smiling to her duo. "Ready?"

"Are you?"

"Yes, why are you looking at me strange?"

"Oh, nothing. You went to the bathroom four times on the plane. Baggage claim is in the lower level. Then we'll get the car."

Looking at the growing crowd, Frank stood closest to the carousel, and they were there before the luggage started to roll. "Move back over there with the carry-ons. I don't want you and Frankie run over." When the ramp started to move, people pushed closer. Seeing Sam's suitcase come around, he pulled hers off. Next, his was a breeze in comparison. He grabbed Frankie's thinking it would be the lightest, and his arm certainly got the jolt of the unexpected. It was damn heavy. What did the kid pack? He signaled to Sam who came right away and pulled his while he took hers and Frankie's.

"What did you pack in here?" he said critically to his son.

"Clothes."

He looked at Frankie with a raised eyebrow. "This feels a lot heavier than clothes."

"Sam helped me. And she used the extra room for her stuff." He glared at Sam. "See? I told you, he'd know."

"Oh, man. You packed for a week. Your cases weren't enough for you?"

"Obviously. My bath and body products and makeup weigh a ton. What's the big deal? We're good. Let's go get the car, King Khaos."

"King Khaos?" Frankie laughed.

"That's his name when he gets bossy."

Frankie, wide-eyed, stared at her.

"Don't you even think it, champ."

Not to Frank's liking, the wait for the rental was a lot longer than anticipated. People complained they didn't get the car they reserved. When he got up to the desk, he preferred not to use his NYPD consult badge, so he opted for his military ID that indicated Special Forces. That caught the eye of the thirty-something guy behind the car rental desk, even initiating a salute. Frank reciprocated in appreciation. A few minutes later, after the clerk spoke with some other people, their SUV appeared.

"John told me the trip is a straight ride—"

"That's good."

"Uh, no. Don't get so excited. It's at least ninety minutes."

Sam's jaws dropped. "Well, I'm assuming there are rest stops."

"Hey. I'm putting on my MD hat here. You're not drinking that much. We'll talk at the house."

Sam chuckled, turned, and Frank saw her sly smile as she pulled her suitcase toward the parking lot entrance.

Yeah, she sure does know something is up. I'll play along. For a while.

❧❧❧

In Prescott, Arizona, in the kitchen of her ranch house, Lauren Berkeley, with her back against the kitchen sink, stared at her son in exasperation as he fiddled with the fried chicken thigh on his plate, the string beans moved to the side and over the edge. She shook her head as she watched him slip a fork filled with chicken to the boxer that lay by his feet. "Henry, you have to eat your dinner. Star already had his."

"No. I don't. And he's my only friend."

For a moment, she turned her back and stared out the kitchen window at the massive acreage she worked hard to build and maintain. All of her knowledge on how to run a horse ranch didn't help her now. Thirty-five horses, groomers, trainers, vets, all with expert knowledge but none on parenting. She turned, pulled a chair away from the table, and sat knee-to-knee to him. "Baby, you've only been here a week. We're going to take you to your school on Monday. Would you like that?"

Henry rubbed his greasy index finger in the knotted holes on the tree-trunk table. Still not responsive, he dipped his fingers into the bowl of brown gravy next to his plate. With his lips sealed, he swiped his fingers over the shiny finish on the table. He looked up slyly at his mother. "I guess."

"Okay. You're done." She pulled the plate away from him and wiped the table with a wet cloth. "Let's go wash you up." She grabbed onto his forearm, and he yanked it away.

"I can do it myself."

Lauren smiled. "Go right ahead, little man." She stood watching him with her arms folded across her chest. The button on the front of her plaid shirt popped off. In a daze, she watched it fall to the floor and bounce under the kitchen table.

This motherhood thing ain't what it's cracked up to be.

He traipsed into the adjoining bathroom and slid the little stool in front of the sink. The three-year-old made a game of jumping up onto it and turned on the faucet. He giggled. The pump-bottle of hand soap must have caught his eye. With his palm on the handle, he pumped the pink soap into his other hand until it overflowed and fell into the running water. Laughing, he rubbed his hands together, splashing them into the sink. Bubbles built up and overflowed onto the oak floor. Hysterical laughing brought an angry mom running in.

"Henry! What on earth are you doing?" Lauren yelled, shutting off the water, and bending down close to his face. "Child, I can't leave you alone for a minute! Do you know how hard it's going to be to clean up this mess?"

"No," he said, pouting. Then, in a whim of mischief, he cupped some of the pink fluffiness into his palm and tossed the soap up into his mother's face.

"Henry!" With a raised palm to swat his behind, she stopped mid-air. *It's too soon for that*, she thought, controlling her hand as she shifted to grab a towel off the oak rack. "Henry, that soap burned my eyes. You hurt Mommy." She bent down and scooped as much as she could of the bubbles into the towel and tossed it into the tub, starting the water.

He stepped off the bench. "I'm sorry," he said as he peered up at her.

"You're a big boy and you have to start to think before you do something. Okay?"

"Yeah."

"Excuse me?"

He crinkled his nose. "What?"

"It's 'yes, ma'am.'"

"Yes, what?"

"Ma'am. It's showing you have proper manners."

Shaking his head, he said, "I never heard that word before."

"Well, it looks like your Uncle Frank and Aunt Samantha didn't teach you manners."

Henry perked up then a moment later started to cry and raced out of the bathroom.

Okay, Lauren, bad move.

She tossed the bathroom mat into the tub.

⌘

John opened the front door of his parent's home inside Bueno Terrace in Serento, holding Alexi over his right shoulder, Zach over his left, and with Duke sitting by his side. Frank and Sam stared at him with their mouths agape.

"Don't, tough guys, don't. They both woke up at the same time, and Vicki's making dinner," John said as he moved over to let them in. "Pick up the suitcases if you can. My mother will freak if you scratch the tiles."

"Smells great in here," Frank said as he came in with both hands loaded.

"It sure does." Sam's gaze shot to the pattern in the flooring. "That design is spectacular."

"Thanks. My mother decorated the whole house, top to bottom."

"She's a match for Henry Slater, where's the bathroom," Sam said in the same breath.

"Right over there. Four steps to your left." John watched Sam race with her legs rubbing together as her aura shouted to him a bright silver and orange. He smiled ear to ear.

"What?" Frank asked, throwing his arms out to the side.

"Nothing. Ricky, Frankie's here. Come take him to your room."

Ricky appeared, yelling, "Come on, Frankie." He grabbed up Frankie's suitcase. "Yikes, this is heavy."

"Let me take that, Ricky. Sam's stuff is in there, too. We'll bring it in later."

The boys ran off with Duke beating them as Sam came back.

John stared and smiled. "Come on, let's go into the kitchen. I'm sure we're wanted in there by now."

"You sure are," Vicki said, coming into the entry hall. She embraced Sam. "How are you feeling, darlin'? Any better?" She walked toward the dining room with her arm around Sam.

"Thanks, Vicki. It's tough. I miss them so much."

"Hey, Sam," Frank said. Sam turned around. "Watch what you say in front of Frankie," he continued. "He's the child in your life now."

Sam paused and nodded. She wrapped her arms around his torso. "You're right, Frank. You're right."

As they sat around the dining room table, Duke was the first to run in and lay down next to Ricky's usual seat. Too bad Sam was in it, getting her thigh pawed by the pup. "Hi, boy," she said, rubbing his head.

"That's not a happy greeting, Sam," John said. "You're in the wrong seat. But stay there. Since we were in New York, Ricky got him used to people-food. I'm trying to train him away from it, but he's winning."

Frank laughed. "Forget about it. Once they have that taste, you're done."

"Hey, Dad. When are we getting a dog? You promised."

Vicki brought platters of chicken Francaise surrounded by grilled veggies to the table. Frank and Ricky inhaled deeply. "That smells so good, Vicki," Frank said as he used the spatula to serve his son. "Right, Sam?"

Sam couldn't answer. She gagged. And paled. All eyes were on here, even the boys.

"Sam, are you okay," Vicki asked as she put a platter of gluten-free biscuits on the table.

"Sam," Frank asked with concern in his voice, "are you okay? What's wrong, princess?"

"I'm just a little dizzy. It was a long day. And I haven't flown in ages." She placed her palms on her lower stomach.

John shot Frank a glance then grinned. Ricky smiled, too.

"What? You know something I don't?" Frank asked.

"Not necessarily," John responded.

Ricky wide-eyed stared at his father. "I know! Sam's pregnant."

A dead silence overtook the room then laughter from the adults, minus Sam. John's gaze took in the massive room, and he concentrated on the faux painted wall in the beige marble pattern. Anything, not to be put on the spot. Sam sure was pregnant. Her aura glowed with the vibrant colors of a mom-to-be.

"Really? Really, Sam? Are you pregnant?" Frankie asked. "I'm going to have a baby brother or sister? Really? Really?" He got up and ran around the table, embracing her.

Sam held him for dear life. "I think so, Frankie. I think so. But I haven't taken a test yet."

"Ricky, how do you know?" Frank asked.

"Grandma Esther told me. She's a doctor that delivers babies. And Mom had the same look on her face when she was pregnant with Alexi and Zach. I know because I came back to live with them right at the beginning. Right, Dad?"

John gave his son a thumbs up. "Well said and very accurate."

Vicki placed a reassuring palm on Sam's forearm. "Sam, eat what you can. No pressure, darlin'."

Sam took a few deeps breaths. "I'm good. Thank you. So what are the plans for tomorrow?"

∽∾∽

Lisa Brandt, sitting behind her desk in the home-office of her condo—in the section of Chicago known as The Loop—sorted through the papers she was given by the New York City Child Protective Services. Her lawyer-brain swirled, not with the information before her, but on the man whom she loved with all her heart, Henry Slater. Not that she'd admit it to them. Those detectives. How intrusive they were. She still couldn't absorb the fact that Melissa wasn't Henry's only child as he told her as well as the others. Luckily, Melissa looked like her—same color hair, shape of the eyes. Her daughter wouldn't be a constant reminder. And that bastard! To lie to her. One thing she doubted was that Henry offed himself. He was too vain. At least he provided for Melissa in a trust. She got good vibes from Frank Khaos and his fiancée, Samantha. They were now in Florida going to confront Henry's biological parents. Guess he was the bastard. *Wake up, Lisa, you're now a full-time single mom, and a full-time partner at Ponte and Brandt. After the funds in the will are distributed, you'll also be a more-than-wealthy woman.* In a moment of self-pity, she threw her pen on top of the desk and slouched in her chair. What a decision. Taking a child-care leave was out of the question. The firm wouldn't grant it, and she'd just made full-partner last month. She swallowed. She'd need a nanny. Then she had an epiphany. *Um, what do I have to do to find out if I'm even in the will?*

She stood, opening the slat blinds, and stared out of the window from the thirtieth floor overlooking the busy residential area filled with high-rise apartment building such as hers. She tried meditating but the serenity didn't come as it always did.

Melissa snuck up behind her mother, jolting her. "Mommy, FedEx is at the door. I asked who it was and they said you have to sign for two boxes."

Lisa smiled. "Then let's go see what those boxes are." She put her hand on her daughter's back and led her through the hallway into the dining room, through the entry hall to the door. "I'm glad you didn't open the door, honey."

Melissa shook her head. "I never would. Daddy told me. I know. It's probably my arts supplies."

"Art supplies?" Lisa asked as she opened the front door. The FedEx driver handed her a clipboard and a pen. "Thank you." One box was huge. The other narrow box leaned against the wall standing about six-feet tall.

"Yes. Daddy had an art room in his apartment, and he was teaching me. I want to be a decorator like him." Melissa stared at the return address, ignoring her mother's reactions.

A decorator? Over my dead body. I want no reminder of that bastard in my house.

"Yes! It's from Uncle Frank. It's definitely my art supplies. That's probably the drawing board," Melissa said, pointing to the box against the wall. She tried to lift it. The box didn't budge. "Mommy, help me slide it into the apartment." She looked up at her mother's frown. "What's the matter?"

"Nothing, honey. Let's get these into the hallway, and we'll open them."

And then I can figure out how to throw everything away when you're at school.

☙❧

He'd made it. The infamous Jarrett Miller made it. He began to love his reputation. Though still wanted for the murders in New York City, he managed his escape. Yeah, that FBI Special Agent Brett Case could kiss his ass. Jarrett made it to the county they'd never think he'd return to— Sun County in Florida. He'd hit other areas in the state, where he had to look over his shoulder a bit, but never here, not in years. One of his contacts in Delaware arranged his ride. The guy actually drove into Lower Manhattan to pick him up. With a new appearance, keeping his head shaved, he bleached his mustache, eyebrows, and beard, a strawberry blond. Big difference from his medium-brown. The beard was curly, too, reaching at least four-inches and still growing. Luckily, he was fair complexioned so the lighter color worked.

To play it safe, he used a real smelly depilatory to remove all of his body hair—the hair not covered by clothes. The pic that his ex and the feds were sharing on social media looked no-way-in-hell like him.

With a change of drivers in each state, starting in Manhattan, they zigzagged through the states, so far west, the feds wouldn't have an eye out for him. He landed in the Panhandle in Florida after driving through Texas, Louisiana, Alabama, and Mississippi. At that point, he got his own vehicle. Why let his stooges know his final destination. Several weeks passed since he spoke to the woman who betrayed him. Once was enough. The next time he'd see her was right here. In her home state. In her county.

He'd read in a local Florida paper that Vicki's dad, the renowned Sheriff Marin was retiring in mid-April. What kind of daughter would she be if she didn't come down for the party of the county? Definitely. His ex, Victoria Elizabeth Marin, would be making an appearance. He had some more time to wait. He'd timed his arrival perfectly. The county was small enough for him to find her. He knew where her house was. Not the one they lived in, in marital bliss, ha, ha, the thought made him burst out laughing, but the house she bought a few years later.

He'd learned about the new house from one of his pain-doc contacts right after he got out. *Glad he had the same phone number*, Jarrett thought. Yep, Dr. Sterling Geod, the doctor—who had offices in a few different counties—was still his best source. And he even formed some really tight friendships in his office back in the day. Camille and Joshua Hunter. Once Jarrett found out they were originally from New York City, that cinched it. A friendship for life. He laughed, friends all right. *Did he even know what friend meant?* Nope to him it was all business. And those two were waiting for his call.

Jarrett hoped that Vicki still had that house, but now she had a new family and her last name was Trenton. So who knew where she was? He couldn't afford to put out feelers now so he wouldn't be counting on anyone but himself, including a select few. He'd just have to guess that after eighteen years, Vicki's likes and dislikes were the same. He'd canvas the areas she'd like to go. Easy-peasy. Then it dawned on him. A lot could happen in eighteen years since he'd last been here. He noticed that driving around—more stores, restaurants, even department stores, though nothing like New York City with whom he had a love-hate relationship. Deep down inside, he was the Florida-boy who loved the sunshine and good old hometown cooking—Vicki's cooking.

He lay down on the bed in his rented trailer in the RV park, still getting used to the name he chose—Fred Crumby—sounded good-ole-fashioned Southern to him. Too bad, he didn't have any of the paperwork to go along with it. Just lots of cash. Enough to keep him from leaving a paper trail for months. It had better not take him that damn long to find that bitch.

CHAPTER 30

Since this was first time he'd be working with cops in another state, Frank decided to dress the part, putting on a denim sports jacket over his black T-shirt, and jeans, and they weren't his usual skinny's. Sam stuck to her corporate casual look, wearing a beige pants suit in a Ponte knit with a light blue blouse, and no jewelry, except for her sugilite and moldavite pendant she kept tucked under her blouse. She carried the jacket over her arm.

John wore his usual—not an Armani suit, but a dressier sport jacket. Yeah, even at the house, Frank looked at him strangely as they left. It was in the high eighties. Guess John forgot about Florida temperatures. When John opened the door, the humidity hit Frank right in the face. Oh, man, was that uncomfortable. And it was only April. He didn't know how long he'd be able to stand this heat.

Frank had never seen so much greenery as on their drive up. Now, with John driving, he was able to take in more of the scenery. A lot of available land. Being used to wall-to-wall buildings in Manhattan, and on his small plot at home in Brooklyn, he wasn't sure if he'd like it here. He felt claustrophobic in Slater's apartment building, but this was the other extreme.

Neither he or Sam had ever been in a relatively new precinct. Walking into the Sun County Emergency Operations Center in Lardo, they both seemed astonished by the white walls, fresh green carpeting, and the huge state-of-the-art war room wowed them. There was room for over thirty officers, each having their own computer on the table in front of their cushioned swivel seats. And that was with the room in its smallest capacity. Freezing from the air conditioning, Sam put on the blazer that hung over her arm.

John pointed in the direction they needed to go. "Nice, Uh?"

"Tell me about it," Frank said. He looked up, reciprocating the smile from a guy at the other end of the room. "That's got to be your wife's twin."

"Both of her brothers are here. Come on."

After the man hugs, John introduced Frank and Sam to Vicki's brothers, Commander of SWAT, Mark Marin, and Detective Brian Marin as they sat at the conference table. Frank didn't waste time, opening the manila folder he carried. Sam removed more paperwork from her tote.

Brian sat opposite Frank and Sam with the screen on his computer lit up. Apparently, he was a no-nonsense guy, too, getting right to it. "Okay, let me get this straight. Dr. Khaos, your brother, a serial killer, wanted you to come down to Florida to confront your biological parents as a stipulation for the execution of his will. Correct?"

"Yes. Exactly."

"For what purpose?"

"Basically, he wants me to give them a message. He blames them for him turning out to be a murderer so that they can go to their graves guilt ridden."

"That's a stretch," the commander said.

"No. Not really," Frank said, pausing. "In Henry Slater's case, his psychopathology is environmental. Yes, he was treated badly, not so much with physical abuse, although some was evident, but more neglect. He felt his parents didn't want him. A head injury, knocked against the wall by his father precipitated bad headaches, and continued when he banged his head against the wall in the closet they locked him in. In addition, he had repeated falls where he hit his head. That damaged the frontal cortex. The autopsy showed that. He's a big as me, so you could imagine the pressure of the falls."

Brian shook his head. "Don't buy it. Feeling neglected isn't an excuse for being a killer."

"No. Of course not. But the brain injury is. He couldn't control his impulses. And in his own warped mind, he chose his target by the neglect."

"How so?"

"What do you already know?"

"Not much. The New York FBI headquarters contacted the Miami office, and an agent contacted me. Special Agent Brett Case was working closely with you. That's it. They wanted you to give us the facts and the documentation. We just couldn't go round up innocent people."

"Okay. Henry Slater came onto our radar with his first killing in the city, Carolyn Baines—"

"Who was my best friend," Sam said woefully.

Brian compressed his lips before he spoke. "Sorry, Detective."

Frank patted Sam's forearm. "He'd gotten careless and his DNA was recovered at the scene. His wasn't in the system but mine is. That's when I learned I had a brother, not one but two. We were placed for adoption. My brother Carl was adopted at birth. I was in the foster care system until adopted at ten. Henry, who was born Benjamin Hunter was the child they kept. The start of his murder spree was when he found out we existed, nine years ago. He did not attempt to find Carl or me. The headaches were intolerable by then. Putting together what his children told us, when he went away for the night, that's when he did the kills, the headaches were gone when he came back."

"Whoa, his children? The kids knew what he was doing?"

"No. No. No. They're young. Sam and I had them for two and half months. They're back with their moms now. But that's another case."

"You said he chose his targets as a result of his parent's neglect?" Brian said. "How so?"

"Now, this is a stretch. He informed me his mother told him all the time that she didn't want him, and she never should have had children. So, he killed women who told him they didn't want to have children."

"Seriously?"

"Yes," John said. "Don't mock it. You guys down here don't have the capacity to deal with a serial killer investigations. Small units. That's why he was able to get away with seventeen murders across fourteen states. They were viewed as isolated murders until he got to New Jersey. The psychology of it only has to make sense to them, not us. Other women told us what a wonderful and compassionate man he was. He seemed to be the perfect man—until you add in the murderer component. His children's mothers adored him."

"You're right," Brian said. "I'm on the job over twenty-three years, and I've never had a serial case. That I knew of, anyway."

"Hold on a second. He's deceased? Was he killed in capture?" Mark said.

"Not exactly. He set us up. We thought we would capture him. We didn't know he knew about me. We underestimated him. By the standard definition, he took Sam hostage. For her release, he demanded to meet me, and our other brother, along with his nieces and nephews. We had a very long meeting. He had the will and told us what he wanted. He had a hundred-sixty-K in hundred dollar bills for each of his victims' families, along with handwritten confessions. He also had a trust for his niece and three nephews. Then John found in his apartment, the trusts for his four children."

"That's a lot of money," Brian said. What did this guy do?"

"A lot," Sam said. "He was constantly trying to prove his parents wrong, that he was good enough. For one, he designed and operated restaurants in casinos up and down the east coast. He had a decorating business for high-priced apartment building dwellers in the city. On his evil side, he spearheaded or controlled a child kidnapping ring and bogus adoption ring. That's the case still under investigation, and the FBI is taking down players across the country. And with all that, he was a protective dad to four, with one on the way."

"Can't pin being a dead-beat dad on him at least," Brian said. "Okay, what are the parents' names and do you have any idea where they live?"

"Somewhere around Crystal River, and their names are Joshua and Camille Hunter," Frank said, choking out their names. "They were seventeen when they had me. They're sixty-one now." He slouched back into his chair.

"Are you sure you want to do this, Doc?" Mark asked.

"I have no choice. After he laid it all onto the table, the bastard swallowed a cyanide capsule. He croaked a couple minutes after. The courts acknowledge this as a deathbed confession. And what's asked has to be carried through."

Brian typed the names into the search for Sun County court records. He let out a deep breath and spun the laptop around for them to see. "Here are your parents, Dr. Khaos. Not exactly in Crystal River."

Frank stared at his father's license photo. He was looking at an older him. For the second time since his adoption thirty-four years ago, he felt abandoned. He blew out an exasperated deep breath. "That was too easy. Where's my mother's?"

Brian slid to the next screen. Prison record. Frank's eyes widened as he read the document. He could tell his mother must have been an attractive woman in her youth, with short dark brown hair and brown eyes. Though her life hadn't been easy—it couldn't have been easy. Not with a three-year prison sentence and then going back to her less-than-moral life.

"Her license is suspended," Brian said.

"How come?"

Brian turned the computer back toward himself and typed some more. "A DUI four years ago, her third. She also has outstanding driving violations."

Frank looked down and shook his head. "Real sweethearts. Okay. What are the odds they're living at the residence you have?"

"Fifty-fifty. Though residents are supposed to change their address on their license within ten days of moving."

Frank fidgeted in his seat. "With the history these two have, I don't think they take anything seriously. Even at their age now, they're sleaze."

"Maybe they just had a hard life."

Sam rested her palm on his forearm. "You know, Frank, we only know what Henry Slater told us from his perspective. His might not be based in reality."

Frank pointed to Brian. "What Detective Marin just told us sort of confirms what Slater said. Three DUIs? Prison term? That's extreme for well-functioning people. I'm tending to go along with Slater on this one."

"Okay," said Mark. "How do you want to proceed? Want us to bring them here, or do you want to go to their residence?"

"Where do they live?"

"In a manufactured home area on the lake."

"Oh, nice!" Sam said.

Brian and Mark laughed. "Don't jump to that conclusion yet, Detective."

"It's, Sam," she said, "and he's Frank. We're informal. Do you mind?"

"Not at all. We're Brian and Mark. So what do you want to do?"

Frank compressed his lips while nodding. "Let's go there." He began to rise. "No." He swallowed hard. "Bring them here. I want to know nothing about them."

John shot Frank his signature look. "I suggest you reconsider."

"Why?" Frank went over to the window and grimaced,

looking out at the expansive green lawn.

John spoke to Frank's back. "Because *you* need closure as much as Slater did."

Frank turned around.

"It's true, Frank," Sam said compassionately. "You haven't slept peacefully since you learned Slater existed."

Frank raised his index finger in thought. "Okay, but I go myself. Not with you, John, nor you, Sam. I want them to know nothing about my relationships. I'm going to pretend I'm delivering news about their son. Now where did you say they were? Not in Crystal River? Though, it wouldn't make a difference to me."

"First, no. You're not going alone," Brian said. "Second, they're in Wilbur. The area mostly houses trailers and manufactured homes. It's not a safe area to go alone. You just can't go up to someone's house. And are you planning not to tell them you're a son they placed for adoption? They'll take one look at you, and they'll know. You definitely need a police escort. For one, you don't hold any jurisdiction here. And secondly, you don't have a permit to carry."

"It's not a criminal matter."

"But they have criminal pasts. Sixty-one isn't old enough to guarantee you'll be safe."

"Excuse me?" Frank asked startled, pointing to himself then throwing his arms out. "You think I can't handle myself?"

Mark put his palm up. "We know your MMA background, but this is a right-to-carry-state, and even though they have felonies on their record, and they're not supposed to carry, we can't be sure they'd adhere to the law."

"Okay, so you two can go with me."

"Yes."

"Okay, Sam, you go back to the house with John and have some fun with Vicki and the kids."

Sam looked at him dumbstruck and didn't move.

"Seriously. I don't know how this Florida heat will work for you now."

John burst out laughing. "And you think pregnant women don't live in Florida?"

"Frank, er, if you're going to be the mother-hen, you'll be worse than my parents!"

❧❧❧

On the phone with the hospital administrator, Sarah Phillips sat back in her office chair in her one-family home in a Salt Lake City, Utah, suburb, aggravated beyond words. She'd taken a week off to settle in with her son, and now she was getting dissension about wanting to rearrange her hours. Never in a million years did she think she'd have this much trouble. Not with her seniority. Apparently, that status was all bullshit. They had told her to work it out with her colleagues. No one in the hospital pharmacy seemed caring enough to want to change shifts with her. She was only asking for a couple of hours different. They gave her the excuse that they'd have to hire per-diem for someone to fill in the slot, and her situation would disrupt the usual shifts. She just needed to end at two-thirty, not five, to be home in time for Benjamin when he got off the school bus. What the heck was she supposed to do? She had no mommy-friends in the neighborhood to have him stay at a kid's house for a couple of hours. At nine, Benjamin was still too young to be a latchkey kid. She heard clicking on the other end of the line. Crap. After ten minutes of holding on for the administrator, they dropped the call. Forget it. She couldn't deal with the hassle now anyway. She'd have to hire a babysitter. She slumped back into her chair as Benjamin came into the room.

"What's the matter, Mom?" Benjamin asked.

"Why must every conversation with you start with 'what's the matter?'"

Benjamin let out a harrumph and walked over to her desk. "Because. You never look happy."

"That's just the way I am."

"No, it's not." He rolled his eyes. "Did you forget what Dr. John told you?"

"What? That you can get inside my head?"

"Yeah, well, I can."

"Well, let me tell you something. Come over here." She pulled him into her embrace. "You want to be a doctor, right?" He nodded. "Well then, start thinking like one. I'm telling you from a medical point of view that none of that stuff you somehow believe in is scientifically proven."

"Dr. John is a doctor, and he can do all that, and he told me he's been like this since he was a little kid, like me."

"Well, Dr. John is out-of-the-ordinary then."

"So why can't I be out-of-the-ordinary, too? Uncle Frank and Aunt Sam understood me."

"All well and good. Your mother, me, does not, and in our house I make the rules."

Benjamin shot her a hard stare. "Then I don't want to grow up in this house." He stormed out of the office.

ℲℲℲ

Frank sat in the back of the police Charger, looking out the window, with his mind wandering. What in the world, was he going to say to these people? These two people who irresponsibly had not one, but two children who they had no intention of raising. Granted, they were only seventeen but, where were their parents? His grandparents. How could a grandma and grandpa not want to have contact with their grandchildren? He knew that Jen's parents and, definitely, Sam's, would do no such thing. His parents probably did do him and Carl favors by placing them for adoption, but saying "Thank you" to them was way out of his comfort zone, shrink or not, and he was a human being first, not to mention someone who went through his own trials and conflicts his entire life. No, he had nothing to thank them for. The only ones he had gratitude for were Theresa and Peter Khaos who changed his life for the better. They were his parents and the only ones whom he'd honor with that title.

It seemed like they drove forever, grass after grass after grass. He'd tire of the color green soon. He finally understood Sam's dislike for the color red after the Aries case. He let out a guttural laugh. Not one store, shopping mall, gas station came into view. Were they taking the scenic route? Where was civilization? They finally crossed over a main road. Frank turned his head fast for his gaze to take in some fast food restaurants. Then one block over, they turned down a country road and slowed. "We there?"

"No, Frank," Brian said. "Take a look out the window. My side." Brian stopped the car.

Frank slid over to the driver's side and rolled the window down. "Whoa, that's a big turtle." He laughed and took a photo of it to show his son.

"That's a snapper turtle. A bite could snap off your finger. They grow to over thirty-five pounds. If you come across one, stay away."

"Thanks for the head's up. What are we waiting for?"

"For that little fella to decide what he wants to do. He's too close to the tire. Sit back and relax. This can take a while."

"You're kidding me, right?"

"No. They're endangered. It's a crime to kill them. And don't feed them either."

Frank chuckled. "Okay, what other kind of wildlife are we going to meet?"

"The Hunters live on a natural lake. You never know if an alligator might decide to go for a stroll."

"How do the residents deal with that?"

"Sort of a mutual respect," Mark said. "When the humans stay out of the lake, the gators stay away from the edge. I'm not saying there aren't any incidents, though." He glanced out of the window. "Go," he said to Brian. "He reached the other side. We're going about another five miles."

Frank's gaze went to either side of the car, looking out into the woods. At some less dense area, he saw run-down wooden shacks and garbage strewn on the ground. It looked like a rather unpleasant place to call home. The surroundings seemed similar to what John explained to him about where Ricky lived prior to his rescue over four years ago. *The Hunters moved down here from Brooklyn, so how did they find themselves here? Unless, they wanted to hide. And from whom?*

Brian turned onto a dirt road so narrow the branches from the trees made their way into the back seat through the rolled-down window.

A heavy branch swiped Frank's face before he could grab it. "Whoa!" In his yelling, Brian swerved the car and came to a halt. The two cops looked toward the back seat where Frank was trying to push the branch back out of the window. It was thick enough that Frank—with all his strength—could not simply break it off.

After the laughter, and Frank reddening, Mark got out of the car, having to push the car door against more foliage. For a man as big as John, he had his own struggle. Mark slid against the Charger to the back of the car. Opening the trunk, he pulled out a battery-operated chain saw. He managed to cut through the branch and Frank snapped the rest of it, leaving a part on his lap.

"Uh, what am I supposed to do with this?"

Mark opened the rear, passenger side door. "Not keep it, that's for sure. There are red ants on that." He pulled the branch across Frank's lap and out of the car. "Check your pants. If you see ants, kill those buggers. Their bite is brutal."

Frank saw a few crawling down his leg. He swatted them as they reached his cuff."

"If you get red, swollen, and itchy as heck, you got bit."

"Thanks, pal. Any more good news?"

"Yeah, we'll be there in a few minutes." Brian drove the next three miles without more interference from nature since Frank rolled up the window. They turned up another narrow road and drove until the dead end.

Frank got out of the car, putting on his shades as he walked to the water's edge. The view that accosted his gaze was spectacular. He breathed in the fresh air. The energy from the dense foliage cleansed him. Wow! He couldn't live in the desolation, but he could understand wanting to live amongst nature. Not one sliver of concrete. His gaze traveled around the edge of the lake. Not rainy season, the water level was lowered, and he saw Lilly pads and heard frogs communicating. He felt they were yelling at him for intruding upon their peace. Their land. Their home. He'd heed to Mark's warning and not get too close to the water. He backed off. A face-to-face meeting with an alligator was as much on his bucket-list as meeting his birth parents. He wondered which would be worse.

Mark called to him from the front door of the run-down home a few feet away from him. Frank turned and grimaced at the structure he previously ignored.

"They're not here," Mark said. "This house hasn't been occupied in months, and there's hurricane damage."

"Damn. I knew it was too easy when you found their address."

"Okay, let's head back to the office and start some investigating. You have a week?"

"A little more. Ten days if we need it."

CHAPTER 31

Benjamin plopped down on the bed in his room, contemplating his life—all nine years of it. No way would this mother love him. Not like Uncle Frank and Aunt Sam. He fell onto his back, staring up at the ceiling. He smirked as he looked around. As much as he told his mother what he wanted—a room like the one he had in his dad's apartment in Manhattan—she didn't get it. The smart doctor—Sarah Phillips—who thought she could tell him how to think couldn't even get the colors right. She painted his room a pale blue and had blue plaid bedding and sheets. Ugh. Boring, with a capital B. He missed his brother and sisters, and his cousin Frankie. He felt lonely, the loneliest he'd ever felt in his life. Even lonelier than he felt when his dad made him stay in that cage-dollhouse for an hour after he pulled that shenanigan with Miss Monty. At least he saw Dad, Melissa, and Henry baking cookies in the kitchen. He'd call Melissa. Benjamin got off his bed and opened the top drawer in his desk, pulled out a piece of paper, and tiptoed into the kitchen. Looking around in the hallway, he saw that his mother was nowhere to be found. He picked up the handset on the counter and dialed. Melissa's mother answered on the second ring.

"Hello."

"Lisa, this is Benjamin. Can I speak to Melissa, please?"

"No, Benjamin. Do you realize what time it is?"

He glanced up at the clock. *Nine o'clock, big deal.* "Well, we don't go to bed yet."

Melissa must have heard her mother and she ran into the den. "Mom, is that Benjamin?"

Benjamin yelled into the phone, "Yes, Melissa, it's me.

"All right, talk to him. Not too long."

Benjamin whispered, "Go somewhere private." He went into his room. "Where are you?"

"In my room. Benjamin, I got to get out of here."

"Me, too."

"What are we going to do? She told me we don't have room for my art supplies. This is a big apartment. There are a couple of extra rooms. She hates me."

"Mine does, too. She doesn't like the way I can tell things. I know. Let's call Uncle Frank. Remember when dad had two people on the phone?"

"Yes."

"I remember how to do it. Hold on." Benjamin put Melissa on hold, dialed Frank, and when the phone rang, he brought his sister in. Frank's phone went to voicemail. Benjamin ignored the message ding. "Should we leave a message, Melissa?"

"No. We need to talk to him in person. Hang up and call Dr. John."

"Okay, hold on." When John's cell rang, Benjamin reconnected his sister.

ↂↂↂ

John answered on the third ring. "Trenton here."

"Dr. John," Melissa and Benjamin yelled into the phone at once. Each one bombarded him with what was going on.

John walked out onto the lanai and sat on his favorite built-for-two lounge he brought over from Vicki's house. "Hold on. One at a time. I can't understand what you're saying. How do you know how to do a conference call?" He paused. "Of course you'd know. What's going on?"

He wouldn't even mention the time. They should have been in bed.

"Okay. Benjamin, you go first," Melissa said.

"Dr. John, it's so bad," Benjamin said, crying out the words. "I can't talk to her. She's so mad all the time."

"Mad about what?"

"Her job. She was trying to change her schedule so she could be home when I get off the bus, and kept calling them, and they got mad at her, and fired her. And now she doesn't have a job."

"Whoa. Hold on, Benjamin. That can't happen with all the time your mom has at that hospital. Are you sure she was fired?"

"Yes. Now all she does is sleep, all day. I even got up myself this morning to go to school, and I met the school bus alone."

"Why do you think she sleeps all day?"

"She'd been taking these pills."

John got that jolt-of-a-memory-moment. Nick told him he thought Dr. Phillips needed her own pharmaceuticals. And he saw that possibility in her aura. "What kind of pills, Benjamin. This is important."

"I know about the bad-drugs from Dad. He never liked to take them, and he told us all about them if we were ever approached by someone in school."

"In your school? Scholars Academy? I doubt if anything bad would happen there." *Yes, it can happen anywhere, but why alarm the kid?*

"Yes. Dad knew. But he said, 'just in case.'"

Frank came out onto the lanai. He mouthed to John, "Benjamin?"

He nodded. "They called me, too." He sat and listened.

"Think, Benjamin. What kind of drugs?"

"She told me they calm her nerves, and I saw her spill some into her hand, and she put a lot into her mouth and drank a lot of water. In the beginning she didn't take that many, but the past week, she's taking a lot."

"Benjamin, this is Uncle Frank. And then what happened?"

Before Benjamin could say anything Melissa cried into the phone.

"We want to come back to you and Aunt Sam. We can't take it here. We're dying. Why did you do this to us?"

Frank compressed his lips, leaned back into the lounge chair, and ran his hands over his face. He stayed with his face covered until John elbowed him. "Guys, it's the law."

Benjamin sobbed. "We don't care about the law. Our lives are more important than any law."

"And my mom hates me doing art." Melissa cried the words out. "I heard her mumbling that she'd throw my art stuff out when I'm in school. I think she was saying it to herself, but sounds came out. I started screaming, and she said, 'Okay' but I can only draw in my free time. And my teacher! She's so mean, even though I'm the new girl in the class. I want to go back to Mr. Bannon. He was teaching me how to sing."

"It's only been a little over a week, guys—"

"A week, too many, Uncle Frank," Benjamin said, weeping.

"And she wants to go back to Italy, anyway," Melissa said, whining the words out."

"Italy? Really?"

"Yes, Uncle Frank. I heard her on the phone, trying to get me a nanny. She doesn't want to be with me."

In the background, John and Frank heard yelling from a pissed-off mom. "Get off the damn phone, Benjamin! I mean it, now!"

The call abruptly disconnected. John and Frank sat stunned, both slumping into the lounge. John spoke first. "Okay, we might be able to do something here. Getting Benjamin away from a drug-addicted mother might be easier. And if Melissa's mother wants to leave the country..." He let his voice trail off. John didn't want to call Brett so late, but he'd send a text. *Melissa and Benjamin are very unhappy. Benjamin told us his mom is abusing pills. Lisa Brandt wants to leave the country. Check it out.*

"I'm not telling Sam about this call for a couple of reasons. I don't want her to get her hopes up, and I want her to bond again with Frankie and give him her attention, not being distracted. That was hard to do with five kids."

"Plenty of parents do it. Plenty of parents re-marry and bring their own kids. The thing is to make him feel important. We prepared Ricky before the twins came, and he's got responsibilities."

"I know, and it was a hard adjustment for him to begin with," Frank said. John nodded. Frank sighed. "I don't know for sure if Frankie's sadness about the kids leaving is genuine or he put it on as the contagious effect. Everyone was feeling it so he absorbed it. We'll need to talk about it, a lot. You know, as long as you texted Case, has he heard anything about finding Jarrett Miller yet? That's gotta be on your and Vicki's mind."

"I spoke to him before we left. So far, nothing. The Bureau lost the trail, which I found particularly shocking. There's no sign of him in New York, and he's got to know the DEA has eyes and ears out for him in Florida, so Case didn't think Miller would be stupid enough to come here, or stay in any of the states with his drug dealings. Case felt he wouldn't commit another murder because he found his original target, which, I'm sorry to say is my wife. As long as Vicki has her weapons, she feels safe here. She's not the woman Jarrett once knew. If Marcus Willtower gets any wind of him, he's supposed to tell Case ASAP. So we just have to let it play out its course. Down here, there are several deputies as undercovers, and they look for drug connections. There's a Drug Enforcement Division in the sheriff's office, with a DEA task-force. The guys here are on top of things. It's a smaller department but they have loads of resources. And they'll be quick to find the Hunters, too." Frank smirked. "Seriously," John said. "It won't be too long, knowing my brothers-in-law."

❧

Joshua was right. Jarrett sent him a picture before he left New York. His bitch-ex-wife was back in Serento, seen at the local Publix. Yeah, she was shopping with a full wagon, without kids, though. But with a redhead. They even gave Joshua a hand-out when he had a beggar's cup in his hand. His go-to person for info was his friend who still had smarts, though living in the woods for six months. Who'd suspect someone his age? Almost old enough for Medicare. It was foolproof. Joshua and his wife, Camille found an empty abandoned shed for shelter in the rain or at night. He'd told Jarrett he was happy to be free from that damn house and his wife's medical bills, anyway. The house had hurricane damage, too much so to live in, and the owner didn't want to bother to wait for FEMA and any repairs. All they had to do was not pay their damn rent for six months, or any bills. They closed their piddly bank accounts and took all the cash out. Now everything was on the government.

Yep. Jarrett could always count on them, especially since he was their supplier for Blue for Camille's habit. She always went through the legit prescriptions for Oxycodone way too fast. And the docs wouldn't give her anymore. They wanted her to go farther south to the "sober living capital of Florida." The nerve of them! She laughed in their faces. What? Leave her cushy income stream. No way. The docs could go fuck themselves she would tell Jarrett.

Jarrett Miller—comfy in his rented RV, inside a park, in the woods in Serento—sat on the cot eating a sub and drinking a can of cheap beer. Everything was so easy to get for cash—never a credit card paper trail. Yeah, he was definitely using his smarts. He made it down to Florida and away from the damn FBI. They wouldn't track him here, especially since he didn't plan to do another murder—until he found Victoria Elizabeth Marin. To him, her surname would always be Marin. He'd never acknowledge the schmuck doctor she married. But he'd sure as hell look him up. Leaning back into the pillow on his cot, Jarrett searched for Dr. John Trenton on his cell. Yeah, he'd done it before but he wanted to see if there were updates. Whoopee fuck! There were. The Trenton's home in Scarsdale had been broken into and vandalized in January. Holy fuck! Even the address was listed, and the suspects had been caught. Trenton had just gone back to his position as department head in forensic psychiatry the end of February. *Perfect. Now the middle of April, it was too soon for them to allow him to take off and go with his wife to Florida. Okay, the bitch had to be alone for sure.* The redhead she was spotted with had to be a long-time friend. No worries at all. He didn't know what to do next. He'd think on it.

He'd never been afraid of the woods, though he'd heard horror stories about the bobcats, and the rattlers. Armed with a revolver he got from one of Joshua's friends—a creep known to make straw purchases--he tucked it into his waistband and carrying a bag with a few beers and a pay-off for Camille, he ventured down the steps of his trailer. Some of those steps were sure rickety. There wasn't a long walk to the shack.

He hadn't seen them for some time, so tonight would be a great reunion. As he walked farther into the woods, he smelled the smoke from makeshift barbecues, cooking the cheap cuts of meat the homeless found in the garbage bins in the back of the chain stores, and fresh food markets. Workers never stopped them. At least they knew the food wasn't going to waste.

Big-guy, Joshua Hunter, named for his physicality, greeted Jarrett with open arms. "Great to see you, man. Come on, eats are up. Glad you made it."

"Yeah, those damn feds were on my tail, but I think I lost them. Thanks for the piece," he said, pointing to the gun in his waistband.

"Sorry, I couldn't get it for you myself."

Jarrett very well knew that felons couldn't own a gun down here. Neither should he. "Don't worry about it." He looked around at all the people in this little community. "You know all those creeps?"

"Don't worry about them, all like us. You don't look half-bad, bald."

Camille came out of the shed, trembling and looking like she needed a fix. Even in the dark, Jarrett could tell. She couldn't walk straight. He approached her with a smile and handed her a baggie. Enough Blues for her to use and sell at her convenience—seven-hundred-fifty—the Hunter's payment for the gun and finding his bitch ex-wife.

⋞⋟⋞⋟

From a good distance away, a group of homeless men sat around a campfire, rubbing their hands together, and observing the Hunters with their guest—every one of them, suspicious. Who came into their territory and why? They looked to their left.

A haggard man with a long ponytail sitting with an old worn blanket around his shoulders pulled out his cell phone, and snapped a pic of the newbie with the Hunters. The couple got into the pic, too. It was sent via text to the task force at the sheriff's office. *I think I might have found Miller. Not sure. He was with our target. Let's move in.*

⋞⋟⋞⋟

Detective Brian Marin was in the war room in the EOC in Lardo, looking at files when DEA agent Paul Curtlin came in with a printed photo and handed it to him. Marin gave it a good look. "The Hunters. How did you find them?"

"They've been on our watch-list for a while now. Tonight we caught them in the act with Jarrett Miller. Your brother and you put him away eighteen years ago."

"Not only that. He's wanted for the murder of five women in New York, and now's he's after my sister, again. The FBI is on the case."

"We know. Agent Willtower was in the office with Mrs. Trenton. He just didn't know if he did, in fact, recognize Miller with his head shaved. He's on the scene now, in the back woods. We just sent in SWAT with a few agents. If my estimate is correct, they'll be here in cuffs within the hour. What do you want with the Hunters?"

"They're the biological parents of a forensic psychiatrist in New York. He came down to find them."

"Why now?"

Brian blew out a deep breath. "Oh, man. It's rough. The Hunters are the parents of a serial killer. He's deceased. They kept him, but placed two other boys for adoption. Dr. Khaos is one of them."

"Khaos, with a K?"

Brian nodded.

"Frank Khaos?"

"You know him?"

"With a name like Khaos, how can I forget? I was in Iraq with him and Marcus Willtower. Wow, an Iraq reunion. Give him a call."

"Do you want to deal with one thing at a time?" Brian asked. "Dr. Khaos knew the Hunters were into shady deals. Trafficking, it's more than he thought. He has to confront them and deliver a message."

"Such as?"

Detective Marin didn't have time to respond. The commotion in the hall caused him and Agent Curtlin to open the office door.

Commander of SWAT, Mark Marin, and his team still in full-gear brought in the Hunters handcuffed and screaming into separate interrogation rooms. It took four men to push six-four Joshua into a room and shove him into a seat.

Detective Marin went into the room with Miller. DEA

Agent Marcus Willtower and another agent shoved Jarrett Miller into a seat in a third room. "You actually thought you could escape the feds?"

Miller just sneered.

Willtower handed Miller's revolver to the other agent. "You can rest easy now, Detective. He's going away for life. Aside from possessing a weapon, which he knew he shouldn't, he was a major trafficker of pain pills."

"And don't forget he's wanted for five murders in New York City. I'd have to agree. He's done. Are you going to be here for a while, Agent?"

"Oh yeah, Agent Curtlin and I will be here through the night. Glad this takedown happened relatively fast. I was getting tired of living in those woods," he said, laughing as he left the room when two deputies came in to guard Miller.

Brian went into his office where the commander waited for him. He nodded to his brother then sat behind his desk. "It's been a long time since we solved two cases in one sweep." He sat back in his seat.

Mark removed his belt with guns, ammo, and Tasers, and leaned against the wall. "Want to call Khaos?"

"Yeah, if he's anything like us, I don't think he'd care about the hour." Brian looked at a folder, found Frank's number, and dialed. While it was ringing, he noticed the clock showed after midnight.

Frank answered on the fourth ring. "Who's this?"

"Frank, it's Brian Marin. We didn't want to wait till morning. How soon can you get here?"

ℓℛℓℛ

Frank was on edge. He kept his posture stiff, clutching Sam's hand as a deputy guided them down the hall in the EOC. He couldn't focus, his vision blurred, not sure if it was because of fatigue or if he was blocking out the inevitable.

John Trenton followed, equally as silent. They were ushered into Detective Marin's office. Mark was also there. "First, sit down, take a few deep breaths, and we'll tell you everything. But you really have to calm down first. I can see it."

Sam interlocked her arm in Frank's and held on tightly. Frank did some deep breathing and held onto Sam tighter. It took him a couple of minutes and the men gave him the time.

"You found them?" Frank asked.

"Yes. They're here," Brian said.

"Oh, man. I wasn't ready for it to be this quick. How did that happen?"

"They were busted in the midst of a drug deal—with Jarrett Miller."

"Seriously?"

"Oh my God," Sam said. "That's bizarre."

"Not really. This is a small area," Brian said then explained. "The Hunters were on a DEA watch list. And Miller was on another list. I had just put in a search for them and the agents made the connection. This is the first time they're in the area together in a long time. We'll find out for sure, but I surmise, Miller wanting to go after my sister is what brought him back."

Frank nodded. "I'm glad you got him without involving Vicki. Now why was it so important for me to come in tonight?"

"Hold on a minute." Brian pressed the intercom. "Come in agents."

Frank furrowed his brows and turned toward the door. DEA Agents Marcus Willtower and Paul Curtlin entered, grinning from ear to ear. "Oh, man!"

Frank got up, nearly knocking his chair over in the excitement, and the three men hugged together. For a long time. Sam became misty-eyed. John smiled and nodded to his brothers-in-law.

"Oh, man. This is too much. The both of you, wow."

"This is why you had to come in tonight, bro," Curtlin said. "We'll be outta here by six. We notified Agent Case about Miller and the Hunters. He just told me some things, briefly. Do you want us to go in there with you?"

"No, man, thanks. John will be with me. And Sam."

John nodded, and Sam smiled.

"I don't think I can do this alone. I thought I could, but I had to take a good hard look at myself. What are they looking at?"

"Because it's their fourth time going to prison, even though it was in their youth, they're looking at life without parole. No bail, by the way."

"Don't look at me. I wasn't planning on paying it."

"Just to be clear," Willtower said. "All right, they're being interviewed separately. Do you want us to bring them in so you can talk to them together? Your dad is as big as you."

"Dad? I never thought of them as my parents, ever. I never met them. I just found out about them in January."

"We'll bring them together for you. How long do you think you need?"

"As little time as necessary. I need some more details to finish profiling our last case, and I just want to deliver a message."

"Give us a few minutes," Curtlin said as he left the room.

Willtower smiled at Sam. "You're still with this guy?"

Sam leaned in toward her man and held his arm. "Yep. We're engaged."

Willtower gave Frank a man-slap on the shoulder. "Congratulations, bro."

Curtlin opened the door and signaled for them to come.

Frank grabbed onto Sam. "I have no idea what I'm going to say, Sam."

"Come on," John said. "You'll figure it out."

CHAPTER 32

Frank stood stunned after his military bros left the office. In a moment, he was going to confront the Achilles Heels of his past. He clutched Sam's hand so tightly she let out an "owe!" He released her in shock that he'd do anything to cause her pain. Okay, it was now or never. He took one step and Sam and John took a step with him. Mark Marin let him have his space. Frank appreciated that.

Vicki sure had awesome brothers. They had her back. Thinking of brothers, would Frank be able to rekindle his relationship with Carl? He certainly hoped so. He left the room, side-by-side with Sam, and John following. They had a short walk. A few doors down. He'd decided not to plan a lengthy conversation. Two minutes and he'd be out of there. He paused, cringed, then knocked. He felt his body become rigid. He'd never felt so stiff. He couldn't even rotate his shoulders. A deputy opened the door and let them in. He went face-to face with his bio-parents. His handcuffed parents. To the woman who bore him and his spitting-image of a father. His gaze escaped them to scan the room—barren with just the table, chairs, and white walls. It was a momentary distraction then he looked straight at them.

Joshua and Camille Hunter—criminals who were now going to do life behind bars—stared up at Frank with a coldness that riveted through him and made him shudder. The hate in their eyes couldn't be mistaken. That expressionless glare.

How can parents act this way? Can they possibly not recognize me?

Frank pulled a chair out from the table and motioned for Sam to sit next to him. John, as he told him he would, stood at a corner in the room, leaning against the wall, hands across his chest, and paying attention.

"Do you know who I am?" Frank asked.

Joshua shook his head. "No. But you resemble me in my youth."

"Um um. What about your youth?"

Camille swallowed hard but looked down and away. "Are you one of our sons who we gave up for adoption?"

"Yes, I'm one of your sons you *placed* for adoption, Francis. I go by Frank. But I'm here to talk about the son you kept."

Camille avoided the question. "Who's this looker?"

"My fiancée, Detective Samantha Wright."

Joshua frowned. "We don't want no cops in our family."

Frank did all he could do to control himself. He didn't know whether to laugh at them, or yell. He decided on neutral. "Well, I'm a forensic psychiatrist, and an NYPD profiler. So you wouldn't want me either. And you didn't. Where did this notion of family come in?"

"You're a fuckin' shrink?"

"Yes. Tell me about Benjamin. What was he like as a kid?"

"Where's our son, Carlton?"

"Why the interest now, Camille? Carl was adopted by loving parents, the way it should be, and he'd had a wonderful life. He's an attorney. Why did you decide to keep Benjamin?"

"He's an attorney? You outta tell him to go meet your grandparents. You, too. They're attorneys."

"Grandparents? They're still living?"

"My mom and pop passed on, but your mother's parents are still with us, those bastards."

"Why were they bastards?"

"They kicked Camille out when she got pregnant with Carlton. Did nothing to help us, nada. Then when we got into shit, they disowned her. What happened to unconditional love? Yeah, that's what it's called. It's bullshit. We learned everything about love through them. But I bet they'd love to see you and Carlton. They're up in their eighties now."

Frank tried to keep the same coldness as Joshua, even though at this moment it was hard. He actually had living grandparents? Stunned, he swallowed hard. "First, maybe they didn't want to enable your bad choices. That's treating adult-age children like adults."

"Whatever."

"Where do they live?"

"Bensonhurst, Brooklyn. We ain't seen them in in forty-four years. Hey, do we have grandchildren?"

"Yeah, but I'm not telling you—"

John let out a guttural cough. Frank stared at him as John hiked a brow. Guess he did need John in the room.

"Yeah, you've missed out on not knowing eight wonderful children."

"Well, I'll be. Can they come to visit us?"

"No, Camille. I'm not introducing them to anyone, especially in jail, who hasn't been a vital part of their lives. Tell me about Benjamin. And then I'll tell you."

"We haven't seen him either since he was seventeen. At eighteen, he legally changed his name. We did try to track him. We saw some art of his in a street fair in Greenwich Village. We knew it was his work, but he didn't acknowledge us. Who cared? We were busy staking out a gas station to hit. So what about him?"

"For one, he's deceased." The parents sat still for a moment. No sense of grief or sadness. Frank continued. "By his own hand."

"Suicide? No, not a Hunter! We're not cowards," growled Joshua.

"Yeah, well, it was after a long search for him and he

was captured. We had him cornered, and he, unlike you two, didn't want to spend his life in prison—or on death row—or worse."

"Death row? What did that lame brain do?"

Frank remained nonchalant. "He murdered seventeen women."

"His one accomplishment in life."

"Actually, it wasn't. He had an MBA and successful businesses, though one was illegal."

"Illegal? That's the spirit. Camille and me are nonconformists. We don't let the law dictate our lives."

Frank had to laugh. "Oh, yeah? Well, how's that working for you?"

"Have some respect. We're your papa and momma."

"Actually, you're not. My adoptive parents were my mom and dad. Okay, I think I'm done here. I have a message that your son wanted me to deliver. It's so that we can execute his will. Detective Wright, and Dr. John Trenton, in the corner, there, will be my witnesses that I delivered that message."

"And what might that fuckin' message be?"

"I can see by your attitudes that he was right. Did you tell him, Camille, that he disgusted you and you wished he wasn't born?"

"Yes, but, every parent gets crazy once in a while."

Frank wasn't fazed. "Was it constant?"

"Yeah, it was. He was in the way."

"What's the message, *son*?

Frank ignored the tone. "He wanted me to 'thank you' for driving him to be a serial killer."

"Wow, Camille, another great accomplishment for our family."

"That wasn't complementary. It was his way of being sarcastic. And to also tell you you're not getting a dime from his monies."

Joshua lit up. "He's got cash?"

Frank let his serious tone sink in. "Shit-loads."

"That's not fair!"

"Yeah, well, life's not fair. And that's what you get for living a lawless life." Frank paused and then glanced up at John. He closed his eyes for a moment and nodded with his lips sealed. "Before I leave, I want to tell you something."

"And what's that, shrink-son?"

Frank stood. Sam rose from her chair. He puffed out his cheeks and blew out a deep breath. He despised these people, so it would be easier. "I want to thank you for placing me for adoption. Because I had a family who loved and appreciated me, despite my faults, and now I have a family whom I love." He put his arm around Sam's shoulders and squeezed.

Sam became misty eyed, and John had a closed-lip smile on his face as they left the room. Frank didn't look back.

❦

Special FBI Agent Brett Case disembarked the plane at the Salt Lake City Airport. The entire trip he'd made plans for the field office to send agents to meet them at Dr. Sarah Phillips home. He fumed that he legally couldn't let the Slater children stay with Frank and Sam. Knowing them, they'd make the best parents, and he trusted they'd do right by the children. Should he have ordered drug testing for Dr. Phillips? As long as she appeared stable, they couldn't authorize it, not without a firm suspicion. Yeah, he knew doctors were among the highest for narcotic abuse, but it wasn't apparent with her. An FBI agent was picking him up. If they were lucky, verifying Benjamin's claims could happen quickly. The car pulled up outside the main passenger gate to the terminal.

Outside Dr. Phillips apartment, Brett and three agents knocked on the door. No answer. Then they rang the bell three times. Benjamin came to the door. "Who's there?"

Brett was surprised. *He's not in school?* "Benjamin, it's

Special Agent Case, from New York. Open the door, please."

Benjamin opened the door and the four agents came in. Brett gave him a moment to settle in while he took in the faux painted mural on the wall. *A Henry Slater original.* Then his gaze went to Benjamin. The kid trembled. The agent hadn't ever seen him look this unsettled. "Benjamin, why aren't you in school?"

"I missed the bus."

"How come?"

"Mom," he nearly choked the word out, "didn't get me up, and she's sleeping so she couldn't drive me."

"Where is she?"

A groggy, Dr. Phillips called from her bedroom, "Benjamin, who's here?"

Brett stormed into her bedroom with a female agent. He looked around for a moment, eying the lavish decor. Paid for by Henry Slater, he assumed. "Remember me, Dr. Phillips? I came out here from New York to see you. This is Agent Massey."

"And why is that?"

"Because your son doesn't need a drug-addicted mother. Get out of bed, go with this agent into your bathroom, and give a urine sample, now."

"Why?"

Benjamin came into the room despite the agents' attempts in the living room to keep him with them. Brett had to continue with the hard questions. "You're humoring me, aren't you? I can tell you're using, a narcotic for numbing out your reality, Vicodin, maybe?" He touched her palm. "Sure, your hand is clammy. You're having trouble focusing on me, blurry vision? Are you vomiting?"

Benjamin confirmed it. "Yeah, she vomits a lot."

"Benjamin, go into the living room and stay with the other agents." Brett stared right at the nine-year-old who had to know by now that he was no-nonsense.

Benjamin let out a huff but obeyed.

"Out of bed, now, Dr. Philips."

"Do you have a warrant?"

Agent Massey took it out of her pocket. "Yes, we do." She abruptly put it onto the bed.

Begrudgingly, Dr. Phillips got out of bed. "Let me get a robe, please." She went into her closet.

Agents Case and Massey guessed what was up. Massey followed her. She caught Dr. Phillips rubbing a vial of urine—just the right amount, forty-five milliliters—in her palms. "Well, what have we here, Doctor? Buy it online, or steal it from your pharmacy? Was that the real reason you were fired?"

"We'll have to check that out, Agent Massey, and that can mean mandatory arrest if theft was from the hospital, let alone losing her medical license. Did you hear that, Dr. Phillips?"

After sneering at Case, Dr. Phillips succumbed to the order—too weak to fight, and minus the desire to do so. She went with the agent into the bathroom.

"I'm sure you've analyzed drug tests at the hospital, correct?" Agent Massey asked.

Dr. Phillips merely nodded.

"Okay, then, we're doing the immunoassay, it's quick. Wash yourself with this cleansing pad. I'm going to watch you."

Dr. Phillips did the job. The agent put the testing strip into the vial. It shot up positive. She showed it to Brett.

He didn't waste time. "Dr. Philips, you're under arrest for endangering the welfare of a child. And that's to start." He read her Miranda but decided not to handcuff her, for Benjamin's sake, and she was so sedated, she wasn't a threat. He led her out of the bedroom. "She doesn't look able enough to get dressed. Agents, take her outside. We'll send over some clothes to the hospital. She needs medical attention first."

Agent Massey and another agent escorted Dr. Phillips out. "Sure thing, Agent Case."

"Benjamin, come sit on the couch with me."

The kid sat next to him, sulking, with another agent taking a seat in a club chair opposite them.

Brett continued. "You and Melissa did great by calling Dr. John. You do realize that, don't you?"

Benjamin merely nodded.

"I know it's been rough for you kids, and I'm going to do my best to fix that."

"How?"

"What do you want to do?" Brett asked, knowing the answer.

"I want to go back to Uncle Frank and Aunt Sam, and if anyone could do it, you can, Agent Case. And I want Melissa, Henry, and Margie back too. Did Dr. John tell you about Melissa, too?"

"Yes. We're having a FBI team assembled to go to her house, too. So for the moment, here's what we need to do. Agent Chester will be contacting Child and Family Services here in Utah."

"No! They'll put me in foster care!"

"Let me finish, okay?"

Benjamin sniffled and swallowed but looked up at Case with tears in his eyes.

"Agent Chester will fill out the paperwork so you can come back to New York with me and stay at my house. I have an eight-year old, a fifteen-year old, a twelve-year old, and a little guy who's Henry's age. You'll have a great time with them until your aunt and uncle come back from Florida."

"When will that be?"

"They'll only be there for spring break, so you won't miss any school. So how about it?"

Benjamin smiled from ear-to-ear. Agent Case had his answer.

"Let's get you packed."

ოჯო

Holding Henry's hand, Lauren Berkeley brought him into the ranch-hand dining room, a barn-size log cabin for the first time. Henry looked around in awe at the twenty men—twenty loud men—who wore plaid shirts, tight jeans, and they didn't bother to take off their hats indoors. All talking stopped when they saw their boss with that little kid. Some laughed. Some looked her up and down, with Lauren knowing their lewd thoughts. Of course they did. She'd hook up with them. Yep. She had her own harem of men. Hot men. "Okay, listen up! This is Henry. My son came back to live with me. It's time for me to introduce him to you clowns."

"And why did he do that?" a ranch-hand teased.

"Yeah, well, his daddy passed. I expect y'all to be nice to him." Lauren sat Henry down at one of the eight-foot long log tables with bench seating. No booster seat, and though Henry was tall for his age, his forehead barely reached the table.

"Come on, Lauren. Get the kid something to sit on," the rancher next to him said. "I'm Robby, Henry. Hold on, we'll fix this." The man looked around the cabin and, smiling, went to the corner and pulled a saddle off a rack. "This should do it, Henry. Ever sit on a horse?"

The three-year old stared at him wide-eyed.

"No, huh, well, you'll now, a pretend horse, until we get you on a real one," Robby said. Henry looked at Robby, panicked. Robby laughed at the boy's expression. "Here we go."

He lifted Henry for a moment, put the saddle across the wood bench, then he seated Henry on top of it. Henry sat with his knees bent on the bench.

At first, Henry was shocked and didn't know what to do. He stared at the men who were laughing at him.

Lauren thought he was about to cry. But this little kid was tough.

Henry started to rock and pretended he was on a real horse. Then he giggled, and it turned to full-blown laughter.

Lauren patted Robby's back. "Ya did good. I owe ya." She winked at him, and every man knew what she meant. "I'll bring in his breakfast."

"I'll keep an eye on him. You like it here, Henry?"

Henry grimaced. "You're going to take out your eye?"

"No, son. It's an expression."

"I not your son."

"That's an expression, too."

Lauren came back with Henry's breakfast and put it in front him.

He crinkled his nose. "What's that?" he said, pointing to two long strips of a brown-something.

"That's bacon, Henry. Didn't you ever eat it? Taste it, it's the best."

Henry picked up a slice and bit off a piece. After letting the flavor set in his mouth, he shook his head vehemently, spit out the tiny bits, and let the bacon fall to the floor, but Star caught it before it hit the ground. "Ugh, that was icky. What's that?" Henry asked, pointing to the bowl.

"That's grits with cheese and butter."

Henry grimaced again.

"It's cereal. You'll like it."

Henry picked up his spoon and tasted the grits. He mushed it in his mouth. "Um, this is good."

"Thank God for small miracles. Getting him to eat is a chore."

"I'll take care of it. Here, Henry, try some biscuit." Robby buttered the bottom half with homemade butter, with a small amount of salt added.

Henry took a bite. He opened his eyes wide and smiled at Robby. He bopped his head up and down. He ate slowly, drank the glass of raw-milk, and for a three-year-old, he consumed a lot of the food. "I'm full," he said, trying to get off the saddle.

Robby smiled at the struggle and lifted him off. Henry

lay down to snuggle with Star who moved to the other side of the cabin near the door.

Another hand watched him with the dog. "Hey, Lauren, he's cute. When are we getting him on a horse?"

Henry heard him. From a distance he, yelled, "No. No horse."

"Why not?"

"They're too big."

Everyone laughed at him. He frowned, having enough of the teasing. Without saying anything, he slipped out of the door that was just open enough for him to fit. Star followed him. The men—and his mother—were oblivious that he'd left.

❧❧

Henry sat down on the steps of the porch that surrounded the expanse of the cabin. He squinted when the sun shone brightly in his eyes. With Star next to him, he got up and walked around the porch to where there were other steps. He sat down again. All he saw was grass and more grass. Then he saw it in the distance.

A bunny.

❧❧

Three FBI agents rang the bell to Lisa Brandt's apartment. She was on the phone and didn't hear the doorbell, or she ignored it. The agents persisted. After looking through the peephole and seeing those blue and gold FBI jackets, she opened the door, still holding the handset.

She looked at them with disgust. "What?"

"We're here to talk about Melissa. May we come in?"

Frustrated, she yelled into the phone. "I'll have to call you back." She slammed the handset down onto a table near the door. "What do you want? I'm having enough of a hard time finding a nanny. Melissa's in school." She pointed to the couch for them to sit.

"I'm Special Agent Farber," he said, handing her his creds. "Why do you need a nanny?"

"I got another offer to go to Italy. I didn't think it would happen so soon after Melissa came home. I can't take her with me. She doesn't have a passport, and my company wants me to go next week."

"How long will you be there?"

"Indefinitely. Last time it was eight months. It can go up to two years."

"Do you think that's fair to Melissa?"

"No, it's not fair, but my life is screwed up at the moment, too."

"We'll make it easy for you. How about allowing Melissa to go back to live with her Uncle Frank and Aunt Samantha? She'll have a loving home again."

"What makes you think I'm not loving?"

"You'll certainly be an absentee mother. Where are her art supplies?"

She groaned. "Now I get it. She spoke to Benjamin. What did those two mischief makers plan?"

"They can't plan anything. They're minors. Show us where her art supplies are."

She got up, annoyed, and showed them into another room. An empty room, with cream painted walls—nothing to foster a child's artistic ability. The boxes were opened, but no attempt was made to set anything up.

"You want an answer to your question?"

"I have a feeling you're going to tell me your opinion whether I want to hear it or not."

"No, you're not giving her a loving home."

❧❦❧

Henry ran down the steps of the porch to get a closer

look at the bunny. As soon as he came into view, the bunny hopped away, fast. Following, and trying to run just as fast at the little creature, Henry ran far away from the cabin with Star by his side. He didn't turn around to see where he was going. The angle the bunny took was away from the house—to somewhere on the ranch. Henry finally collapsed on the grass, not being able to run anymore. His breathing labored, he lay flat on his back on the soft grass. He spread his arms out making angel-wings, like his cousin Frankie taught him in the snow. The memory triggered tears, and he started to cry, holding tightly onto Star. Star licked away the boy's tears and rested, lying over Henry's body. Henry sat up and finally looked around. He moved all around. He couldn't see the house. Where was he? He had no idea. He decided to walk and talk to Star. "Take us home, Star."

Star didn't respond. Not the way Henry meant. Star started running, and Henry yelled for him to slow down. The dog didn't. Henry saw nothing—no cows, no horses, none of the ranch-hands he met at the cabin. *Where is everyone?* He walked a long time, not knowing where he was going. It was getting dark. It started to get windy, and he became more scared by the moment. Bales of hay blew past him. One knocked him down. His sneaker slipped off. After struggling to get it on, he gave up and left it. He yelled, "Star!"

He hobbled more, and it became too windy for him to walk against the pressure of the wind. He finally saw it in the distance. The cabin. He'd make it. After walking a long time, he was exhausted. He pulled off his other sneaker, feeling more comfortable in his socks. He tossed the shoe. He reached the cabin. *Yes! I'm back!* The door was open a bit, just like this morning.

When he entered the building, he was surprised. The wind was so strong it slammed the door shut behind him, leaving Star outside. The horses in their stalls started to whinny. Henry screamed. Loud fearful screams. He crept by the horses on tiptoe, some bucked, trying to get out of their stalls. He raced to the other side of the barn where he saw the ladder. His way to escape those horses. He looked up. He'd climbed higher than this before. He remembered at the policeman place when everyone got mad at him. Step by step, he ascended the nine-foot ladder to get up to the loft. More of that stuff that knocked him down in the wind. But he was away from the horses. As he lifted his foot off the ladder, something snagged onto his sock and pulled it off before the ladder fell down. He lay on his belly and watched it land with a smack against the wall. He saw part of a step break off.

But he was safe. Away from those horses.

CHAPTER 33

Relieved Jarrett Miller was out of the picture, though she was upset that she didn't bring him down herself, Vicki made plans to take Sam around town while the men and kids were doing their thing. John wanted to take them to the wild life park in Homosassa. He always wanted to do things to enrich Ricky, Vicki told Sam. She did, too, but today she'd needed her girlfriend time. And so did Sam, Vicki decided.

If it was one thing she'd work out in her marriage, it was her-time. Sans kids time. John's parents would be babysitting the twins. Since they'd returned to Florida, the senior Trenton's couldn't get enough of them. Couldn't blame them. Their only son finally gave them grandchildren. Three wonderful grandchildren.

They'd finalize their plans for the day at the breakfast table, where Vicki prepared a true country breakfast, the likes of which Sam and Frank probably had never seen. When they came to the table, her guests saw fluffy fragrant homemade biscuits with a jug of natural honey, and a pot of homemade butter next to the platter. To hell with gluten-free this morning. Or sugar-free. She served a Southern-style frittata with eggs, cheeses, turkey bacon, and turkey sausage, and home fried potatoes. It was huge, and filled a thirteen-inch three-inch deep rectangular stoneware pan. A jug of fresh squeezed orange juice and a fresh pot of hot coffee sat on trivets.

"Good morning," Vicki said, greeting the crew as they

sat down. "Hope you're all hungry, especially after last night."

"Oh my God, Vicki, this amazing! Thank you!"

"My pleasure, Sam. And don't forget and *fattening*. After last night you all needed a treat."

Frank and John laughed. "We sure do, at least I know, I do," Frank said, digging in and serving Frankie. "Oh, man, Vicki this is amazing."

"It sure is, babe. We're not going to talk about it now, but I'm glad Mark called you last night."

"Oh sure, it was peachy, interrupting my nursing Zach, but he said he knew I'd be up."

"Yeah, Dad, where did you and Sam go last night?"

Frank paused. "Well, Vicki's brothers, one is a commander of the SWAT team and the other is a detective, and after talking with them the other day, they knew I was in Iraq. Two of the DEA agents that work out of their headquarters were in Iraq, and Vicki's brother mentioned me to them. Turns out, they knew me, too. So we went to see them. After all these years, it was great meeting my military brothers."

"That's cool."

Vicki smiled, knowing Frank got out of that one gracefully. "Sam, how would you like to go see one of our classrooms? Mark's wife, Jaimie, said we could come visit her. She teaches fifth grade."

"I'd love to! That was my grade, my last year. I'll have to change, though."

"Uh, no you don't. What you're wearing is fine."

"A T-shirt with cropped pants? No. That would never fly in New York."

Vicki laughed, a little insulted. "Well this is the South."

"Oh," Sam said, getting the message. "But I'll be more comfortable."

"Sure, darlin'."

Frank grabbed a second biscuit. "Vicki, these are wonderful. We can't get these in New York."

"You probably could but they'd be rock-hard. Frankie, are you excited to go to the park today?"

"Yeah, Ricky told me about it, it's cool! Especially, the alligators."

"You'll see lots of things you'll find very interesting. And let them take some of the programs. It's an all-day affair."

"Don't worry, babe, we'll give you gals a long day of girl-time. No worries."

Sam helped Vicki clear the table and then she scooted into the bedroom to change into a short-sleeved blouse and wide-bottom embroidered-up-the-leg blue-denim jeans.

"You look very *teacherly*, Miss Wright," Vicki said.

"Thank you!"

"Let's go. Boys, we're leaving. Have fun," Vicki yelled as she and Sam bolted out the door. "The school is right down the road."

"That's great. I had a forty-minute commute. Most of us did."

"And you'll love these classrooms. Eighteen kids, max, and very hand's on," Vicki said. Sam looked startled. Vicki affirmed. "Yes, not like in New York with thirty-five or more in a class."

As soon as Vicki drove into the school's parking lot, Sam sat up with dropped jaws. "Oh gosh, I can tell already it's going to be amazing inside. All on one floor?"

"Yes. None, of those dreaded stairwells." Vicki pulled into a spot.

After pressing the buzzer on the wall outside the door, and entering, Vicki took Sam into main office to get visitors passes. They knew Vicki, this was her school, too, but Sam had to show ID.

Sam walked through the hall in amazement. Vicki noticed. "It's a great place to work."

"I see that. It's immaculate." Sam peeked into an open classroom door. She stopped and smiled. Vicki saw her expression melt, seeing the kindergartners, all working in center activities.

"Come, on. Jaimie's class is around the corner." They walked around the bend, and reached the classroom.

Jaimie greeted them with smiles. She hugged her sister-in-law then interrupted the children who were working in various centers in the room, at the computer station, reading area, writing center, making story maps. "Boys and girls, you remember Miss Marin, don't you? Who was in her class in kindergarten?"

The kids got excited to see their former teacher, yelling out to her.

And this is our friend, Detective Wright. She's has a big-time job in New York."

"But before I entered the New York Police Department, I was a teacher, in your grade."

A charming little girl raised her hand. Sam acknowledged her with a smile. "I never saw a lady detective before, ma'am. What's it like?"

Sam glanced toward Jaimie, smiling that she was asked so politely, Vicki thought.

"Take it away, Detective," Jamie told her as she and Vicki took seats. The children scrambled back to their desks, excitedly and very well behaved.

Sam grinned from ear-to-ear. Vicki assumed she felt at home in her element.

ɞɷɞɷ

Frantic, Lauren, her ranch-hands, and the deputies from the sheriff's office of Prescott, Arizona, some on horseback, some on foot were in the midst of a search for little Henry, who had now been missing for five hours. How could he have disappeared right from under their noses and with twenty adults in the room? Star was nowhere, either. She was some responsible mother, all right. The sheriff informed her if they didn't find Henry soon—and un-harmed—she'd be arrested and charged with neglect. It was neglect. How could she expect her ranch-hands to do her job? That wasn't in their job description. She ran out from the living area in her house after the harsh scolding from the deputies. They'd taken some of Henry's things for their dogs to sniff when they called in the K-9s. She paced back and forth on the porch then grasped onto the railing and stared into the emptiness of the terrains.

The horse teams came back to the house, without Henry. Robby ran onto the porch. "Lauren, we found one of his sneakers. This is it, right?"

She took it and broke down crying. "Yes. Where on the property did you find it?"

"In the north, easily a mile, but the wind-storm could have blown it. I doubt he could have walked that far."

"There's eight square miles on this ranch," a deputy chimed in. "No telling where that young'un went. But we're keeping the search close to the house, no more than five miles around. No way could he have gotten that far."

"Yes, he could have. His uncle told me he's athletic. He can get into mischief, and he's a climber."

Robby blew out a breath of frustration. "Lauren, why didn't you tell us? It's all land out there. No place to climb." He paused a second then yelled to the ranch hands, "Saddle up, we'll check every barn on the ranch. If we're lucky, he found shelter." He mumbled to himself, "If a rattler didn't take him out before he did." He was off the porch and on his horse without saying another word to Lauren. "Split up, we have twenty barns to cover. Move it! And watch in the high grassland." The men sped off, each knowing the direc-tion to take around the house.

Another deputy came onto the porch. "Ma'am, your son's been missing over five hours now. I have to call it in."

༄༅

John and Frank entered the park lobby and already Frankie was excited. Ricky pulled him over to the tank with the two-headed turtle. Frankie and his dad were both astonished. "That's amazing." Frank spoke to the turtle, "Hey, little guy."

John laughed. Today was going to be a great day and nothing was going to change that. Both cases were satisfied and John wanted to make sure he'd take Frank's mind off things. He was confident Vicki would do the same for Sam. "Come on, there's more great things in there. My treat." They paid at the desk, and Frankie ran to the large manatee statue. It was surrounded by bricks and palm trees.

"What's this?"

"Ricky, tell him."

Ricky was all smiles. "That's a manatee. They live here. They're part of the elephant family, but live in water. They just got a new one, named Betsy, and she's twenty-four hundred pounds!" Even other visitors smiled at the boy's enthusiasm as they poured in.

"No kidding," Frankie exclaimed.

"No kidding. Come on. Dad, I want to go to the alligators."

"We'll see it all, champ." They walked down a cobbled stone path, with wood railings on each side, with large screen enclosures blocking the visitors from the creatures.

As they were walking down the wooden path, John's cell rang. "Trenton."

"Brett Case. Are you alone?"

"No, what's wrong? Watch the kids," John said and then mouthed to Frank, "Brett." He walked to a bench and sat down.

"All right, listen. Good and bad news. I'll tell you the bad, first."

"Oh, man." *Here goes something to ruin the day.* "What happened?"

"Henry went missing. He ran out of one of the cabins. It's seven hours now. They sent horse-teams out covering the ranch. They brought in the K-nines a couple of hours ago. CPS called me when they saw the paperwork I sent in."

"Damn it, how long does it take to find a three-year-old?"

Frank perked up and sat next to him on the bench while Frankie and Ricky watched the flamingos entertaining park visitors.

"Stay put, guys, don't wander," Frank said, then he mouthed, "What happened?" He leaned in to hear the conversation.

"It's a ranch with a huge expanse," Case said. "They're also concerned that someone could have come onto the property to abduct him."

The men felt like exploding, but had to keep their composure for their sons. "Do you want me to fly out there? Like ASAP?"

"No, John, too much time for that. Can you do what you do long distance?"

"I know what you mean. Yes, remote viewing, and I can astral travel, but not with these crowds. It's wall-to-wall people. Hold on. I have an idea." He turned to Frank. "Can you entertain them here, while I try this out in the car?"

"Of course. Go. Now."

"Ricky, stay with Uncle Frank, and show him and Frankie around. I have to get something in the car."

"Okay, Dad."

John ran out, past the desk. "I'll be back in." He sprinted through the parking lot in the rear. All of the spaces were taken. Still on the phone with Brett he said, "Fill me in. What does the area look like? I've never been out west." He entered his car and turned on the air.

"Me neither, but we have field agents on the premises now. I'll connect us. Hold on."

Less than a minute later, an agent made contact. "Dr. Trenton, Agent Mayberry. We have horse teams and K-nines searching. No sign of the family dog, either, and he's not responding to a call out. He's a pup, so he hasn't developed skills yet. Miss Berkeley told her ranch manager, who attempted to build a relationship with Henry that he likes to climb. So they're searching over twenty barns."

"Oh, man. Let me see what I can do. Yes, he's a climber. I can't promise, but I'll try my best. I have to disconnect. Electrical interference stops the process. I'll call you back. Stay close." John disconnected. He sat back in his seat and did his deep diaphragmatic breathing. Real deep. It was a good thing his breakfast was digested. When he was solid in his focus, he concentrated. This was the third time he had to use his psychic vision in this case. The first with the birth certificates, then in Locklear Henderson's closet, now this. *They say it comes in threes. Come to think of it, so does Henry's climbing. Has to be. The first time was in Frank's house, the second time in the precinct, and now, here. Definitely, that's the natural order of things. Yes, definitely, he climbed to escape something. This isn't a shy little kid. So he must be terrified.*

All right, Max, I need you big time, now. You gotta help me find Henry, Max. He's three years old. He's on a large ranch, and he went far away from the house. I'm zoning out to see it, Max. I need you to help me push the vision. Give it all you got. Max came to in front of his third eye. An expansive ranch came into view. Grasses, barns, no Henry.

John lay with his head back on his headrest. He wasn't getting any messages—too stressed in a life and death situation, not in comfortable surroundings.

Come on, Max, do this, buddy. All of a sudden, the message came out. *HORSES.* Then it evaporated, as a security guard knocked on the window of John's SUV, startling the bejesus out of him

"Are you all right, sir?"

John rolled the window down. "Yes, just resting. I had a late night last night."

"I need to see your ID, sir."

"Listen, I have to get back to an FBI Agent in New York."

"Yeah, sure. Your ID."

"Yeah, but hold on a minute. I'm a forensic psychiatrist. Sheriff Marin is my wife's father." John called Brett. He answered immediately. "The only clue that came through is *horses*. Tell them to check in all of the barns with horses where there's a loft for him to climb up to." John disconnected. He pulled out his ID from his wallet and handed it to the guard.

The guard nodded and handed his ID back, giving him a strange look. "Have a great day, sir."

John blew out a deep breath, and leaned his head back again. One word, *HORSES*. Max gave him a three-word clue in the Gemini case, *CASTOR AND POLLUX*. But he wouldn't knock it. That clue helped him solve the case. He prayed from the bottom of his soul that clue of *horses* could help find Henry.

Brett called back fifteen minutes later. John needed that time to rest. "We found him! They narrowed the search to barns with the horses, and lofts, three. He was fast asleep on the hay. Star was outside the barn, barking. Henry knocked down the ladder, so when the agents went in there, they noticed immediately his sock was hanging from a broken rung. They climbed up, and there he was. Thanks, John. They should have called me right away. They're taking him to the hospital for a check-up. He woke up in the ambulance and started screaming for his Uncle Frank."

"How would they have known? What's the good news?"

"I'm assuming that Frank and Sam do want the kids back, correct?"

"Definitely, and?"

"We're working on it. I have Benjamin with me now at my house in New York, one mother arrested. Melissa's mother is going to be off to Italy next week. We closed up Melissa's boxes of art supplies, and they're on the way back to Frank's house. Our agents will travel with her on the plane. Now with this situation, with Henry, I think I can get him, too, by telling Berkeley it's this or prosecution for neglect. What day are you due to fly back?"

"We're staying longer for my father-in-law's retirement party. Do you want me to tell Frank they have to leave sooner than Saturday, that something came up?"

"Benjamin desperately wants to go to their house. He's fine with my kids, but I'm too strict," he said, laughing. "Frank and Sam will have to be tougher with them. Melissa's mother is so busy packing and making business plans, the kid's being ignored."

"Do you want me to tell them?"

"No. Let me see what happens with Henry. How long the hospital keeps him. They want to make sure nothing bit him. I'll call Frank later when everything crystalizes. Keep this under wraps."

"Will do." John put his head back. He wasn't a great actor. How would he keep this secret? He'd better get back into the park.

CHAPTER 34

Frank wasn't planning to tell Sam about Brett's phone call concerning Henry. She'd want to pack up right there and then and fly to Arizona. He felt like doing that, too. He said a silent "Thank you" up to God for them finding him. Over seven hours, his little guy was missing. Seven hours. That could have been disastrous. Frank lay back on the double lounge, under the starlit night. He spoke a message to his mom, Theresa, in thought language. *Mom, I don't know how you're going to do this, but bring those kids back to us. I saw my bio parents last night. They're despicable human beings. I'm glad they refused to raise me, and I'm blessed that you and Dad did.*

Sam came onto the lanai and cuddled next to him. "Penny for your thoughts?" She lay her head down on his chest. "It's nice out here under the stars on a clear cool night."

"It certainly is. John told me this is his favorite lounge."

"Yeah, why?"

He smirked, in a teasing mood. "This is where he and Vicki first had sex."

Sam jumped up so fast she became dizzy. "*EWWW.* With capitals!"

He pulled her back down, laughing. "Relax, it was over five years ago. I'm sure it's been cleaned and rained on plenty."

"But still."

"How did your day go with Vicki?"

"The school is so beautiful, and Jaimie is an awesome

teacher. And those kids. Just precious. They asked me questions about being a detective, and Jaimie let me teach a lesson."

"Very cool, princess. Very, cool."

"I think I do miss teaching, more than I ever thought I would."

"It's something to think about when you're on childcare leave." His cell rang. He grimaced. "Hey, Brett."

"Listen, something came up. We need your documentation from your meeting with your parents and in person. We can't move forward without it."

Sam listened to the conversation. "Come on, Brett. We're having such a great time. Frankie and Ricky are getting along amazingly. We're scheduled to fly back up on Saturday."

"No can do. Both your allegiance to the FBI for this case takes precedence. It goes with the territory, Detective."

Sam let out a deep sigh of exasperation. "When do you want us to fly up?"

"Wednesday. Day after tomorrow. The Bureau will pick up the tab for the fee for changing your flight. Do first class if you have to. No standby. Just let me know the flight. Got it?"

"Yes, Agent Case," Sam and Frank said together. The call disconnected.

"He's a great guy, but when it comes to the job, he's a hardass."

"That's why he does what he does," Frank said. He sat up and Googled the airline. It took him over two hours to find another flight for Wednesday, noon, and it was first class. An extra three-hundred bucks. He appreciated Brett's dedication for the job. He'd sacrificed plenty.

Frankie wasn't a happy camper leaving Ricky. They'd become close. Frank and John told them they'd be seeing each other in New York, and they'd arrange sleepovers. John had plans to go with Vicki to make the final arrangements at the restaurant for her dad's retirement party so he couldn't drive them to the airport. They took a car service.

Mid-week during a school vacation, the Tampa airport was mobbed. They'd gotten there early, checked in, and had time for breakfast. It was fast food. Something Frank hated. Nonetheless, breakfast tasted real good, having it for the first time, in like forever.

They relaxed on the plane, and to be honest, for a man as big as he was, first class was just a tad more room. Frankie leaned against Sam and dozed. She fell asleep, too. Frank kept thinking about Henry and what was going through his three-year-old mind. The two-hour-twenty-minute flight seemed to have dragged for him.

They landed. Back at JFK. Now the fun would begin. The crowds were about ten times worse than Tampa. Sam made her usual trips to the ladies' room. He sure hoped she was pregnant. No test yet. But her girls seemed a little swollen. That was a sign for sure.

They made it down to baggage claim, and their luggage took over forty minutes to appear on the carousel. Then they heard it.

"Paging, Dr. Frank Khaos and family. Pick up a white courtesy phone, please."

"Who the heck is that?" Frank and Sam exchanged long stares. "Ah, maybe my in-laws came to pick us up." They walked to the white phone behind the check-in desk. He picked up the phone. "Dr. Khaos."

"Dr. Khaos, you're wanted in the visitors' lounge at the other end of this floor."

"Why?"

"I don't know, Doctor."

"Okay, come on guys." Dodging the crowds and zigzagging through them, they walked the length of the second level, and after looking in through the glass window on the lounge door, no one was in there. Frank opened the door, and they went inside."

❧❧❧

"If your in-laws were coming, Frank, they wouldn't put us in here. But I haven't flown much, so you can't go by me." Sam sat down on a long leather couch, and crossed her legs. She looked around, admiring the lounge area. It was first-class, that was for sure. She loved the exotic paintings on the wall from locations many people didn't get to travel to.

Frankie cuddled next to her. "Why are we here, Sam?"

"I haven't a clue, sweetheart."

Frankie got up and looked out the window of the door. "It's Agent Case and two other people."

Agent Case opened the door and moved out of the way to let Benjamin in.

"Benjamin," the three of them yelled at once.

He ran into Frank's arms then Sam's then hugged Frankie, his best buddy. "I'm here for good." They all hugged together and wouldn't let go.

Through tears, Sam cried out the words. "Oh my God, Brett, how did you pull this off?"

Brett sat on an adjacent smaller couch, relaxed, and leaning back. "Take a few deep breaths and calm down. Just wait."

Another agent opened the door, this time with Lex and Bella. They stepped aside to let Melissa in. Melissa ran to Sam who held onto her little girl. The crying intensified. "Brett, I can't believe you accomplished this." Through the screaming children, Sam didn't know if Brett heard her. He did.

"I took an oath to make this world a better place and to do what's right. This is what's right." Sam gasped. He continued. "It's my mission in life. I'm a Libran, too. Take a few deep breaths and wait."

The new family didn't let go of each other. Frank's arms were long enough to embrace all of them. Nick opened the door with another agent, and Henry came charging in. "I ran far away, and climbed, and was lost, and I was in the hospital," he yelled as if proud as he ran into Sam's arms.

"You were what?"

"Sam, he's okay," Brett said, "but you," he said as he wagged a finger at Henry, "better not pull that stunt again."

Henry hid his face between Frank's legs then looked up at Brett from the corner of his eye. "I won't," he said, turning his head back onto Frank's lap.

"So what's the deal, Brett?" Frank asked, somewhat suspicious.

"I'll give you some papers to sign, and you're their legal guardian until they're eighteen and can make their own decisions. After the marriage, Sam, you'll be added. We have a limo here to take you home. The kids' luggage is in the car. Melissa's art supplies are already at the house. Both your parents were there to accept delivery, and they set up the bedrooms. They're there waiting for you."

Both Sam and Frank looked at him with dropped jaws. Sam mouthed "Thank you" with tears flowing.

Melissa lit up. "Yes! We can plan the wedding!"

Sam hugged her. "We're all going to plan the wedding."

"Wait, where's Margie?" Benjamin asked.

"Margie is with her mom. You know she was only with you four months."

"Ooh," Melissa said, whining. "But we want a baby."

Benjamin got excited. "Wait! We'll have Miss Monty's baby!"

"No, Benjamin," Case said. "We spoke to her. Miss Monty married her boyfriend, and they're keeping the baby. They're very happy."

Benjamin looked despondent.

Frankie chimed in. "We *are* having a baby, Benjamin. Sam's pregnant."

"Really, Sam? Really?" Benjamin and Melissa yelled together.

Benjamin stared at her tummy, almost trance-like. "You *are* pregnant, Sam, and you're having a girl!"

"Come here." Sam took him in her arms. "Yes, I think I am!"

The agents and the detectives stood, just as emotional, even Bella. She had to walk away to compose herself.

Agent Case had to snap them out of it. "Let's get this family home."

Sam could barely get up. She was so weak in the knees Frank had to lift her. The agents grabbed their luggage. With the children, surrounding them, holding on, Frank and Sam left the lounge.

The End

About the Author

Ronnie Allen is a New York City woman who transplanted to Central Florida eleven years ago. A teacher for thirty-three years in the New York City Department of Education, as well as Board Certified Holistic Health Practitioner, she has an MS Degree in School Psychology and a PhD in Parapsychic Sciences. Ms. Allen holds children and family close to her heart and includes stories of survival in her plots. She specializes in healing on the spiritual, mental, emotional, and physical levels which appear in threads running through her books.